FRANCIE'S STORY

By

Sandy Ross Jacobs

ISBN 9798611923573

Cover photo by Dave Souza, his own work.
Loch Fyne, Scotland

Major Characters

Francie O'Conner Hanson

Francie's parents are Eileen and Dan O'Conner.
Francie's brothers are Denis, Brian and Thomas.
Francie and Pat Harrington have one child: Katherine Louise Mullins (Kate).
Francie marries Michael Hanson and has two children: Timothy and Audrey Hanson.

Pat Harrington

Pat has one child with Francie: Katherine Louise Mullins (Kate).
Pat marries Moira and has twin boys: Josh and Flip Harrington. Pat and Moira divorce.
Pat marries Giulia and has one child: Sophia Harrington.

Kate Mullins Walsh

Kate's biological parents are Francie O'Conner and Pat Harrington.
Kate's adoptive parents are Grace and James Mullins. Her brothers are Tommy and Leo Mullins.
Kate's has three half siblings from Pat: Josh, Flip and Sophia Harrington; and two half siblings from Kate: Timmy and Audrey Hanson.
Kate marries Sean Walsh and has twin children: Violet and Finn Walsh.

Other notable characters:

Robert Dugan, Kenneth Samuels.

Dear Reader,

Let me tell a little secret. I didn't know Francie until I wrote this story. One night while I was between wakefulness and sleep, Francie came to me out of nowhere. I had no idea who she was, but she said she wanted me to write her story. I ignored her—in fact, I ignored her for a long while. But she kept coming to me at night. When she pushed her way into my life in broad daylight, I relented and opened a new file in my computer. I called it "Francie's Story," and the words poured out. Francie continued to visit me, mostly at night, and I raced to my computer every morning to capture her. For six months, she was my best friend, and then her visits became shorter and farther apart. She wanted to prepare me for her departure. I miss her now that she's gone from my life, but the lesson she came with lingers: Every life is a story and it's up each of us to fill in the details. I did it for Francie and now I'm doing it for myself.

Read on....

Prologue

The letter came on a cold, rainy Tuesday marked with the return address, P. Harrington, London, England. The cold metal of the mailbox chilled Francie's hands, but when she saw the letter, a warm flush spread throughout her body.

She couldn't bring herself to open the envelope—she was afraid of what it might say. She put it aside, trying to calm the feeling of immediacy she felt about what he might have written.

She hid it in her middle bureau drawer, covered by her underwear.

Sometimes she held it up to the light but was unable to see through the thick paper. Sometimes she traced her finger over the handwriting she had not seen for twenty-three years.

By Friday morning, she was desperate to open the letter, but she didn't give in. She tried to distract herself, though her thoughts kept returning to Pat. She could see his grin, hear his laugh, smell his delicious scent. Everything she had put out of her mind for all those years came back to her.

PART I

Chapter 1

Francie O'Conner grew up in Ireland, the fourth of four children in an educated middle-class family. She was born with the gifts of a bright smile, a bright mind and a way of relating to everyone she met. Her father was the district manager of a transportation company, climbing the ladder to a more important position. Her mother was a reading specialist in the public school system, traveling from school to school four days of the week and seeing private clients at their homes Fridays.

Without any coaching from her mother, Francie taught herself to read when she was three. Her family thought she was remarkable, but Francie spent the rest of her childhood regretting her skills. It was not easy to live up to the expectations other people held for her. Her parents often complimented her, saying they had no doubts that her accomplishments would be outstanding. The nuns at school assumed she would be a top achiever. She smiled and thanked them, but inwardly she felt pressured not to disappoint them. Her friends turned to her for advice and support, and, although she insisted she was no more experienced in life than they were, they wanted to hear what she had to say. She was grateful for the gifts God had given her, but sometimes she just wanted to be an ordinary, average girl. She loved her family and she loved learning—these were primary in her life—but she was aware that if she slipped, she would be letting everyone down. Her favorite place of respite was the public library where she found the quiet privacy to spend uninterrupted hours with no one to question her about her academic progress or pass judgment on her choices of leisure reading. At home, her mother frowned upon romance novels, but at the library, Francie was in charge—and she read about romance, in all its stages.

Her greatest pleasure at home was a simple one—to spend time with any or all her three older brothers, Denis, Brian and Thomas, each a year apart from the other. Thomas, the brother closest to her age, just two years older, was her favorite. Her brothers taught her to play sports like a boy—no sissy skills for her—and, on the side, she learned what makes boys tick. Consequently, she always felt relaxed with the opposite sex and confident on the athletic field. Most importantly, her brothers gave their little sister unconditional love.

Because of her academic excellence, Francie skipped a year of school and graduated when she was sixteen, seven months before her seventeenth birthday. Her parents and brothers were all graduates of Trinity College in Dublin, but when The University of Edinburgh offered her a scholarship, she was thrilled to accept. The lure of walking the halls where greats such as author Sir Arthur Conan Doyle and philosopher David Hume had trod impressed her. And being the first to go away to college gave her a feeling of adventure to add to the loosening of the family strings. The O'Conners were bursting with pride—their gifted daughter was going to one of the best universities in Great Britain—and on full scholarship. Francie's accomplishments kept her mother busy on the phone for hours, telling all the aunts, uncles, cousins, and friends about her daughter's achievement. Her heart was full of pride, and though she tried to be discreet, she couldn't help but show her joy.

The Bible warns that "pride goeth before the fall," and Francie's mother wanted to avoid bringing any jinx to Francie's good fortune, so she and the rest of the family didn't spare the lectures and warnings:

Remember that studies come first.... Eat a healthy diet.... Don't stay up too late.... Always behave like a lady.... Beware of college boys—they drink too much and they expect too much.... Maintain your virtue.... Go to Mass every day.... Above all, make the family proud.

Armed with advice from her parents, her brothers, the nuns and the priest, she packed her bags and said her tearful goodbyes at the Port of Dublin. She took a deep breath to inhale the familiar smells of the Irish air and boarded the ferry to Wales. In Holyhead Port in Wales, she would transfer to the train to Edinburgh. From the window of the ferry, Francie watched the port retreat in the distance until she sensed that her former life was behind, and her future was rushing to greet her. The entire journey would take a little over three hours.

And in those three hours, her life changed forever.

"Is this seat taken, Miss?" he asked. She looked up and saw a mop of black curls tumbling over the most alluring blue eyes she had ever seen.

"It's yours," she said.

The two fell into an easy conversation. As they shared their stories, the coincidences were so remarkable that Francie thought the boy might be teasing her. They were both headed to University, they both had parents who expected great things from them, and they both were going away from home for the first time. The most important thing, they came to agree, was the new freedom from their parents' unrelenting expectations. He was going to St Andrews University on the east coast of Scotland, only an hour's bus ride from University of Edinburgh. Hallelujah!

She felt a bit nervous and thought she was talking too much, so she forced herself to quiet down and listen, but in less than a minute, she couldn't help herself—she wanted to share everything with him. She smiled when she spoke, and he retuned her smile with a mischievous grin. He reminded her of her third brother, Thomas, and before long, she was flirting with him—in a very subtle way—but still flirting. She had never done that before, but now it came naturally. Something about him was irresistible.

"So," she said, "now that we're going to be living in a foreign place, I guess we should tell each other our names so that at least we'll know one person in Scotland. I'm Francie O'Conner."

"And I'm Pat Harrington. I'm pleased to meet you, Miss O'Conner—my best and only friend in Scotland."

They talked and laughed all the way to Wales, interrupting their conversation only to buy sandwiches from the wheeled food cart. "Ham and tomato," they said simultaneously, which brought on a fit of laughter between them.

The ride went too quickly—they had so much more to say. When the ferry was about to dock, they exchanged addresses, said quick goodbyes and ran for their trains—hers to Edinburgh, his to Fife.

Once she was alone, her thoughts assailed her. *Was that experience real? Is it possible to fall in love in three hours? Will I ever hear from him again?* She hoped she would know the answers within a few days, but after ten days, Francie decided that he probably forgot her already and was into his new life at St Andrews. She would get on with hers.

She easily conquered the routine of college life. She liked the girls on her floor in the dormitory, and she enjoyed her classes. Some of the boys' dormitories had reception rooms for parties, and Francie and her friends went to a whirlwind of mixers. They met a couple of nice boys and enjoyed slow dancing and jitterbugging to music on L.P. records, but she had Pat on her mind and wondered what it would be like dancing with him.

At the end of her second week of classes, she came back to her dorm to find Pat waiting outside with a handful of daffodils and his confident grin. Her legs turned to rubber. They hugged as if they were old friends and went to a campus coffee shop to talk, and, as it turned out, to flirt.

He told her of his family. Despite his Irish coloring, he was from England. His father was a doctor and his mother a hospital administrator. They moved to Ireland when his father accepted the position as head of surgery at Blackrock Clinic, a suburban hospital close to Dalkey, where they lived. His mother was from a background of high social standing, with a member of the House of Lords in her bloodline.

Francie began to squirm a bit—*How can someone from my modest roots hope to have a boyfriend from a family of his social standing?*

Pat continued. "My father is a product of boarding school, then Oxford, as were most of the males in the family. My brother William is ten years older, a plastic surgeon living in England with wife and two youngsters." He described his brother as being staid, like his father. Because of the ten year age difference, they had little in common—they were brothers, but they felt more like distant cousins. His brother's interests were like those of his father, centered on science, particularly biology. Their father groomed him to become a doctor and to share a life of medicine with him. He started by teaching him how to dissect small creatures and insects and to name all their parts. Next, he taught him the basics of human anatomy. William learned quickly—at a young age he was proud to point out and name many of his own body parts to his father.

Ten years later, when Pat was born, his father had little time for a baby in the family. He was devoting most of his interest to his medical practice. William continued to find the subject fascinating, and his father encouraged him by discussing particularly interesting medical cases with him.

Pat's mother was his main companion in the family. From the day of his birth, he captured her affection and became her favorite—her baby, the sunshine of her life. When he came to be a young man, she balked at the idea of his going away from home to University. Pat knew better—he had to get away to live his own life and make his own decisions. When his mother reconciled herself to his intentions, she warned him, just as Francie's had, of the temptations of college life and directed him to honor his ancestry by surrounding himself with quality people, to which his father added, "Of the same caliber as your family."

Francie listened closely then said, "Oh, so you're a dignified Englishman."

"Guilty," he replied, "but there is a lot of Irish in me, so I'm not too dignified. I've been living in Ireland since I was eight years old."

She held her breath and asked, "Are you a Catholic?"

"Church of England—does it matter to you?" He reached across the table and ran his finger over the back of her hand, then covered her hand with his, squeezing it lightly. She felt a tingling go through her body, all the way to her toes.

She looked him in the eye. "For one thing, my parents would forbid a relationship between us. And for another, my family all went to Trinity College. Oxford and Cambridge were completely out of reach financially, so your family would probably forbid a relationship, too. Is it possible for us to ignore that now?"

"For me it is, so if it is for you, let's not think about it. This is just between us, here and now. Let's not worry about the future—we've only just met." She was sixteen years old and he was eighteen, much too young not to dream.

They talked for six hours, sometimes seriously, but mostly they were playful. Pat caught the early evening bus back to St Andrews. When they said goodbye, they were drawn together as if magnetized, chest-to-chest and thigh to thigh. They shared their first kiss, gentle at first, lips together, slowly parting, with tongues searching to know each other better. Francie had never kissed like this, but the feeling that shot through her body came naturally, and she knew this was special. She wanted the kiss to go on forever. Pat was more experienced. He had first-hand knowledge of the feelings eighteen-year-old boys had for girls, but this was different. It felt deeper, more real.

They met every weekend during the fall and winter, exploring Scotland and each other. The days were cold, rainy and dark, but now and then, the sun would penetrate the clouds and produce a blinding sparkle on the sea and an almost supernatural glow to the moors. The freshness of the air was invigorating, and so was the feeling of young love. Their conversations flowed freely, about their goals, their dreams, their strengths and weaknesses. Pat wanted a career in the law. "My mother put the idea into my head that I should be a judge, but I can't think that far ahead. Right now, all I want to do is spend time with you—and show off my muscles. Does that fit the qualifications for me to become a judge?"

"If it does, and if I ever commit a crime, I'd like you to be the one to hear my case," she said. "As for me, philosophy is my main interest. I love to read about the thoughts of the ancient Greeks and Romans who shaped modern-day thinking. Maybe someday I could put my studies to practical use, but, right now, all I want put to practical use is admiring your muscles."

"Then we're in perfect agreement," he said. "But I have to give you credit, too. Forget the philosophy lessons, it's those dark green eyes of yours that snagged me."

When the weather turned bitter cold, they went to lectures, musicals and plays. Both universities had indoor tennis courts, and they liked to play singles. He had a muscular body and was a good athlete, but, thanks to her brothers' teaching, she clobbered him on the tennis court the first time they played. She promised that when they played again, she would let him win a set or two.

Pat was an excellent dancer, and she loved to dance but had not inherited the easy rhythm of her brothers and parents. When her parents danced, others on the dance floor stopped to watch. She enjoyed dancing with Pat and tried to fake her abilities, but Pat was a natural and could easily pick up that dancing was not one of her talents. Pretending condescension, he said, "Your dancing is much worse than my tennis, but don't worry, I promise to teach you not to step on my feet too many times if you would actually let me do the leading."

"I'll ignore the insult if you accept my excuse to blame it on genetics—the dance gene passed me by."

They kept their courtship secret from their families. When they were home for school vacations, they stayed apart and told no one of their romance, knowing that their parents would forbid it.

From the time Francie was in grade school, she kept a journal. Sometimes there were lapses between entries, but now she had to record her feelings—she never wanted to forget any of the joy she felt. She wrote, with a little drama, *I am in love with the man I want to share my life with. I love his wit, his intelligence and his spirit—and he is so handsome, I feel fuzzy all over every time I see him. I don't know how I could ever tire of him. We are keeping our romance a secret for now and my biggest challenge is not telling Tommy. We have never had secrets from one another, but I have to hold my tongue because he'd tell our brothers.* She was dying to tell Thomas—they had shared everything—but this time she kept her secret.

They went home to their families in Ireland for Christmas vacation and didn't see each other for ten days, until the end of winter break was approaching. Planning to head back to their universities a few days before classes were to begin, they each told their parents they had advanced projects to start, and each set of parents was delighted their child was so devoted to academics.

With *Merry Christmas* a memory and *Happy New Year* behind, Francie and Pat boarded the ferry once again on their way to romance.

They felt as if they had been apart forever, and once they got on the ferry, they could barely keep their hands off each other. *Is this my life, or I am living in a romance novel?* she asked herself.

When they disembarked in Wales, they spotted a hotel across from the port, and, dizzy with young passion, crossed the street. While he checked in, she perused the lobby gift shop. She unfolded a cashmere sweater, fingered the silk scarves, and inspected a few greeting cards until she peeked into the lobby and saw him mouth the room number, *B-8*. She casually walked across to the stairs and ran to the next floor to wait for him. He took the elevator, and they arrived at the door to the room at the same time.

She undressed without embarrassment, accustomed to her three brothers sneaking peeks at her from the time she was a toddler. Once, when she was about twelve, her oldest brother, Denis, walked into the bathroom just as she was getting out of the tub. She quickly turned her back to him, but he was so embarrassed, he ran out of the bathroom, red faced and screaming, "Oh my God, what have I done?" while she laughed and reached for her towel. He couldn't look her in the eye for days.

Now, in the hotel in Wales, she realized that Pat had never seen a girl fully undressed. She saw the astonishment on his face when he looked her up and down, trying to be casual about seeing her naked body. She was perfectly proportioned with high young breasts, a tiny waist and curvy hips. He told her she was more beautiful than he ever imagined. Then he undressed, slightly awkwardly, and they drew together. He caressed her, then broke the spell by laughing.

"What's so funny?"

He made several attempts to answer her, but each time he started, he laughed even harder. Finally, he was able to get out, "How could this little body have beaten me so badly on the tennis court? It's not possible—I must have been having a bad day."

She countered with, "Really? I went easy on you. Double or nothing next time."

Their lovemaking, like their first kiss, was gentle and loving at first, gradually becoming passionate. Their days together in Wales were enchanted. When they weren't making love, they were finding fun in everything they did, laughing at the smallest details and the large ones, too. One day the hotel staff forgot to supply towels, and Pat ran from the shower and jumped into bed soaking wet. She jumped under the covers with him.

One night they went to a café for dinner. "When in Wales, do as the Welsh," they decided, as they ordered Welsh Rabbit, labeled a traditional dish.

When the waiter served them melted cheese on toast Pat said, "Excuse me, we ordered Welsh Rabbit, not melted cheese."

"This is Welsh Rabbit, though some tourists actually expect rabbit," he replied. "You're not one of those, are you?" Nonplussed, they looked at each other, and this time they roared.

They fantasized about their future. They would live in Scotland, they would have two children, Katherine (Kate), and Philip (Flip). Over and over, they talked about being married as soon as they graduated.

They spent three days in Wales, then boarded their separate trains to take them back to school in Scotland.

On January fourth, for her seventeenth birthday, Pat took Francie to a formal restaurant in Edinburgh, a sharp contrast to the school cafeterias where they usually ate during the week. He had called in advance and requested that a small vase of daffodils be on the table for this special occasion. Francie looked at the flowers, then at Pat, and sat down misty eyed. Pat ordered two glasses of champagne, and in a flourish of exaggerated moves, the waiter opened a full bottle in front of them with a very loud pop.

"Congratulations, young lady, and best wishes for a lovely birthday, compliments of the house," he said. Feeling like celebrities, they clinked their glasses and toasted the waiter, each other, and their future.

Without looking at the menu and not wanting to duplicate the Welsh Rabbit experience, Pat simply ordered the specialty of the house. "An excellent choice," said the waiter. Their dinner arrived, beautifully arranged on the plates, and even though they weren't sure what they were eating, they enjoyed it—they would have enjoyed sausage rolls as long as they were together.

When dessert came, the waiter presented an extra plate for Francie, with an ornately wrapped box on it and a card that read, "To Francie—my first and only love." Inside was a gold, necklace with a heart-shaped charm. Francie looked at Pat and thought she would never stop smiling.

"Francie," he said, "I thought I had everything. And then I met you and realized nothing else mattered except our future together."

When they rose to leave, the waiter bowed slightly, tented his hands and said, "It was a pleasure seeing two people so much in love." He wished them good luck. Francie kissed him on both cheeks.

For the next few months, they alternated weekends between Edinburgh and St Andrews. They found a charming bed and breakfast in nearby Dundee. Their room was barely heated and they had to cuddle under the down comforter to keep from shivering until their intimacy warmed them.

They awoke the next morning to sunbeams playing on their skin. The sun shone through the slats of the window blinds drawing horizontal lines across their bodies. They faced each other and Pat said, "No matter what happens these lines will join us forever in the Universe."

Sometimes the fierce cold near St Andrews took their breath away, and they hunched their shoulders against the cold. But they both loved the outdoors and persisted in their walks. One bright February day, when the weather was calm, they decided to explore the trails at Glen Tilt, starting in Blair Atholl, a village two hours away by bus and train from St Andrews. They walked the windy lanes of the town. Most of the neat rows of houses were painted white and adorned with now empty flower boxes under the windows—and a cat looking out from inside. At a tearoom in the village, they bought a picnic lunch and filled their thermos with hot tea. Most of the stores were shuttered for the season—clearly not a winter destination.

The day was sunny and bright, perfect for an adventure, so they followed a sign pointing to the start of a eleven-mile loop of the town on a series of trails in the woods. Francie took her hat and gloves off and enjoyed the warm air on her skin.

"What do you think?" he said, "Are you up for the challenge?"

"On a day like this, what could go wrong? I'm up for if you are. I vote 'yes.'"

They walked briskly for a little over an hour, covering what they estimated to be four or five miles, when they noticed the clouds rolling in over the hills. They could smell rain in the air. Almost immediately, the wind picked up and the icy rain began. By then, Francie was bundled in her hat and gloves which offered almost no protection from the weather. They decided to turn back, but their progress was much slower because they had to walk into the wind and rain.

The muddy forest trails made for slippery footing and wet shoes.

Francie felt her body stiffening as she hugged her chest and shoulders against the cold. "Pat, I'm freezing," she said with teeth clenched.

"Come in here with me," he said, unzipping his parka for her to enter.

"There's not much room in here, so just let me warm up for a few minutes, then we can drink our hot tea," she said.

The tea warmed them temporarily, and Pat suggested they jog to keep warm. "Think of a hot summer day in the south of France," he suggested.

"Pat, this may surprise you, but I've never been to the south of France—or the north of France, either. I'll try my hardest to imagine it, though."

So they jogged, swinging their arms, pulling their hats down against the rain and tightening their wet scarves around their necks. What had been beautiful scenery before the rain and cold now was a dark, dreary vista. Occasionally they stopped to have a few more sips of tea and to jump in place. "Is this how they do it in Cote d'Azur?" she asked, shivering and trying to keep moving. Gradually, their blood circulated to warm their bodies, but they knew they might not be able to keep up their energy to make it back to the village of Blair. They had eaten their sandwiches and drunk all their tea; most of their energy went into trying to keep warm. They spotted a small, weathered sign hanging askew on a post, almost covered by the brush *Thomson Cottage one mile ahead.*

The sign was old and battered, and they were skeptical that the cottage still existed, but they agreed they didn't have much choice and should try their luck. They veered off the trail and followed the rutted path. Now at a slow walk, they concentrated on just putting one foot in front of the other.

After a while, they saw white smoke rising in the distance, a huge relief to the freezing couple, and, fifteen minutes later, they found the source—a stone house with *Thomson* painted on a panel next to the front door. The barking dogs inside announced their arrival. An elderly woman holding back three anxious dogs opened the door, and when she saw the condition of the young couple, she called for her husband to help get them inside and take off their wet clothes.

"Don't mind the dogs," the man said. "They're friendly to strangers, glad to see them, unless they sense danger."

"What in the world made you hike the woods on a day like this?" the woman asked. "You're nearly frozen. Didn't anyone warn you about the sudden weather changes here?"

When their breathing returned to normal, they told them they were students at St Andrews and U of Edinburgh and had no idea that the rains of Scotland could be so icy cold.

"It was so beautiful this morning, we decided to hike and have a picnic lunch," said Francie. "We're both from Ireland and this is our first winter in Scotland."

Mrs. Thomson told them that occasionally a lost hiker knocked on their door, but never anyone as cold and exhausted as the two of them.

"We've lived in our little cottage with our ever-changing brood of Labrador retrievers since the first day of our marriage sixty years ago. It's not often that we have visitors, especially in the winter, and we're glad for the company," she said, "so warm yourselves in front of the fire and let your wet clothes dry. We'll drive you back to Blair Atholl when you're ready, but don't make the same mistake again—you might not be so lucky the next time. While you're in Scotland, remember the saying, 'If the weather in Scotland is nice, grab your raincoat, because within an hour the weather will change.'" Then she and Mr. Thomson went to get hot tea and biscuits.

They came back with the tray to find Pat and Francie—and the dogs—in deep sleep in front of the fire. Mrs. Thomson left the tray on a small table and tiptoed out of the room.

When they awoke, the older couple heard them moving around and told them they had better be on their way because darkness sets in around three o'clock and they didn't like to drive in the dark. "So have your tea and biscuits quickly—oops, the biscuits are gone, and I think the dogs are smiling—I'd better get more biscuits. We don't want to turn you away hungry."

Within fifteen minutes, they were back in Blair Atholl, hardly believing that such a short distance could have made them so miserable.

Francie and Pat thanked them repeatedly for their kindness.

"We were once young, too," said Mr. Thomson, "and we had stars in our eyes, just like the two of you. Stay safe and happy...."

When spring came, Francie and Pat continued their walks. They visited coastal towns and watched fishermen haul in their catch at the harbor of Thuro. They walked the cliffs and the heather-filled bogs and hills. They became part of the scenery throughout the Kingdom of Fife where they explored ruins of old castles and ancient towns. They had learned from their winter experience that when the weather was wet and windy—which was often in Scotland, regardless of the season—to shorten their walks and spend time in tea rooms and cafés to wait an hour for the weather to change.

Every weekend was like a honeymoon for them. They reveled in the intricacies of one another, enjoying the love and passion of youth, never thinking that anything could ever stand in the way of their future.

Most starry-eyed lovers feel invulnerable to anything outside of their world, and Francie and Pat were no exception. But, inevitably, reality intruded into their magical lives. By the beginning of April, Francie realized she had missed two periods. Her mother had never explained "the facts of life" to her, and Francie thought that if she washed carefully, she could not become pregnant. When she confided in Pat, he, too, was naïve about birth control and thought that quick withdrawal was the way to avoid conception. One thing they did know—they wanted to get married. But first they would have to face their parents. She was sure that when her parents met Pat, they would recognize his intelligence, charm, and good family background, and see for themselves how much in love they were. She thought she could convince her parents that the differences of religion didn't matter. At semester's end in May, they would tell their parents. They hoped their high grades would help soothe their news. In their own minds, they were responsible, young adults.

The reality was that she was seventeen, legally underage, and he was barely nineteen.

At the end of the semester, on their return journey to Dublin, Pat got up from his seat on the ferry, knelt in the aisle, and with his most serious face, said "Francie, my love, please marry me so we can be together in a little cottage in the woods, with three dogs, until our old age." He gave her a velvet box with a gold ring inside, set with a stone the color of daffodils.

She said, "Yes, yes, yes, of course, yes!" and stood up, pulling him up with her, and hugged him. He slipped the ring on her finger. Everyone within hearing distance applauded. Pat acknowledged them with a deep bow.

They wished they could stay on the ferry forever and not have to face their parents, but despite their wishes, the ferry plowed through the water on its inevitable journey to Dublin. The sun penetrated the windowpanes of the ferry painting a pattern of stripes. "Look, Pat," she said, "remember—we'll always be together in the Universe." Dizzy with the love and scared of what might happen, they kissed goodbye before the boat docked. Francie returned the ring to its box and hid it in her handbag until she could gently break the news to her parents. With a squeeze of hands, they stepped onto dry ground in the busy port of Dublin. She watched Pat's parents greet him with hugs and pats on the back before they whisked him away in their shiny black sedan. He managed to look past the crowds of people to have one last glimpse of Francie. She tried but could no longer find the car in the flurry of people on the quay.

Welcome Home, Honor Student! read the sign that greeted her outside her house when the taxi pulled up. Her parents and brothers were waiting outside for her.

The table in the dining room was set with their best linens and a buffet spread with a sugar-glazed baked ham, sliced turkey, cheeses and salad and Francie's favorite dessert, the famously rich Bailey's cheesecake. The house was open to friends and family to join in welcoming Francie home after having conquered her first year at University of Edinburgh. Francie smiled despite the chaos she was feeling inside, thinking about the news she had yet to announce. She would tell them tomorrow.

That night, as she was getting ready for bed, her father knocked softly on her door and came into her room. "Francie," he said, "you have done the family proud and we love you for it." Guilt washed over her and she decided to wait a few more days to tell them of her pregnancy.

Ten minutes later, her mother opened Francie's bedroom door and walked in without knocking. "You don't have to tell me, Francie. I knew that you were pregnant as soon as I saw your eyes." Francie had never heard her mother speak in such a stern, unloving tone. "Tonight's party was a sham, a humiliation for all of us. Your purity is gone and with it, you have fallen from grace."

Francie was shocked. She moved toward her mother to find the comfort of her hug, but her mother backed away. Francie reached for her. "Mother, I'm so sorry, but it's not what you think. We're engaged," she said, and showed her mother her ring. Her mother did not look at it. "Wait until you meet Pat—he's wonderful—and I know you'll love him. We are going to be married as soon as he tells his parents. Both families can meet and make the arrangements together." As she said this, she started to cry, softly at first, then sobbing.

With vehemence, her mother continued, "Do you think your tears will make me change my mind? Your tears mean nothing to me, Francie. How could you have done this to us after all we have done for you? I'll call Father Grady in the morning and you and that boy will be married by week's end. Shame on you—you have disgraced the family."

Francie lowered her head and barely whispered, "Mum, there's something else I have to tell you."

"No, don't tell me anything else. Nothing could be worse than this. We'll talk in the morning."

Francie was miserable all night. She would have to see this through by herself without Pat there to help. In a day or two, when the situation with her parents calmed down, she would call him.

The next morning, the house was unnaturally quiet. Francie walked into a silent kitchen and found her parents and brothers waiting. Her mother had told them.

The doorbell rang—the priest.

"Good morning to you all," Father Grady said.

They all nodded back and mumbled "Good morning." Father Grady looked at Francie with sadness in his eyes and said, "Okay, now, Francie, if you and the family are willing, let's sit down together, and we'll all hear the whole story."

She started, telling of her first meeting with Pat, their devotion to each other, their honest and strong love and respect. She told them of Pat's background, that his family was English, but had lived in Ireland for over ten years. His parents were well-established in the medical and social community in their town. She added that Pat was brilliant, an all-A scholar with a solid future.

"What parish is Pat's family's church in?" asked Father Grady. "I'll speak to the priest and try to arrange a meeting together with the boy's family so we can plan the wedding."

Crying uncontrollably now, knowing what might happen, Francie told him that Pat was not a Catholic.

Two days later, her parents sent her to live with the nuns until after the baby was born. The child would be adopted. Francie was forbidden to contact Pat. Her parents would reject all calls and destroy all mail from him.

Instead of saying goodbye, her mother said, "You are no longer my daughter. I never want to speak to you or hear from you ever again."

Chapter 2

The church's Home for Unwed Mothers was in a semi-remote part of suburban Dublin, with a black iron fence around it, surrounded by woods. It was on the grounds of a cloistered convent. The girls were free to roam the garden, but the fence remained locked. They could go to the nearby village, accompanied by a chaperone, for an hour each week. No phone calls were permitted.

Francie shared a cell-like room with a girl her age named Rosemary. The room had a cold-water sink with a rust-stained ring around the drain and a rubber stopper on a chain. There was no mirror. The only decoration was a crucifix over each bed. A broom, a dustbin and a mop stood in the corner, and the girls were required to sweep and mop the floor daily. By five thirty each morning, they had to straighten their beds with sheets pulled tight, blanket folded and pillow smoothed, in time for Mass.

All the girls were required to keep their conversations to a minimum and to avoid small talk and socializing. Reflection, repentance and work were required. Silence during meals was expected.

Francie wrote in her journal, *There are no bars, but I am in jail and the nuns are my keepers. The sisters here show no kindness—they are nothing like the ones I knew at school in Dublin.*

Rosemary and Francie's backgrounds were quite different, and they had very little to talk about except how they got into their situations, their families, and their resentment of the harsh demands of the sisters. However, she and her roommate liked each other and were glad to have the other for company. They had a relationship and respected each other's space.

The story of Rosemary's pregnancy was shocking to Francie. Rosemary and a friend had met two nice-looking boys outside a movie theater after the show. "We all started to talk, and one of them, Guy, told me I was pretty. Me and Peggy were wearing mascara for the first time and thought we looked so cool and grown up in our mini-skirts and boots. She talked to the other boy, Mac, and he asked us if we wanted to go for a ride in his car. Guy and me got in the back, and Peggy sat with Mac. We drove to a road that ended near the woods. Peggy and Mac got out of the car and took a blanket with them, and me and Guy were alone in the back seat. He kissed me and told me I was beautiful, and then he touched me under my blouse. I wanted him to stop, but it felt good, so I didn't say anything. While he was kissing me, he reached under my skirt and into my underpants. That felt really good, and he started to tell me how special I was and he was going to do something to make me feel great. Then he was on top of me and started to put himself into my body. It hurt a lot. I told him to stop, but he said that was normal for the first time.

When he was done, he told me, "Now you're a woman."

I said to him, "How could I be a woman? I'm only fifteen."

He said he thought I was older than that, at least seventeen, and that when I got home, I should wet a washcloth with water and vinegar and clean myself. That way I wouldn't have to worry.

"A few minutes later, Mac and Peggy came back to the car and we drove to the movie theater. They dropped us off, said good night and drove away. They didn't even ask for our phone numbers.

"A couple of weeks went by and Peggy told me she got her period. I still hadn't and after another month, I figured I must be pregnant. I didn't tell my parents, but after two more months, my mother could see for herself that I was. She called me a slut and said I would never be clean again. Three days later, my father drove me here to the Home, called me a whore, and said not to come back until the little bastard came out.

"So here I am—miserable, lonely, and crying myself to sleep every night. As soon as I'm old enough, my parents told me I have to quit school and get a job."

"Rosemary," Francie said, "we're both in this place for the same reason. We just got here different ways. You can depend on me if you need help."

"Me, too, Francie," she said.

The next day, the routine the girls would follow every day began. After morning Mass and a breakfast of porridge and milk, the forty or so girls worked in the kitchens making communion wafers for daily shipment to churches throughout Ireland. The work was grueling, and the routine never changed—the girls carried heavy, five-gallon buckets full of a thin flour and water batter from the mixing room to the kitchens. The kitchens were excessively hot from the high temperatures of six large griddles. The girls ladled batter onto each griddle to make one large twelve inch disk, then covered the pan to bake. The baked disks were quickly removed and stamped with small crosses. The girls sprayed them with water, stacked them into piles of seventy-two and loaded them into a humidifier until the next day when they cut them into small coin-sized wafers. All the work was done while standing up. Francie found the job to be mindless and tedious—the heat was more daunting than the work. She was constantly thirsty. There was a one-minute break for water every hour. Occasionally a girl had a weak spell or fainted and was given water and a half hour of rest. The sister in charge told the girls that during their work, they should think of their faith in Jesus and the sacrifices He made for them. Francie spent most of her time thinking about Pat and planning the life they would share when she left the Home.

They were offered a small lunch, usually a cheese sandwich and an apple, or, occasionally, a hard-cooked egg, before returning to the kitchens to continue the next step of production. Using the disks that had been stored in the humidifier the day before, they quickly loaded the stacks of seventy-two onto a cutting machine. It required a great deal of strength to press the foot pedal with enough power to cut through a stack of seventy-two wafers, making about five thousand small wafers with one cut. They did five cuttings an afternoon yielding about twenty-five thousand wafers each day. The girls who ran the foot pedals were exhausted quickly but had to keep up with the work. Francie was lucky—she was strong—she had been raised on nutritious food and lots of activity—but many of the others were not as lucky as she. Some of the girls, including Rosemary, struggled to get the work done. Although conversation was not permitted,

Francie could sense when her roommate needed help. At times, when the supervising sister was not looking, she'd whisper to Rosemary, "Quick, Ro, switch places with me. My job is easier than yours today." She tried to give her encouragement by smiling at her when their eyes met, helping to raise Rosemary's spirits a bit. Francie's resentment toward the sisters and the church grew each time she saw one of the girls treated poorly. *Where's the Christian charity?* she thought.

The girls whose babies were due within the next month had the easiest jobs—packing, labeling and loading boxes of five hundred wafers for shipping. This was the only step in the process that was done sitting down. Every day they made a new batch. The work never ended. At week's end, they had made and shipped one hundred twenty-five thousand wafers to Catholic churches all over Ireland, to be blessed and received by one hundred twenty-five thousand faithful Catholics as the body of Christ.

If they only knew who made these, Francie thought.

She was constantly homesick, not just for her home and family but for the fairytale life she and Pat had during the past year. Letters she wrote to her mother came back unopened. She knew no way to communicate with Pat and assumed he had the same problem trying to find her. She sent a letter to him care of St Andrews University, but it was returned to her saying that he was no longer enrolled at the school. She tried calling him at his home in Dalkey but heard a recorded message that the phone had been disconnected. The two people she needed most—her mother and Pat—were beyond her reach. When the baby she carried stirred within her, she knew that a part of Pat was inside her, and she ached to hear from him. From time to time, she got mail from her father and brothers, but they kept it to a minimum due to her mother's insistence. Her brother, Thomas, wrote to tell her that their parents refused Pat's calls and letters.

Her suffering and loneliness never let up.

The nuns constantly reminded all the girls at the hostel of their guilt. Francie lost her faith in God and family and swore she would never attend church when she was free. By day, she hid the ring Pat had given her, but she slipped it on before bed, running her finger over the yellow stone remembering their last ferry ride together when he asked her to marry him.

Around her neck, tucked into her clothes, she wore the gold heart—his gift to her for her seventeenth birthday. Each night she and Rosemary cried themselves to sleep, muffling their sobs.

On weekends when the weather was fair, Francie walked outdoors to find quiet places to write in the latest of the journals she'd kept since she was fifteen. Writing her thoughts, experiences and observations calmed her, especially now, and served as an outlet for her emotions.

She seldom went into the town because the pregnant girls accompanied by chaperones drew stares from the townsfolk that made them feel like outcasts.

One evening she wrote to her former advisor and to the Dean of Students at University of Edinburgh, informing them that she would not be able to return for the next semester. She asked them to send her records to her current address. When the information she requested was returned to her, she was flattered by the accolades written in letters she received from her professors and the administration. For safekeeping, she put the letters in the box where she kept her journal.

In addition to making wafers, the girls were required to complete a project needed by the hostel so that when they left, it was a better place than when they came. Francie chose to start a library from the many books girls left behind. She cross-catalogued them by author and subject and arranged them on a spare shelf near the dining room. She wrote book reviews of the ones she read and presented summaries when asked. This activity was limited to only fifteen minutes each week, but even that slim distraction made Francie and the girls grateful. For their project, others knitted or crocheted baby blankets, or made sock dolls for the hundreds of babies and children who lived in or passed through the church orphanages.

In October, Rosemary, went into labor. The two of them had been asleep for a few hours when Francie heard Rosemary moaning.

Francie was terrified and could see the fright on Rosemary's tear-streaked face, but knew she had to do something to help. Rosemary was sitting on the side of her bed in great pain, so Francie went over to her, encircling her in her arms. "What can I do for you?"

"Just hold me, Francie," Rosemary said meekly, in the voice of a frightened child. "I rang for the midwife, but I'm so scared."

Francie continued to hug her, trying to allay her fears, saying that it would be over soon and that she would be able to see her baby. But the truth was Francie was scared for herself, too, and even lonelier now. Her time would be coming soon, and there would be no one, not even Rosemary, to give her comfort.

A sister took Rosemary from the room in a wheelchair and that was the last time she ever saw her. When their labors started, the girls were taken to a part of the Home that was more like a hospital until their babies were born. Then, a few days later, the girl left through a back entrance, suitcase in hand, but no baby in arms.

A week later, on the morning of October 25, more than a month before she was due, Francie's waters broke, and her pains started. Before she called the midwife, she hid her necklace and journal in a zippered compartment of her suitcase and then rang for help. The midwife took her to the birthing room, and after several examinations and tests told Francie that the baby was most likely premature, and the birth might be complicated. They had to be very careful not to stress the baby during the birthing process. Francie didn't want to let go—the baby was her only connection with Pat, and she wasn't ready to face the emptiness she knew was coming. She tried to delay the birth, but she soon gave up, knowing her efforts were futile. The baby was determined to be born. The midwife told her point-blank that the baby came first, and Francie had to do everything in her power to cooperate. When it was apparent that Francie's delivery was going to be difficult, the doctor took over.

The labor pains were coming more frequently, merging into one long almost unbearable pain, but the doctor would not jeopardize the baby's life in any way by allowing anesthesia. After ten hours of hard labor, Francie gave birth to her tiny daughter. The midwife showed her to Francie for just a few seconds, then took her away. Francie was not permitted to hold her, but in those few seconds, the baby opened her eyes and seemed to look at her for just enough time for Francie to see two tiny blue eyes, identical to Pat's. Those beautiful eyes were the last things Francie saw before she lapsed into unconsciousness. She had no awareness of how close to death she had come. Her body required a transfusion of three units of blood to keep her alive. Twelve hours later, she regained consciousness. Her first thoughts were of the baby. "Is she alive?" she asked the nuns, "Is she healthy?"

"The baby is very tiny. She is premature and requires close monitoring until her nervous system matures. Right now, she is struggling, but she's a little fighter and we hope she'll make it. We're all praying for her."

"Please, please can I see her? She must feel so alone without me to hold her," she pleaded.

"That is not permitted, but all babies are God's gifts, and the tiny, premature babies get special care until they reach normal maturity and are ready for adoption."

"I don't know how my baby gets her name, but is it possible to name her Kate?" Francie asked, wanting desperately to give her daughter the name she and Pat had chosen in the fantasy they hoped their life would become.

"I'll suggest it, but the adoptive parents are legally permitted to change their baby's name when the new birth certificate is issued."

Francie spent ten days recovering her health after the trauma of childbirth. Whenever a nurse came into her room, she asked about her baby. The nurses always had a positive response, saying that the baby had stabilized but needed close monitoring.

Two weeks after the baby's birth, the doctor authorized Francie's discharge. The Reverend Mother summoned Francie's father to take her home. When her father's car arrived, one of the sisters gave Francie her small suitcase and showed her to the door. She knew she would never see her baby again. Sobbing now, Francie ran into her father's arms, but he gave her only an awkward hug in response. He asked about the baby and Francie told him that the baby was a girl, but the birth was complicated, and she was fighting to stay alive. "I don't know for sure if she will make it. I pray for her and hope you will, too." Her father had no further comment.

They started driving, but her father turned in a different direction from where the family lived.

"Where are we going?" she asked.

“I’m taking you to the airport. Your mother and I decided that you would not be living at our home again. Your Aunt Agatha, my older sister in America, agreed to take you in. You can make a new start in the U.S.” He cleared his throat and seemed to want to say more, but all he said was, “I’ll send her a check every month to pay for your board.”

He drove to the airport, showed her to the proper gate, and gave her a quick hug, a passport, and a suitcase packed with her things from home. He had nothing to say as he handed her a ticket to Philadelphia and two hundred American dollars in case of an emergency. Then he said goodbye and told her to be a good girl. She felt like old rubbish being thrown away.

Francie boarded the plane in a state of shock. Her body was sore, and she was still weak. She didn’t know if she would ever see Pat, or her family, or Ireland again. She thought about her uncertain fate, turned toward the window, covered herself with her allotted blanket, and cried quietly into her pillow, eventually falling asleep for a few hours. When the plane landed in Philadelphia, she braced herself for what was to come.

Chapter 3

Aunt Agatha was waiting with a frown and a cold greeting. She took Francie home to a row house on a treeless street in West Philadelphia. Every place looked the same except for the few that had a tiny patch of garden next to the three concrete steps. Over the front door hung a sign with the numbers 5834, the 3 hanging sideways, making it read 58m4; its peeling brown paint showed layers of colors from years gone by. Her aunt opened the door and led Francie inside to a small gray entryway with a worn rug and a few coat hooks on the wall. She hung up her coat and nodded to Francie to do the same. The house smelled stuffy and old, as if the windows had never been opened. There were no welcoming cooking smells, no aromas of dinner stewing or bread warming, or any of the odors that Francie loved in her home in Ireland. There was a small lounge and an old kitchen with a table, big enough for one, a tight squeeze for two. Upstairs were two small bedrooms and a tiny bathroom with a toilet and tub. The stale body odor of the previous resident lingered in the room that was to be Francie's.

"I'm not a wealthy woman," her aunt told her, "and your father has provided a meager amount for your care. I usually have a boarder in this room for additional income to my small salary at the store where I work. When you regain your strength, you will have to find a job as soon as possible. I am fulfilling a family duty by giving you a place to live, and I'll see to it that you are on a tight leash with no chance to repeat your sin while you are in my care."

Francie tried to tell her aunt that she was not that kind of girl, and she and Pat were in love, with plans to be married, but her aunt would not hear of it.

"No excuses, missy—you are what you are." She titled her chin up and looked down her nose at the crestfallen girl. "You will be expected to clean the rooms you use and take care of your laundry. I will provide porridge in the morning and a small supper at six every evening. Anything extra is up to you to. You may use the kitchen as long as you leave it the way you found it. I expect you to leave the bathroom spotlessly clean." She looked around as if trying to find other things for Francie to do. "I work downtown in the stockroom of Wanamaker's Department Store, Monday to Friday. I leave here at seven thirty every morning and am home by five. You can convalesce for a week. After that, I expect you to straighten and clean the house every day. You can continue to rest for part of each day. Dinner is promptly at six. We will leave here every Sunday morning to attend ten thirty Mass."

The long speech left Francie exhausted. Even though the bed and pillow smelled old and used, she wanted only to crawl under the covers. Her body was sore from the baby's birth, and her breasts were leaking, constantly reminding Francie that her baby would not receive the mother's milk nature provided for a healthy baby. She foresaw life at her aunt's house to be as bad as life at the Home, barely tolerable, loveless and dreary.

She started her cleaning duties slowly, at first cleaning only her room, the bathroom, and kitchen, resting between cleaning the next room, trying to heal her body and trying to deal with her loneliness and sadness. As soon as she could, she washed her bedding and hung it to dry. By the following week, her duties increased to cleaning the entire house.

It had been slightly over three weeks since she gave birth, and several times a day, Francie prayed that her daughter had survived.

Her journal was the only outlet for her emotions, and every night she wrote about her feelings. *I never imagined I could feel so empty inside. The homesickness is with me all day, from the time I wake up until I fall asleep at night. There is no escaping it.*

When her aunt came home after work, she would inspect what Francie had done and nod. Then they would share a meager dinner, usually eating in silence and retiring to their rooms for the night.

During the first week of December, Francie left the house for the first time. The fresh winter air energized her—she took deep breaths, trying to swallow the delicious air. This first outing made her realize she had to get out of the house as much as possible or she would suffocate. She was a keen observer and started to familiarize herself with the neighborhood. Her aunt's house was on the shady side of the street, facing north. She went out the front door and turned right, walking east to Fifty-Seventh Street where she turned left. After a few blocks, she came to Market Street, a wide thoroughfare lined with businesses and dominated by the structure holding an elevated train track overhead. She stopped at a fruit stand and used some of her emergency money to purchase two apples and two bananas for her aunt and herself. She asked the fruit seller to explain some of the street patterns to her. The woman was friendly and eager to help.

"The streets on the west side of Philadelphia are divided into straight blocks. The number streets run north and south, and the named streets run east and west. Don't worry—it's very logical once you know the names of some of the east-west streets. In this area," she said as she pointed, "if you walk straight south on, say Fifty-Seventh Street, when you leave Market Street, you will cross a series of streets named for trees—Chestnut, Walnut, Locust, Spruce, and Pine. There are a few minor streets in between, but if you memorize those major ones, you can find your way around most of the downtown area, too."

"Thank you—I'm going to try it right now, so if you hear on the radio that a hopelessly lost girl was found roaming the streets of West Philadelphia, you'll know it's me," she said with a smile.

"Come back again and I'll tell you more—good luck."

Francie walked a short way down Market Street, stopped in a store that sold stationery and bought a small packet of airmail paper and a few stamps. Then she successfully navigated her way back to the fifty-seven hundred block of Locust Street, repeating *Market, Chestnut, Walnut Locust, Spruce, and Pine* in her head until she had it memorized. She had no trouble finding the house.

She put the apples and bananas on a dish in the kitchen. When she told her aunt to help herself, the reply was hardly a thank-you. "Well," her aunt said, "aren't you the extravagant one."

In her room, with the door closed, Francie wrote a long letter to Pat, telling him all the details about her time at Home for Unwed Mothers, the birth of their daughter, and her anxiety about whether their baby was still alive. She went on to write of her banishment to the home of her unloving aunt in the U.S. and her determination to finish her education. "Pat, I miss you so much. I feel that I am ripped in two and will never be whole until we're together again. You are everything to me, my love."

For weeks, Francie waited for his reply. Then one day, her letter was returned marked, "No Longer at This Address—No Forwarding Address." She put it in the drawer with her journal.

Evcry Sunday her aunt expected her to go to Mass, and Francie complied. When she entered the church, the familiar scent of incense and candle wax that once comforted her now nauseated her. She felt empty when she was in church and empty when she left. Her only prayer was that her baby was alive. After church, she and Aunt Agatha went straight home. There was no such thing in her aunt's routine that included going out for lunch or even for tea and a pastry.

Chapter 4

She knew that to keep her sanity and to make her own way in America, there were two things she must do—find a way to continue her studies at University and get a job so she could pay her aunt a stipend and save for her future. Philadelphia was easy to navigate. The bus and subway system linked many sections of the city. The area of West Philadelphia where she lived was a short bus ride away from the verdant Benjamin Franklin Parkway. Francie knew if she were going to be a Philadelphian, visiting the city's answer to Paris' Champs-Élysées would have to be at the top of her list. Starting at the world-renowned Greek Revival-style Philadelphia Museum of Art, the Parkway was lined with flags from every nation of the world leading one mile into the heart of the city. The sight of the flag of Ireland momentarily brought tears to Francie's eyes. All along the way, other classically designed stone buildings housed the Rodin Museum of Sculpture, the Franklin Institute Science Museum and the mammoth Philadelphia Public Library, her first destination of the day. Though it was well into December, the weather was moderate, and the remainder of the falling leaves swirled in zephyrs to the ground.

From the time she was a small child, libraries were a magical place to her. They opened a world of other people, places, and things—true and imagined—everything. Libraries gave her the opportunity to seek knowledge of anything she desired—and offered more solace than the Church had ever given her. The library was her first stop on the road to independence. She walked through the double door of the huge stone building and entered the high ceilinged, hushed reception rotunda. A feeling of belonging came over her—this was her turf, her safe harbor, whether in Ireland, Scotland, America, or probably any place in the world. She breathed in the smell of ink, paper and glue and felt them strengthen her. After registering for a library card, Francie went to the reference room to research universities in the area. And there she learned that University of Pennsylvania was one of the top academic institutions in the country. It was a short bus ride away.

Francie made a beeline for the bank of public telephones and called the Office of Admissions.

When a woman answered, Francie immediately started speaking, racing through what she had to say. "I hope you can help me. My name is Francie O'Conner. Less than one month ago, due to a family crisis and with no advance notice, I was sent from my home in Ireland to the U.S. to start a new life. My only relative here is an aunt who has given me a room in her house in exchange for household duties. I met her last month for the first time. I am finally over the shock of my situation and ready to formulate a plan for establishing myself here. My first priority is to continue my education at a top university, so I can make a place for myself in this country. Last spring, I finished my first year at University of Edinburgh, summa cum laude. I have recommendations from the President of the University, the Dean of Students and the head of the Classics Department, my area of major studies. I know this is an unusual request, but I would like to speak to the Dean of Admissions. Every day counts to me. Would it be possible for me to come in as soon as possible to drop off my credentials? Could I come today?"

"Wait a minute—slow down. You covered everything in one breath, young lady. Your first step is to talk to Mrs. Chester, the assistant to the dean. She may be able to help. I'll forward your call to her....and good luck!"

The receptionist buzzed Mrs. Chester's office and asked her to take this unusual query. The office seldom took calls from hopeful students, but the receptionist told Mrs. Chester that this applicant was extraordinary. "She is sincere and well qualified. And she is desperate."

Mrs. Chester said she'd accept her call.

This time, Francie spoke slowly, more in control, but still with genuine emotion. She introduced herself and repeated her appeal to speak with the dean. Mrs. Chester told her that the request was quite out of the ordinary and that the dean did not see students except under very unusual circumstances. Francie gathered up all her nerve and kept talking. She repeated her academic record, adding, "My circumstances are very unusual, but deeply personal. I have been in this country for less than a month after leaving Ireland. I am virtually alone, trying to regain what I lost." Then, with a tremble in her voice, she said, "I would rather not explain my reason over the phone, Mrs. Chester. Could I come to the office and speak to you and let you decide if I could see the dean?"

Mrs. Chester, too, heard the desperation in Francie's voice, and using her professional judgment, asked Francie if she could come today with her credentials. She would show them to the dean and let her know if he would see her.

"Could I? Oh, yes, yes, yes, I can," Francie said, her voice now thickening with tears. "Mrs. Chester, this is the only good thing that has happened to me in months. Thank you so much."

She hung up the phone, fortified by the compassion of the women in the Admissions Office and hurried back to the reference librarian to find the city's bus and train schedules. She circled the key points highlighting her present location, that of the University, and of the street where she lived. Having grown up in Dublin and traveled all over Scotland, she found Philadelphia's public transportation system easy to master, especially now that she knew the mantra, "Market, Chestnut, Walnut, Locust, Spruce and Pine."

She rushed back to the house to get her credentials and within an hour entered the Admission's Office.

"I'm Francie O'Conner," she told the receptionist. "Mrs. Chester said she would see me today."

"Oh, yes, I'm so glad Mrs. Chester agreed to meet with you. Have a seat and I'll buzz her to let her know you're here." As she picked up the phone, she said to Francie, "And I'm so pleased to meet you."

It was obvious that this was a very busy room—the phone rang almost constantly, and the carpet and chair seats were well worn. The table next to her held brochures about the University. She leafed through one and in less than a minute knew this was the place for her.

The door to an adjacent room opened, and a middle-aged woman with a welcoming smile extended her hand and introduced herself as Mrs. Chester. She said, "What took you so long?"

Francie immediately relaxed. "How do you do, Mrs. Chester? I'm Francie O'Conner," she said smiling and speaking with her melodic Irish lilt. "Thank you for seeing me and for making me feel so welcome."

"Oh, my, I didn't expect to see such a young girl."

"I was sixteen when I entered University of Edinburgh, and I'll be eighteen in January, but in the past few months, I've had to grow up fast. I'm afraid my carefree youth is over."

She handed over her credentials, and Mrs. Chester quickly looked them over. "Impressive," she said, "but I must warn you that all of our students are high achievers, so Dean Ross will be looking for something a little extra that will impress him. I'll do what I can to convince him to grant you an interview. I see scores of applicants, but there is something about your impassioned request, accomplished record and confident way that make you stand out as a perfect match with the University. If he agrees to see you, I think that you will make as good an impression on him as you have on me." She paused, looking with great interest at the young woman. "Stop back here in two hours to find out if he has made his decision. Meanwhile here's a guide to the campus—you might enjoy exploring it."

"Thank you, Mrs. Chester, for everything you're doing for me. I can feel the energy of the University and can hardly wait to stroll around the campus—and buy a soft pretzel from a vender. This is a new experience for me, the pretzels, I mean. I'll try one for lunch."

For forty cents, she purchased a soft pretzel and a Coke. The vendor asked if she wanted mustard on her pretzel, and she said, "If that's the Philadelphia way, sure."

Pretzel with mustard? It was delicious, like nothing she had ever tasted. She walked around the campus, visited the bookstore and athletic fields, went to Houston Hall—the social building for students, and, of course, the library—then sat on a bench beneath a spreading chestnut tree to watch the students hurrying to their classes. The campus had the vitality of youth mixed with the traditional old stone and mortar buildings of a prestigious university. The air hummed with a vibration of social and intellectual stimulation. Francie felt that this was her natural environment, and she was eager to return to it.

Two hours later, she was back in the admissions office. The receptionist buzzed the dean to tell him of Francie's arrival, and a few minutes later, Dean Ross opened his door and asked her to come in.

He looked like one would expect an academic to look—tweed jacket, dark slacks, bow tie. On the wall were four diplomas from various universities as well as portraits of past university officials. A framed picture of a woman and grown children sat on his desk.

"Miss O'Conner," he said. "It's a pleasure to meet you. Of the hundreds of applications from students all over the world, your credentials, commendation and letters of recommendation are some of the most impressive I've seen. I know the University of Edinburgh well and have walked its hallowed halls. Several generations back, my great-great grandfather was a professor of history there. Most of my father's family is still in Scotland, but as for our branch, my great grandfather immigrated to the U.S. almost a hundred years ago and settled in Philadelphia. I am curious, though, because you don't sound Scottish. In fact, you sound Irish."

Francie had been listening attentively. She spoke up, charming him with her smile. "Dean Ross, Scotland is wonderful, but I didn't intend to mislead you. The reason I don't speak with a Scottish burr is because I'm Irish, from Dublin." Then, with a mischievous smile, she added, "Is it possible that you have some Irish in your background, too? It's said that the combination of Scottish and Irish is unbeatable."

The Dean smiled broadly and said with humor, "Well, I guess that makes me unbeatable, because I'm half Irish. My mother's family was rooted in Ireland before they came to this country."

The hour-long interview was more like an informal discussion. By the time it was over, Dean Ross seemed as if he were a welcoming uncle. Francie told him that she preferred not to talk about the reason she left University of Edinburgh, but she assured him it was a personal family matter and had nothing to do with academics. If it were an absolute necessity, she would tell him the particulars of her move. "I have always loved learning, and when I matriculated at the U of E, I felt my academic life transition to a new level—one with unlimited possibilities of advancement with outstanding faculty and fellow students.

"I felt the same excitement in the air today when I explored the campus. I felt at home, especially this time of year when anticipation of the holidays is everywhere, and the students are wrapped in their navy and red mufflers, the same colors as University of Edinburgh."

The dean laughed. "Well, begorra, they are—not something I ever really thought about."

Francie grinned at him and went on with her story. "As my records from U of E show, my major was Classical Studies. I loved the way the Greek philosophers shed enlightenment on the thinking and behavior of humankind over the centuries. Heraclitus said, 'The path up and down are one and the same,' which puzzled me at the time I read it. I was so happy then. My life had been up, up, up." She shrugged, smiled at him. "I hope you don't think I'm a complainer, but after being so miserable for the past few months, I am finally optimistic about this chance to start on the way up again. Now I understand more fully what Heraclitus observed—I am actually living it—the flow of life takes us up and it takes us down over and over again—and right now, I'm flying."

"Miss O'Conner," he said, "for a person so young, the wisdom you exhibit amazes me. I won't ask about the situation that sent you on the road down, but I assure you that you are on the road up now."

He flipped through her dossier quickly again and held it up, gesturing it as a salute to her.

"Your record stands on its own. As does this interview. The University welcomes a select handful of outstanding foreign students by offering a one-year scholarship, extended yearly if your academic progress merits its continuation.

"My decision today is an easy one. Welcome, Francie O'Conner, to the sophomore class at University of Pennsylvania." He stood, extending his hand. "Our student employment office will help to find you a part-time job on campus, if required."

Francie was overwhelmed. "Thank you so much, Dean Ross, for giving me this chance. I promise I won't let you down." It was all she could do not to hug him.

The Dean congratulated her and assigned an advisor to guide her with course selection. He pointed her in the direction of the student employment office. "The winter term will be starting on January ninth. You still have time to choose your classes. Your guidance counsellor will advise you how to make up the semester you missed, and student employment will help you find a job that starts as soon as possible. I'll be watching your progress," he said with a fatherly grin. "Stop in whenever you need advice from a Scots-Irishman."

That night she wrote, *My favorite day of the year is always the first day of a new school term. I'll get myself a U of P scarf and be ready on January ninth for opening day.*

Chapter 5

On her way home, the church near U of Penn beckoned to her. The door was open, and it was suddenly difficult for her to pass; she needed to go in to give thanks. She felt a tiny stirring inside her. *Could it be that my faith is coming back?* She peeked into the church. The familiar odors of candle wax and incense that had nauseated her before didn't bother her quite so much. She gingerly entered, knelt and crossed herself, then proceeded to the confessional. She buzzed for the priest and began, whispering her story to him—her love for Pat, her resentment toward her parents, her hatred for the foul treatment from the sisters, her awful separation from her baby, her dislike for her aunt and the terrible feeling of living without love.

The priest listened without comment. When he was sure she had finished, he said with a gentle tone, "There are many students who come here, some as lost as you, and I welcome them, as I welcome you. I can tell that you were raised in a good Catholic home. You have a particularly difficult problem to deal with, and I hope your faith will lead you back to the Church. Please come to see me whenever you feel the need."

"Thank you, Father, for keeping the door open."

She knelt in front of the altar and gave thanks to God for healing her body and spirit and for giving her the opportunity to start again. She lit a candle for her daughter and prayed for her health and happiness, wherever she was.

That night she wrote in her journal, *I continue to doubt my faith. I feel that my Church has let me down. But at the same time, I feel the need to connect with God so that He can hear my prayers. I want to thank Him for giving me a second chance at life. The resentment I feel is not with God but with the Catholic Church and the way I've been treated because of its doctrines.*

Christmas Eve in Aunt Agatha's house was like nothing she had ever experienced. There were no decorations, no kind words, no happiness—just the instructions from her aunt to fix something to eat for herself and to be ready to go to midnight Mass. Her aunt marked the occasion by turning on a light in the window before they left. They went to church, spoke to no one and came home immediately following the service.

On Christmas day, Francie took a walk and saw the Christmas decorations on nearly every house she passed. At least somebody's happy, she thought. That night, Christmas supper was potato and bacon soup and an omelet.

"Thank you, Aunt Agatha," she said. "I have something for you." She handed her aunt a red envelope and watched as she opened it and took out the poem Francie had written. She had spent several hours working the poem and choosing the appropriate words so that it wasn't overly sweet, just a nice sentiment telling her aunt how much she appreciated allowing her into her house and wishing her Christmas cheer and a happy New Year. Francie recited the poem in her head as her aunt read it, hoping she would look up and smile at an amusing phrase. Instead, Francie watched Aunt Agatha read it dryly, put it back in the envelope, nod her head and stuff it in a kitchen drawer. No kiss, no hug, no gift and no thank-you. Francie went to her room, slammed the door and wrote in her journal that she had the saddest Christmas of her life.

Thoughts of not knowing if her baby were alive and well haunted her. She hoped a family who could give her a good life had adopted her. She could deal with that once she knew her baby was alive.

On the fourth of January, she spent her eighteenth birthday in disbelief that so much had happened in the one year since she and Pat had celebrated her last birthday. Unbridled joy had turned to dismal emptiness and sadness. That night she wrote in her journal, *I am so lonely, but I know I have to shake off my negative feelings and concentrate on my future. Once I get past the next few days, I'll be on my way to a new beginning, a better life at a new school, and a part-time job so that I can earn some spending money. After seven months of misery, my life is back in perspective. I am starting to feel my youth return and am ready to make new friends. I can see a purpose now.*

She wanted to share all this with someone. "Would it be all right if I correspond with my brother, Tommy?" she asked her aunt.

"All communication mailed to your home has to be approved by your father. I'll write to him to see if he will allow it," her aunt answered coldly.

Two weeks later, Francie received a letter from her brother. She opened it as if it were the most wonderful gift she had ever received—knowing she was part of a family.

Tommy told her that a pall had descended over their home.

It's not the same place you left, Francie. There is no happiness here. Mum is relentless in her condemnation of you. She never speaks your name, and she leaves the room if anyone mentions it. I think she has lost her mind. Da is moody and resentful but doesn't talk about it. He's loyal to her, but I think he blames her for spoiling what was once a happy home. Denis and Brian have moved out and hardly ever come home, so I am stuck here trying to add some sense to our parents' lives. Right after I graduate in June, I plan to get a job and find a new place to live. Life goes on and I have to think about my future.

Francie, please believe me when I say I'm not writing to complain. You have it much worse than I do. I just want you to know the truth about what is happening here. I miss you so much, my little sister, please write as soon as you can. I will always be on your side, no matter what."

With all my love, Tommy

He included the address of the local post office and told her to write to him there in care of general delivery so he would be sure to receive her letters.

Throughout the reading of Tommy's letter, with joy and nostalgia, she wept.

Fortified with the knowledge that her brother was there for her, Francie felt energized. Her future beckoned once more, and with her familiar positive attitude, she began again. Instead of feeling old before her time, she felt her true age—eighteen—and was ready to return to the world of her peers.

Francie was back in action, and the University of Pennsylvania welcomed her.

At orientation, Francie learned about the University's tennis facilities. She was eager to get back to the game that had provided such fun for her and her brothers. During one of her breaks between classes, she stopped by to check out the courts. On the typically frigid January day, six matches were being played by hardy souls on the outdoor courts. She didn't have the winter garb to even consider playing in the cold. The indoor courts were her destination. She wasn't sure how to enter the facility, so she stopped a young man, who said he was going inside, too. He introduced himself as Noah, one of the four pros.

"You're just the man I'm looking for," she said, introducing herself. "I'm new in this country and new at the University. How would I go about finding people to play with?" she asked.

"If you have time, I could spend a few minutes hitting with you to assess your level," he offered. "Then you could put your name on the sign-up sheet according to ability for those looking for games or substitutes. I'll find a demo racquet for you, and you can grab a pair of old shorts from the lost and found bin."

"Are my trainers okay?" she asked.

"Your trainers?"

She pointed to her feet.

"Oh, I should have known—we call them sneakers in the U.S."

"Darn," she said shaking her head. "I knew that, but I forgot. I'm finding that old habits die slowly, but from now on, sneakers, it is." She looked at him with a wry smile. "It's been more than a year since I held a racquet, so be ready."

"Duly noted," he said smiling back at her.

He was in for a surprise. Once she got into the rhythm, he saw that her groundstrokes were extraordinary. She had power and accuracy and could slice and spin the ball. He tested her at the net and was impressed by her reflexes and put-away shots.

"Francie, I think you're a ringer. You must have been putting me on. How did you learn to play like the boys?"

She grinned at his compliment, eager to tell him. "By playing with the boys, how else? My three brothers were fierce competitors and showed me no mercy, especially when they needed a fourth for doubles. They deigned to play singles with me when they were desperate, but once I started taking sets from them, they upped their game and whipped me with their strength. My finesse was no match for their power. One of my brothers is a ranked player in Ireland and plans to become a pro."

Noah encouraged her to go out for the tennis team, but she said that between work and school, the only time she could play would be early in the morning or after five in the afternoon.

She told him about her financial situation and asked if the pro shop sold secondhand tennis racquets. "Could you find a group for me? And one more important question—how much does it cost to play?"

"Don't worry, Francie. Once I find a group for you, we'll supply you with one of the demonstration racquets the big manufacturers send us. After that, all you'll need is a tennis skirt or shorts. We sell them here, new or used. Your sneakers—or trainers, as you call them—are fine. I'll let you play at no cost for the first month. After that, we'll negotiate to find the right price, but let's keep the deal confidential—I'm making an exception for you."

"Thanks so much, Noah," she said. "There is so much generosity here—what a country, and what a school. And, of course, what a pro! Thank you again." As they walked out, she said, "I work at the school's business office every day, and you can leave a message for me there."

Two days later, she got the call. "I found the perfect mixed doubles for you with two male graduate students and a junior girl with abilities like yours. They want to play on Thursday night at five thirty. How's that sound?"

"Like music to my ears—angels singing. I'll come a few minutes early, straight from my job so I can look over the lost and found to find something that fits."

Francie walked onto the court alone. This feels like home. The familiar sounds of balls popping off strings and players' calls of "out," or "good serve," as well as the grunts, brought back memories of good times. Even the sweaty smell of the facility made her happy.

They were a good foursome and had fun because they all played to win, taking no prisoners. It felt so good to be back. After the game, they went to Fonzo's near the campus for pizza and to get to know each other. The two graduate students had been friends since their undergraduate days at Penn. Anders was in Law School and Charlie was studying for a PhD in an esoteric field called "bryology," the study of moss. Annie's comment about that was, "I guess you have two very unhappy parents. Are there any jobs in that field?"

"Maybe one," he parried, "but I have a lock on that, I hope. What's your major?"

"Anthropology—another field with one job available," said Annie.

The three of them turned to Francie, and she said in the tone of a question, "Classics?" At that they all laughed.

"Another losing proposition," one of them said.

They made a date to play the next week.

From then on, they were Thursday night friends. For Francie, it became the highlight of her week, the only luxury her meager salary allowed.

Chapter 6

And so, her first year of exile continued. Slowly, the intensity of her losses faded, and she accepted the life thrust on her. She went to church with her aunt every Sunday. She got no pleasure from the rituals, but she felt the joy of God in her heart while she was there. Each week, she lit a candle for her baby—always Kate to her—and included her in her prayers every night, never knowing if her daughter was alive, if her name was changed, if she was cherished.

As the months went by, the clarity of her memories of Pat faded little by little. She had left her carefree youth in Scotland when she was seventeen, and now, though she was just eighteen, she strove to regain at least some of it. She had made friends with a few classmates, male and female, but she seldom dated. When she did, she felt no romance. Her devotion to Pat became a misty memory but no longer a reality. She could think of him now with smiles instead of tears, and she became herself again. Her outgoing personality began reemerging from the cloud she had been under for the past year and a half.

The correspondence she so treasured continued between her brother, Thomas, and herself, as they sent letters back and forth every few weeks. Describing her new school in her new city, she told him that her mission was to make a new life for herself in America.

The University of Pennsylvania is a microcosm of life in a big city, Tommy. The school encompasses several campuses. The interior quadrangle is surrounded by red brick and stone dorms, classroom buildings, offices and a massive library. Students are strolling or rushing in every direction, and American touch football games are being played on the grass. This is a happy place. Laughter and shouts of activities pepper the sounds on campus all day. Our kind of football is called 'soccer' here, and black and white balls are in motion all over the green. The outer campus houses graduate schools, a major hospital, shops selling everything from sailing hats to formalwear. I won't go into more detail, Tommy, but you get the picture.

All over the city, the supermarkets are staggering. I usually shop at the A&P. I have never seen so much food and so much variety. I made a great discovery—Shea's canned tomato soup (fifteen cents a can) and grilled cheese toast (practically free)—a delicious combination. AND I can afford it! It's my main comfort meal at home.

Restaurants and cafés have all kinds of food—Chinese chow mein, Italian pizza and huge sandwiches called hoagies, southern fried chicken and biscuits, and food from every country in Europe. The street venders sell soft doughy pretzels with mustard on top—and they're delicious! The people I see are unbelievable. All shades, from almost jet black to pale white, Chinese, Japanese—all ethnicities and sizes and shapes. There is such a big world here—nothing like little Ireland.

I suspect that Aunt Agatha finally has a goal in her life—to make me as miserable as she is. But now that I have you to tell, I can laugh about it.

Tommy, you are the most-loved person in my world now. On lonely days, I read and reread your letters and hope that someday I meet someone here to love. I'm ready to fill the hole in my heart.

Love, Francie

Tommy wrote back to her about what was happening at home, both good and bad. The good—Margaret. He met her at a victory party after a football game at Trinity, and now they're in love.

We're taking it slowly but have stopped dating other people. She's everything I ever wanted in a girl—sense of humor, intelligence, and adorable—black hair and blue eyes—a sharp contrast to us O'Conners with our light red, dark red, and bright red hair!

Denis and Brian share a place downtown. They are both robustly healthy, competitive as always. Still fierce tennis opponents, but Brian is starting to edge out Denis from the winner's circle. Denis has his architect's license and is now going through the motions required to advance from drawing blueprints for humdrum, boxy, cheap housing to something he actually creates. It takes years of technical and financial strain to navigate the ranks. Brian is plugging away at his journalism and now has a small weekly column in the "Post." No love interests for either of them—at least any that last.

The bad news is that Mum and Da are struggling. She is bitter all the time and has made him bitter, too. She is disappointed with all of us boys for not giving her grandchildren. Any mention of you is still forbidden.

I miss you too, Sis, and hope you find happiness.

Love you, Tommy

Francie read his letters over and over, seeing his face, hearing his voice on every page. She would add his letter to the pile in her drawer tied in a ribbon and titled, "Letters from Home." Occasionally, she would get short notes from her other brothers telling her that Tommy shared her news with them. They always apologized for the long intervals between their brief missives and hoped Tommy let her know how busy they were. She loved hearing from Denis and Brian, but Tommy was her number-one brother.

At the end of her sophomore year, Dean Ross congratulated her on her perfect grades and extended her scholarship. She beamed and thanked him for his faith in her and for continuing her scholarship. "Because of you, I can continue to become the person I always hoped to be."

"Francie, even when we first met, I knew you would be able to achieve anything you wanted. You sailed through all the additional courses you needed to bring you up to date and still earned top grades. The University is lucky to have you."

"Dean Ross, since you know me better than anyone here, I would like your opinion about something. Could I ask you for free advice? I'm thinking of making a change."

"I'll do my best."

"I spoke to my advisor, but I'd like your input, too, as a mentor and a friend.

"Philosophy and the arts have always been my favorite subjects, but now I think I am ready for a more practical pursuit. Ever since I began working in the business office here at the University, I have become fascinated with the intricacies of what it takes to run a business. I never knew there were so many facets to it. I've observed that putting those parts together to create a successful business requires a broad knowledge of many subjects and an ability to coordinate them in the proper order. Many aspects of the liberal arts come into play here—sociology, psychology, philosophy, history, politics and more. I've begun to realize that my study of the liberal arts is a valuable steppingstone to another field of education. What would be your opinion about changing my major to business administration?"

"Francie, this is quite a surprise. I'm impressed by your presentation. You sound like a super-salesperson already." He beamed at his favorite protégé.

"Changing your major will require quite a bit of additional work for you. You'll need some prerequisite business courses to make up for those you've missed. Our Wharton School of Business is world-class, and you'd be hard pressed to find a business school anywhere in the country with the quality education you'll find here. As I said before, I have no doubt that you will succeed in anything you put your mind to, Francie."

This time when she thanked him, he shrugged off the offer of her hand and hugged her instead. "I'm privileged to be a part of your present and future. I feel as proud of you as I do of my own children."

Francie's eyes started to tear up, moved by what he had said. "Dean Ross, you are like my guardian angel." She kissed him on the check and told him he had a special place in her heart. "I promise, I'll never let you down."

During the summer between her sophomore and junior years, she worked in the office full-time, saving her money so that eventually she would be able to afford a place of her own. At summer's end, she started her junior year as a student in the Wharton School of Business. She continued to be grateful to her aunt for taking her in, but they had very little to talk about, and her aunt was happy to keep it to a minimum. On the weekends, Francie supplemented her income by waitressing at the Irish

Pub in downtown Philly. The Irish-American owner hired her to add some authenticity to the restaurant, and her Irish lilt and smiling eyes served her well, as did the generous tips she accumulated. The clientele loved to hear her say, "And what can I get for you blokes tonight?" with her slightly exaggerated Irish accent. She loved her business curriculum—and she loved her jobs, both at school and in the Irish Pub. Now when she played tennis, she could pay for her court time without any great sacrifice. She was definitely on the upswing in this part of her journey through life.

She continued to eat and love Shea's canned tomato soup when she needed a tasty, affordable pick-me-up, and for the warm feeling it gave her. As the end of her junior year approached, she wrote to the company to tell them how much she enjoyed their soup—and that she had practically lived on it for the past two years.

"Would you consider hiring me for summer employment? I think that any company who makes a product that can sustain a college student for two years at such a low price must be doing something right! My studies at Wharton School are teaching me the theories of business, but I hope I could learn something from your company about how to apply those principles."

She included her resume and requested an interview. A week later, a letter came inviting her to the company's offices and manufacturing plant in old city Philadelphia, just across the Delaware River from New Jersey.

The interviewer asked her if she had any experience in the food industry. She hesitated, and then plunged in. "When I lived in Ireland, I worked in a church run business, learning all phases of production, including mixing, baking, packaging and shipping of communion wafers. We produced and shipped twenty-five thousand wafers every day all over Ireland.

That sealed the deal, and she was hired.

That night she wrote in her journal, *Who could have predicted that my forced labor making communion wafers would serve as my entrée into the business world? This is beyond ironic, almost laughable.*

Shea's Soup Company and Francie were an excellent match. The company treated its employees with respect and generosity, and in return, they worked with pride and efficiency no matter what their job. Before her senior year began, she had banked several hundred dollars and tasted every one of Shea's products served in the employee cafeteria.

During her last week of work, she made an appointment to meet with someone in the personnel office. "I'll be graduating from Wharton School next May," she said, "and after spending the summer working here, I'll be looking to find permanent employment as an executive trainee after I graduate. I am willing to start at any level. Would you take my application under consideration?"

She was answered with a smile and a handshake. "Send the completed application with the letters of recommendations you have, and I'll personally deliver them to my department head. Good luck with your senior year—we'll wait to hear from you next spring."

Her senior year went well. All her classes were stimulating, and she gleaned a wide range of knowledge, but the subjects of merchandising and marketing particularly fascinated her. These areas required social skills, and she thought hers would be an asset. The two subjects became her senior year area of concentration. Before graduation, she interviewed again at Shea's Soups for their executive training program and was hired to start work two weeks after commencement. She was elated. She called her tennis buddies to help her celebrate—her treat. Though she was still under drinking age, one of the gang sneaked her a beer, which she raised in a toast to friendship and the future.

With some of her savings and the promise of a steady salary, she rented a small apartment and planned to move the day after graduation. Life in the drab and cheerless house with her aunt was ending, and both were more than ready for it. Their relationship was one of tolerance and civility but positively no warmth. Sometimes Francie wondered why her aunt was so miserable. Maybe her life had been loveless. Or, was it possible that old Aunt Agatha had not been permitted to marry the man she loved? Whatever the reason, all Francie could see were the dregs of a wasted life.

She finished University at the top of her class and was asked to be Valedictorian. She accepted with pride and wrote a speech containing the themes that were her story—new beginnings, respect for one's self, letting go of the past, adjusting to adulthood.

"My studies began at University of Edinburgh, where I majored in classics. I most loved Greek philosophers. Their insights into the human condition impressed and inspired me to think deeply about how the world around me came to this level of civilization. I also learned that understanding some of the most brilliant philosophers the world has ever seen takes more than memorizing theories and getting an A on an exam. It takes living day by day, year by year, adjusting to meet the circumstances life brings. Many philosophers believe that life and its meaning is a circular process, always changing yet remaining the same. The Greek philosopher, Heraclitus, studied this paradox and formulated a philosophy based on his observations and experiences. He recognized that the pattern of the human condition is circular and travels in waves. The paths we follow constantly go up and then down, repeatedly, swerving with our life's rhythm. Although I am very young, I can see in my own life how what he said is true. I recognize it in myself. I have been to the heights and I have been to the depths in my short life. I have learned not to give up when down and not to be complacent when up. The goal of our education at this outstanding university should not simply be the knowledge we gain from books, but the rational manner in which we put that knowledge to work to make ourselves and our world a better place—expecting ups and downs along the way.

"For me, and for many other graduates, these past years at the University of Pennsylvania have transformed an uncertain future into one we can approach with confidence and pride.

"Thank you to the administration for the generosity and warm welcome you gave me; thank you to my advisors who guided me to find my way; thank you to my esteemed professors for the knowledge they imparted to me; and thank you to my fellow students who befriended a lonely immigrant. I will do my best to pass it along, and to appreciate that there is nothing as valuable as human kindness."

Her aunt listened with no emotion, a blank stare on her face. After the ceremony, Francie thanked her for providing her with a place to live, and she moved closer to her in order to give her a hug, but her aunt backed away. They said their goodbyes, and she saw her aunt smile for the first time.

Probably because Francie would be moving out that day. After three years of small steps, Francie was taking a giant step to reach one of her goals—moving to her own apartment, her first real home in her new country.

Chapter 7

All her professors congratulated her, but her economics professor lingered. He asked her if she and her family had plans for lunch. She told him she had no real family here.

"Done!" he said. "I would be honored to take you to lunch to celebrate."

"How could I say no to that, Dr. Hanson?" she asked. "It's the most surprising offer I've had in three years!"

Within walking distance of the University, he ushered her into a quiet restaurant, the kind that uses starched, white cloths and napkins and doesn't rush you from the table. She told him that her main diet for the past few years had been Shea's tomato soup and toasted cheese. Would he please order for her?

"Champagne first?" he asked, and she accepted. He asked her to call him Michael. She blushed, and he laughed. "There's nothing as bright as the blush of a redhead."

When she had been his student, she barely noticed him, but now she saw how appealing he was—tall and slender, with broad shoulders and a shy grin. His hair was sandy-colored, probably much blonder when he was a child, and his eyes were hazel, narrowing when he smiled, making tiny wrinkles at the edges.

They started a conversation filled with small talk, gradually becoming more personal. She realized that she was flirting—this for the first time since she met Pat—and he was, too. Something had clicked, and they both felt it, an attraction. They had a happy conversation full of funny anecdotes, optimism and increasing interest. Both of them were barely aware of the food.

"I listened closely to your valedictory speech, Francie. It was as if you were speaking directly to me. I have been on the down path for so long, and now I think I am heading up—at a run. Let me explain....."

Francie smiled her encouragement and picked up her champagne flute.

"I'm thirty. Right now, that might sound old, but believe me, in ten years, you'll be thirty and you'll think you're still a kid—like I feel right now with you."

He didn't want to hold back his exuberance about her, but first he wanted to be honest with her about his past.

"Five years ago, I married my college sweetheart, Emmy. We were so much in love, and marriage was such fun—like playing house, only we didn't have to play at it—it was real. The first year of our marriage was charmed—I finished my PhD, and the University offered me a full professorship. The G.I. Bill had been passed in 1944 and was extended into the Fifties to include veterans of Korea. Enrollment was way up at all the colleges and universities. Additional professors were needed, and I was lucky enough to be hired by Penn. Our luck continued—a month later, Emmy was pregnant. We bought a little house downtown and started to decorate and shop for baby furniture."

He paused and looked down, then looked up at her with the saddest eyes she had ever seen. Francie looked at him with concern.

"Three months later, our luck gave out. Emmy was killed by a drunken driver. Our baby died within her."

Francie nearly dropped her glass. She held her napkin to her face, gasping at what he had just said. She automatically reached her hand across the table to take his.

He held on tightly. "I was away at a seminar in New York when I got a call from my parents. They told me that Emmy was in the hospital, and I should come home as soon as possible. They didn't tell me that she and the baby were already dead."

He was in control of his emotions as he continued, but tears rolled down Francie's face. He continued to grip her hand as if he needed her support to go on. She covered it with her other hand, tucking one finger into his cupped palm. He placed his other hand over their clutched hands. They both seemed to be hanging on for dear life.

"I went straight to the hospital where the doctor broke the news to me as gently as he could. I asked to see her. They recommended against it, but I insisted, and what I saw appalled me. This couldn't be Emmy—this was a shell, a mutilation of what she had been. The car had knocked her down and the rear wheels had run over one side of her face. I broke down. How could I never hear her laugh again? How could I never feel her touch or feel her against me while we slept?

"I couldn't leave her there alone and go home to an empty house.

"She was my wife, my constant companion, a part of me. I sat with her for hours until the doctor gave me a sedative, and my parents led me away in a drug haze to their home. The next day we talked about the funeral. The whole day is a blur in my mind. I never returned to our home. I couldn't bear the thought of what I'd lost. All I can remember is the coffin that contained Emmy and our unborn baby.

"My parents took over the sale of my house. I spent a year with them. The president of the University and the head of my department were exceptionally kind and told me to take as long as I needed to recover before coming back to work. I went for long walks, forcing myself to go out now and then with friends and colleagues. I read, I watched mindless TV."

"How awful it must have been," she said with tenderness. "I can feel your grief even now."

"It took six months for me to return to work and another six months to move from my parents' home to a place of my own, a small apartment on campus where I still live. It has taken years for me to think calmly about losing Emmy, but now I can finally picture her, as she was before the accident—young, beautiful and happy—a bit like you."

Francie gave him a grateful smile and petted the hands she still held.

"I didn't think I would ever be normal again," he continued. "But one day, when you spoke up in class, I felt a stir inside of me, the first inkling of a return to normalcy. Your smile, your intelligence and your wit charmed me. By the end of the semester, I was smitten with you—and you had no idea of the effect you had on me. I was frightened that you would find someone else. I wanted to meet you the right way in accordance to the rules of student-teacher ethics. I didn't want to scare you off or put you on the spot, so I tried to act very casual."

Francie looked at him quizzically. She in fact had had no idea.

"It was all I could do to wait until the ceremony was over today to speak to you. So here I am, my heart on my sleeve, eager to get to know everything about you."

The words he spoke gave Francie chills, followed by a feeling of warmth that brought a blush to her face. "I am honored to even be considered in the same breath as your Emmy," she said.

He smiled when he saw her blush, and he touched her cheeks with his fingertips.

Francie's voice was thick with emotion when she told Michael how sorry she was for all of the unhappiness he had endured. "I know a little about unhappiness and loneliness, too. When we first started talking today, I felt we had a bond, but I didn't know why. Now I do. We have both suffered the loss of what we thought was our only love. Right now, today, we are taking a giant step on the long path back up."

She took a deep breath.

"As you said, I'm only twenty. My tragedy is not even close to what you experienced, but, at age seventeen, I felt as though my world ended. What I do know is that I am attracted to you, excited, even. It's been three years since I felt this way about anyone. I haven't told anyone my story, but I'd like to share it with you."

As she told him about her past, she started to feel trepidation about whether to include her pregnancy and banishment to the Home. She wanted to be honest with him but, at the same time, didn't want to scare him away. She decided to wait to see his reactions before she told him her darkest secret.

"I graduated from upper school when I was sixteen. I had the usual short relationships with boys, mostly friendly, nothing serious. The most important boy in my life until then was my brother Tommy.

"The day I left Ireland to go to University of Edinburgh I was sixteen. This would be my first time away, a milestone in our family who all spent their college years living at home and commuting to Trinity College in Dublin. On the ferry on the way to Scotland, I met a boy on his way to St Andrews. Something clicked and we fell in love. For Pat and me, it was a first love, and we expected it to last a lifetime. I'm smiling inside when I tell you that for my seventeenth birthday, he took me to a fancy restaurant and I asked him to order for me, which he did, with champagne first. The same as you did today."

"I guess by now you're used to underage drinking," he said with a big grin.

"Cheers to that," she said, lifting her glass before she returned to the seriousness of her story.

"Our love was amazing, like something you would read in a fairytale—we liked the same things, laughed at everything. We spent every spare minute together and spent long days traversing Scotland on foot, bus and train. We were bursting with love and passion, and when we made love for the first time, it seemed like the natural thing to do. We knew we would have to face challenges from our families when we went home at year's end. My family is Catholic and his is Church of England, a very big problem for both families. On the ferry, on our way back to Ireland, he knelt and proposed to me. He slipped an engagement ring on my finger. When I said 'Yes, yes!' everyone in hearing range applauded. We hated to leave the ferry, because we knew we would face difficulties with our families. When the boat docked, his parents whisked him away, and I never saw him or heard from him again."

This time it was Michael comforting Francie, holding her hands, rubbing them gently.

"When I told my parents that I was engaged to a Protestant, my mother was furious. She had expected me to be her perfect daughter, one who would live a life within the structure of the family and the Church."

Francie took a long time before she continued her story. Michael remained silent, giving her time, and she decided not to tell him about her baby, Kate. She was ashamed about the pregnancy and her time at the convent. She would tell him later, if their relationship became serious. So, she skipped one of the most important details of her young life.

She continued with, "Because I was only seventeen and still a minor, my parents had the right to dictate my immediate future. They banished me from our home and sent me to live with my father's older sister in Philadelphia. My aunt never wanted me to share her home and made it known to me every day for three years. My parents have had no contact with me since I left Ireland. They no longer consider me a member of the family. They had cut off all means of communication between Pat and me, and I entered this country alone and scared, to live with a stranger, my childhood over."

Michael's eyes were damp. He shook his head at the cruelty.

"I have become accustomed to homesickness and the hurt I feel every day for what my parents have done to me, and I've accepted that Pat and I will never be reunited. I have been in limbo since I left Ireland and thought I would never get over the loss of my first love."

She looked him directly in the eyes. "Today, at this lunch with you, I feel alive again," she told him.

They talked for hours, which turned into weeks, then months, and finally for years during their very happy marriage.

When Francie and Michael's courtship became serious, he wanted to share his joy with his parents, Elizabeth and Michael, senior. From the get-go they got along famously. Michael's parents embraced her and told her that they were delighted, adding that they could see why he fell in love with her, because they had, too. They encouraged Francie to call them Mother and Dad, as Michael did, but said they would understand if she'd rather use their first names. Francie told them she would be honored to consider them her parents and call them Mother and Dad.

The wedding was an intimate affair in the chapel at University of Pennsylvania. Francie's brothers Brian, Denis, and Thomas and his wife Margaret came to Philadelphia for the occasion. Francie and Margaret met for the first time and had a natural affinity for one another—they both loved Thomas and knew they'd be good friends. On the spot, Francie asked Margaret to be her matron of honor. Thomas had the honor of giving away his sister and Dr. Ross served as Michael's best man. The "Thursday Nighters," Francie's tennis gang, were among the few friends who were invited to share the happy event. They had all graduated and moved on to the world of ex-students. Miraculously, they all had good jobs—Anders with a top law firm and, like many other freshman lawyers, worked sixteen hours a day. Annie and Charlie were officially engaged and living in Washington. Their educations served them well—Annie was employed by the World Bank as an anthropologist in their social development department, and Charlie, now a PhD in Bryology, worked at the National Institutes of Health overseeing research into the healing powers of sphagnum moss.

At the reception, Dr. Ross proposed a toast to the bride and groom, saluting their accomplishments—the highlight of which was blending their lives into a perfect union. Francie raised her glass to Michael's parents, thanking them for accepting her as their own and for being so gracious and loving ever since she met them. There were more toasts all around, culminating with Michael's tribute to his bride for giving him another chance at life with the most beautiful, brilliant and light-hearted person he had ever met. Francie responded by speaking of the vicissitudes on the path to happiness, saying because of Michael, once again, both their lives were at the summit, and they planned to stay there together in a long, happy marriage. When she raised her glass this time, she announced that she was finally of legal drinking age.

When they returned from their honeymoon, their first priority was to move from Michael's tiny apartment to their own home. Francie's choice was to live close to Michael's parents. She loved the sense of family they provided and wanted to raise their future children near their grandparents. They bought a fairly large house in Haverford, hoping to fill it with a team of four little ones.

After a few months, they learned that plans don't always work, and wishes don't always come true. Francie and Michael seemed destined not to have children. Francie told her doctor the secret she had never told Michael and asked the doctor to keep her story in confidence, between only the two of them. The doctor told her that probably the birth of her tiny baby happened prematurely because her cervix was not strong enough to hold a fetus to full term. "Not being able to conceive again may be nature's way of compensating for your weak cervix," she explained.

That evening, with a voice full of emotion, Francie told Michael. "I have a weak cervix and probably will never be able to carry a baby."

Michael held her. They accepted the sad reality of their childless situation and made the best of it, becoming more devoted to one another. Their love was a mature one, different from their first loves, wonderful in its own way. Francie felt a thrill every time Michael lightly touched her shoulder when he walked past her chair, and Michael loved the way Francie kissed him hello every night when he came home from work, as if she hadn't seen him in ages.

Michael's parents became a large part of their lives. They were fine people—highly intelligent and quite accomplished, but never boastful. His father was a publisher of textbooks used by universities and secondary schools, a business that had been in the family for generations. His mother was a top editor for a major literary publishing house. Michael was their only child, and his parents had hoped to become grandparents, but they accepted the inevitable. Francie and Michael invited them for dinner once a week and met them at their private club in Haverford for Sunday brunch after church. The conversations were always lively and they all enjoyed the comradery of the two generations. The senior Michael and Elizabeth were regular churchgoers, but Francie and Michael seldom attended except for Christmas and Easter, when they all went together.

Francie was grateful that Michael's family welcomed her unconditionally, regardless of her religion. Her mother-in-law became her best friend and surrogate mother to whom she turned for advice and comfort. Once a week, usually after Sunday brunch, they tried to have an outing together, sometimes to the city for a theater matinee, sometimes to Longwood Gardens to wind around the acres of verdant outdoor paths and in the sultry, tropical atmosphere of the greenhouses. Husbands were invited, but they usually opted to watch sports and spend father and son time together. On Sunday evenings, they all looked forward to take-out dinners—steak sandwiches, hoagies, pizza, Chinese, deli.

Michael rose to head of the economics department at the University, and Francie found satisfaction and success in the world of business. She was an adept manager with a facility for understanding the balance sheet, and she, too, rose in her career. After twenty years and many advances in her positions at Shea's Soup Company, she became Vice President in Charge of Marketing. The company was family owned, but they welcomed certain investors. Francie was one of them, and slowly but steadily, she accumulated a sizeable amount of stock.

She loved her work and admired most of the people she worked with. The company implemented many of the projects she recommended, and the business became more and more successful during the years since she had joined the company. She was instrumental in developing a robust overseas market, and Shea's Soups had become a staple on pantry shelves all over Europe and parts of the Middle East.

She introduced franchised Soup and Sandwich Bars to hundreds of college towns. Shea's tomato soup and grilled cheese combo became the top seller among students looking for nutritious, filling, inexpensive food. A poster with Francie's picture and personal endorsement appeared in every shop. To extend communications between the administration and the employees at the company, she hired a promising journalism graduate to develop a newsletter highlighting outstanding employees and showing the personal side of some of the executives. She suggested that management host a yearly company-wide event at a Phillies game including free tickets, refreshments and souvenirs for all employees and their families. Employee and management relations at Shea's had always been excellent, but the Family Event Day and the newsletter made them all feel like they were part of a big family. Employee loyalty and production reached the highest level the company had ever seen.

Francie had stopped writing in her journal after their first year of marriage. She had Michael to confide in and no longer needed her journal. The memory of her teenage love affair with Pat dimmed, and Michael became the center of her life. Their marriage was one of love, mutual respect and admiration, and most important, one of happiness and laughter. Occasionally she felt guilt for not telling him about her teenage pregnancy, but she still carried the shame of being an unwed mother, and now her guilt was compounded by the fact that she had never told him.

The uncertainty of her daughter's existence was always with her.

Chapter 8

Weekends were always difficult for Francie. She desperately wanted children, and on weekends, most of their friends were busy with theirs. She and Michael always found something to do, usually chores that they didn't get around to during the week, but those jobs never filled the hole in her heart of having no children. She hoped that one day she would find Kate, but she knew the chance of that happening was slim. She still hadn't told Michael about Kate, and at this point, she thought she never would. What good would it do?

One Saturday afternoon when Francie and Michael were purging their closets of winter clothes, Francie went out to the garage for a can of mothballs. She was sick of cleaning and was disgusted with seeing Michael's old bike for the hundredth time, taking up wall space. "Can I ask you why you're saving your old bike?" she asked with a challenge in her voice. "It's been hanging in the garage untouched since we moved in. Why don't we put some shelves out there?"

Ignoring her tone, he answered, "I can't throw it out—maybe I'll want to ride it someday. And anyway, I'm sentimental about it—I used it for my newspaper route when I was a kid. I made big money, five bucks a week delivering sixty papers every day. I was really cool—an expert at throwing newspapers from a moving bike. It was all in the folding technique. Mine was excellent." He gave her the superior look of a successful entrepreneur.

She put her hands on her hips. "Okay, Mr. Big Business, how about going to the bike shop to get it serviced? I'll go too, and while we're there, maybe I'll get a bike. I used to ride no hands when I was a kid." Her mood perked up and she offered a truce, "Instead of cleaning closets, we could ride together on weekends."

"The neighbors will think we're hippies—no adults ride bikes around here—but what the heck, let's do it. I hate cleaning as much as you. I only do it because I thought you liked it."

They drove to the bicycle shop, the old Raleigh tied to the roof of their car.

"I can try to save it," the repair man said. "I'd have to take it down to the frame—new tires, new gears, new seat, new wheels—you'd be smarter to trash it and buy a new one. It'd be a whole lot cheaper."

Francie suggested, "We can give it a proper burial, say a few parting words and dump it. It's your decision."

In the end, they bought two new bikes, black for him, maroon for her, each with three gears. Helmets, too. And a bike rack for the back of the car. And a mirror for the handlebars. And side baskets. "Enough!" he said. "All this because you wanted me to get rid of my old clinker."

The bikes turned out to be a good purchase. They started riding in the neighborhood, but it seemed as if they were invisible to cars and had a couple of close calls. So on Saturdays, they'd load the bikes up and drive down to the Schuylkill. On weekends, the drives were closed to car traffic, so bikes and walkers could move unimpeded along the river from City Line to downtown Philadelphia through Fairmont Park. The scenery was luscious—miles of picnic grounds on the west side and the swift-moving narrow river on the east. Competitive crews rowed racing shells, pulling hard and fast with their sculls, practicing. University of Pennsylvania had its own boat house and crew and frequently competed with area colleges.

Francie always found time to spend in the regional public library in Bryn Mawr or in neighborhood bookstores, and one day she came home with a travel magazine featuring bike paths and bed and breakfasts in the Mid-Atlantic States. When Michael came home from work, she practically assailed him. "Look at this, Michael, let's do it!" She'd found a historic home with a five star rating in a small town in Maryland not far from Chincoteague Island. The book says, 'a home on the historic register surrounded by country lanes winding through farmland, perfect for bicycling.'"

"Is Chincoteague the place where horses run wild?"

She nodded, pointing out the pictures. "I already called Worthington Hall, the place recommended in the book. They have four colonial style bedrooms upstairs—the owners live downstairs. I spoke to the wife."

The deal was done. Two weeks later they left for Snow Hill, Maryland for a weekend stay, bikes loaded on the rack for the two-hour drive. Check-in was informal, owners Irene and Arthur carrying their guests' luggage upstairs. Irene had made a reservation for them at a local crab shack a ten minute walk away. "This is a small town and places here close early. I hope that six o'clock isn't too soon for your dinner?"

"We're ravenous, so nothing is too early. My mouth is watering just thinking of Maryland crab cakes. It's just five now, so we'll be down by ten of six.

"Our garden is open to all our guests. Gardening is my hobby—I've marked the names all the plants. Please wander around and use our garden chairs and hammocks if you'd like.

A few minutes later, Arthur rapped on the door to say he was leaving a snack outside their room, and they heard him walk downstairs. Francie was partially undressed, so Michael cracked the door and saw what Arthur had left. "I'll say!" The tray held homemade cheese puffs, three small wedges of berry goat cheese, gruyere and Irish cheddar along with a small bunch of grapes and some almonds.

"Look, Michael, there are two robes in the closet." She slipped hers on. It smelled of a potpourri of roses and cinnamon. In the pocket was a sweet-smelling little bag wrapped with a green ribbon and a note saying "Compliments of Irene."

"This place is the find of the year," he told Francie. "Good job."

When they started in on the wine, Michael got romantic. "Do we have time for a quickie?"

"No, dear, save it for tonight when we can take our time," she suggested. "Let's eat instead."

His lower lip went out, but she wasn't buying that act.

They sat at the small table by the window overlooking the neat little garden, sipped their wine and nibbled on the refreshments. They wanted to leave plenty of room for dinner—and they were glad they did. The simple, homey restaurant's crab cakes were first-rate, even for Maryland, the crab cake capital of the planet. Michael had three, and Francie limited herself to two, slaw and French fries on the side. Michael added a side of black-eyed peas cooked southern style with a ham hock. Ice cream, of course, then a digestif of Amaretto on ice, or Amaretto straight up, the only two choices.

After dinner, they took a long walk around the town. The summer night was wonderfully cool, with none of the city's mugginess. Francie couldn't get enough of the sweet smell of the surrounding meadows.

As predicted, when they returned to the room, they made love slowly, missionary style as befitted their colonial room, but at the end, they added a modern flair.

They slept until almost ten, quickly showered and ran downstairs for breakfast. "Are we too late?"

"In Snow Hill, you're never too late," Irene said. "One of the other couples hasn't come down yet, the other two are gone for the day." She brought them a basket of fruited muffins, bacon and eggs and fresh blackberries from their vine. Francie had her usual tea, and Michael had a glass of cold milk. The other pair, a couple from Delaware, showed up, took a look at Michael and Francie's breakfast and groaned.

"There goes my diet," said the woman as she pulled out a chair. "I'm Ginny and this is my husband, Paul." Introductions were reciprocated and light conversation began. Ginny wanted to know if that was their car with the bikes on the back. Michael said it was and told them they planned to pedal in the area for most of the day. "Sounds wonderful," she said. "The last time we cycled was on our honeymoon twenty-five years ago. Our kids are always goading us to buy bikes, but I think we're too old."

Paul jumped into the conversation saying, "Teenagers! They're always giving advice. How old are your kids?"

Michael knew that this question would come up—it always did, and they had a standard answer. "We don't have any yet. We've been married ten years and we're waiting until we're sure our marriage will work." That stopped him in his tracks. Francie, fighting off tears, thought, *I'll never get over not being able to fill our home with children.* She forced herself to shake it off, just as she had been doing for the ten years she'd been married.

Other than that one question, an amiable conversation of small talk ensued—their jobs, their hobbies, their backgrounds. When it was time to shove off, they told the others they had a lot of ground to cover. "See you at cocktail time," they said.

That seemed to be Arthur's cue to come in to announce that he would be cooking dinner. "Does everyone like lamb?" The answer was unanimously affirmative.

Irene gave them a send-off with a shopping bag packed with fresh rolls and last night's cheese. "In case you get hungry," she said. "And here's a map of the area with some of my favorite places circled."

Francie was enchanted with the country lanes. They rode for a half hour without seeing a car, but once in a while a tractor came in the opposite direction hauling a load of fresh peaches. They passed a cloth covered stand stocked with radishes, a jam jar and a sign saying, "Bunch of radishes, 25¢ Honor System."

Just to be congenial, they put in a dollar and took only one bunch.

Farther down the road they saw a girl of about ten selling tomatoes, with a sign "3 for a dollar, just pict." They bought six and cushioned them in Michael's basket surrounded by the radishes. For a stretch of a few miles, they passed long, low buildings with high windows covered with wire. Francie started to cough. "Do you smell what I smell? she asked. "How could anybody live here? It smells like the elephant house at the zoo, only worse. What do you think is inside those shacks?"

"Maybe slaughterhouses? Pigs?" They peddled as fast as they could for almost a half hour until they got past the area and could finally take a deep breath without gagging. Further down the road, they saw the sign, *You are now leaving Purdue country, home of America's best poultry.*

"Remind me never to buy chicken again," Francie told Michael.

About two hours into the trip, they came to a crossroads with a combination gas station and grocery store. "We have wine, rolls, radishes and tomatoes. All we need is mayonnaise, and I'll make you the best tomato sandwich you ever ate," Michael told Francie.

"And the first since I left Ireland."

They entered the store, stiff from being on their bikes, and picked up mayo and Cokes. Francie asked the man behind the counter if there was a road back to Snow Hill that didn't pass the chicken coops, and she showed him her map. He circled the best way back, "It's a little longer than the one you just took, but I think you'll like it. There's beautiful country to be seen."

They turned right as directed and picked up a road bordering horse farms. The horses frolicked freely, foals playfully running with them. Francie admired what had to be miles and miles of double picket fences, keeping the horses enclosed without a feel of isolation. Tomorrow they'd go to Chincoteague and see the truly wild horses.

They entered an area that seemed parklike and stopped just off the road and found a flat spot to spread out their jackets on the velvet grass. Michael pulled out his keychain knife with a flourish and sliced the tomatoes. Francie was impressed. "That little knife really comes in handy, doesn't it?" He told her he used it all the time, a white lie. She had given it to him for their first Christmas and today he was finally using it.

He spread the rolls with mayonnaise, layered on the tomato slices. "Would you put some of that cheese on mine please, Michael?"

"Absolutely not! Real tomato sandwiches consist of tomatoes, mayonnaise and bread. Anything else is on the side."

"Sorry, excuse me for asking," she said freshly.

They gobbled down the sandwiches, cheese, fruit, and radishes, leaving nothing. They agreed they got their four bucks worth.

They wended their way back to Snow Hill and the Hall in time for a shower and snooze before cocktail hour.

The dining room table was set for ten, and after cocktails on the patio, the four couples and the host and hostess sat down. Apparently, Arthur had been a professional chef during his other life, and he had grilled a butterflied leg of lamb. A buffet was set up on the sideboard with the meat, roasted red new potatoes, grilled fresh summer vegetables and chilled applesauce. Crispy sliced baguettes and sweet butter were on the table for passing. Dinner was impressive.

The four couples talked about the different things they did that day—one went fishing, one went antiquing, and one stayed at the Hall reading, sunning and swimming in the lap pool. Irene and Arthur explained how they came to retire from the mad scene in New York. They had always wanted to renovate a historic house to use as a bed and breakfast and had been looking for years. When they found this one, it was love at first sight. Three years of painting, plastering, replacing and polishing, and the house was ready for action. Last year was their first. They were written up in a national magazine and guests started to pour in. They were booked all spring, summer and fall until Thanksgiving. Then they closed a bit for a short vacation and opened again for three weeks around Christmas and New Year's. In February they spent the month in Florida and started up again late in March.

"We thought we were semi-retiring to a slower pace, but this is a twenty-four hour job, seven days a week. Now we have a rotating staff of five. We are living our dream and want to share it with people like you who appreciate what small town country life has to offer." The hosts raised their glasses to the guests. "We hope you come back to see us."

Everyone around the table reciprocated and said, "Amen."

Next day was Chincoteague Island, on the Maryland-Virginia border. Checkout included hugs, then they loaded their bikes and left for the twenty mile trip east. Francie thought about how much America offered, and she had only been in a tiny part. "Michael, I would love to see more of the area. Maybe we could take a trip like this more often," she said touching his thigh lightly.

"Francie, you always make me want to say 'yes' to anything. Where'd you learn that?"

"Practice," she said. "I've been watching you and somehow I learned that you're a sex maniac disguised as a stuffy professor."

"Don't be so sure of yourself, babe—if you only knew how many grad students were after me, you'd take extra special care of me."

"Well, 'babe' yourself. Tell me more." Now her curiosity was up. It sounded like something was cooking behind the scenes of academia.

"A lot of hero worshiping goes on by graduate students, and when they make too many appointments for advice, it's obvious they're there for another reason."

"Oh, my God," Francie said. "Pull into the next parking lot so I can service you."

He laughed and kept driving. "Not now, 'babe,' I have a headache. Maybe in ten minutes."

They drove into the visitors' parking lot at the entrance to Chincoteague, untied their bikes and followed a fenced bike path running through the park. Francie loved the complete lack of mechanical noise. Only the sounds of the breeze ruffling the leaves and the trill of songbirds were heard. Michael felt it too, and they kept silent during the ride. It was tranquil and energizing at the same time. The hilly, scenic trail gradually started to change. The trees became scrubby and mounds of sand appeared. Francie's senses quickened when she heard whinnying from somewhere near. A pack of about twenty horses raced by, close enough for them to see manes flying. The thrill of watching the strength and speed exhilarated her. Michael pulled up to stop next to her and when they looked at each other, all they could do was shake their heads in wonder of what they were witnessing.

They knew they were getting closer to the coast when they got a whiff of salty air. Just before the Atlantic came into view, they passed a small meadow where mares and their new foals were grazing. Tears started to roll down Francie's cheeks at the sight of the mares with their babies. If only, she thought, turning away so Michael couldn't see her crying.

In the town of Chincoteague, the tourist stores carried beach supplies and souvenirs. There were several small motels.

"Let's lock our bikes here," Michael said. "I have something I'd like to do."

She gave him a questioning look and locked her bike. He took her hand and looked deeply into her eyes. "Let's pretend we're lovers—I'm in the mood," he said and walked her toward the closest motel. "You owe me one, remember?"

She was nonplussed, but game as always. She started to skip alongside him. "I'll race you," she said.

The room was crummy, the sheets were limp, the floor was gritty and the windows were grimy, but for them it was a lover's paradise. An hour later, they checked out, rode back to the car, tied on the bikes and headed home into the sunset, just like in the movies.

Chapter 9

Ten more years went by—and then the letter came.

On the third day, she opened it.

Dear Francie,

I never thought I would find you again, but here I am, after so many years, with a story you won't believe.

After your parents sent you away, I didn't know what happened to you and the baby, or if we even had a baby. They refused all contact with me. For years I tried to find you, hoping we could live our dream to be married. I finally accepted that you had started a new life somewhere and didn't want to be found.

Can you believe we're in our forties? Wasn't it yesterday that we were roaming the hills of Scotland? I still miss you. Do you think of me every now and then? I hope so. But I'm happily settled into a good life and expect you are too. Take a deep breath, because what I have to say will rock your world.

A young, British woman named Kate Mullins came to my office today.

Seeing the name "Kate," Francie's heart skipped a beat. She put the letter down and walked into the kitchen for something, anything, to ready herself for what she hoped would be good news. She filled a glass with water, set it down and returned to the letter. She reread the line with the name "Kate Mullins" and forced herself not to read too quickly. She needed time to process each word.

She was well-dressed and intelligent, and I thought she was looking for a job. I asked her if she had her resume with her. She smiled and said that was not the reason she had come to see me.

"I'm glad you're sitting down," she said, "because I have something important to tell you."

She hesitated, then said, "I think you're my father."

I felt the air go out of my body.

Francie, there is no doubt that she's our daughter. She has your light reddish hair and my blue eyes. The more we spoke, the more I felt like I was speaking to you—the way she smiles when she talks is so much like you.

Francie's hands started to shake so violently she couldn't focus on the quivering words. She took deep breaths to quiet her trembling hands and racing heart so she could read on.

She told me about her background. As an infant, Grace and James Mullins adopted her through the Catholic Church. She grew up in London with two older brothers who always treated her as if she were born into the family. She was very close to her them, just as you were to your brothers, Francie. She even said that she got her athletic abilities from her brothers, who honed her techniques to rival theirs.

All her life she'd been told she was special, a wanted baby—that was why her parents had adopted her. She hardly gave her adoption a thought until she was a teenager, when she began dwelling on her origins. She didn't want to hurt her parents by asking about her "real mother and father" so she kept her feelings to herself. By the time she was fifteen, her family noticed a change in her moods. At first, they chalked it up to her being a teenager, but then they realized they had to get to the real reason for her pulling away from them. She finally told them that she'd like to try to find her birth parents but didn't want to hurt their feelings. Her mother embraced her and assured her that it was natural for her to want to find us. They told her they would be happy to help. Then her mother added that they would love to meet them, too, to thank them for the miraculous gift they gave them, their special daughter.

At this, Francie put the letter on her lap, and weeping, she fell onto her knees clasping her hands in prayer. "Thank you, God," she said, "for bringing us together."

Kate told me it felt so odd hearing the words "birth parents." She considered her adoptive family her real family and always thought she was one hundred percent English.

They told her that the church arranged the adoption and brought her to England from Ireland when she was six weeks old. One of the qualifications for the adoption was that the adopting family be Catholic and raise the baby in the faith. The family was in full agreement. They received a blank birth certificate and were asked to fill in their names and the baby's name and date of birth. The church authorities told them they could not reveal the history of the baby's birth, except to say that she was born prematurely and kept in an incubator for weeks until her development was acceptable. The sisters called her Katy, or sometimes Kate, and she seemed to respond to the name. When Grace and James Mullins came to collect their new baby, they named her Katherine Louise Mullins. They called her Kate.

The names of her biological parents were in the sealed adoption papers, so Kate and her parents could not make any progress trying to find us. Then, finally, when she was eighteen, Ireland liberalized the laws, and Kate was able to trace her place of birth to the convent in Ireland—the one that you were in, Francie, for all those months. The original birth certificate was on file there, with the name of the mother as Frances O'Conner. The name of the father was misspelled, and instead of "Patrick Harrington," it said, "Patrick Harrigan."

For five years, Kate tried to trace your family and mine as best she could, starting with the Dublin phone book, then expanding her search to all of Ireland, calling as many "O'Conners" and "Harrigans" as she could reach. Those who answered said they didn't know anything about us. Now, five years later, via the miracle of the internet, she was able to find me by looking for names somewhat like "Harrigan" in the entire Great Britain. The computer listed several "Patrick Harringtons," and after further research and phone calls, my name came up as most likely. She made the appointment to see me.

Kate said that as soon as she saw my eyes, she knew right away that I was her father. She had been looking at those eyes in her own mirror for twenty-three years.

We talked for hours. I told Kate about our romance and our forced separation, and about the years I tried to find you. I told her that for all this time, I didn't know if our baby was a boy or a girl, or even if it was alive. And suddenly, here she was, a beautiful young lady, sitting in front of me!

She gleaned from her research that you had moved to the U.S. I had searched all over the UK for you, never dreaming that you had left the country. I didn't try to call your brothers—I didn't want to put them in the position of going against their parents' wishes. When Kate showed me her information, I gave it to a young researcher in my office.

A few days later, he found you listed you as "Mrs. Michael Hanson," living in Pennsylvania, USA.

Francie, even after all these years, my heart dropped to hear that you were married. I know how irrational that sounds, but my emotional reaction was that of an eighteen-year-old boy to his first love, not that of a forty-two-year-old happily married man with two children.

We have so much to catch up with—and I know you must be eager to meet Kate. How soon can you come to London?

Wire me at my office and I'll meet you at the airport.

I'm not sure how to sign this, so I'll just say,

Pat

He had enclosed a business card that said Pat Harrington, Barrister, followed by an address and phone number.

Francie tried to process the information. She walked from room to room in a daze, heart beating out of control. She spent an hour thinking about what to do and what to tell Michael, then she called his office and left a message for him to come home as soon as possible. She gave no details except that she needed him.

"What happened?" he asked when he burst into the house to see Francie curled up on the sofa crying. "What hurts?"

She stood up and hugged him, clinging to him for support. "Nothing hurts, but when I tell you my story, the one I should have told you the day we fell in love, you will be the one who's hurt."

She poured two glasses of wine, asked him to sit close to her. She gave him the letter from Pat and watched with trepidation as he read it. Michael's expressions went from interest to disbelief to shock.

When he finally looked up, she began the full story—all of it—her pregnancy, her banishment from the family to the Home for Unwed Mothers, her loneliness, her resentment of the nuns who told all of the girls they were sinners, and the exhausting work in the kitchen. She told him about her difficult delivery, and the birth of her tiny, premature baby.

"The baby was fighting for her life when they put her in an incubator and took her away. I was so weak from loss of blood that I went into a coma immediately after Kate's birth. I was close to death. Once I regained consciousness, I cried constantly. My only thoughts were of losing our baby, the embodiment of our love. Remember, I was seventeen years old, living a teenage romance. I spent three weeks recuperating until I was well enough to be discharged. My father came to pick me up and I met him in the driveway, alone, holding my suitcase. I left the Home not knowing if my baby was dead or alive, and as for me, I felt more dead than alive. My father barely talked to me. I thought he was taking me home, but he told me I was no longer welcome there, and repeated that my mother never wanted to see me again. He put me on a plane to Philadelphia to live with his older sister who was clearly not happy to have me with her."

Michael was sitting next to her, a bit separate on the couch. They were both crying.

"Weeks later when I recuperated from giving birth, I set out to take control of my life. I started at the library, which led me to the University, and you know the rest of the story. For the three years I lived with Aunt Agatha, she barely tolerated me. The last time I saw her was at my graduation."

She looked up at him, almost shyly, begging him to be okay with the sad tale she'd kept from him for so long. He was not looking at her. She choked out, "And then you came to my rescue. Michael, I was lonely for so many years—then I met you, and love returned to my life."

They sat in silence, Michael's head in his hands. Then he looked up. "Why didn't you tell me, Francie? I thought we were always honest with one another—with no secrets."

She shuddered at the accusation in his voice. "I felt so ashamed, and when I fell in love with you, the shame didn't go away—it just got deeper. I never wanted to exclude you from my past, but my feelings of guilt still run deep. I lost my parents, my home, my baby, my first love, and my faith. I was afraid that if I told you the truth, I would lose you, too."

He still could not look at her. She had to keep talking. "Michael, my wonderful husband, I hope you'll understand that I have to go to London to meet my daughter. All of these years I prayed for her to be alive, but until I opened the letter from Pat, I didn't know if she had survived. Can you forgive me?"

He said nothing, shaking his head from what she had told him, or not told him. Was she the same person he thought he married? Abruptly, he stood up, went into his study and closed the door.

And Francie waited, glassy-eyed, not knowing what to expect. Her feelings were conflicted—she was overjoyed with the knowledge that Kate was alive, but terribly disturbed about the pain she caused Michael. Would finding Kate mean losing Michael? The thought of not having him beside her was unbearable. She walked back and forth not knowing what to do. She sat down, she got up, she picked up a book and stared blankly at the pages, then closed it. Her head felt like it would explode. She went into their bedroom to lie down and get her thoughts in order. *I must go to England to see Kate—that is my first priority. Michael is so kind, but would his kindness extend to this—a secret I kept from him for twenty years? Will he ever trust me now? Will he leave me? How could I bear that?* Again she thought, *Is it possible that I gained Kate and at the same time lost Michael?*

She stayed in bed for almost two hours. Then she heard him come out of the den and call her name. "In the bedroom," she said.

He sat down on the bed and handed her a reservation for a ticket to London for the next evening. With a look of love and concern on his face,

Michael said, "I want you to spend some time alone with your daughter, and then I'd love to meet her. I reserved a seat for myself three days after you arrive in London. Of course, I forgive you, Francie."

She burst into sobs and grabbed him around the shoulders. She felt as if he had handed her the most valuable gift of her life. Over and over she thanked him, hugging him so tightly that he cried, "Enough!"

"Having you as my wife fills my cup to overflowing, Francie. You made the mistake of a young girl, then you let your secret fester inside of you for all these years. I love you with all my heart. From the first day I met you, my spirit felt renewed after years of loneliness, self-pity and resentment. I don't know if I could go on without you."

"Michael, you will always be my hero." They cried together, hugging one another, unsure of what the future held for them, but knowing their love was secure. She was happy, frightened and excited to meet the future.

PART II

Chapter 10

Pat was there to greet her at Heathrow. She saw his face, and time stood still. He was carrying a bunch of daffodils just as he had the first time he came to see her at University of Edinburgh. They ran to each other and embraced, and the years fell away. They both laughed at the absurdity of the situation, then with no hesitation and no questions asked, found their way to the hotel at Heathrow Airport.

He asked for the best room the Hilton offered, and they barely got there in time to lock the door before they began to undress. "Be prepared," Francie said. "I've gained a few pounds in the past twenty-three years." He looked anyway and told her that instead of the thin, angular eighteen-year-old girl he remembered, she now had the soft, rounded form of a woman, but with the same adorable face and freckled nose that he fell in love with so many years before.

"I see you changed your style in underwear. I guess you discovered Victoria's Secret. What happened to the white cotton panties and bra?"

"Nice of you to notice," she said.

She looked at Pat's boyish face and shockingly blue eyes, but when he undressed, instead of a wiry boy, she saw the body of a fit, well-developed man. She couldn't take her eyes off him.

"And I see you changed your style, too. You replaced the sexy, tight, jockey shorts with baggy, old man boxers."

They kicked their underwear aside, lay down on the bed, and caressed one another, making new discoveries and remembering old ones. He told her that he remembered the fresh smell of her hair and would recognize it anywhere. She turned to him and they kissed with the passion of so many bottled up years. She told him that the taste of his kiss was still delicious, and they kissed again. He started to explore her body with his hands and with his mouth. She moaned, remembering his touch, and she touched him in all the old, familiar places.

He rolled on top of her, and they looked into each other's eyes—and realized this was a mistake. There was no use trying to relive their time together as teenage lovers. The innocence of their young love that seemed so real in the past seemed shallow compared to the depth of the love they had for their spouses and the lives they had built around them. Even as they felt helpless before their passion, they knew that for them, as they were now, this was wrong.

"We can't do this," they both agreed, almost laughing, falling away from each other, still on fire, still wanting each other as they had when they first met.

"Do you think I can get my money back for this expensive room, or do you think they have an hourly rate?" he said, with his familiar grin.

"Maybe they'll give you a discount if you tell them we reached a dead end."

She decided she could use a long, shower. "Mind if I come in, too?" he said. She made him promise *no funny business* and he climbed in, gradually making the water colder to discourage any feelings of passion. When they were finished, they encountered a familiar problem.

"Can you believe it—no towels!" They both ran into the room to wrap themselves in the sheets. "History repeats itself," she said, barely getting the words out through her laughter.

"Wales all over again," he said.

Just before they left the room, they came together and kissed again, reluctantly letting go, knowing that this would be the last time they shared their passion.

On the drive to London, they started to catch up with what had happened since they parted so many years before at the port of Dublin. She told him of the overwhelming loneliness she felt for him and for her family, the grueling routine at the Home for Unwed Mothers, and the awful feeling of not knowing if their baby had survived.

"I couldn't contact you, Pat. It was as if you and your family had vanished. All that remained of you were the engagement ring you gave me on the ferry and the gold heart you gave me for my seventeenth birthday. For three years, I wore them on a chain around my neck, but when I fell in love with Michael, I put an end to trying to contact you, and I put away the ring and necklace and that whole part of my life. A new chapter was beginning.

Pat reached over and without looking at her, took her hand. She picked up his hand, still clasped to hers, and kissed it, knowing she should have more control over herself but couldn't resist. She could hardly take her eyes off him, she loved him so much.

After a moment she said, "The first time Michael and I felt an attraction, I told him about you. But I never told him about our baby. I was too ashamed and was afraid I'd lose him.

"Francie, my darling, we both did the same thing. Yesterday was the first time I told Moira about Kate, though she did know about our teenage love affair. She was resentful that I had withheld one of the most important parts of my past from her. I think it may take her a long time to forgive me."

"Pat—until recently you didn't know that Kate had been born. Did you explain that to Moira?"

He told Francie that he did, but his wife didn't accept it as the full truth. "She was right, it wasn't the full truth. I always had hoped that our child was alive and that you and I would find her one day."

"Pat, the problems that we both had are so complicated. My hope is that you and Moira work things out and restore the happiness in your marriage. I'm lucky that Michael is so understanding, and I love him even more for it. You and he are the only two men I ever loved, and after nineteen years of marriage, Michael and I still treasure our time together. The only thing missing is children—after Kate's birth, I could never conceive."

Francie sighed and looked out the window, not focusing on anything, just going over the thoughts in her head. Pat reached out to squeeze her hand again. She clung to it, turned to him and continued her story.

"When your letter came, I held it for three days without opening it. I was certain that whatever the contents, I would have to share them with Michael. Once I'd read your words, I trembled at the thought of telling him about our daughter and the misery I endured in Ireland. I knew that this could permanently change our marriage, and it did—but for the better, with no secrets and no more guilt. Michael has been my greatest supporter since the day we met, and he didn't let me down in this most difficult decision involving all of us. He said that he would love to include Kate in our family if it's all right with her."

Pat's first reaction was sorrow about the life that could have been theirs if only his parents had not been so selfish and secretive about refusing Francie's calls, and if only her parents had not been so rigid, so unaccepting of religious differences.

Now he began his story. For years, he tried to contact her parents, but they refused all calls. He tracked down the address of their home, and he drove there only to find they had moved and left no forwarding address. He had no knowledge of Francie's banishment to the convent, or the birth of their baby girl.

Pat's family had moved, too, back to England, to a town called Sunningdale, outside of London. Their phone number was private, probably the reason that Francie couldn't find them. Pat's parents, especially his mother, were distraught when they learned of Francie's pregnancy. They were sure that Francie had arranged it so she could snag a boy from a wealthy family. They only hinted about this to him, but he knew that they didn't think that Francie was good enough for him. To them, pedigree was preeminent. This was not something he would ever tell Francie. When they refused to pay his tuition at St Andrews, he surrendered to their insistence and transferred to Oxford.

He knew he had to continue his education and reluctantly matriculated at the university all the Harrington men attended. He concentrated on his studies, blocking out social contacts with everyone but his dons. When he graduated with the title of *Barrister*, his parents' dreams for him to become a judge were in place. Nothing was too good for their handsome, brilliant son.

He dated off and on for eight years, but he never came close to a compelling relationship that measured up to the one he had with Francie.

"Francie, you were in my thoughts and dreams every day. I never thought I would feel the same for anyone that I felt for you. Then I met Moira, and something clicked. I thought I might have a second chance at real love. We've been married for eleven years and we have twin eight-year-old boys, Philip and Joshua. We have a happy family full of so many good things. I had a lot of explaining to do when Kate showed up. Then after I contacted you, I told Moira that you were coming to meet Kate. When I told her that I was picking you up at the airport, Moira's expression changed to one I had never seen before—resentment mixed with jealousy. A few seconds later, her face softened, and her strength of character showed through. She put on a brave front and told me that together, we could work things out. I told her I was certain we could and reassured her that I loved her and was confident that our marriage was strong enough to include my daughter in our family."

He was quiet for a few moments, evaluating his feelings. Today, from the minute he saw Francie at Heathrow, something he had hidden from himself for years came to the surface. He realized that he had settled for Moira, that he would never have the thrill with her that he had with Francie. A shadow came over him, knowing that his life with Moira had been a distant second to the one he could have had with Francie. He loved Moira and didn't want to hurt her, and he loved the family they and their boys had made together. He saw no solution.

"Francie," he continued, "when Kate Mullins stepped into my office after all those years and told me who she was, I was completely shocked. I couldn't speak, but when I regained my composure, Kate and I began a long, long conversation, and, I hope, a lifetime relationship.

"In my letter to you I told you the details of how Kate found us after more than five years of searching. When she finished the story, I reached across my desk, took her hand and told her about how she got started, and why she had to be given away for adoption.

"Shortly after, we put our heads together, fed all of the information into a computer, and we found you." He patted her knee, not daring to look at her. "And here you are, Francie, my love, with so much for us to learn about our daughter and about each other. If our three families, yours, mine and Kate's, have hearts big enough to make room for all of us, this could be a beautiful continuation of our story."

"Let's try to be positive," said Francie, "and expect everyone involved to be reasonable. We're all in this together, and the situation can have a happy ending if we move ahead openly, honestly, and with love—and no more secrets."

Late afternoon, they arrived at Claridge's in London. By now Francie was quite jet-lagged. She insisted that Pat drop her at the hotel and not come in. "My mind and heart are racing, but the one thing I know for sure is that I'm dying to meet Kate. Could the three of us have some quiet time together tomorrow after I sleep off my jet lag? Maybe brunch at the hotel around eleven?"

"Yes! Gladly," he said. "I'll make the arrangements and see you here in the morning."

She could not leave without touching him. "Pat," she said, her hand on his arm. "I never thought I would see you again. My life is so rich with memories. This is more than I could ever have asked for."

He looked at her with love and whispered good night.

Chapter 11

The next morning, Francie woke up late, free of most of her jet lag, and got into a cool shower. Under the stream, she thought of Pat and went over the events of yesterday. She smiled when she thought of their almost culmination in the hotel room and knew she—they—had made the right decision. She turned her thoughts to the big day ahead. Foremost in her mind was the excitement—as well as the fear—of meeting Kate for the first time. Her *daughter*—the word rolled off her lips like a blessing when she said it aloud.

The phone was ringing in the bedroom, and she hastily wrapped herself in a towel and rushed to answer.

"Hello," she said with a grin, "I hope it's you."

"Yes, it's me," said Michael. "I'm miserable, been up all night waiting until a decent hour to phone you."

Francie's smile disappeared. She was so disappointed. She had expected the call to be from Pat and was shocked at her reaction to Michael's voice. She sat down, took a deep breath, and forced herself to squelch her disappointment.

He sounded shy and tentative, and so lonely. "I never thought I'd I miss you so much. I didn't want to intrude on your private time, and I promised myself not to call, but I just needed to hear your voice."

"Oh, Michael, I miss you, too. I wish you were here to help me deal with my nervousness about meeting Kate. We're having brunch at the hotel this morning." She didn't tell Michael that Pat would be coming. Or that he had picked her up at the airport the day before. Or that they had jumped in bed together. Just thinking about that made her loosen her towel to cool off. Now completely naked, she threw the towel on the floor and fanned herself with her hand.

She fell silent, thinking about new secrets she was already keeping from Michael. *Will I be telling lies to myself my whole life?*

Michael sensed there was more to the story but knew this was not the time to ask about Pat. He told her he loved her and wished her a wonderful reunion with Kate.

The guilt she felt made her ask Michael if he could possibly change his ticket and come today. "I feel like half a person without you."

"If I have to ride on the wing of the plane, I'll be there. I'll let you know my new reservation plans as soon as I have them."

After they hung up, Francie thought about what she had said to Michael about being glad he called. Although she said she felt like half a person without him, the truth was she had not thought of him since she left Pat the night before. She stood, leaving the wet towel on the floor and headed toward the bathroom. She needed more time to get her head together. She hoped Michael would not be able to find a flight until the next day. Although she knew that her love for Michael was deep and true, she hoped Pat would knock on her door and find her undressed. To her naked body in the mirror, she silently admitted, *My love for Michael is real, but the thrill I feel with him is nothing like what I felt yesterday with Pat.*

She finished dressing and was about to head for the lobby when the phone rang again. This time it was Pat. "We're in the lobby," he said. She could hear the smile in his voice. Her knees went weak, making her smile at the sensuality of it all.

She ran from her room to the elevator, and when it reached the ground floor, there they were. Mother and daughter saw each other and connected instantly. Francie was looking at a younger version of herself, but with Pat's bluest of blue eyes. Kate looked at Francie and knew there was no denying that she was looking into the face of her mother, a more mature version of herself. They hugged, and cried, and laughed, all within the same instant while Pat looked on with a heart about to burst. He stretched his long arms around them and right there, in the busy lobby of the staid Claridge's, they cried together.

When the emotion settled, they went into the dining room holding hands. Pat had requested a table in a quiet, secluded area, and there they sat, with so much to talk about.

Kate was the first to speak up. "I've been thinking about what to call you. Is it okay if I call you by your first names?"

Francie and Pat looked at each other and, for no apparent reason, they burst out laughing. "Yes," they said in unison and laughed some more.

"Of course," said Francie, looking at her girl. "That would be lovely. The title of mother and father belongs to the parents who raised you"

Their brunch lasted more than three hours, with lots of laughter, and more tears. They talked and interrupted with so much to say about what had happened during twenty-four years of separation.

Back and forth, filling in blanks and recalling names of places, Pat and Francie told Kate the story of their magical romance, and then separately, everything else that had happened during the twenty-four years until today.

When it was Kate's turn to tell her story, she told Francie what she had told Pat about her happy childhood with parents who put family first, and her two older brothers who taught her to excel in sports, especially tennis.

Francie smiled; she was thrilled to tell Kate that her older brothers, too, had taught her how to play sports, especially tennis, like a boy. "How's that for a coincidence?"

At that, Francie, shaking her head in mock despair, looked at Pat. "Your father was pathetic on the tennis court. In all our matches, he lost to me every time, except for the games that I threw."

To save his male pride, Pat had to defend himself against Francie's story about her tennis superiority. He drew himself up and said, "So, Kate, my graceful daughter, how are you on the dance floor?"

"Damn good, if I have to say so myself."

"Aha," he added, turning to raise his eyebrows at Francie and then speaking to Kate again. "You have me to thank for that. Francie has two left feet."

Francie harrumphed. "Pat, you'll be happy to know that I have finally admitted that I am an awful dancer, so, Kate, I'm glad you didn't get my dancing genes. I wish I had gotten my parents' and brothers' abilities on the dance floor, but, with the right partner, my dancing isn't too bad." She eyeballed Pat as if her bad dancing was his fault, then looked over to Kate and asked her if she had a beau.

"I haven't met the man of my dreams yet, but I'm not giving up—more about that later. I was a good student, started Cambridge at seventeen and learned that I liked the study of economics because it involved so many fascinating disciplines—history, sociology, math, statistics, politics. I'm in the process of writing my doctoral dissertation on how the world economy incorporates all these influences, and I'm loving the subject even more. That might sound kind of nerdy to you, but my goal is to become a professor—not the boring kind, but one who takes what is usually a dry subject and adds excitement to it."

"Another coincidence," chimed in Francie. "My husband, Michael, is a professor of economics, so you should have plenty to talk to him about—and, like you, he is far from nerdy. You might actually understand him. I just pretend. He was my professor when I was a young student. I never dreamed that he and I would become romantic, but apparently he did. Maybe that was one of the reasons I got a decent grade in a subject that I didn't comprehend. I was a business major, but my concentration was in marketing."

Pat couldn't get enough of listening to his girls' conversation and watching their twin-like expressions, gestures and reactions. He could not get a word in, and he liked it that way.

Eventually they looked around the room and realized they were the only ones still there. It was three o'clock when Kate said, "Maybe you have all day to talk, but I have to get back to reality and work on my thesis. At least for a little bit today." When they rose to leave, Pat and Francie noticed the late day sun shining through the window making patterns of horizontal lines on the table. Pat looked at her, knowingly, and in response, Francie blushed. *The Universe is getting smaller* came to her mind.

Kate conveyed her parents' invitation to come to dinner the night after next, with all family included. Francie said that Michael would be here by then, and Pat accepted for Moira and the boys. When they exited the dining room to the lobby, the three of them were so lighthearted, and their smiles were so broad, people in the lobby smiled, thinking what a happy family they were. But inside, Pat and Francie worried about what might happen at the meeting with their mates. Kate left before they did, gliding gracefully into a taxi to rush back to her apartment.

The desk clerk hailed Francie and handed her a message. Michael had been able to get a mid-morning flight and would be arriving at Heathrow that night at ten o'clock. He ended with, "Can't wait to see you, my darling girl. I'm so lonely without you." Wordlessly, she showed Pat the cable.

"We have to talk," she said, and they headed for the elevator.

They barely made it to the hotel room when Francie started to cry. That she was suddenly in Pat's arms made her cry even harder.

After a few seconds, she controlled her tears and broke from their hug. "No more of this," she said. "We need to have a serious conversation about the future."

"Last night was miserable," Pat said. "I told Moira a shortened version of our meeting at the airport and our drive to London to drop you at Claridge's. I didn't have the heart, excuse me, the nerve, to tell her the truth, so I told her that the meeting was awkward—that you were happily married, and that you were glad to know that I am, too, and that Kate was the primary subject on our minds."

He shrugged, looking guiltily at Francie. "I don't think Moira believed a word I said. After a two-martini dinner, I told her I was tired, and we went to bed early. Francie, I love her and the boys, but all I could think about was you and how I love you with an excitement I had forgotten existed. We have a connection I could never have with anyone else. This morning I woke up and could barely wait to see you again. I felt like I would burst with happiness."

He reached for her hand and drew it to his lips.

Francie responded. "This is not the conversation we should be having." She moved away from him. "I feel guilty, too. I lied to Michael when he called this morning to tell me how much he missed me and how lonely he was. I told him I was lonely, too, and needed him here. I asked if he could arrange an earlier flight—that's why he's coming tonight instead of tomorrow. The truth is I have not been lonely for one second since I saw you at the airport. I was actually disappointed when Michael called this morning—I thought it was you calling. So, you and I have the same dilemma. I love my husband and you love your wife, but we love each other so much more. We have been apart for twenty-four years." She looked mournfully into his beloved blue eyes. "Will we ever be together?"

They decided it was too soon to consider anything other than their current lives. Francie would go home with Michael in a few days, and Pat would go back to his family, and they'd try to sort things out and do the right thing—for everyone.

For now, absolutely no romance. They agreed, but when it was time to say goodbye, they kissed as passionately as they had a quarter of a century ago.

Francie led him to the door. and he closed it silently behind him as he left.

She stayed in her room until the daze of being with him wore off, and then decided to go for a long walk. She headed toward the library on St James Square, a place where she hoped to find the comfort and tranquility she always felt when exploring the stacks. She had some deep thinking to do about what was at stake and expected the atmosphere in the library would put her at ease.

It helped calm her, but she came to no conclusions.

It was well into evening when she returned to her room. She had called Tommy from the U.S. to tell him about Pat's letter and finding Kate. She told him her travel plans and asked him to call her brothers. She hoped they could all come to London. "After a day or so, I should know my schedule and I'll call you as soon as I can," she'd told him. Now she dialed Tommy's number.

He answered on the third ring.

"Hi, Tommy. It's your favorite sister."

"Do I have a choice?" he said with a chuckle.

She started right in, "Guess what? I had lunch with my twenty-three-year-old baby, Kate, and I'm walking on air. We had the most wonderful day—I can't wait for you to meet her. I'm not sure how long I'm staying, but I definitely want to see you and Margaret, and the family. How does tomorrow sound? Is that too soon for you?

"Francie, are you on drugs? I haven't heard you this happy since that last Christmas before you left. Denny and Brian are expecting me to call so we can arrange a reunion. Margaret and I can make it tomorrow, but I have to see if that's too early for the boys."

"Is there any chance at all that I could see Mum and Da? Do you think that after all these years, they'll finally relent?"

"I'll do my best, but I'm not very hopeful. Is Michael with you?"

"He'll be here tonight—he wanted to let me have some private time with Kate and Pat before he came. You know, until two days ago Michael never knew about my pregnancy and the birth of Kate, so this has been a lot for him to digest."

They spoke for about an hour, barely waiting for one to finish a story before the other had one to tell. "Oh, Tommy, it's so much fun to talk to you like this. When I was living with horrible Aunt Agnes, I never would have believed I could be this happy again."

"On that note, I have to hang up. I have lots of calls to make and lots of explaining to do to the family. No one else knows you're here and that you found your daughter. I'll call you tomorrow as soon as I come up with plans for all of us. Welcome home, Sis. You've been gone too long."

By the time she hung up, Francie was more than hungry. She ordered a tray from room service and included a bottle of wine and a cheese plate to have with Michael when he arrived.

A short while later he called. "I'm here! Just landed—the plane was early."

"I'm waiting with wine and cheese and open arms. The taxi should have you here within the hour. Room 242."

She was in turmoil, trying very hard to sound natural. She loved him so much, but she couldn't block out the overwhelming joy she felt with Pat.

An hour later, he was knocking on her door. They shared a long embrace. "Forget the wine and cheese," he said, "we'll have it later." He carried her to the bed. They were gentle with each other at first, as they usually were during lovemaking. But their excitement mounted, and they made love as never before. She felt intense heat searing through her body and a feeling of urgency culminating in a climax she had never imagined possible. Michael was so happy to be with her, so thrilled with their expression of love, he told her he never wanted to be separated from her again. She squeezed his hand, told him she loved him.

"I'm suddenly starving," he said. They polished off the whole bottle of wine, finished every crumb of cheese, and called room service to send up ice cream.

What she didn't tell him was that during their lovemaking, she had been fantasizing that she was making love to Pat.

Chapter 12

The next morning Francie and Michael ordered a full course English breakfast for two from room service. The waiter arrived with a cart containing a round table, starched white tablecloth, heavy silverware and bone china. He set up the table, and another waiter brought in a large tray, followed by another waiter with another large tray.

"You must have the wrong room," Michael said. "We ordered breakfast for two, not ten."

The waiter was used to this reaction. "No mistake, sir, this is a breakfast for two. I hope you and Madame enjoy your meal. Please let me know if there is anything else you need."

"What we need," said Michael "is about eight more people to help us eat this."

"Welcome to the British indulgence—the famous full English breakfast," Francie said, smiling broadly. "Any questions, or should I just start identifying unknown items?"

"Just that black slice of something, please."

"Bloodwurst. But don't let the name scare you, it's quite good."

"Thanks for the recommendation." He eyed it suspiciously as he tucked in his napkin. "If we start now, maybe we'll be finished in time for lunch," he said to Francie.

During their breakfast, Tommy called. "Are you up for a visit from your brothers? Margaret and I can be there for a late dinner tonight. Brian and Denny can't skip work today but can get to Manchester tonight. Then tomorrow they can drive over to London in time for a late lunch."

"Oh, Tommy, thank you, thank you, thank you for arranging this."

She could hardly get the words out to say, "Do you realize that this is the first time in over twenty years that we'll all be together? Bring pictures and please ask Denis and Brian to bring them, too. And don't say "no" when I say we're booking a room for you and Margaret as our guests at the hotel tonight."

"Francie, you don't have to do that."

"Tommy, what better way to spend our money than to treat you and Margaret to a luxurious love nest?"

Laughing and skipping any more objections, he accepted. "See you soon, a few hours."

"You have a long drive ahead of you. Drive safely and don't rush. Can you call when you're about an hour away?"

"Sure, Granny," he said.

Chapter 13

Francie and Michael spent the day exploring London. Michael had been there once, right after college, and Francie, too, had been there once, as a child on vacation with her parents and brothers. So they did the tourist thing—hired a driver for a whirlwind tour; walked with dozens of other tourists around the Tower of London; watched the changing of the guard in their tall, bearskin hats at Buckingham Palace; strolled through Hyde Park; and visited key points at the British Museum, including four of the nine famous *must-sees*: Rosetta Stone, Parthenon Sculptures, Lewis Chessmen, and the King of Ife.

At four o'clock, Francie asked Michael if he had enough culture for the day. "Ready for a brew?" she said. He stuck out his tongue and panted. They high-tailed it to their last stop, a typical pub, and sent their driver on his way. They skipped the ploughman's lunch and shared an order of fish and chips with two mugs of beer, their preferred version of high tea at the Savoy.

They taxied back to the hotel, hung the *Do Not Disturb* sign on the door, shared a quick shower, an unsuccessful try at lovemaking, and a long nap. They were both exhausted from the long day and night before. Francie's only thoughts were about how good it felt to be with Michael. No matter where she was, when he was with her, it felt like home.

The phone rang at seven p.m. "It's Margaret! We're about an hour away."

"We're eager to see you both," said Michael. Francie is over the top! We'll meet you at the bar in the lobby."

An hour later, there they were, looking a little worn from the long ride, but such a wonderful sight to Francie.

Conversation burst from all of them, and pictures of home and kids were passed around Every drink brought another toast to each other's health and happiness. The familiar Irish toast, "Slainte," brought Francie to tears, and the four of them took out their handkerchiefs and joined her.

She told them she was going to try to arrange to have Kate meet all of them at lunch the next day. She was glowing when she said, "My world is so full right now. I have a husband I love with all my heart, a reunion with my brothers and their families, and a daughter I never thought I would know."

She looked directly to Thomas. "Let's talk about Da and Mum. Have you asked them about a visit from me?"

"Truth be told, none of us sees them except for holidays, Francie. The kids hardly know them. They hate to visit their grandparents because the house is so full of gloom and doom. They have only themselves to blame. I will never figure out why Mum is so vindictive and why our happy Da turned into a miserable stranger to us all.

"I asked the priest to give them counsel, but nothing worked. They only listen to the voices inside their heads and find no reason to change.

Francie shook her head, her eyes sad. Michael took her hand.

"I called them this morning to tell them you were in London and the news about Kate. I told them you wanted to see them. Mum said, 'Absolutely not,' and hung up on me. I'm so sorry to have to tell you this, Francie, but I think you should know the truth. So many years have gone by since they chose to change our family, and I fear they'll never reconsider."

Michael put his arm around Francie, and she could barely clear her voice to tell Tommy how sorry she was that her actions had broken up the family.

"Francie, our parents are irrational. There must have been something wrong all along for them to act this way, but I don't think we'll ever know. Please don't blame yourself. You're the glue that always held us kids together. When we didn't have you, we weren't complete.

"Let's talk about good things."

Michael had been quiet throughout this discussion, but now he spoke up. "I could write a book about all of the positive things your sister has done since she arrived in the U.S., but I'll start from the day we were married nineteen years ago, when you gave her away to me.

Francie and Michael smiled at Tommy.

"Even though she was young, the philosophy student in her deduced that along with the absolutely necessary qualities of love and attraction, there is another necessity for us to base our married life on—recognizing that there are three important entities in a marriage—the husband, the wife, and the marriage. Sometimes one of us has to step aside for the other, and sometimes we both have to step aside for the sake of our marriage. Because of her wisdom, our marriage started as a partnership, rather than a competition, and continues to do so to this day. She charmed me and she charms everyone she meets with her smile and good nature." He brought her hand to his lips, still talking. "When our neighbor had daily hospital treatments, Francie looked in on her every day for a month and helped with meals, driving her kids, and just holding her hand. She volunteers at the local food bank and delivers meals on wheels to those in need. In our town, people know she's always willing to help, and she's the one they turn to in an emergency, And she continues to impress her peers at Shea's Soups with her logical and forward thinking." He raised their hands together as if they were the champions in the ring. "She gave me life again when I thought I would never recover from losing my first wife and our baby. I am what I am today because of her."

"Michael, that's enough!" Francie kissed his cheek.

Margaret said, "Well, let me tell you about your brother Tommy and what a rock he is." She gave him an air kiss and told her in-laws all about their lives. "We're blessed with happy, healthy children who actually like each other. Tommy has set a great example by helping around the house—not just in the yard, but with the household chores, too, and they follow in his footsteps. We all help each other, sometimes a bit grudgingly, but we know we'll get back what we give—that's what makes us a family, not just parents and children living under the same roof.

Tommy sat there smiling at Margaret's description of family life, knowing that without her subtle encouragement, their family would not be as successful. Then he gave her a big hug and a long smooch, turned to the group and announced, "There have been some changes since the last time we spoke. I am still a tennis pro, but now, I own fifty percent of a tennis academy."

Francie and Michael gave him a thumbs-up and Tommy responded with a proud grin.

"I handle everything to do with tennis, and my partner, Felix, takes care of the business end. The Dublin Tennis Academy, called the DTA, has eight indoor courts and four outdoor ones. We employ six pros and twelve junior staff." Everyone at the table applauded, and Tommy stood up to take a bow.

Margaret said, "Enough with the boring stuff!"

Tommy laughed and ended with, "The bottom line is that I love it, and, so far, we're successful—always booked and always having fun, and always looking for ways to keep our business vibrant."

"As for me," Margaret chimed in, "a year ago, I was promoted to senior surgical nurse. The operating room has been my domain for five days a week, but I wanted more. Now that our kids are teenagers, I applied and was accepted to medical school, so next fall, I will be back at the books!" Now it was Margaret's turn to curtsy to the applause.

Francie leaned over and hugged her. "Wow. That is such a big deal, Margaret. I hope you love going to school as much as I do."

She returned Francie's hug then said with a big smile and crossed fingers, "The jury is still out on that one, Francie."

She went on, "Tommy and I have so much to say about our kids, but this is not the time for it—it's yours, Michael's and Kate's time. We hope you can visit with our kids soon. They are so much fun, and remarkable to watch as they progress, if you can stand the big voices and constant eating. We can't wait to meet Kate, and our kids are excited to have a new cousin.

For the next few hours, they ate, drank, talked and laughed and finally stumbled to the elevator to go to bed. "No fair calling before nine," they all agreed. "See you in the morning."

Chapter 14

Francie and Michael awoke to a rare, sunny spring day in London and called Tom and Margaret. "It's one minute after nine," Francie said. "Let's go for a walk before breakfast."

"We've already had our breakfast, but we're up for a walk on this gorgeous day. We've heard from Denny and Bri, and they should be here by twelve thirty. I told them we'd meet them down the street at The Painted Hat Restaurant. They can't wait to see you and to meet Michael and Kate."

They started walking toward Hyde Park, making a stop along the way for pastry and coffee to go. They spent the rest of the morning weaving along the well-used paths. Tommy filled them in on what to expect from Denis and Brian.

"Both of their careers are progressing," said Tommy, "and both have love interests but are still single. They'll tell you more when we see them."

They headed back to the hotel for a quick wash-up before they went across to the restaurant. They found the boys were there already, waiting at the table with identical grins.

"Well, Jesus, Mary and Joseph!" Denny said, "You are still the freckly faced, teenage sister I remembered."

Brian rushed over to hug her. "Francie, our baby sister, you are still a beautiful young woman. What happened to us?"

Despite what Francie knew to be true, she was shocked when she saw them. "Oh my God! You grew up! I was expecting to see two boys, but I'm looking at two of the handsomest Irishmen I've ever seen."

Michael piped up to introduce himself. "I'm Michael. I came with Francie. She's the main event, I'm only the husband."

"Ah, so you're the guy we've been hearing so many good things about for the past nineteen years. I'm sure you must feel like you're standing on the sidelines watching the show unfold, but I assure you, you will be in act at lunch with us today."

"Don't worry, I'm enjoying the show, so carry on," said Michael.

Francie saw Kate making her way through the crowded restaurant. "Kate's here!" she said. "The real star of the show."

Francie began introductions. "This is Michael Hanson, my husband—the rest are O'Conners—Denny, my oldest brother, Brian, the middle one, Tommy, the youngest, and Margaret, Tommy's wife, my one and only sister-in-law."

She hugged Kate. "And, everyone, this is Kate Mullins, my daughter," she said with pride—your niece."

The greeting looked like a rugby scrum of hugging and touching.

When they all sat down, the boys just stared at Kate. "There is no doubt about whose daughter she is," said Brian.

"She looks just like you, Francie," said Denny.

By then, everyone in the noisy pub was looking at them, the noisiest ones there. They didn't care and kept on talking, laughing and crying.

"Michael and I are pretty well up to date on Tommy and Margaret, and you know a bit about what Michael and I do, thanks to our annual Christmas letter, but what's new with both of you?" she asked Denny and Brian. To Kate,"Listen carefully, my daughter, this is complicated."

Kate smiled at her brand new uncles. "I'm all ears."

Denis started. "Here's the thing, Kate, from the eldest brother who has always ruled the roost. Francie told us a little about you on the phone, and first I want to tell you how thankful we are to your parents for raising you so right. Then I want to thank them for encouraging you to leap into our family, too. I can personally assure you equal membership in the O'Conners' crowd, whether you want it or not."

Kate gave him a little bow of the head.

Denny then looked at Francie. "I want to apologize to you, Francie, for letting so many years go by without keeping in closer touch. Brian and I let Tommy do the job for us, but you were never far from our thoughts.

It has taken years for us to loosen the hold that our parents had on us, and we're still working on it."

There was a short, almost awkward silence. Then Denny turned to Michael. "To you, buddy, thank you for guiding Francie out from under her cloud by bringing love back into her life. We love you for it."

Denny saluted him with his beer, smiled around the group, cleared his throat and said, "Here we go! As far as I'm concerned, my story is easy to tell. I graduated from Architecture School and started work as an apprentice in a company that built low-cost housing developments. After two years of the monotonous task of drawing blueprints of the same units with slight variations, I got an invite from my boss to make suggestions for improving the layouts of the units. Fortunately, he liked what I suggested, as I was at my wit's end by then. I was promoted and assigned to improve existing blueprints by using my own designs. That was my first step to becoming my own designer."

"Do you have pics, Denny?"

"Nah. Maybe someday you'll see the actual buildings." He shrugged, blushing. "Anyway, meanwhile, I found Dublin's social life to be too fast for my liking—too many bars, too much drinking, and too little time for substantive conversation about the world outside Dublin. I was a bit of an oddball in that respect, as most of the people my age were into the bar scene. I had casual friends, and I went to some parties, but I never entertained at my place. On the pittance that I earned, I couldn't afford a decent apartment in the city, and there was no way I would move back home. For ten years, I stayed in that tiny place while I climbed the ranks of my company. I finally reached the level of designing larger buildings and shopping centers. My salary increased as my projects increased. I moved to a decent two-bedroom flat that I furnished with real furniture, not thrift shop discards. I was happy to put all that in the junk heap and start living like an adult. Instead of going to bars, I joined a bicycle club where I met a new group of people with interests similar to mine. There was one woman, Carol, who particularly attracted me."

Brian leered at his brother, his eyes wide and round. In sotto voice, he said, "Carol was a looker."

Denny ignored his brother and went on. "We started a relationship. She was a manager in a new tech startup. We both enjoyed the outdoors, sports, politics, and we loved doing those things together. Our relationship became a serious romance, but something wasn't right. We both knew how much we enjoyed what we did together, and, as we approached thirty, we began talking about moving in together. She knew I was a practicing Catholic and I knew she was not. She never spoke of her religion until it was time to combine our lives. She stopped me in my tracks when she told me she was Jewish. I didn't know what to say."

"Well, what's wrong with being Jewish?" Francie asked.

"Nothing for you, but everything for me, Francie. I'm sorry that Carol and I never talked about it before. I just assumed she was Catholic, albeit non-practicing." He looked around the group. "You know that our parents and the Church made sure that as children we were sufficiently indoctrinated to feel guilty if we married outside the faith." He sneaked a sheepish look at Francie, and she was stone faced. Her early life had been ruined because of the faith. And her life now was with a Protestant. She squeezed Michael's hand under the table to let him know what she was thinking. "Eventually Carol and I had a long talk about religion and the differences in our upbringing. We loved each other, but we both realized we should have talked about this from the start. Marrying a non-Catholic was never anything I could consider, and for Carol, conversion to a faith she didn't believe in was never a consideration. We tried to carry on without thoughts of marriage, but we both agreed that if marriage was not our future, we had no future. When we broke up, I was actually relieved. And she probably was too. I knew that a certain thrill was missing anyway. We are friends now, and I was so happy for her when she married someone who was perfect for her. I still have not been able to find the perfect one for me, but I'm not giving up."

"You seem like a perennial bachelor to me, bro," teased Brian.

Denny once again ignored Brian. To the rest of them, he said "So that's all my news and now it's time for the real "newsman" to tell his. You're up, Brian."

Another familiar grin, making Francie smile, and Brian, nodding to her, said, "I'll jump right to myself, since Denis covered the excuses and accolades to Francie and Kate, to which I heartily agree."

He moistened his throat with a long swallow from the mug in his hand, and plunged in. "When I studied journalism at Trinity, my advisors warned me that it was difficult to get a job unless you were tenacious in your search and didn't take rejection personally. Or peanuts for a salary. I'd been editor in chief of the *Trinity News*, so I thought I would step right into a great job, but I learned that the real world was more difficult than the womb-like college world."

His brothers laughed, and he laughed with them. "I had sold a few freelance articles to several major newspapers throughout Great Britain. I moved from home to Dublin, poorer even than Denny, and he let me share his tiny hovel while I looked for a job. I got a resume together and started knocking on the doors of every major and minor newspaper in or near Dublin. I was willing to start at the very bottom, and I was successful—I was hired for a job at the very bottom."

Brothers clapping, which he ignored.

"Maybe I should have wanted more, but a job offer was enough for me. I started at the *Herald* as news reporter and stringer, and, pretty soon I was on features. After a year and a half, I was able to afford my own hovel, around the corner from Denny.

"It was worse than mine," whispered Denny, raising his mug.

"When I became Bureau Chief, I moved to a one-room apartment in a decent building." He gave a superior look to Denny. "Unlike my cerebral brother, I loved the bar scene. I would meet my mates at the end of the day for a pint at the local hangout for reporters. We'd laugh at some of the news of the day and worry about some of the serious happenings. Mostly, we would gloat about our assignments. One day a group of women came into our domain, all magazine writers, mostly fashion. One look did it—and Rosie and I have been together ever since."

Here Denny cut in. "She's cooler than Carol."

"Her work as associate editor for *Teen Life* involves travel several times a year. She specializes in new looks for teenagers, a constantly changing field, including visits to fashion houses, on-site interviews with high school students, photo layout approvals, and monthly articles for the magazine. She would be here today, but she's on an assignment in Milan."

"I'm impressed, said Francie, and Kate agreed."

"Now for my two announcements that even my bros don't know: I have been appointed Managing Editor, and Rosie and I decided that we both want kids and it's time to be a properly married couple. So, the big announcement is that we are getting married on October 20, and we invite you all to Dublin to celebrate with us."

Tommy and Denis jumped up to pat him on the back and offer congratulations and the girls gave him hugs and kisses.

"Champagne all around," said Michael. "A toast to the reunited family and the bride and groom-to-be. Congratulations to Brian and to Rosie, in Milan, probably hiding from her fiancé and his raucous family."

They sipped their champagne, and then Denny said, "Okay, Kate and Michael, let's hear what the two of you have to say. Since you're both economists, maybe you could tell us how to balance our checkbooks."

Kate said, "Economists can only tell you the theory for balancing your checkbook, but we usually are as bad as you at balancing our own."

Kate was so relaxed and so down-to-earth that they all felt an immediate affinity. "She's definitely family," they thought, raising their glasses with a "Hear, hear."

She told them about her background, noting the coincidence of having older brothers to mentor her, just as Francie had, and issuing a tennis challenge to any of them. "Except you, Tommy—no pros allowed." She went on to tell of life in her happy family with no real constraints. "As long as we pursued what we believed in, completed our education, and finished our dinner every night, we were one big happy family." She smiled and continued.

"I have two mothers to thank for my personality. I am lucky to have inherited their easygoing natures and senses of humor, especially around this group," she said, eyeballing her uncles. "My social and romantic exploits have been great and horrible, you know, the usual; and I have a full range of friends who have enhanced my life. As far as romance goes,

I'm on my third true love. For the past two years, this one, Ned, has been a keeper, and we're beginning to see a future for us."

"More wedding bells?" asked Brian.

Kate raised her shoulders in an I-don't-know way and continued on a different track. "You might say I take after Michael, because I'm a PhD candidate with hopes of teaching economics at Cambridge, and maybe you think I'm nerdy, but to me, watching the ongoing global fluctuations and their impacts is exciting. Isn't it amazing that the theories formulated in the past two centuries still apply?"

Here Michael applauded as her brothers booed. "Right on, Kate," he said. "A traditionalist just like your half stepfather. Or whatever I am." He clinked his glass against hers.

Francie spoke up. "If I didn't know better, I'd say you both sound like nerds, but since I do know better, I hope both of you come up with a new earth-changing theory and share the Nobel Prize, so we can all come to Norway to embarrass you at the ceremony."

Kate said, "In two minutes, I covered my life, so this concludes my resume. I hope I earned a place in the family!"

"Hired," they all said and held up their glasses to her.

When it was Michael's turn, he said that Kate had covered the field of economics and he didn't want to bore them with more of the same. "I just want you all to know how I feel about being a part of this family. I was an only child until I married Francie. Now I'm part of a team of brothers, something I spent my youth dreaming about. You have made me feel welcome, and are succeeding in teaching me to be raucous, a quality I am coming to value." Here he had to stop until the hooting group settled down. "I love your sister and am thrilled to be one of the boys, and—if you let me—an honorary Irishman."

Francie watched Michael as he spoke—his gestures, his way of looking everyone in the eye, the expression of joy on his eyes. She fell in love with him all over again. She stood up and kissed him, then kissed him again to show everyone how much she loved her man.

In spite of all the talking, somehow the waiter was able to take their lunch orders and with the minimum of disturbance, serve the platters to the right people.

Michael paid the entire chit, saying that the happiness this reunion gave Francie doubled his enjoyment of being part of it.

Francie added, "I wish you all could stay longer, but I know you have long trips home. The next time we come to England, I promise to give more advance notice."

By now, it was five p.m. and they said their goodbyes and went their separate ways.

Francie realized that for the past two days, she hadn't thought about Pat at all.

Chapter 15

Dear Reader,

If you're a writer, and you've just finished a Planter's Punch, then immediately returned to continue writing, some wacky thoughts might occur to you. So, read on....

"Francie, I've never seen you look so happy and so beautiful," Michael told her as they were on their way to dinner at the Mullins' home. Francie was wearing a chiffon dress with a matching cashmere scarf in the shade of green that most redheads rely on when they want to look their best.

"Having a tall, handsome man on my arm doesn't hurt," she said as she looked up at him with a smile. Kate opened the door for them, kissed them both and introduced them to her parents, Grace and James. They smiled warmly and extended their hands, followed by affectionate hugs. "Now we know where Kate gets her good looks, Francie," James said with a courtly bow. "The resemblance is remarkable."

"Thank you for welcoming us to your home." Francie beamed at the two of them. "And thank you for raising Kate. For twenty-three years, I prayed that she would be part of a happy family, and my prayers were answered because of you both."

"Well, come in and meet our sons, Kate's brothers."

Francie said to Tommy and William, "I'm so glad that Kate has older brothers—I have three and know how wonderful they can be. Kate raves about you—how you take care of her and protect her, and how, just because she's a girl, you don't give her any slack as far as sports are concerned. My three brothers were my closest friends and taught me how to play tennis like them, just like you boys did for her. Coincidentally, one of my brothers is named 'Tommy,' too."

A thumbs-up sign from Tommy.

"And this is Ned, not a relative, but a regular around here," said Kate, introducing her boyfriend to Francie and Michael.

"It's so nice to meet you, Ned," said Francie, giving him a hug. "I'm sure you're confused about the situation, but just wait, it gets more confusing, I guarantee."

Ned answered, "Don't worry, Kate's been prepping me for two days, and I have a cheat-sheet in my pocket."

"Great," said Michael, "I might want to borrow it."

The doorbell rang again, and Kate welcomed Pat and Moira and their twin boys. Francie froze when she heard Pat's voice. She tried to act as normally as she could in front of Michael and Moira, and now she knew for sure that it was not going to be easy. *Please let me get through this in an adult way*, she said to herself.

Introductions were made all around, and they settled down in the large living room while the maid served drinks and hors d'oeuvres. Moira and Francie were overly cordial to one another as were Michael and Pat. Underneath the façade, the women were sizing up each other and so were the men. Michael was taller, with dignified good looks, and Pat was broader, with ruggedly handsome looks. Moira was pretty in a reserved way, and Francie was cute in a vivacious way. Francie and Pat sneaked a glance at each other and could see that they both thought the situation was either laughable or dangerous. The host and hostess knew how awkward it was and tried to make it easy for everyone to feel comfortable, especially Kate, who actually seemed oblivious to any tension. She was just so happy to see the families together—her families.

She kissed Pat and turned to Moira saying, "I'm pleased to meet you, Moira. I hope that we become friends." Moira forced a smile, trying to look pleasant under the circumstances.

To her new brothers, twins Flip and Joshua, Kate said, "How lucky can a girl get? I have two more brothers to add to my collection of favorite people."

Josh spoke for both of them, "It's so cool to have a sister—Flip and I always wanted one, and we're glad you're too old to bug us."

Kate laughed. "Wait till you meet my other brothers. They have stories to tell." She asked them how they felt about being hugged, and they reluctantly agreed, Flip saying, "We can do it once."

The whole room laughed, easing tension at least for Francie and Pat.

"I feel honored," Kate said. "And don't worry, I won't do it again unless I ask permission first." She looked around. "Now that we've all been introduced, I'd like to propose a toast.

"To all of us—the Mullins, the Harringtons, and the Hansons—here's to happy, healthy relationships in our unique family.'"

"Hear, hear," from the crowd.

Kate flitted from group to group with light conversation and a big smile, happy that everyone was there because of her and in her happiness felt no tension. Or ignored it if she did.

"Dinner is served," said Grace.

Place cards positioned them randomly with the exception of the young boys who sat next to each other with one parent on either side. Conversation flowed freely. They discussed a range of serious subjects including politics, drugs, education and life in the States compared to England. Michael and Kate had interesting things to say about the world economy, and both concluded that although they might be considered experts on the subject of macroeconomics, they both had trouble making decisions about how to budget their own money. "You have that right," James commented. "Even as a child, Kate was withdrawing money from her piggy bank more often than she was depositing."

The group was quite congenial. Light conversation interspersed with laughter continued.

Pat and Francie sat on different sides of the table and tried to avoid glancing at each other, but, inevitably, their eyes met. They could feel the passion stirring. Pat's eyes filled with longing for her. She looked away, and then she was drawn back. Slowly she felt a tightening in her groin. She shifted her position slightly, but the feeling didn't go away. She tried to concentrate on the food on her plate, but she could still feel his eyes on her. Her nipples started to harden. The feeling became more intense, and she realized she was on the verge of an orgasm. She looked back at him with desperation. When he realized what was happening to her, he looked away and tried to make small talk with his son, but the boy was busy joking with his brother. Pat looked back at Francie, who excused herself from the table. She got to the powder room just in time to hold a wad of tissues to catch her juices while she shivered in full orgasm. Nothing like this had ever happened to her before.

After a few minutes she regained her composure, cleaned herself as best she could, splashed water on her face and returned to the table. Since Michael was sitting on the same side of the table as she was, he didn't see what had happened. However, Moira did, and made it obvious in the look she gave Francie. Everyone else was involved in conversation and apparently had not noticed. Pat knew it wasn't funny but still had to force himself to stifle a laugh.

As soon as dessert was finished, Moira said it was way past the boys' bedtime and apologized to everyone for leaving early. She had had enough of trying to be congenial in this very difficult situation. Pat thanked the hosts, kissed Kate good night, shook hands with Michael and said they hoped they would all keep in touch. Then he quietly said to Francie as Moira was saying her goodbyes to the hosts, "We made a beautiful girl, and we had a beautiful relationship, but I don't think we're finished yet." He held both of her hands in his and said, "Good night."

About an hour later, Francie and Michael left the group and taxied to their hotel. Francie couldn't bring herself to speak a word in the taxi. Her world was shaken.

"What's the matter?" Michael asked when they were back at their room. "We had a wonderful day with your brothers, and the party started off happily, and then something changed."

"What changed, Michael, is my life. I thought everything would be wonderful once I found Kate, but everything is so mixed-up now. I don't know what I feel. I think it would be best if we fly back home tomorrow. I'll come back here when this all sinks in."

"I can only imagine how difficult this is for you, Francie," he said. "I don't know what I'd do, if by some miracle, Emmy came back to life, but there's one thing I do know—I would love you no matter what."

"And Michael, I love you, too, no matter what." She took his hand and led him to the bed. "Michael, I need you more than ever now. Your love means everything to me."

That night they made love gently, with a passion generated by love, familiarity and understanding, and she did not think of Pat until right before she drifted off.

PART III

Chapter 16

Dear Reader,

Michael woke me from a sound sleep to tell me that I was making him look too much like a wimp, so I decided to give the poor guy some credit. Read on....

When they arrived back in the U.S., their marriage began anew, very different from what it had been before. Michael pumped himself up with resolve to become a man of action.

Francie returned to work, exhausted physically and mentally from their trip, but in a few days she recovered from her jet lag and settled into her usual daily rhythm. She convinced herself that what happened in London was an aberration, and she filed her thoughts of any future with Pat in the Roladex in her mind under "F" for "Finished." The early chapters of her life were over. Kate was the point, not Pat. Now when she thought about her daughter, there was a live person, a lovely face to the name, and she was ecstatic. Kate was alive! Kate was happy! And after twenty-four years of worrying about Kate's survival, Francie was at peace.

She never wanted to forget the joy she felt at this moment, so she decided to take up writing in her journal, the alter ego of her youth. For nineteen years, her old journals had remained untouched in a locked cabinet in the basement. She felt the time was right to reminisce. All through one night, she pored over what sometimes read like a stranger's life. She laughed out loud when she read, *Pat makes me feel like a woman, an object of desire.* She never thought of herself as a drama queen, but her writing as a seventeen-year-old seemed like the dialogue of a school play.

For almost a year after she had come to the U.S. she had written about her unhappiness and the loss of Pat and her family. Now the words seemed unreal to her. It was almost as if she were reading about a younger sister, not herself. She picked up a subtle change taking place. As she read further, she could see the growing maturity of her thoughts. When she rediscovered the entries about her studies in philosophy regarding the vicissitudes along the path of life, she saw those of a young student who didn't trust her own instincts. Her conclusions were based on someone else's theories. *How could I have believed that the explanation of life's experiences was so simple? Maybe the philosophers I studied weren't as brilliant as I thought. Why did I have to read philosophy to learn that my* personal *journey was the human journey, the one that everyone travels. The only variation is in the details.*

She brought her journals up to the present with a quick skim of the past nineteen years, the experiences and emotions of an extremely happy wife and businesswoman. Putting the words on paper about her feelings toward both Pat and Michael made it even clearer to her that her choice was right. She wouldn't contact Pat—he would remain in her past.

Michael had done some serious thinking on the way home from England about the age difference between Francie and himself. She was still a young woman, just beginning her forties, beautiful, vital and sensual. And he was fifty, the age when some men start to see a decline in their virility. He couldn't ignore the electricity he observed between Francie and Pat and would be a fool to think they had not been affectionate to some degree during the time before he arrived in London. He trusted Francie's fidelity to him and chose not to discuss the subject with her. He was an even tempered man, and thought things through with deliberation, looking for logical answers. He reasoned that he had to make their marriage more exciting, and he would have to come up with a plan.

The first thing he knew he had to do was to get into shape. He had always been athletic—played squash at Penn for the past two decades—but he knew he needed more muscle and less spare tire. He hired a handyman to put up a basketball backboard and hoop on the garage. At six feet-two he'd often played hoops at the gym at Penn but not for the last couple of years. He called some of his old buddies, and they began a twice-weekly half court game at his house. Francie had only seen basketball played a few times, and she found that she liked watching the men. She soon became fascinated with the game. Her memories of the sounds and smells of boys grunting and sweating brought back thoughts of her brothers…which led to thoughts of the home and country she left…which led to a touch of homesickness.

In her journal that night, she wrote, *It seems like it would be easy to make a new life in a country that offers everything, and I'm grateful for what I have, but my real home is where my history is, where I lived my childhood and formative years. Michael, his family, and my friends have given me a wonderful life here, a life rich with love and security. But just once I would love to bump into someone I knew when growing up—that will never happen here. My friends tell me they love to hear my Irish lilt, and I'm flattered, but sometimes I feel they see me as different. I long to hear the same Irish lilt as mine spoken from people around me, but I seldom do.*

Enough whining, I sound like a spoiled brat.

"Michael," she said one day, handing him a warm brownie right out of the oven, "could you teach me to play basketball?" *How could he say no once he'd taken a bite of the brownie?* She had carefully laid the trap.

He drew himself up, and in his new macho persona said, "Francie, we're just a couple of guys having a good time."

Rather than bristle at being brushed off at his cocky statement, she said coyly, "I know, dear, but I don't want to play with them. Isn't there a way just you and I could play?" She vamped a little, played with her hair, curling it behind her ear and moved toward him, salaciously licking her lips from the brownie she had just nibbled. "We'll be alone on the court. It will be a bonding experience."

"Maybe," he said slowly, then perked up. "But first, for the next couple of weeks, you'll have to practice taking shots at the hoop from all over the court, especially from the foul line. If you miss, you'll have to run to the ball and shoot from wherever you pick it up." *That should discourage her.*

She smiled slyly and gave him another brownie.

He thought he knew his wife, but he didn't know her at all.

She was outside every day after work taking shots over and over, running the length of the driveway and into the backyard. After three weeks, she was in better shape than he was, and she challenged him to a game of HORSE.

"What—where did you learn about HORSE?"

"My secret coach," she said. "Wanna play after dinner or before? We can put the outside lights on."

End of story—she beat him. She had a great eye and rarely missed. He was so overconfident he actually threw a few air balls. However, they laughed a lot, had a great workout and decided to make HORSE their Tuesday night date. From then on, he gave nothing away and won the majority of games. She never failed to give him a run for his money, and he had to play hard to stay ahead.

Continuing with his campaign to make their marriage more exciting, he approached Francie two weeks later, on a warm Sunday in May and invited her on a road trip.

"Francie, my Irish colleen, since you never lived through the teenage car experience, I decided that it would be good for us to spend part of every Sunday taking a road trip, an adventure for the two of us—to make us feel like kids again. It's an American tradition for young folks, and we're still young." He kissed her on the forehead." At least you are! To make it more interesting, I'll plan a surprise, and every week we'll drive to a place neither of us has ever been. We'll explore, have lunch, then later pick up pizza for dinner."

"When do we start?"

"Today," he said. "Now."

"I can be ready in five minutes. Is that too long?

"Sounds good to me. Wear comfortable clothes and bring an extra pair of sneakers. No more hints—I'll see you in the car."

Off they went. From their home in suburban Main Line Haverford, they headed south on U.S. Route 1. Michael, the inveterate teacher, told Francie it was the first major interstate highway in the U.S., running for roughly 2,500 miles from the Canadian border of Maine to Key West, Florida.

Francie, the inveterate student, listened carefully, noting every detail.

"Once the high-speed turnpikes were built, the road became a minor highway, and sometimes a local road, like it is in this part of the Philadelphia suburbs. Then after a ten mile stint as a highway, it becomes a rural road with lots of local charm."

"I'll let you know when I see the first cow," she said looking out the window.

He put a tape in the CD player, and they got into the rhythm of their tunes. Francie loved the songs from *Saturday Night Fever*. She sang along, word for word, with the Bee Gees "Stayin'Alive," and "How Deep is your Love," snapping her fingers to the disco beat and swaying with the romantic ones. Michael liked everything from *Grease*, especially, "You're the One that I Want" which he sang to Francie with his fist in a make-believe mike.

Four songs later, they passed the magnificent Longwood Gardens, originally owned and developed by Pierre S. du Pont, and now recognized as one of the most breathtaking horticultural gardens in the world.

When Francie saw the sign over the stone entryway, she told Michael she loved his choice. She didn't remind him that she had visited there several times with his mother.

"Nope, good guess, but that's not it," he said, and drove farther south. Francie marveled at how quickly the scenery turned into farmland, cow pastures with groups of sleepy cows and dairies touting *Homemade, fresh-churned ice cream made from Guernsey cows.*

"I see there are a lot of black and white Holsteins here. Did you know that Holstein Friesians are the most popular milk cows in Ireland?" she asked, attempting to teach the professor. "But those brown and white cows ahead are Guernseys. They give the richest cream for butter and ice cream. That cow seems to want us to stop here. Can we? I know we just had breakfast, but I don't want to disappoint old 'Bossy.'"

Michael jammed on the brakes and made a sharp turn into the dairy's driveway. "Great suggestion, Francie. Never let it be said that I disappointed a cow."

"I'll spread the word," she said.

They ate their cones while they meandered around admiring the baby calves and their solicitous mothers. Michael took a picture of her showing a cow her ice cream cone.

"What beautiful dreamy eyes," he said.

"Thank you, Michael."

"Yours are beautiful, too, Francie."

Back in the car, they picked up another minor highway that led to Brandywine Creek State Park. This was old, old territory, an area of hiking trails, historic buildings and artifacts from the Revolutionary War. When they came across a re-created village of the times, Michael parked the car and they strolled through a field, peeking in huts and admiring volunteers dressed in clothes of the period. Francie was fascinated by the skill of a woman in a ruffled hat baking bread in a stone hearth, using a bellows to keep the fire going. The sound of hammering drew them to a shack where a well-muscled man blacksmith pounded horseshoes on an anvil. Kids in puffy shirts and knickers pumped their legs on swings hanging from tall oaks. Some rolled hoops along paths of packed dirt.

Francie liked this part of Pennsylvania, and they spent twenty minutes back in time in the tiny village, holding their breath to avoid temptation when they walked past the stand where popcorn was being made over an open fire.

"If I hadn't eaten that big ice cream cone, I would have popcorn," she said.

"My thinking exactly, Francie. But I'm so full—maybe the best cone I've ever had. You were right about the Guernseys."

The day was mild, with a light breeze from the west, one of those days that make one glad to be out and about. Francie breathed in the aroma of fresh grass and newly planted crops in the freshly turned earth. "Michael, we should spend more time in the country. The air is so fresh and delicious." She took a deep breath and let out a series of sneezes that left her with a runny nose and itchy eyes. "Oh, my God I hope I'm not allergic to the country air. I couldn't stand that!"

They got back in the car, and her symptoms were alleviated. "Better?"

asked Michael. Francie crossed her fingers and nodded. They drove down the road approaching the Andrew Wyeth Museum built on the banks of the meandering Brandywine Creek.

She immediately recognized the landscape around her as the setting for so many of Wyeth's paintings. It gave her chills to realize that she was looking at the same scenery the painter made famous in his dreamy tempura masterpieces.

"Michael, this is perfect."

"Think again, and keep your seat belt buckled, we're not there yet."

"But I would love to see the museum, Michael."

"We'll save that for another trip, but this time you're not getting off so easily."

She scooted closer to him and gave him a kiss. "Michael, I trust you. If you say that where we're going can top Andrew Wyeth's works, I'm all for it."

"I accept the compliment and the kiss, but we're in for a nautical trip. Maybe someday we'll take a cruise around the world, but today we're canoeing down Brandywine Creek."

"Uh, oh, we're in trouble. I've never been in a canoe in my life."

"Well, then I can show off the skills I learned on a pond in camp when I was ten. The Brandywine looks tame—it can't be too different from paddling in a pond. If I mess up, you probably won't even notice. As for you, there's always a first for everything, and I'm willing to meander down the Brandywine if you are. It's easy, you'll catch on quickly. Then we can shoot the rapids in Colorado."

She grinned, eager to get started. "You know I never turn down a challenge, but let's keep Colorado out of the picture for a while, like maybe a decade."

At the Brandywine Canoe Company, they were greeted by a man with long hair and a grizzled beard, dressed in well-worn hunting clothes.

"We'd like to rent a canoe. Are you the man we want to see?"

"Any experience?"

"A little from when I was a child, but my wife has none."

"Okay, here's the deal," he said. "The water's pretty low, so you don't have to worry about a fast current. Since you're stronger and have some experience, you sit in the back and basically power the boat. Your lady can steer with her paddle and warn you of anything ahead—low branches, shallow areas and such. You pay by the hour. The crick's runnin' slow. No worries. Look out for the first stop-off about an hour ahead. If you miss that one, or if you want to go farther, there are two more, each about another forty-five minutes downstream. I have crew at each dock to help pull your canoe in. Our van drives you back here to your car. Each canoe has two lightweight lifejackets. We prefer that you wear them, but it's your choice. The deepest water should be less than two feet deep.

"Fifty bucks an hour in advance and leave your driver's license here in case of damage to the equipment. No refunds."

"Sounds easy. I'm game to go," said Francie, and started to climb into the canoe assigned to them. "Wait a minute!" they both yelled, but too late, Francie had rolled the boat to one side and ended up one ankle deep in the water.

She tried to sound carefree, "I still have one dry foot and another pair of shoes in the car. You ready or not?"

Michael got in and the canoe *meister* said, "You're on your own—good luck." As soon as they turned their backs to him, he rolled his eyes and shook his head muttering under his breath, "I sure hope the crick don't rise."

It took only a few minutes to get the hang of it. As soon as they were out of hearing range, Francie said to Michael, "How'd you like Mr. Friendly?"

"I don't think he has job satisfaction," Michael answered sarcastically. "Maybe he should take it up with personnel."

The conditions on the creek were ideal. They meandered past woods of oaks, sycamores, maples, and pines and saw groves of fruit trees in full flower. Farther downstream, they noticed outcrops of a greenish rock. The teacher in Michael couldn't resist. "That's green gneiss—there's lots of it in Pennsylvania. We have some in our garden in the stone retaining wall."

"How do you say that again? Green nice?" Francie said, feeding Michael's ego.

"It's pronounced *nice*, though it's spelled *g-n-e-i-s-s*. Sometimes it has a glitter to it—the Germans named it after the word for *spark*. It's very common in Pennsylvania."

Francie pretended to study the green rock as they glided past. *It's almost lunchtime. When do we get to the refreshment stand?* she thought, a trifle bored.

"Here's another piece of information for you, Francie. I read somewhere that the Indians planted sycamore trees near water so that when they were in the woods, they could look up to search for whitish limbs with the peeling bark of the giant sycamores—and expect to find water nearby."

"Michael, I never knew you were such a nature buff. I'm learning more about you every day."

"I'm a regular font of knowledge. You ain't heard nothin' yet," he crowed.

Francie turned around to look at Michael to make a snide remark, and they ran into a pile of stones and branches in the middle of the creek. They couldn't work the canoe loose, so Francie said that since it was her fault and she already had one wet foot, she'd jump out and free them.

Shin-deep, she pulled on the back of the boat while Michael pushed with the paddle. It worked. Just as the creek picked up some speed and depth, the canoe glided forward with Francie sloshing after it. Michael did his best to dig in while Francie caught up, waterlogged from the knees down. By then they thought the whole thing was a riot, and they laughed so hard that Michael lost his grip *and* the paddle. He grabbed the other one while Francie headed off downstream chasing after the lost paddle.

A couple of guys fishing on the bank watched the comedy unfold. "Hey, city folk," one of them yelled, "welcome to the country."

Francie caught up to the paddle snagged on a branch, grabbed it. The water had become shallow again, so she signaled Michael to come get her. Looking like a wet mouse, she climbed into the canoe. Wet shoes, wet sox, wet jeans.

"How do you like canoeing so far?" Michael asked her.

"Can you believe it—I love it! I'm having a great time."

They got to the first dock and decided to keep going. Bad mistake. It started to drizzle, followed by big, heavy drops. The creek ran faster, and they zipped up their life jackets. Within a few minutes, they seriously had to learn how to handle the canoe.

"Watch out for the branches ahead!" Francie warned.

"Duck!" said Michael. "I can't steer away fast enough."

Lucky for them, they ended up with only a few scratches, but Francie's hair had caught in a branch that ripped out a small tuft from her head. "Ouch!" she yelled, rubbing her head. Without looking around, she said, "Quit laughing, Michael! I've been scalped!"

They were soaked to their skin when the rain stopped as quickly as it had started. They looked like they'd survived a shipwreck in the Atlantic.

"I suggest we follow the sign and dock up ahead, unless you want to keep going to the final stop," he said.

"We can't. If we miss the last stop, we may end up in the Delaware River, then the Atlantic and then, maybe Europe. So far, we haven't navigated this damn crick very well, so I vote, pull over now—we can't go to Europe without our passports."

When the dock came into sight, they didn't see any crew, so they started yelling, "Hello, hello—somebody—anybody—pull us out."

Two characters appeared, both bearded, wearing khaki camouflage hats, tank tops and jeans. They brought them in with long hooks.

"Hey, folks, ya' have fun?"

"Sure," Michael said shivering, "we'll be coming back again someday when we get over our pneumonia."

A dilapidated van took them back to their car. Francie tried to get some words out, but her laughter held her back. On her third try, she managed to say, "I hope women with bald spots turn you on, Michael."

"Never tried one before, but the idea shows great promise." He rubbed his hands together like a wicked guy in an old-time melodrama. "Does this mean that we won't be shooting the Colorado rapids?"

"Not in my lifetime," she said, pulling off her wet shoes, socks and jeans. Her thighs were bright red and goosepimply with cold. "Drive carefully, if we get into an accident, remember I'm almost naked. How could you explain that to the police?"

They turned the heat on high, drove through McDonald's and ate in the car.

Once home, they took long, hot showers, got into bed and both fell into a dead sleep.

He awoke before she did, turned to her and started to caress her breasts. She stirred. "What a nice way to wake up," she murmured, enjoying the warmth of his touch.

He mounted her, moving his hand lower on her until he felt her wetness. He repositioned himself even lower, adjusting her legs over his shoulders. She wasn't sure what he was doing, but she knew she liked it. Her body accepted his mouth. He parted her downy lips with his tongue and licked her. She moaned, then quivered, quickening to convulse in a heightened orgasm. He moved up on her and kissed her mouth and inserted himself into her body slowly moving back and forth inside her, then more quickly. They orgasmed together. She let the wave of rapture wash over her until it slowly receded.

"What a delightful afternoon," she said. "Can we do this part again next Sunday?"

He laughed. "How about tomorrow?"

That night she wrote in her journal, *Something wonderful has happened to Michael. He's become young again, playing basketball with the boys, taking road trips, and best of all, our lovemaking is electrifying. We both seem to be teenagers again, and it's great fun. It's almost too good to be true—maybe we should pace ourselves so we don't burn out too soon, but we're having too much fun to stop.*

For the next two Sundays, they continued their trips, one to Chestertown, Maryland on the Chesapeake Bay for their famous hard shell crabs, and one to Bay Head, New Jersey to see the grand estates on the beach and have lunch in a quaint tearoom. Each week he gave her one or two clues as to their destination, usually having to do with what to wear and what to take with her. Their *afternoon delight* lovemaking when they got home on those late afternoons made a great double feature for the day.

On the fourth Sunday, his hint was, "Wear hiking clothes."

They drove east on the Pennsylvania Turnpike, then took the Northeast Extension. Francie had no idea where they were going. After about an hour, she started to see signs advertising the Pocono Mountains. "Aha," she said, "I figured it out. We're going mountain climbing."

"Something like that. We're headed for an area of the Poconos where I've never been but always wanted to see—the Delaware Water Gap, famous for its trees, trails and falls. "Our destination is Dingmans Falls, a small mountain town. I mapped out a ten mile hike. We can climb alongside the falls up to the top and down again, have lunch, then hike to the car. Are you game for a ten mile hike?"

"Are you kidding? Do you think you're married to a lightweight? I hiked all over Scotland, so I certainly think I can conquer ten miles in Pennsylvania!"

They continued driving, and after an hour or so, the topography changed. The hills became steeper and the woods denser. They left the main road and followed a series of small, winding lumber trails heading round, round, round and up, up, up. "Francie, keep an eye out for a sign to Dingmans Falls—you should spot it pretty soon."

"I'm looking," she said, "but I'm getting pretty dizzy. Are you sure we're on the right road? There's absolutely nothing here but woods."

Michael was almost at the point of turning around. "We'll give it another five miles, then give up."

About two miles ahead, Francie said, "I may be seeing a mirage, but I think there's an arrow on a sign that says *Dingmans Falls, straight ahead.* We must be here," she said. "Keep going straight."

They drove, and drove, and drove, sure the sign was a hoax. There was not another car on the road. After a half hour and what seemed like miles of winding roads, they pulled into the Dignmans Falls' parking lot. A sign pointed to a series of hiking and climbing paths: "*Welcome! Yar here.*"

"Ta-daa," she said, adding, "Wahr here!"

"Now I know how Columbus felt when he finally discovered America," said Michael, slowly unwinding his long body as he pulled himself out of the car.

"And I know how his crew felt," she said. "I think I'm going to be seasick." With that, she hurried to the side of the parking lot and vomited onto the grass.

"Are you okay to go on?"

"We have no choice—there's no way I'm getting into that car right now to go back down that winding road. Now that I'm on solid land, I feel better, so lead on."

They started on the trail to see the falls. There were small, unobtrusive red and green slash markers on the trees to show the long route and the short route. They wanted the long route, so they followed the red markers over hills, through meadows, crossing small creeks with stepping stones. Late June was an ideal time to be outside in the clear mountain air. It was cool in the shade, but when they entered a clearing, Francie loved the way the sun felt on her face on this spectacular June day. Occasionally, they met other hikers returning from the falls, all friendly, raving about the views from the top.

They knew they were close when they heard the roar and felt the moisture-cooled air on their skin. Around a bend, they suddenly caught sight of the tumbling falls. As they got closer, they were awed by the sheer volume and force of the roaring water rushing one hundred and thirty feet to the frothy stream below. Wooden steps, two hundred and fifty in all, lined the falls from top to bottom.

"Let's go," said Francie, and she was off to climb the steps along the falls.

"Francie, pace yourself—you may be younger than I am, but you're not sixteen anymore."

She gave him a dirty look and kept going. After climbing about fifty steps, she was breathing heavily, and she sat on a step to wait for him.

"I hate to say, '*I told you so*,' but I take pleasure in saying it anyway. I told you so!" He winced as he sat down next to her. "I think my knees may be giving out, but after seeing that gray haired couple up ahead, I'm resigned to make it to the top."

They slowed their pace and hiked steadily. When they reached the top of the falls, they felt like champions. Looking down was even more impressive than looking up. The constant plunge of the millions of gallons of water was hypnotic, and they were drawn into watching rainbows in the sunbeams that danced on the droplets.

“Oh, my God,” Francie said, “now we have to walk down!”

Francie started sneezing as they descended. By the time they reached the bottom, her eyes were running, her throat was itching, and she was still sneezing. Aside from that, they were ready for new knees and new hips. Francie headed for the refreshment stand and took a stack of napkins for her runny nose. “This is much better than using my sleeve,” she said, “but the paper seems to be made of tree bark.”

They had hot dogs and drinks from the lunch stand and agreed that they deserved a slice of coconut custard pie.

Taking the shorter path, they dragged themselves back to their car.

“If we started exercising today, do you think we could get our old bodies back?” Francie said. Michael’s response was a groan.

“Just think, in three short hours we’ll be home, ready for our *afternoon delight*.”

Francie grunted her response. “I didn’t know I married Superman.”

The road was as twisty going down as it was coming up. Francie tried to hold back her nausea, but the hot dog had a mind of its own. She covered her mouth and pointed to the side of the road. Michael stopped while she watched the lunch become food for the raccoons, topped with coconut custard pie for dessert.

“Well, that’s one way to keep the weight off,” she said as she got back into the car. “Let’s see if I can hold off a repeat performance.”

Francie slept the rest of the way home.

When Michael pulled into their garage, he turned to her and said, “How’d ’ya like it?”

“It was fun and educational,” she said. “The fun part was being with you and seeing the falls; the educational part was learning that I’m never going back.”

They took scalding showers and got into bed, but this time they had to skip the *afternoon delight*—too stiff, too sore, too sleepy.

Francie slept straight through until morning. Michael had an early class to teach and woke her up when he left. She was still groggy. “If you feel lousy now, wait until you see how stiff you are when you try to get out of bed to go to work,” he said and kissed her goodbye.

For one of the few times in her life, Francie called in sick. She was exhausted and still nauseated from the lunch. She tried to eat a slice of toast, but as soon as it touched her tongue, she gagged and ran for the toilet. As the day went on, she felt better, had her reliable grilled cheese sandwich, this time with cream of chicken soup instead of tomato, to help keep her stomach settled. When Michael came home, she was still a bit lethargic, so he offered to make dinner.

"Something light, please."

He made his specialty—poached eggs on toast, which she found perfect.

They went to bed early and decided to watch T.V. in bed, something they seldom did. Halfway through *Wheel of Fortune*, she fell asleep.

They next morning she had no appetite and still felt weak all over. She ate a few peanut butter crackers for breakfast with a cup of tea.

"Francie, this is not like you," Michael said, concerned as he watched her. "I'm calling Dr. Mitchell. I think you might have food poisoning."

The doctor could see her at nine that morning, which was perfect for Michael. He cancelled his first class and his next one wasn't until two.

"Fine," she said, barely keeping the crackers down.

Michael stayed in the waiting room while Francie went in to see the doctor. Twenty minutes later, the nurse told him that the doctor wanted to see him in the examining room. Francie was shaking her head, saying over and over, "I can't believe it, I can't believe it. Are you sure?"

Michael went right to Francie and gripped her hand tightly. He turned to the doctor in a panic. "Is it serious?" He steeled himself and said, "Please, tell me everything."

"Yes," she said, "it's serious."

The doctor paused, looking serious herself, then grinned. "Your wife is nine weeks pregnant, Michael. She's in good health and normal in every way. Now I've told you everything."

Wide eyed, he looked at Francie, and both of them beamed. He put his arms around her and squeezed, then quickly stepped back. "Oh, God, I forgot already. Did I hurt you?"

She and the doctor laughed. "Don't worry, Michael, the baby is well protected."

"I know you've been married almost twenty years, and this is quite unexpected. When Francie first came to me years ago, she told me about her former pregnancy. I told her that her difficult delivery and erratic periods made it unlikely for her to conceive again, but surprises like this happen more often than you think," she said. "I'll recommend an obstetrician who specializes in cases such as this. I doubt that Francie will have any problems, but best to be careful. You're lucky, Francie, the nausea was late in coming and should be over in the next couple of weeks, but don't be surprised if you're tired for a while. You can go to work but try to take it easy in the beginning. The tiredness should fade, too."

The doctor closed Francie's file and handed her a slip of paper. "If you have more allergy attacks, here's the name of an allergist, but usually allergies disappear as pregnancy advances—and, if you're lucky, they won't come back.

Hand in hand, they practically danced out of the office. "Well, that explains the nausea and exhaustion," said Francie "I was sure the coconut custard pie at Dingmans Falls was poisoned."

The first telephone call was to Michael's parents. He was teary when he gave them the news.

"Would you repeat that?" asked Michael's mother. "Did I just dream that you said a baby was coming? Are you sure?"

"One hundred percent sure and certified by the doctor, and we're appointing you both as our chief babysitters."

"Stop right there, let me tell your father." She put the phone down and ran to get him.

He heard their voices in the background and then a loud *whoop!*

His dad got on the phone, and he yelled into the receiver. "Congratulations, Son, when can we babysit?" Michael told him they'd have to wait about seven months."

Francie called her brothers, and, of course, Kate.

"I'm so happy for you both, and for me, too," said Kate, with a smile so big that she could barely get her words out. "A baby brother or sister—can I come stay with you when you have the baby?"

"Kate, neither of us has ever taken care of a baby, so we're even. I only had a few minutes to see you on the day you were born, and I can't think of anyone else I'd rather have with me—we can learn together, and Michael can help us fumble along. Keep your calendar clear in January."

With a huge smile on her face, that night she wrote, *I'm pregnant! Just when I thought I was the happiest woman in the world, I found one happier—my mother-in-law! She has spread the word all over the Main Line. Her excitement adds to mine and we're all looking forward to the start of the new generation. Even I can't believe this turn of events. What did I do to deserve such happiness—and how can I give it back? After the baby is born, I'll turn my thoughts to improving the world, or at least the world around me.*

Chapter 17

Within a couple of weeks, just as the doctor had predicted, Francie's nausea ceased, and her energy returned. After the past month of coming to work at noon, she returned to her original routine, taking time off when needed. When she'd told her colleagues the news, they were almost as excited as she was. One of them planned to start knitting that night.

She and Michael continued their Sunday road trips, but they kept them tame. During the summer months, they drove to different beaches on the Jersey shore. In Cape May, they took an architectural walking tour past ornate Victorian, Gothic and Italianate houses. Francie stuck her nose in the air in mock snobbery and remarked, "Victorian here is a replica. In Ireland, Victorian is authentic."

They ate just-caught fish on the dock and capped off the afternoon by taking the ferry to Lewes, Delaware for souvenirs.

One Sunday they drove to Atlantic City to walk the boardwalk and take a ride on a rolling chair. Nate, the rolling chair pusher, introduced himself, offering his white-gloved hand to shake. He gave them tidbits of the history of the "good old days" of Atlantic City. Francie listened closely, telling him this was her first time there.

"It's people like you who make me love my job."

She told Nate, "I love this experience, but don't you think boardwalks were meant for walking, not riding?"

"I'll answer that one, Nate," said Michael. "When I was a kid, riding in a rolling chair with my parents was one of the coolest things I ever did. That and having french fries in a paper cup from one of the stands," he added.

Nate said, "We're coming up to one of the best. Do you want me to stop there?"

"Most definitely," said Michael, telling Francie, "This is a gourmet experience, the best potatoes you'll ever eat."

"Michael, I'm Irish. I've had every kind of potato invented." But she had to agree, those hot, greasy, salted fries in a paper cone really were the best. "You have to admit that eating them outside in the sea air doesn't hurt the experience."

Pennsylvania has a slew of antique stores, so one Sunday they followed an "antiquing" trail to New Hope where they made several *can't resist* purchases and ate double-decker ice cream cones, coconut and mocha for him, pistachio and strawberry for her. "Can we come back tomorrow?" she asked Michael.

"Do I detect a theme to our road trips, Francie? Wherever we go, we seem to enjoy the food more than the scenery." She agreed he had a good point and continued licking her ice cream cone.

Despite her growing silhouette, Francie's hormones were soaring, and Michael was the beneficiary. He loved looking at her throughout every stage of her pregnancy and found her irresistible, especially on Sundays.

Her obstetrician was pleased with her progress, and she got the go-ahead to travel to Ireland in October for Brian's wedding to Rosie. The entire O'Conner family would be staying at the same hotel in Dublin for the three-day celebration. Michael had booked a room next to theirs for Kate, and, the three of them were in keen anticipation of spending time as a family. Francie's brothers were quiet on the subject of whether their parents would be there, and Francie left well enough alone. As far as she was concerned, this was Brian and Rosie's weekend, and nothing was going to put a damper on that.

Chapter 18

Francie and Michael arrived at the hotel in Dublin late afternoon on Thursday looking radiantly happy. Kate was in the lobby to greet them. "Look at you—you look gorgeous," she told Francie, "and you, Michael, look like the proud father-to-be."

"Darn right, I'm proud. I've waited twenty years for this."

Francie told Kate she was as vivacious and adorable as she remembered. "And there's no denying that you're one of us, a real O'Conner, except for the English accent."

"I've only been here a few hours, and, accent or not, I feel like I've been a part of the family forever. They're so much fun and so easy to be with. Hurry up now, everyone is waiting for you to join us at the party."

"As soon as we check-in and drop our bags, we'll be there. Just give us fifteen minutes."

"Your room is just next to mine. The rest of the family has us surrounded on the same floor, so this may be our last moment of privacy. See you in fifteen," Kate said, and flit back to the dining room.

"Michael, the first thing I have to do is brush the moss off my teeth—at least that's what the inside of my mouth feels like."

Michael assured her she wasn't the only one. "Air travel hasn't solved that problem yet."

Their luggage had been put into their room, and they both dug in for their travel kits and shared the sink for a vigorous brushing and quick face washing.

They left their packed clothes askew and set out for the dining room. No time to deal with wrinkled suits and dresses. Family came first.

A refreshed Francie and Michael followed the sound of laughter to the private dining room. "It's a good thing my raucous family is tucked away from the normal people who enjoy a nice, quiet dinner. I hope you're not embarrassed, Michael."

"That was the old me, Francie, the staid one. Now that I'm a part of this family, I've learned how to party *to the max.* It's such a pleasure to be with your brothers. I hope that we all stay close so our son can feel part of a big, happy family."

"Or daughter," she said.

They entered the room and immediately were at the center of a crowd of huggers and kissers. "We're lucky we didn't get smothered in the welcome," he whispered to Francie when things settled down."

"May I present my beautiful Rosie, my bride-to-be," said Brian, holding hands with his bride, a green-eyed Irish lass, her ebullient personality shining through her smile. "Francie, I'm honored to finally meet the one that I've been compared to ever since I met Bri," she said with a smile and a hug. Francie hugged her, then warned her brother, "Brian, you devil, promise me you'll treat Rosie better than you ever treated me, with all of your dirty tricks."

"Don't worry, girls," he said. "If I pulled the stunts on Rosie that I pulled on my baby sister, Rosie would beat me up!"

"And so would I," said Francie. "I'm a big girl now."

Denis clinked a spoon on his glass. "Welcome all of you to the groom's dinner, hosted by my brother, Tommy, my brother-in-law, Michael and me."

Francie looked at Michael and whispered, "Why didn't you tell me you were in on this?"

"Family secret," he said with a wink.

There was hooting and cheering around the room. Tommy called for quiet, and he introduced Rosie's father, who said grace.

Then Michael offered the first toast. "I'm sure everyone in this room except me has heard this toast hundreds of times, so please join me in congratulating Rosie and Brian with some good Irish whiskey and this grand Irish wish,

May God be with you and bless you,
May you see your children's children,
May you be poor in misfortune, rich in blessings.
May you know nothing but happiness from this day forward.
Sláinte!"

The room went wild.

By the time he returned to the table, all of Francie's eye makeup had run down her face. She took a small sip of his wine and a big gulp of her pregnant-lady-special Virgin Mary and told him his blessing was outstanding.

Almost all Irish parties are happy and fun, but this one ranked with the best of them, a night of dancing, laughing, and bonding. It was almost midnight when all the guests left, and the family stumbled upstairs to their rooms to have a good night's rest before the big day.

A wedding celebration lasting three days is not unusual in Ireland, and Francie was used to prolonged Irish parties, but for Michael and Kate, that night was a first, and they both felt giddy with champagne and with the thrill of their new family. The three of them got into the elevator singing. Kate kissed them both good night at the door to her room and said she this was the best party ever. She had danced with all the men there—and some of the women. Michael agreed, saying he had the time of his life and could not imagine that the celebration could continue for two more days. What he really meant was that he didn't know if he could continue for two more days. He had never had so much to drink in his life.

After traveling all night and morning and partying all afternoon and into the night, Francie and Michael dropped their clothes to the floor and collapsed on the bed without even brushing their teeth. The room looked like a tornado had hit it.

They slept for twelve hours until a knock on the door brought them back to their senses. "Wake up, sleepyheads," said Tommy, "we're on our way to lunch."

Francie opened the door and said, "No way, Tommy. It will take us hours to get ourselves together after yesterday. Michael never saw so much whiskey flow at one time, and even though this pregnant lady didn't drink, jet lag still has a grip on me."

"I think that you both have earned a day off to adjust to the time, so we've arranged an early dinner for all of us tonight. Margaret will let you know the details. Just remember little sister, the wedding starts at three on Saturday and we all plan to leave here at two to walk to the church, then afterward, back to the party!"

Michael appeared from the bathroom looking like something from the Planet of the Apes, badly in need of a shave. "We'll call you later to let you know if we're up to walking ever again, but by tomorrow we should be fine."

They ordered a very late Continental breakfast from room service and relaxed in bed, still drowsing when the waiter knocked on the door and picked his way through the mine field that was on the floor.

Michael restored himself to a semi-human state by gulping two cups of coffee while Francie slowly sipped hers. They found they were ravenous and devoured all the toasted soda bread, croissants, fruit and pastry, washing it down with more coffee and a pitcher of water. They hung up their mangled clothes and hoped for the best, then dressed and left for a short walk to Saint Stephen's Green to try to get their blood circulating. They talked about the party and Francie went over the cast of characters expected at Brian and Rosie's wedding the next day. "Let's start with the ones you met yesterday—the bride's parents and four siblings and their spouses, then my three brothers, and my sister-in-law, Margaret. Oh, and Kate, of course. Next, the ones you didn't meet—my eleven aunts and uncles and their spouses, then my thirty-eight first cousins. Do you want me to go over all of their names?"

"Spare me, please, I'm begging."

"That leaves a horde of friends who will make themselves known before the night is over, and that's a guarantee."

"So yesterday's party was just a warm-up?" he asked.

"Righto!"

"And what about the marriage ceremony?"

"I'm not sure that I can explain it in three hours, but here goes." At least three months before you pick a wedding date, you have to post your banns at a registrar's office, the official way of informing the public that you plan to be married. Next, for three Sundays, your banns are read aloud at the bride and groom's churches, nearby churches and the church where the wedding will take place. Then you have to take a premarital course, usually from your parish priest, and show a signed document stating it's been completed.

"If there is a Mass scheduled at the time of your wedding, all of the people who are there for the Mass can stay for the wedding."

"Even if they're not invited?"

"Yup. The ceremony takes about an hour with lots of hymns, prayers, kneeling, standing, sitting, readings, homilies, and the marriage vows. Expect a mixture of Latin and English.

"After the wedding, there will probably be informal congratulations, and then the guests go to the hotel for cocktails while the photographer takes pictures.

"Do you think you could cut it short, Francie? My attention span is waning."

"Hang on, I'm almost done. Eventually everyone goes to the ballroom for dinner. Then scores of toasts begin and continue all evening. After dinner, the band comes, and dancing begins. This could go on into the early morning when the staff puts out a buffet breakfast for the survivors. That's about it…."

Michael's only comment was a droll, "Just like ours."

That evening, as promised, the immediate family had a small, intimate dinner in the private room of a café. Francie, Michael and Kate had a chance to meet the up-and-coming O'Conners for the first time—Tommy and Margaret's four children—one at Trinity, two in upper school (all boys), and one bonus, a daughter age thirteen. The children were as irresistible as their parents—smart, funny and loving.

In bed that night, Francie had trepidation about seeing her parents the next day for the first time in so many years. Of course, Brian's wedding was a major event in their lives, and she expected that they would be overjoyed. They would be sitting in the first pew, a place of honor for the parents of the bride and groom. Francie and Michael would sit with the rest of the immediate family close to the front of the church.

Francie hardly slept that night. She was troubled with thoughts of how her parents would react to seeing her, and she was conflicted about how she would react to seeing them.

Chapter 19

The front pews at the church were reserved for the immediate family, some of whom arrived early. Rosie and Brian's' brothers and nephews served as ushers. The older nieces were bridesmaids, and Rosie's sisters were matron and maid of honor, and since Brian couldn't chose one brother over the other for his best man, he chose his best friend, Sean, for the honor.

As Francie expected, the bride and grooms' parents were seated on either side of the first row. Francie, Michael and Kate sat two rows behind with her other brothers and close family. She was shocked to see how old her parents looked, especially her mother, who used to be so pretty, but whose face now showed frown lines of bitterness.

At precisely three o'clock, a string quartet started playing "Oh Promise Me," and the processional began. The bridesmaids wore lavender dresses, Rosie's favorite color, and the groomsmen wore lavender ties. The smiling groom and his best man came down the aisle and took their places. The flower girls sprinkled violets and gardenia petals. When the bride appeared, the music changed to "Here Comes the Bride," and radiant Rosie and her father entered the church. Everyone stood and turned to watch them. When Francie's parents stood, they caught sight of her watching them. She smiled, and her parents nodded to her—which was more than she had hoped.

The service went as expected. Rosie and Bri said their vows, kissed each other, then faced the congregation with hands clasped, raised high. The men laughed and, as always, the women cried.

Some of the guests drove to the reception, but most walked across the green to the reception hall. The cocktails began flowing and everyone was ready for the next act. By the time the wedding party finished with pictures, most of the guests were feeling no pain. To announce the arrival of the bride and groom, the pianist played the Beatles song, "All You Need Is Love," and everyone sang the simple lyrics in a refrain that lasted for fifteen minutes, a free for all of dancing, singing, kissing, and drinking.

At six o'clock, the crowd moved into the ballroom for dinner. Dancing would come later. During the meal, guests made toasts, told stories about the bride and groom, made more toasts, recalled their own weddings, and made more toasts. The four course dinner took four hours. Michael's tuxedo was getting tight—he was sure he'd gained five pounds during dinner. Around ten thirty, the waiter wheeled in the cake, and the bride and groom made speeches thanking their friends and families and told some of their own stories about themselves and their guests. Then they cut the cake, sharing the traditional first piece, and the waiters served the guests the delicious pound cake with white icing, with a tiny square of another tradition on the side—the dreaded fruitcake.

The dancing started with Rosie and Brian alone on the dance floor. The band played the couple's special song, U2's "One," then the bandleader invited their parents and siblings to the dance floor. Again, Francie and her mother made eye contact, but nothing was said. Francie's parents were still excellent dancers, and anyone who watched them could see that they had natural talent. They did their duty and sat down as soon as the song was over. The rest of the guests joined in, and Kate became the belle of the ball. Thanks to Pat's genes, she was a wonderful dancer, and just about every single man danced with her at least once.

When they returned to their tables, Denis called Francie aside. He put his arm around her. "Mum and Da would like to invite you, Michael and Kate to meet them for breakfast tomorrow morning. He squeezed her shoulder and said, "Take some time to think about it and then let me know your answer."

She came back to the table, and Michael could see that she was clearly shaken. Her face was pale, and her lips were trembling. She told Michael about her parents' overture and added, "I don't know whether to laugh or cry." This was the first communication from her parents in almost twenty-five years.

"Francie, it sounds as if they want you to be part of their lives again. How do you feel about that?"

"Confused," she said. "My parents made my life miserable for so many years, I don't know if I could ever have a relationship with them again. There is nothing they can say to make it right. I need some time to think this over."

"Would you like to talk to Kate about it," Michael asked.

"Yes, could you find her for me? But wait a few minutes—I need to get my head together." Michael sat with her until she signaled him that she was ready.

He cut in on Kate's dance partner, and, after a few minutes of dancing, he led her to their table telling her that Francie wanted to talk to her.

"Kate took one look at Francie and said, "You look like you're in shock. Are you okay? What's going on?" Francie struggled to get the words out about her parents' invitation and asked Kate for her thoughts about it.

Kate reacted by saying, "It's all my fault—if I had never been born this never would have happened." Francie was appalled to think that Kate felt that way.

"No, no, no, Kate, there is nothing about this that is your fault. I loved you from the day I discovered I was pregnant, and so did Pat. The word *love* is written all over you for us, and I would not change it for the world. My parents are the ones who made a terrible choice for me, for you, and for the unity of our family. Maybe in the beginning I could have forgiven them for making that choice, but after all these years, I can't. I'm not going to accept their offer."

She held Kate in her arms. "Kate, being able to share my problem with you has given me more relief than you know. I hope you don't feel burdened by it."

"Don't worry, Francie, sharing your thoughts with me is an honor. It could never be a burden. I'm just happy that we're here for each other."

Francie told Denis her decision and asked her to relay the message to their parents. "If they really want to see me, they'll keep trying. Maybe someday they'll convince me to change my mind, but it's going to take some time and effort on their part."

The wedding reception went on all night until a dawn breakfast appeared for the holdouts. Francie and Michael were long gone by then, and by mid-morning, they were downstairs having breakfast along with some of the other survivors. A bleary-eyed Kate joined them when they were almost finished and ordered a black coffee, very strong. "What a party and what a night," she said. "Being a part of this family has added a whole new dimension to my life. If this is how it goes, I can't wait for Denny to get married!"

Michael nodded, "Neither can I."

"Don't give me any credit," said Francie, "I'm just the soft spoken, reserved American sister."

After breakfast, Francie and Michael went back to their room to pack for their return trip later that afternoon.

Before they reached their room, Francie and Kate said they wanted some time alone, so they went to Kate's room while Michael went to pack.

"Two things," said Kate. "First I have to ask advice from someone who knows the excitement of love." They sat down on the bed and Kate continued. "Ned and I are starting to get serious. We have so many common interests and have fun doing things together. When we're not working, we spend most of our time together at my apartment or his. Or taking short trips. We have fun and laugh a lot. He would make the ideal husband and I think I could be happy with him for the rest of my life, but I don't know if I love him enough. When I hear the way you talk about Pat and he talks about you, I'm not sure I could ever feel that way about Ned. How did you know you loved Pat—and how did you know you loved Michael?"

"Kate, this is the first mother-daughter talk I've ever had, and I hope I give you good advice. I'll speak right from my heart." She took her daughter's hands in hers as they sat on the bed. "First, I have to say that you didn't smile when you spoke about Ned. That gave me my first clue that maybe you're not as happy as you want to be. She paused for a moment to gather her thoughts. "I've had two men I love deeply, and still do." Her smile was reflected in her eyes when she said, "Each love is entirely different from the other. Believe me, I don't have all the answers, but I can tell you what I've experienced.

"When I first met Pat, it felt to me that I was struck by lightning. I had never felt anything like the attraction I had for him from the moment I looked at him. Of course, I was only sixteen and my hormones were just starting to come alive. The amazing thing is that he felt the same thing happening to him. Maybe all teenagers feel this for their first love. I wouldn't know, but I can't imagine loving anyone the way I loved him. The touch of his hand made me dizzy. We lost all inhibitions about kissing or holding hands in public. It was as if we were the only ones in the world. Every day was exciting, and fun, and romantic—and we thought it would never end." She laughed just thinking about it. "Our conversations were inane—I can't remember one thing of importance that we talked about. When we were together, it was as if the rest of the world faded away. We started to fantasize our lives together." Her face brightened even more when she said, "We chose names for our children—Kate for a girl, Philip for a boy. We'd call him "Flip" for short."

Kate said, "I knew you named me on the day I was born, but I never heard the story behind how you decided on the name. And Pat got a 'Flip,' too. I hope he never told Moira why he wanted that name."

"You can be sure that he didn't," said Francie, raising her eyebrows. "He's too smart to do that. Maybe they agreed that each of them would choose a name for one twin—Philip was his choice and Josh was hers."

She fell silent thinking about the complications of life, then continued her story. "We created a dream world about so many things. A son, a daughter, a dog or two, a house in the woods in Scotland—we were still kids, and everything seemed possible. Although we knew there would be problems because of our families, we were sure we could overcome them. Maybe our romance would have run its course, but we never had time to find out, because our families rebelled and separated us after we had known each other less than a year. All we had to live on were the dreams of two kids imagining that their love would continue forever."

Kate's face was so somber that Francie leaned over and gave her a hug.

"When I was in the Home for Unwed Mothers, I lived with the hope of us being reunited. It was the only way I could survive my loneliness. When my labor pains began, I tried to stave them off because you were the only part of him I still had, but, of course, nature took over and out you came. I only saw you for a moment, but I knew you were ours, Pat's and my creation."

Kate smiled at that statement.

"I looked at your little face, the most beautiful baby I had ever seen, and I saw recognition in your eyes. I knew that we had a bond that only the two of us would share.

"You know the rest of the story. I lost you and Pat, and thought I'd never see happiness again. I never stopped loving him and I never stopped loving you. That will never change."

Francie paused and reached for a tissue for herself and one for Kate, then smiled and said, "But one day a new man came into my life and I discovered that I could love him, not with the intensity of a teenager, but with the depth of a woman. I was only twenty, but my experiences of the past few years had matured me before my time.

"Michael was my professor, and the thought of him being a social person never crossed my mind. He was attracted to me, but never hinted at it while I was still a student. On the day of my graduation, he made his feelings known to me. He knew that I had no real family at graduation and asked if he could take me to lunch to celebrate. I can't say it was love at first sight, like it was for your father, but I felt a familiar stirring in my heart. We talked and talked, and I realized I felt a romantic attraction for the first time in three years." Her eyes shone when she told Kate, "I was alive again and slowly stopped thinking of Pat. My love for Michael grew and grew, and it's still growing."

Again she took her girl's hand. "Kate, I trust you enough to admit to you, and no one else, that the intensity I feel for Michael is not the same that I felt for Pat. First love can only happen once. But now Michael continues to sweep me off my feet with passion and love beyond what I felt for your father. I feel happy every time Michael walks into the room.

"So, in the way of advice, what I can tell you is that if Ned is the man for you, you'll feel that you can't live without him. Every time you see him, you'll feel excitement." She stroked her daughter's hand in hers. "Can you have a happy marriage without excitement? Yes, but at this stage in your life, don't settle for someone who offers love if you don't feel a thrill every time you're with him. If you have doubts, keep looking—you may find someone when you least expect it. Tell me honestly, have you thought about Ned since you've been here? Do you miss him?"

"Well, now that you have told me your story, I am really confused. But the answer is "no—I am having a great time and I don't miss Ned. In fact, I'm glad he couldn't be here tonight. I realize now that we needed some time apart and he couldn't miss his grandmother's ninetieth birthday weekend celebration, so this separation was quite natural. I danced with a dozen partners at the wedding, and I liked them all, especially Sean, ironically the "best man," and the one I danced with three times. Something happened between us while we danced. We both felt it, I could tell. When he called this morning to ask me to dinner tonight, I felt dizzy, just like you described. I am more excited about that call than I have been in years, no matter whom I was with, including Ned. I told him I'd call him back to let him know. I don't want to be disloyal to Ned, but I really want to go."

"My darling Kate, you have to decide what makes you comfortable; if it were me, I'd go. You're not married, not even engaged. For now, follow your heart, not your head, and see where it leads you. It may be a dead end, but you won't know unless you go. Whatever happens, don't promise to marry Ned until you are absolutely sure, and if you decide that he's not for you, let him down gently."

The phone rang before Kate could respond. She had a few private words with the caller, then Francie heard her say, "Yes, she's here," and handed Francie the phone. "It's Pat," she said.

Francie's reaction showed in the bright red blush of her face.

"Pat, you tracked me down."

"I knew all along that you were there—remember, Kate is my daughter, too, and she told me that you would be here for your brother's wedding. I think I showed admirable self-control in not calling you the minute you arrived. I have some things to tell you about the change in my life. Maybe it will help you think about your situation with Michael."

Francie held back both fear and anticipation.

"Moira and I are separated."

Oh, no, Francie thought.

"The night we all had dinner at the Mullin's house, Moira noticed the way you and I looked at each other, and she knew exactly why you left the table, though, I must say, you did a good job keeping it a secret from everyone else. Francie, I wanted to take you in my arms and never let go, but I played my role as devoted husband and tried to overcome my feelings. None of this is Moira's fault. I thought I loved her enough, but my love for her pales next to the way I feel about you."

Francie felt her heart pounding, but she wanted to hear him out before she said anything.

"Two weeks went by, then, Moira told me that she couldn't sleep in the same bed with me. She couldn't erase the picture she had in her mind of seeing the way you and I looked at each other. I actually felt relieved when I realized that the charade I'd been living since that night was over. I moved into the guest room and our relationship got worse. She was so hurt, and I couldn't make it up to her by lying. We know each other too well. Bottom line is I took a small apartment in the city.

"Francie, I feel so much guilt about this, but I have no control over my true feelings. I see the boys as often as possible and I'm welcome at home for visits, but we no longer live as husband and wife. We have both decided to put the boys first, but we know that it will not be easy. I hope we're big enough to sustain our relationship, but it's hard to live with a fractured marriage. I understand her reasons to be hurt, and she understands my situation. Neither of us can see any resolution, so we will probably get a divorce."

Francie was speechless. What could she possibly say to help heal the wound Pat felt? After a few seconds, she said, "Pat, I have no solution. People say that time heals all wounds, and I hope it will for you. That part of your life is over—it could never be the same. I know this sounds like nonsense but deep down I feel that you'll find another love, as strong as ours was. As for you and me, we can still dream, but our time to imagine a life together is over. Do I still love you? Yes. Does my body want you?

Yes. But I also know for certain that I love Michael, in a different way than I love you, but just as deeply, and now that I'm finally pregnant, we are happier than ever."

"Pregnant! Francie—I had no idea. Kate never told me. I'm sorry if this call upset you."

"I'm not upset, Pat. I'm happy to share our news with you." She lowered her voice to a whisper. "And to know for certain that this baby couldn't be yours. Thank goodness we stopped when we did, Pat. You should see Michael—he's so proud. He's told everyone he knows that he's expecting a baby. It's as if he's the first man ever to father a child. I have such joy that Michael and I have this happiness together. I could never live with myself if there were any deception."

Her voiced cracked when she said, "As for us, we have Kate, the product of our love."

There was no answer from Pat.

"Yes, we'll always have that. But now we have to move on with our real lives and leave our memories behind." She whispered, "Goodbye, my love," and quietly hung up the phone.

She sat quietly for a moment, holding back tears and spinning the wedding ring on her finger.

She and Kate hugged each other tightly and cried. Kate said, "After hearing that conversation, I realize I have to end my relationship with Ned and find the right man whose love I can't live without."

"I think you are making a good decision. I wish you that kind of love, darling, and I know in my heart that you will find the right man."

When she returned to her room, Michael was packed for the airport. Francie quickly threw everything in her bags and off they went, back to their life together in America.

On the long trip home, Michael raved about the fun he had with her family. "By now you know that my family is fairly prudish in their behavior. Their standards of having a good time are nothing like what I witnessed in

Ireland. It was spectacular. I hope it runs in the family so that our baby is like his Irish mother."

"What do you mean 'his'—maybe it will be a 'her.'"

"Not possible," said Michael. But if it happens, I'll teach her how to play shortstop."

"Tell me again, where is the shortstop? Between first and second or between second and third?"

"Francie, for someone who calls herself an athlete, you're impossible!"

PART IV

Chapter 20

Francie's pregnancy was going well, and she felt perfectly fine, so she continued to work. She was eager to oversee the plans she had put into effect for the company. She wondered if she were too ambitious, but the pride she took in fueling the growth of the business encouraged her to continue. She pondered over whether her pride was a good trait or, as she had been raised to believe, a wicked one.

Big things were happening at Shea's Soup, and Francie was a major part of them. She was instrumental in taking them from a top name on the household shelf in America to a player in international markets. A variety of Shea's best-selling soups started to appear on shelves in the U.K., Scandinavia and Germany, requiring a division of international sales to be added to the Philadelphia offices.

The company's great success on college campuses snowballed to become a major source of income off-campus, too. Shea's drive-thru restaurants, and their soup and grilled cheese eateries, sprang up all over the city. Service was courteous and quick. The employees were well trained to meet rigorous standards of cleanliness, cheerfulness and speediness. Menus were expanded to include grilled cheese with avocado, smoked meats, egg salad, vegetables and tuna. Seventy-five percent of the restaurants were company owned, and the remainder were franchises. Most of the franchises catered to the tastes of the ethnic groups of the neighborhood.

When the Shea family decided to take the company public, Francie received multiple shares of stock; additionally, she and Michael invested a great deal of their own money. Michael continued to teach, but instead of being on a steady classroom schedule, he cut back on his work schedule to teach a month-long seminar each semester. He wanted to be able to spend the balance of his time with his growing family. He went all the way—learning about the benefits of breast feeding and participating in natural childbirth classes with Francie. In his "New Father" class, he learned how to comfort a crying baby, how to dress a squirming baby, and how to help an overworked, frustrated wife.

Every time Michael came up with a pointer for Francie, she listened closely, laughed on the inside and called her mother-in-law to report her son's progress on becoming an expert househusband and father. They both had a good laugh, knowing that even with the best intentions, plans often go awry. Babies have minds of their own and often their behavior is not as predictable as fathers think they should be.

After seeing how much Michael enjoyed his free time, Francie cut back to a shorter work week and left the office at three. This gave her time for some friends and to engage in female activities—shopping, grooming and relaxing, but no sitting around eating Oreos in her spare time. She kept her trim figure and except for her developing womb, she barely looked pregnant.

After looking at herself in the mirror one night, she said, "Michael, do you think my belly is exactly the size and shape of a basketball?"

"Now that you mention it, I do. Maybe you spend too much time shooting hoops."

They began a routine of walking the hilly lanes of Haverford for an hour before dinner every night. Their neighborhood was what some might call posh, but on their walks Francie and Michael made some not so posh discoveries.

"Did you notice how many driveways need blacktop?" she mused.

"How about overgrown gardens and peeling paint?" he said. "Isn't it amazing what you discover when you're on foot? I guess if we looked more closely, we'd see that ours could use some work, too, at least a paint job—it's been at least ten years since we had one. I'll call a painter—that'll be my first handyman job."

This made her laugh—Michael's idea of doing handy things around the house was calling a handyman.

“I think we should get a dog,” she said, “perhaps a Lab. There are so many in the neighborhood, and they’re so friendly.”

“Francie, this is the worst possible time to get a dog. Let’s get a baby first, then in about five years we can think of getting a dog.”

Her lower lip went out in a disappointed frown, but she knew he was right.

Their walks didn’t get in the way of their weekend excursions, which now became short outings to include furnishing the nursery and choosing items for the baby’s layette. After a couple of times shopping with Michael, she told him gently she was going to ask his mom instead. Francie never forgot how important becoming a grandmother was for her mother-in law. She treated her as if she were her own mother, and she meant it.

“Mother, I am going to need a lot of help choosing the right things for the baby. Can you help me shop? I don’t think we need Dad, and I know we don’t need Michael to help with shopping. You’re the one I want. Another set of eyes would be a big help. The “boys” can stay at home.”

“You know that I consider you my daughter, Francie, and I would be honored to serve the role of your mother.”

They all tried to ward off memories of the loss of Michael’s first wife and baby by staying as positive as possible about the new baby. After they ordered the furniture and layette, they told the stores to keep them on hold until the day the baby was born. The stores were happy to comply. Many of their clients were superstitious about furnishing a nursery before their babies were born, and there was a system in play to deliver the furnishings on the same day.

Each night Michael put his ear to Francie’s belly to talk to the baby. “Now, look here,” he would say in all seriousness, “you better not give your mother any problems. When you’re ready, you’d better come out quickly and smoothly, with no fighting.”

Francie told Michael that she believed the baby heard what he said. “I’m not sure the baby understands English. Could you say the same thing in French?”

Affecting a French accent, Michael said, “Mais oui, Madame, anything pour le bébé boy.”

They both thought this was wildly funny, so the next night Francie made the same request in Spanish, followed by Italian on the next night.

"Francie, why don't you ask me to say it in German—you know that German and Latin are the only foreign languages I know."

"German is too harsh, and Latin is an unspoken language, except in church. Anyway, why didn't you take French, like most prep school boys do?"

"Unlike you, I was an intellectual," he said.

"Touché!" she retorted, snuggling her head in his chest before turning to go to sleep.

As her pregnancy progressed, Francie started to remember small details about her own childhood. Her mother was a source of fun for Francie and her brothers. She could turn the most routine experience into a game. *Find the Goodie* was one of their favorites. Their mother made a fun game of the never-ending job of sorting, folding and putting away their clean clothes each week. She would hide a treat in each one's pile of clothing. They'd find bubble gum, or a whistle, an apple, a piece of candy, or even a deck of cards. Francie once found a whole candy bar hidden in in one of her socks. Even now, Francie could see the scene before her of her pretty mother smiling when her children found their surprise mixed in with their laundry.

Another picture in her mind was of Mum on one knee, opening her arms to hug Francie when she came home from school. Francie felt so loved in those childhood days.

She remembered the time she had chickenpox and her mother stayed home from work to care for her, and how two days later, Tommy got the chickenpox, too. They both stayed in their parents' bed during the daytime when they were sick. Mum would go to the corner store every day to bring them a surprise, sometimes cutouts for Francie or a comic book for Tommy, all along they both knew that the worst was coming—the bitter tasting powdered medicine mixed with a teaspoon of water. Their mother did the best she could to disguise it and always gave them a hard candy to suck on afterward.

These remembrances would be fleeting, probably less than a few seconds, but they always made Francie feel lucky to have had such a kind and fun-loving mother. Then, of course, she would be close to tears when she thought of the rift that formed between them.

Michael and Francie's baby was due around the end of January, and Kate planned to come to the U.S. a few days before the due date.

The baby had other plans.

On the twelfth of January, Francie started to get twinges. She woke up Michael to alert him, telling him not to worry, they had a few hours to go before the pains would get worse. No need to rush.

Disregarding her advice, Michael dressed in record time, retrieved Francie's packed suitcase from the closet and ran downstairs to put it at the door to the garage. From the kitchen, he called Francie's doctor who said to him, "Wait until the pains are about a half hour apart, and then leave for the hospital."

"No way. We'll wait at the hospital if we have to."

Francie was in the bedroom getting dressed and concentrating on how to calm down Michael, when she had one huge contraction.

"Michael!" she yelled, "Oh my God! Come quick—the baby is coming!"

He took the stairs three at a time and ran into the bedroom to find Francie on the bed in a soggy pool of watery fluid.

"Wait a minute, I have to go downstairs to boil water," he said.

"The hell with the water, just take a look and tell me what is happening down there!"

"I think I see a tiny head!"

Francie had another strong contraction.

"Oh, God, the baby's coming out!" Michael yelled.

And out it came, took its first breath, and howled a hearty cry.

"Francie, what do I do? Should I get the water?"

"Forget the water—call the doctor. NOW!"

Within minutes, the doctor was on the phone. Michael was a wreck and could barely speak intelligibly. "Hand the phone to Francie and go take a shot of whiskey for yourself, Michael."

The doctor told Francie not to worry—people had been having babies at home long before there were any hospitals. "Just tell Michael to leave the cord alone—do not pull on it, just keep the baby lying on your chest. Be sure to cover the baby—a clean pillowcase is fine. Ask him to lightly massage your stomach and let nature take care of itself."

Francie relayed the message to Michael. The doctor called for an ambulance, and within minutes, they heard the siren.

Michael ran into the bathroom and vomited into the toilet.

Then he ran into the bedroom, saying "Francie, I'll be right back—don't panic." He ran out of the room and Francie almost laughed out loud watching his state of panic.

When he got back upstairs, Francie said, "Michael, you raced out of here so fast, you didn't tell me if the baby is a boy or a girl."

"Oh my God, I forgot to look." A big smile spread all across his face. "It's a boy!" he yelped.

The EMTs finished the job by cutting the cord and removing the afterbirth. They propped Francie on pillows and placed the baby in her arms so she could have a look at her son.

"He's long and lean and darling—just like you," she said to Michael.

She settled into a room at the hospital while the doctor and nurse in charge cleaned the baby, tested him, weighed and measured him, dressed him in a diaper and undershirt, then wrapped him in a receiving blanket and snuggled his perfect head into a tiny blue stocking cap. And so, pronouncing him "perfect" and congratulating Michael and Francie on a job well done, they left the new family alone.

"A miracle happened in our home," Michael said. "Can you believe it, Francie?

"Barely," she answered. He kissed her and thanked her for the best baby ever born. "I was so frightened when I first saw him. He looked like a turtle out of his shell, but now he looks like a real baby," Michael said. "A human one."

"A special delivery by you, darling," Francie mumbled, smiling. "He's a very obedient little boy—you encouraged him by talking to my belly every night and telling him to make it 'quick and smooth with no fighting.'"

Before drifting off to sleep, she said, "Don't forget to call your parents, my brother Tommy, Kate, the baby furniture and clothing stores, and most important, order a new mattress for our bed." Now she could sleep with a clear mind.

Chapter 21

They named him *Timothy Conner Hanson.* They would call him Tim. At eight pounds, he was a giant compared to tiny Kate at birth. Michael and his parents had supplied the house with all the baby's needs—enough for triplets. Three days later, Francie and the baby come home, and everything was in place, including Michael's parents, who couldn't wait to help.

The first thing Michael told them was that they had to wash their hands before they touched the baby. His parents gave each other a look.

"Well, why don't you get him settled in his bassinet, then we'll see what we can do," his mother said.

Francie and Michael took Timmy upstairs and after a few minutes, Michael came to the top of the steps and sheepishly asked his mother to come up to show them how to get the diaper on.

"You're lucky—it's easy to change a baby now with disposable diapers with sticky tabs. We had to use diaper pins for you and your cloth diapers."

Within a minute, the fresh diaper was in place and the baby was wrapped in his blanket and ready to be nursed. "Michael, why don't you go downstairs and talk to your father so I can spend some time with Francie. Try to relax, and don't worry, you'll get the hang of it soon."

"Okay, but promise to call me if you need me."

"I think we can manage," his mother said.

Five days later, Timmy was thriving, and Michael and Francie were totally exhausted.

"Do you think we're too old for this?" Michael wanted to know. "It's not exactly going like they taught me in class. He sure cries a lot, especially in the middle of the night."

"I guess I'm not as maternal as I thought," Francie added. "This isn't as much fun as we planned it would be. I think we ought to call a nanny service first thing in the morning."

Once the nanny moved into the spare room, life became easier. Between nursing times, Francie could sleep, and Michael learned to ignore the middle of the night mewling of the baby. After two weeks at home, Michael was delighted to go back to work to preside over a new seminar, and Francie was equally delighted to have him out of the house.

Kate came to visit her new brother when he was almost six weeks old. She had wanted to be there for the baby's birth, but when Timmy came before his due date, time didn't allow it. When Kate could come, the timing was better. Thanks to the nanny, the situation was under control. The baby was on a feeding schedule and the nanny had taught Francie the basics of how to keep the baby clean and calm. Timmy was a fine little boy who was starting to sleep through the night.

Michael met Kate at the airport and drove home to find Francie waiting at the front door with Timmy in her arms. Kate gave Francie a quick buzz and put her arms out for the baby. From the moment she saw him, she was overcome with the feeling that they were part of the same family. She cuddled him as if he were her own baby, and Timmy stared into her eyes as if he knew her. Francie and Michael beamed with pride at the show of love between siblings. For the rest of the day, Kate hardly relinquished her hold on him. Once he was in bed for the night, Kate, Francie and Michael started their real visit.

"You've seen us, you've seen the baby, you've seen the house, now tell us about you."

Kate's smile turned into a shy grin. "I was waiting until the time was right to tell you. I wrestled with what you had told me about love when we had our mother-daughter conversation in Ireland, and I have since admitted that Ned is not the one for me. Breaking up was not easy. I didn't want to hurt him, but I didn't want to string him along, either. We both had expected our relationship to turn into marriage, but I had to tell him that my doubts outweighed my certainties. I let him make the decision to separate for a while to see how we felt when apart. Eventually I told him that I was seeing someone else, so we ended our relationship."

With a broad, beaming smile, she said, "I started to see more and more of Sean, the man I met at Brian's wedding. Of course, he's in Dublin and I'm in London, so the logistics are not the greatest, but we see each other every weekend and phone each other every day, at least once. The way I feel about him is almost identical to what you described—he's always in my thoughts and I live to see him, just like you do with Michael," she added for Michael's benefit and to rule out Pat from the mix.

"He told me that he never felt this way before about anyone else. We talked about a future together and have started to make plans." She gestured, squeezing thumb and index finger together. "We're this close to becoming engaged. Our careers are complicated—I'm about to get my PhD and was offered a job on the staff of Cambridge, an honor I can barely believe but may have to reject. Sean is still in school, nearing the end of ten grueling years of medical study to become a pediatric surgeon. Where we live will depend on where he's hired to practice medicine, probably in Ireland. How's that for ironic?"

"I love it! The daughter takes her mother's place. What do your parents think?"

"They like him very much, and so do my brothers. He's very easy to like—good natured, smart, handsome, funny. And we're both Catholic, which should rule out lots of complications."

"I'll say," said Francie.

Michael was fascinated with the whole mother-daughter conversation. "Congratulations, Kate, I couldn't be happier. My almost-daughter is engaged, and I feel like an almost-father of the bride, regardless of the other two fathers involved! And the topper is an offer from Cambridge, a fine reflection on your almost-genetics from me."

The mother and daughter laughed. "The power of testosterone," Francie said. "Yours is world class, dear," she said over Kate's laughter. "Now let's get to bed early. I have some plans for us tomorrow, Katy, my girl. If you can pull yourself away from Timmy and let him spend some time with Nanny for her last full day here, I want to show off my new country to you and show you off to my new country."

Kate yawned.

"Jet lag be damned. Do you think you can be up by eight tomorrow morning?"

"Of course, I'm a grad student—I'm used to being exhausted all day."

They left Timmy with his nanny for Francie's last day of freedom, and she and Kate drove to center city Philadelphia to tour the Old City highlights—historic buildings in Independence Plaza, and the Liberty Bell, then a trip to the Benjamin Franklin Parkway headed by the massive Art Museum. They ran up the seventy-two stone steps leading to the entrance. Francie had to stop twice to catch her breath, "Still not bad for a forty-one year old mother," she said to Kate, panting.

"Okay, you proved yourself," Kate answered, panting herself. They used better judgment when they slowly walked back down the steps to get their breathing back to normal. From there, they strolled along the parkway to Francie's favorite spot—the hallowed Philadelphia Library. A quick look there, then out to lunch for a Philadelphia tradition—cheesesteak. Kate had never had a sandwich as large or gooey as a Philly cheesesteak with roasted peppers, tomato sauce and fried onions. "Could I have one for dinner, too?" she joked. "These are amazing."

On the way home, Francie drove around the rolling suburbs that came to be called the Main Line—named for the main line of the Pennsylvania Railroad track that led west from the city for about thirty miles. She pointed out estates owned by famous people and stopped at *très chic* shops in towns along the chain of railroad stops that linked Philadelphia to Paoli.

By mid-afternoon they were happy to go home to take off their shoes and entertain Timmy. Francie gave Nanny a warm send-off and told her she was always welcome to stop by for a visit and hoped they would see each other often. With tears in her eyes, Nanny said goodbye to baby Timmy, and whispered in his ear, "Remember me, my Timmy."

When Michael came home from work that night, the girls assailed him with their day's exploits. His retort was, "While you were running around the city, I spent the day amusing myself about your upcoming wedding, Kate, trying not to make a fool of myself because of the big smile on my face. I couldn't help but think that if your wedding is as much fun as Brian and Rosie's, I better start catching up on my sleep right now."

That night they had their first dinner since Nanny left, Francie managing to prepare cereal, toast and scrambled eggs. "Uh-oh, looks like trouble ahead," said Michael.

"I just have to get back into the swing of things. It may take a few days, so be patient, Michael. I promise tomorrow will be better," she said, knowing that her mother-in-law was bringing dinner.

The girls stayed home the next day, took the baby for a walk in his pram, and yakked the whole time. Francie felt she was with her best friend—and so did Kate.

When the baby went in for his nap after lunch, they took the time to nap, too, waking up in time to set the table, prepare a salmon dip and a cheese plate for appetizers, and welcome Michael's parents.

Kate was so warm and good-natured, it was hard to resist liking her from first meeting. "What should I call you both?" she wanted to know.

"Why not Papa and Grammy—that's what we'd like Timmy to call us, too."

"I would be honored. I've never had grandparents that I've actually met. I'm thrilled that you're the first."

They talked in a steady stream about so many things, laughing freely about funny incidents and talking just as freely and with intelligence about world issues. When Michael came home, he could hear the laughter before he opened the door. "Well, I see you all met, and I guess you didn't need my input for any lapses in conversation."

"We're having a wonderful time, son," his father said. "The package that came with Francie is amazing. She gave us two grandchildren, Timmy *and* Kate."

When they sat down to dinner, Michael told them that Francie had promised a good dinner tonight, and she certainly delivered. That brought giggles from all of them until Michael asked, "What's the joke? I don't get it." More laughter, no explanations.

The next day Francie took Kate and the baby to Shea's Soup Company so that she could introduce both of her children to her colleagues. Kate was astounded when she walked into the lobby of the building and saw Francie's picture on a poster for soup and grilled cheese.

"Francie, I knew you were successful, but I had no idea how important you are to this huge company."

"It didn't happen overnight. I started in this country at the very bottom—no money, no friends, no visible future—I could only go up from where I was. I took control of my situation and pressed to continue my education. With eyes wide open, I worked myself into a job with a good future. It started with a letter to the company praising how the combination of Shea's tomato soup and toasted cheese sandwiches kept me nourished as a poor, starving student."

When Francie introduced her children to her co-workers, they were greeted with oohs and ahhs for the baby and welcoming gestures for Kate, along with some questioning looks. "We know that you're confused," Francie said, "but just go with the flow for the time being. I'll explain another time."

When they returned to the car, Tim started fussing, and the three of them got into the backseat so Francie could nurse the baby while taking advantage of the opportunity to have a personal conversation with Kate.

Averting her eyes to appear casual, Francie asked her daughter about Pat, saying that the last conversation she had with him was on the phone in Kate's hotel room in Ireland.

"I see him about every two weeks, and, the truth is, he's a mess. It is difficult for him to lose hope of reuniting with you, though he knows it's impossible, and, on top of that, his relationship with Moira is disintegrating. He and the twins are close, and sometimes I see them when we all go to lunch. It's difficult for him to maintain a family relationship with them. Of course they're loyal to their mother, and they're not sure how to treat me. I'm hoping that in time, we'll feel a bond."

"Kate, I know Pat so well, it's almost like he's a part of me. I can feel his pain, but I know I can't do anything about it." Now looking at her directly, Francie said, "I count my blessings, but as I've told you before, I will never get over my first love. I would never trade what I have now for a different life. How could I ever have more—a husband I love, a new baby and a long-lost daughter?

"There's no sense talking about things that will never be. I'm sorry to hear he's suffering, Kate. But I know him—he will get over me, probably in the same manner than I have gotten over him. He will love again."

The two women, so closely connected to Pat Harrington, hugged over the nursing baby.

After dinner, Michael and Kate talked about economics, noting the differences in approach between their two generations. Most of their discussion led to the same conclusions, though they reached them quite differently. Michael invited her to spend the next day with him at his seminar and to be prepared to speak up with her viewpoints. She agreed—like her mother she loved the challenge to show her stuff.

The next morning, stepfather and daughter took off for University of Pennsylvania's campus. First stop was to see Dean Ross, now emeritus but still with a private office. The dean was confused at first. He thought he was seeing Francie again as a young student. Michael introduced Kate as Francie's Irish daughter, the girl she gave up when she immigrated to the U.S. "It took them twenty-four years to find each other, and they have already formed a very special bond."

The dean said, "I never pressed Francie to tell me why she left Ireland, and, until this second, I never knew the answer. But I had my suspicions. Welcome, young lady, you have some big shoes to fill."

"Thank you, Dean Ross. I'm so proud to be Francie's daughter. She told me how important you were in her life—that you were the one who gave her a fresh start in a new country."

The dean smiled shyly at that, and Michael proceeded to tell the dean of Kate's academic achievements. "She's coming to my seminar today to see what she can add from a new generation's point of view, but I wanted you to be her first stop on campus. Next week, Francie will be coming by to show you our special delivery—Timothy Hanson."

The dean said, "Don't tell anyone—I'll pull a few strings and sign him up for the class of 2024."

"Now we're off to find the pretzel vendor to make Kate's introduction to Philadelphia official."

The semi-circle of chairs was full, with Michael's lectern in front. All twenty of the elite students were there. Michael started his presentation with a short introduction. "We have a guest speaker today, Kate Mullins, honors graduate of Cambridge University and London School of Economics and currently, a doctoral candidate in the field of global economics, with an offer to join the faculty of Cambridge.

His introduction was interrupted by a standing ovation from the students and thank you from a blushing Kate.

Michael continued. "She will be adding her point of view to my presentation and will be happy to answer your questions when she finishes blushing."

Immediately, a hand shot up. "Ms. Mullins, I have a question. Are you free to have dinner with me tonight?"

Laughter followed, and Kate gracefully declined.

Kate found Michael's lecture fascinating. Usually a dry subject, advanced econ taught by Michael made it all seem like a game of logic and wits. She could see why the students loved his seminar. Their questions were well thought out, and his answers required a great deal of knowledge, but Michael never faltered. The students directed a few questions to Kate, and Michael was impressed with her answers and her manner in answering them. She showed the students respect and managed to draw out the best in them the Socratic way, by giving them confidence to deliberate, then come up with their own answers. Michael admired her style and gave her a not-too-secret wink.

When the period was over, Michael thanked Kate, and the class gave her another standing ovation; this time she conquered her blush and reached out to Michael to shake his hand. He told the students that he was especially honored to have Kate there, "Not only because she is an up-and-coming expert economist, but also because she is my stepdaughter." Then he hugged her and said, "The handshake is for my colleague, the hug is for my daughter."

With class was over, Kate showed her elation with a skip in her step as they headed across campus to the car. Her mood was contagious. Michael could hardly wait to get back home to describe their day, and Francie was thrilled to hear every detail.

After dinner, Michael gave Tim his evening bottle, and the girls visited together in the kitchen while cleaning up the dishes. "Francie, Michael is terrific! I can see why you fell for him. He is charming in every way. You should see how his students idolize him. But watch out—I think some of the girls have a crush on him."

"I have no worries in that department—I keep him quite busy at home," she said with a sheepish grin.

"It's hard for me to believe that my visit will be over tomorrow, and I'll be back to the world of being as student again," Kate said, putting away the dried glasses, "and you two lovebirds can be alone."

"It's been such a treat having you here, Kate. I know that your life is in England—or maybe Ireland—and mine is in the U.S., but let's try to get together a few times each year. I won't hold you to it, but let's try. I know you're my daughter, but you seem so much like my friend, too." She leaned over and kissed her daughter's cheek.

"I've been thinking the same thing, Francie. You and Michael act so young, I feel as if we're in the same generation. Sean will feel that, too."

Francie grinned at that. "It's so nice to be considered part of your age group," she said. "I hope Sean will be on that page, too."

"Speaking of Sean, he has surgical duty for the next two days. After that, I have a week to bone up on my dissertation before I defend it. I will need some time alone for that, so we'll be apart for a while. Then, about ten days from tomorrow, glorious freedom!"

Knowing that they would miss Kate, but looking forward to being alone, Francie and Michael were ready to have their privacy back.

Michael walked into the kitchen with the baby. "Did I overhear someone say 'lovebirds'?" He turned to Francie. "When do we start?"

Francie and Kate looked at each other, and laughing, said in unison, "Tomorrow!"

Chapter 22

Life was returning to normal for Francie and Michael. They lost their fear of every whimper the baby made and started to enjoy the role of Mom and Dad. The teenage daughter of one of their neighbors, the oldest of four, visited the Hanson's home at least once each week so that she could play with the baby. She was a natural as a babysitter, and Francie hired her whenever she and Michael wanted to go on a date.

Michael's parents visited often, usually stopping to pick up a meal for all of them. They loved bundling Timmy against the winter weather and taking him for short walks in his carriage. During those times, Francie and Michael would run up to their bedroom and set speed records with their lovemaking.

Within a short time, Tim was on a schedule made in heaven, and Michael and Francie started to invite their friends over on weekends for pizza, talk and a few rounds of cards. Their fiercely competitive games of Hearts always ended with laughter and accusations that the winner cheated, follow by the losers paying for the delivered pizza.

Francie was never one for spending too much time with women—she had grown up with boys and gravitated to them—but a mothers' group was forming in their neighborhood and one of the mothers invited Francie to join. There were five other women in the group, all with babies around the same age as Tim. She decided to give it a try.

They met every Thursday morning from ten thirty to noon with their babies and their lunches. In the beginning, most of the talk was about the babies and their progress. Some of the mothers had older children and offered tips about being able to have a life without babies dominating their every thought. To that, they all lifted their glasses of Diet Coke and said, "Amen!"

The women in the group were all different and all much younger than Francie—one was young enough to be her daughter. Amy was a lawyer, Meg was a textile designer, Sue was a physician's assistant, and Lisa was a stay at home mom, the job that never ended. All of them except Lisa had taken from four to six months' leave from their work. Lisa's job with her other three kids kept her busy around the clock—the baby was the easy one.

A month later, by the end of the fourth meeting, the women had begun to know each other very, very well. They discussed their husbands, their in-laws, their complaints, their personal histories, their recipes and their mutual problem of trying to find enough free time for their husbands when they weren't too exhausted to make love. No two of the women were alike, but the mixture of personalities led to raucous laughter.

It took six months for Lisa and Meg to break out of their shells and reveal a few secrets about what went on behind their closed doors. After a revelation from Lisa, Francie said to her, "You must read a lot of romance fiction—no one really does that!" Lisa's reaction was a knowing wink. The squeals of the group were out of control.

For the first time since she was sixteen, Francie had girlfriends. She was the eldest of the group by at least fifteen years, but she found that the girls who had come of age after she did had much more confidence and savvy than she had at that age. She realized that being first in her class was not the best way to navigate her teenage years—and growing up in insular Ireland was nothing like growing up in diverse America. Yes, the group loved to have a good time, but they were also worldly. They discussed politics, books, and contemporary art. They had deep discussions about ideas and ideals. Her American girlfriends were so easygoing, so free to speak their minds, and so full of laughter, Francie felt she hit the jackpot when she was invited into the group.

Before long, the babies recognized each other. They delighted in playing together. When the first one started laughing, one by one they all followed. When one started crawling, the more placid ones observed, and one by one, they all followed, some on all fours and some pulling themselves along on their elbows and dragging their legs behind. Amy's daughter was the first to walk, a marvel at six months; Francie's son was the first to talk—Mama, Dada, Baby—at seven months; Sue's daughter was the first to get teeth; Meg's son was the first to pick up food—a pretzel—to feed himself; and Lisa's daughter had the biggest smile and best nature of all. Month by month, the other babies caught up with one another, and by the time they were a year old, their development was almost identical.

When the mothers started to go back to work, their meeting day changed to Saturday. Sometimes the fathers came and sometimes the babies' siblings came. A relaxed, anything goes social life developed around their families. The husbands were as interesting at the wives. They had to be, in order to keep up with them. The group developed a sense of loyalty, and someone was always there to help in case of emergencies, sickness, or babysitting. Remarkably, there was no jealousy about social relationships in the group. They enjoyed the company of one or more of the couples at sports events, dinners, movies or card games. Saturday mornings became family time for all of them—mothers, fathers and children.

Francie wrote in her journal, *I have discovered what I've been missing by favoring men over women in my social life. My new friends are modern, knowledgeable and funny—we've come a long way since life in the Fifties. Sometimes our conversations are out of control, beyond funny. These women have as much or more to say about life as the men, and they're wide open about it. They know how to make fun of themselves, their men, and their society.*

Francie went back to work part-time when Timmy was six months old. She rehired Nanny, and Michael's parents came when Nanny couldn't. All of them thought Timmy was the smartest, cutest, happiest child ever born. Michael and Francie had a perfect balance of home and work, and they were able to arrange their schedules so that they could spend plenty of time with their son.

Kate and Francie continued to speak at least once a week, and Francie usually had a new outrageous story about her group of friends. Meg and Sue were actually Kate's contemporaries, closer in age to her than to Francie.

Kate made Francie promise to introduce her to the group the next time she came to America.

"You'll love them, and they'll love you, I promise," said Francie.

"But it won't be too soon. I have good news for you! Ready?"

"Shoot," was the reply.

"I'm engaged!" she said.

Francie started to cry. "Oh, my darling girl. I'm hugging myself pretending that it's you. I wish I could hug you in person. Congratulations to both of you!"

"It was so romantic, Mom. We had been bicycling in the countryside, and we stopped at a pub to have lunch. Sean took off his jacket, reached into his pocket, knelt before me and slipped a diamond engagement ring on my finger. Then he looked up at me and told me that I made his life complete and as long as we are together, nothing else was important. 'Please say yes,' he said. It was almost a plea, Mom. So funny. As if I'd say no!"

"Oh, you lucky girl—he sounds amazing! And what a lucky guy Sean is!" Francie said, smiling into the receiver. "Congratulations again. What happened next? I want to know everything."

"I was so surprised. I knew we would be getting engaged, but I didn't know when. I was completely flabbergasted. After the hugging and kissing was over, Sean said he hoped he would get along with all the mothers, fathers, brothers and half brothers that I bring into the marriage. His side is a little more traditional—two parents and two sisters."

"So, when's the wedding, and where?"

"The wedding will be in England, probably around the end of May, after he graduates and I have my degree in hand. The details are complicated, but we'll work it out."

Francie called to Michael to come to the phone, and they both beamed with smiles and happiness for Kate and Sean. "I wish you could see us now," she said, "we're smiling all over!"

"So are we," Kate said.

Chapter 23

The next day, as she was getting dressed to leave for work, the phone rang.

"Francie, it's Pat. Don't panic—I'm just calling to congratulate you on our daughter's engagement, and also because I can't bear not hearing your voice."

There was a long pause, and Francie finally spoke up. "Don't say another thing just yet. I need time to breathe."

Suddenly, she felt as if nothing had changed. She needed a full minute to think.

She heard the longing in his voice when he said, "I hadn't plan to say this, but now that I hear your voice, I can't help myself. I miss you so much. Whenever I see Kate, I am reminded of you, and now that she's getting married, I think of what our life would have been like if only…."

She interrupted him. "Pat, we can't think of that." She forced herself to say, "What's done is done. I can't think about us anymore. You have to get over it. We can both love Kate—she reminds us of how we were. That's enough for me. Please don't make me question my decision. I couldn't be happier than I am today with my husband and baby." She paused for a moment. He said nothing. She went on. "We have to face reality. Our daughter is getting married, and we will all be at the wedding. You and I have to put the past behind us and think of the present."

Pat remained silent on the other end of the phone.

"Please don't call me again. It stirs up too many old longings and feelings that I'm trying to forget."

Pat finally spoke. "I understand, my love. I'm so sorry," and he quietly hung up the phone.

She held the receiver in her hand, trying to hold onto Pat as long as it took to control her tears. Then she kissed the mouthpiece and hung up.

Chapter 24

Michael and Francie, with Timmy in tow, arrived in England two days before Kate's wedding so they could acclimate to the time difference. Traveling with a baby made the transition a little difficult, but Timmy turned out to be a trooper. Kate's mother hosted a "Girls' Breakfast" on the morning before the wedding. The only male present was Timmy, who was glad to be passed around the table for everyone to cuddle. Kate eased the awkwardness of so many strangers in the room by telling all the guests not to be overwhelmed by the complicated family relationships. "We can barely keep it straight ourselves. Just assume we're all related," she said.

The party was intimate and friendly. Conversation flowed freely and naturally. The very feminine array of delicate china and lacey flowers made all the women feel special, a fine way for Francie to renew ties to Kate's mother and to meet the women of Sean's family as well as all the friends.

That evening, Sean's parents hosted a party, with the opposite feel of the ladies' brunch, though a lot less raucous than the one for Francie's brother, Brian, the year before. Still, there were humorous toasts, risqué jokes, and abundant beer. A young crowd of brothers, sisters, and friends of the bride and groom dominated the party. Many of Sean's friends were medical school colleagues, some were mates from his teenage years, and some, including Brian, were older friends who had all played on the same football team since college. Pat was noticeably absent.

Timmy was fussing and couldn't settle down because of the noise, so Francie and the baby left early, but Michael stayed for the entirety. He could not get enough of the Irish sense of fun. He saluted the happy couple with a toast and asked if it was possible for him to convert to "Irish."

When Francie got back to the hotel, she nursed Timmy and put him to sleep next to her until he was ready for his crib at the side of the bed. At around ten o'clock, just as she was falling asleep, the phone rang.

Her first thought was that it was Michael. Who else would be calling her this late? She answered the phone quickly so as not to wake the baby.

A very quiet and shaky voice said, "Hello, Francie, this is Mum" Then, barely whispering, she continued, "I'm sure you are shocked to hear my voice, but I hope you have the time to listen because I have so much to tell you."

Francie had the feeling that she was talking to a ghost with the voice of her mother.

She swallowed hard, feeling as if she were in an out of body experience, "What can I say, Mum? For so many years I waited to hear your voice, and now that I hear it, I feel like you are a stranger."

Her mother spoke nervously. "Francie, I pray that you can forgive me for what I did to you. I was a foolish, prideful mother, so afraid of offending the church that I gave up my child. Please let me explain before you judge me."

"I'm listening...."

"I'm very nervous, Francie, and I might stumble when I tell the story, but it goes back quite a few years. I'll start at the beginning, before you were born."

Francie propped herself up and pulled the covers up to her chin. She took a few tissues from the box near the bed, feeling she had to be prepared to hear anything.

"Da and I started our marriage with very little money. I worked as a teacher, earning a small salary, and Da had just started his career at the *Irish Coach Company*. Your brothers were born in quick succession, and we crowded into our tiny quarters until Tommy was born, and then we moved to a two bedroom flat in Dublin. We needed two salaries, so I went back to work. We paid a girl a small amount to watch the boys. Da and I were tired most of the time and were so busy with the boys and our jobs that we had little time to pay attention to each other.

"Along with teaching reading in school, I made house visits in order to tutor students who needed extra help. The school received a request for tutoring from a man in the district, a professor of history at Trinity College named Robert Dugan. His wife had suffered a massive stroke during childbirth and been hospitalized for three years until she passed. For four more years he was a single father, raising his son, Robby, with the help of various nannies and housekeepers. Robby had dyslexia and needed extra help with reading."

"By the time I met him, I found a lonely seven-year-old boy who felt deserted by his mother, as well as by the parade of nannies and housekeepers who had taken care of him. He needed lots of praise and lots of love. I saw him twice a week during that year and brought him treats from our home as often as possible, the same treats I gave your brothers. His progress was slow, but steady, and after a year of tutoring, he started to make strides in reading. His father, Robert, usually came home as our lessons were ending, and little Robby was proud to read aloud to his father to show him how much he had improved."

The expression in her mother's voice changed, and she continued haltingly. "Francie, I did a terrible thing, but it overwhelmed me. It started slowly, after I had been there about six months. One afternoon, when our lesson was over, Robert followed me to the door and said he was always sorry to see me leave. It said it brightened his day when he came home and saw me with Robby. He squeezed my hand and said good night.

"A familiarity developed, and before long, we fell in love, which led to an affair."

Francie's breath caught in her throat when she heard what her mother just said. *My mother had an affair? How could she? She had a family and children.*

"I was young, I was foolish, I was overworked, and I was ready for some excitement. I loved, and still love, Da, but our marriage never had any excitement for me. I accepted it, and I didn't expect things to be different. But when I was with Robert, I felt the excitement of a sixteen-year-old girl again and within a short time, we became lovers. I knew what we were doing was wrong and that the Church would not accept it. I could never confess my sin to Father Grady, so I started to go to other churches, just to go to confession. I lived with guilt every minute of the day, but we didn't want to give each other up.

"When I discovered I was pregnant, I knew that he was the father—he had to be. Da and I were hardly ever together during that year, and we both knew that he wasn't the father."

"Stop right there," said Francie. "Oh, God, do you mean that Da is not my father? The man who took care of me and played with me, and taught me so many things? The man I adored? Mum, how could that be? How did you stay together?"

"I broke off my relationship with Robert very abruptly, without telling him that I was pregnant. I told him and that I could not live with guilt anymore. Our love affair was over.

"I said goodbye to little Robby as gently as I could, telling him that I couldn't come anymore. I hugged him and told him I would miss him. I became another woman on the list of those who deserted him.

"After you were born, Da accepted you as his own with no questions asked, and I will always be grateful to him for that. He told me that he loved me no matter what, and our marriage actually became stronger because of our secret and because of the extraordinary pleasure you brought into our home.

"From the day you were born, I saw in you what I always had wanted to be—happy, carefree, accomplished and loving. I was living my life through you and I loved you for it. I wanted you to be perfect, and, to me, you were—until the day you came home from university, no longer the perfect daughter but a girl fallen from grace, a reflection of my own fall from grace.

"I couldn't look at you without feeling my own guilt and without trying to hide from God. I sent you away.

"For years, my mind was sour with resentment and guilt. Da accepted my decision to send you off. As life went along, our home became a miserable place. Your brothers and our grandchildren did not want to be with Da and me, and I don't blame them. We offered them no happiness.

"Two years ago when I saw you with your husband and daughter at Brian's wedding I took a good look at myself. Francie, what a terrible, selfish mother I have been to expel you from the family. Since then, I have thanked God every day that you have overcome your situation to become the woman you are today.

"I never stopped loving you, Francie, and I love you today more than ever.

"Could you find it in your heart to be my daughter again after what I have done to you?"

Francie took in all her mother had to say. She was still in a state of shock to have learned that her Da was not her real father. He had been such a loving father until the day they banished her from their home. Had he really loved her all those years? *Was he punishing me for the same mistake that my mother made?* His Catholic responsibility was to remain loyal to his wedding vows. The vow was to his wife, not to me, another man's child.

"Ma, can you imagine what it was like for me to be sent away? I was so lonely and scared. I needed you more than ever. I was young, pregnant, and abandoned. I had a painful, difficult time giving birth, and no one was there to comfort me. My baby was born premature, and the nuns took her from me within minutes of her birth. I was not permitted to see her again. When I arrived in America, I had no idea if she were alive or dead. My breasts were still swollen with milk that I couldn't give her. I didn't know what to do. I had no one to turn to. Aunt Agnes never said a kind word to me. The only thing I wanted was to hear from you."

Everything Francie said brought sobs from her mother.

"It took years for me to get over longing for you, but I finally did.

"And now you ask me to forgive you? And tell me that your treatment of me was because I reminded you of yourself? What do you expect me to do?"

Francie was sobbing now. She tried to compose herself by taking a sip of water from the glass next to her bed, then dipped her tissue into the cup and wiped her face with the cold water. Without realizing it, she was scratching her arm over and over, driving her fingernails into her skin until she drew blood. She took a deep breath, trying to quiet her nerves and force her sobbing to retreat.

She continued. "Forget all those years? Forgive you? Well, I can't—it's not that easy. I lived at home in Ireland for seventeen years. Since I left, I have lived in America for twenty-five years and have made a life for myself. America is my home now. I'm happy—I found my daughter, a part of your flesh and blood that you rejected when you rejected me. I have a strong, self-assured, generous husband whom I love and can rely on. We have a healthy baby son." She took a deep breath. "I have no room in my life for you, Mum. Maybe I will someday, but not now, I am not ready.

"I hope contentment comes to you—you know it's not my nature to wish ill for you or Da. You became the way you are because of the guilt that was bred into you by the Church, and I want no part of it. I refuse to feel that guilt and I refuse to pass it on to my son. Your only guilt should be for discarding me like old trash and abandoning me when I needed you most. I can hear you crying now, but for years you never heard my tears.

"So, I respect that you called to make amends, and I accept your story. But, right now, I can't accept you in my life."

Francie hung up the phone and cried. She stayed awake, repeatedly going over what her mother had told her, confident that she had made the right decision for the time being. If her feelings changed, she would contact her mother, but for now, she was at peace and her head was clear.

When Michael came home from the groom's party, Francie and Timmy were sound asleep. He brushed his teeth and slipped under the covers fully dressed.

They both slept late. Francie had taken Tim into their bed for his early feeding, and then they all fell back to sleep until ten. Francie woke up first, with Timmy still sleeping soundly between them. A few minutes later when Michael woke up, she said, "I hope you don't mind that Sean's brother-in-law is in our bed this morning." Michael was taken aback for a moment until he had the laughable realization that she was talking about Timmy.

They had lots to tell each other about the night before, but they decided to hold their conversation until they had breakfast downstairs. Many of the wedding guests were there, and others were slowly drifting in, some looking decidedly hungover. There was a long table and a buffet set up for them, so Francie decided not to tell Michael about the call from her mother until later. Michael joined the others in conversation, and they recanted the hilarious time they had the night before. Michael said that he never met a group of so many drunken doctors. "If I get sick here, put me on a plane to the U.S. where the doctors are all stodgy. How can I trust any of you after last night?"

They finished breakfast close to noon. Francie and Michael had a few hours until they had to leave for the wedding, so they loaded Tim into his stroller and went for a long walk. Michael started the conversation by telling Francie the ridiculous fun that went on at the party.

"A rock band showed up at midnight, and everyone sang, danced and drank some more. There were some homegrown musicians at the party, and they joined the musicians onstage, playing mostly on key, but not always. Three of the women imitated The Supremes and almost started a riot.

"Pat was there—he must have come pretty late. He came over to me and shook my hand and asked about you and the baby. He spent most of his time with Kate and Sean, but I think he felt awkward. He was very quiet. Francie, I'm not sure how I feel about him. But, believe it or not, I'm not at all jealous. I feel he was connected to you way before I came along, almost like a distant relative. I feel sorry for him.

"Kate's father, James, called me aside to tell me he would be walking Kate down the aisle and invited us to sit in the parents' pew. Pat will be there, too. How would you feel about us sitting there?"

"I would be honored, but how do you feel about it?"

"I think it would be a great thing to do for Kate."

"I'll ask Rosie to hold Timmy for us until after the ceremony."

"Which one is Rosie again?" asked Michael. "Oh, now I remember, she's your brother Brian's wife. We went to their wedding."

"Wise guy," she said.

Haltingly at first, Francie started to tell Michael about the phone call from her mother.

She told him all the details, leaving nothing out, including her response. "I hope you don't think I'm vindictive for the way I spoke to my mother, but I told her the truth about the way I feel. Maybe I'll change my mind someday, but, until then, I don't want her to be in my life."

Michael was gentle with her, putting his arm around her to let her know he agreed with her decision. "Darling, I trust you and your judgment. I have a feeling that you will accept your mother someday, but until that day, you will do a lot of soul searching until you reach the right conclusion. I love you no matter what, but I have something to add."

He hugged her tightly and let her go to look into her eyes. With a wry smile, he said, "If you weren't so emotionally involved, the whole menagerie of your family would be comical."

"It is comical, and I am emotionally involved, but, after what I've been through for so many years, I hardly feel affected by the news, except that now I know why I didn't inherit Da's talent on the dance floor. Wrong genes."

She thought for a minute, and Michael watched the wheels turn in her brain until she spoke up. "Eventually, I'll try to track down my biological father. My mother told me his name is Robert Dugan, and he was a history professor at Trinity College twenty-six years ago. His son, Robby, was about seven when I was conceived—another brother to add to my collection!"

"And two more relatives to add to my list of names," he said with a sigh.

Chapter 25

The church was full of spring flowers, lush blooms in pastel colors. Kate was a smiling, relaxed bride in a gown of yards and yards of organdy, and Sean, the perfect mate for her, stately and serious in his tuxedo with a boutonniere of violets. *All in all, a picture-perfect wedding fit for a girl like Kate*, thought Francie.

James escorted Kate down the aisle, lifted her veil and kissed her cheek. Then he shook Sean's hand and gave her over to the groom. When the couple reached the family pew, Kate broke with tradition, approached Pat and lifted her veil for a kiss from him, and Sean offered his hand for a second handshake. They did the same for Michael. Then they continued with the traditional Catholic ceremony. It was a wedding of joy and love, with no secrets, and no shame.

The reception and party went off without a hitch. Kate called for a toast to her family, introducing her two mothers, Grace and Francie; two-and-a-half fathers, James, Pat and Michael; her two brothers, Tommy and Leo Mullins; and her three half brothers, Flip and Josh Harrington, and baby Tim Hanson—the one wearing the white bib with a black bow tie. "I'll save you all confusion by not introducing my aunts, uncles and cousins," Kate said to the crowd.

Then the groom toasted his family. "My side is more in control. May I present my parents, Daithi and Mary Beth Walsh, and my two sisters, Faith and Hope—easy to remember—and my brothers-in-law, Peter and Joseph. I toast to good family relations always, because mine is outnumbered. However, Kate, if I ever have to take on one of your brothers in a fight, I'll choose Timmy."

Pat and Francie were standing near each other during the introductions. He turned to her for a brief moment and kissed her on the cheek. “Congratulations—what a beautiful bride we made,” he said.

“We did,” she said squeezing his hand. “One of a kind.”

Then toasts all around and the dancing began. The party lasted until the next morning when the bride and groom left in a shower of rice for their honeymoon in Guernsey.

Francie and Michael returned to their hotel just after midnight with a sleeping Timmy in arms. He had behaved like a gentleman during the wedding and slept soundly for most of the loud evening.

They transferred the baby to his crib. He stretched his neck, yawned and went back to sleep.

Michael and Francie looked down at Timmy and their hands naturally found each other.

Michael said, “This has been such a romantic weekend, Do you think we could have our own, private celebration without waking Timmy?”

“Come to Mama,” she said.

Timmy did his part, and their weekend was complete.

Chapter 26

Two days after they returned to the U.S., they were back to their regular routines. Francie's very capable assistant at her office assumed a great deal of Francie's duties and delegated jobs to various departments. Francie oversaw these activities, reviewed sales and recommended changes, if necessary. In the twenty-plus years she'd been with Shea's, many of the old guard had retired, and the newer executives were in their forties and fifties. Francie was still one of the youngest. *Shea's Soup and Grilled Cheese* fast food restaurants continued to be a big success, and Francie was still the face behind the concept.

Much as she loved her job, she was ready to give her domestic life equal time. Not only did she want to be there for Tim, but she also had Michael's parents to consider. They were in their late seventies and starting to slow down, but they were such an important part of Francie's life. Even if she had not been estranged from her parents, she would have treated her in-laws as her own mother and father. She loved them, and the feeling was mutual. They considered her their daughter and were forever grateful to her for making their son happy and for giving them Timmy, the grandchild they thought they'd never have. They loved the bonus of Kate who maintained an ongoing monthly correspondence with her "Grammy."

Michael's parents decided that the time was right for them to sell their large home and move to a senior complex. There were a few nice ones in their area, and Francie helped them choose a large apartment at Westfield, with a spare room for Timmy's overnight stays. They were one of the few couples living there who had a crib in the guest bedroom.

After the sale of the old place they'd lived in for nearly fifty years, the monumental task began—sorting, selling, donating and keeping. Many of the Hanson's possessions had been passed down for six generations. When the first Hanson arrived on the shores of America, the family publishing business began, and, with every generation, the family's fortune and prestige increased. In keeping with their Scandinavian roots, they never flaunted their extraordinary wealth. All the Hansons lived well but quietly and conservatively. The generation of Michael's grandparents sold the business to a large New York publishing house. His father served on the board during his working years, and his mother, who was always interested in the written word, continued to edit. Michael had no idea of the scope of the family's wealth.

In her in-laws' attic, Francie discovered a trove of paintings and antique books and furniture that his parents wanted to sell. She called in a top auction outfit to appraise the furniture and artwork, as well as the silver and linen accoutrements in cupboards and drawers. The appraised value of their furnishings was high. The artwork alone was estimated at over a million dollars. Francie could hardly get the words out. "Michael, did you know your parents were rich?" He scratched his head and shook it in disbelief.

Michael's parents told them to choose whatever they'd like to keep. As for themselves, they would keep some of their favorite things and buy new, lighter furniture for their new home. The only thing of value to Michael was a wooden stool that he had made in fourth grade woodshop at school. That meant more to him than any of the valuable paintings in the attic. Francie was tempted to choose a sunny painting of daffodils by van Gogh, but she didn't think it would be fair to Michael to have a painting in their home that would constantly remind her of Pat. She chose to keep a small Renoir oil of a mother and child that would like nice over her desk. The antique furniture and Old Masters' paintings were not Francie and Michael's taste, so aside from the few other things they wanted to keep for sentimental reasons, the family turned everything over to the auction house.

Once the items were authenticated by domestic and international experts, they were photographed and featured in the appropriate Sotheby's catalogues. The date for the auction of 19th Century European Painting and Sculpture was set for two months later in New York. This would be the first auction in which the Hanson's collection would appear. Other pieces of art and heirlooms—furniture, linens and incidental items—would be shown in auctions of different periods, but this one would contain the majority of their art. After months of sorting, Michael and Francie were finished and ready for a vacation, so they decided to stay in New York for a few nights during week of the auction.

Michael's parents were comfortably settled into their new home with lovely, bright new furnishings and didn't want to go to Sotheby's to watch the family's possessions pass to strangers, so they offered to babysit so that Michael and Francie could have their first vacation away from Timmy, assured that he was in loving hands. Michael had no attachment to the furnishings he grew up with and was glad that the items would have a new life with people who valued them. He and Francie were excited at the prospect of attending the auction at the famous Sotheby's and decided that one or two nights away from Timmy would not be a disaster. They gave them four typewritten pages of instructions and firm orders for them to call if there were any problems or questions. Of course, his parents did not bother reading the instructions. Instead, as most grandparents would, they trusted their instincts and spoiled him.

A day before the auction, Francie and Michael took the one hour train ride from Philadelphia to Manhattan. They checked into the Plaza Hotel, dropped off their bags and went straight to Sotheby's. All the items for auction were on display for twenty-four hours before the day of the sale. The Hanson Collection of paintings was labeled, numbered, and allotted to its own space behind red velvet stanchions. A large number of people came and went from early morning to late night to review the displays. People from all over the world circulated, speaking a variety of languages—Chinese, Japanese, Russian and Arabic, along with Spanish and the rest of western European languages. Some were taking copious notes, others marveling at what they were seeing. Francie was overwhelmed to think that Michael's family was responsible for this exhibit that was in demand by complete strangers from worlds away..

They left the exhibition in great anticipation of the auction the next day. As they merged into the flow of people on the sidewalk, they could feel the frenetic passion New Yorkers seemed to have from just being alive in the city. The buzz was intoxicating, a thrilling place for Francie and Michael to have a second honeymoon. They walked a few blocks, watching people from all walks of life from street performers to women laden with packages from the three "B"s—Bloomingdale's, Bergdorf's and Bendel's. Francie was fascinated to hear nannies conversing in Spanish, Polish and Filipino gesturing with their hands while pushing double strollers and wagons loaded with kids gobbling pizza slices and having a wonderful time. *Probably a daycare taking a lunch break*, Francie surmised. *To think that everyone around us has a unique story and a unique set of gestures according to their cultures.*

After walking about six blocks, they hailed a cab to take them back to the Plaza. Dinner at seven, quite early by New York standards, would be perfect for them. They wanted to spend a long relaxing time in their room after dinner. Michael asked the concierge to make a reservation for them at one of the newer, popular restaurants. The latest "in" place was within walking distance of their hotel, and the concierge took care of the details. Apparently, the restaurant was very popular—every table was taken, even at this early hour. Their specialty was a revival of a style popular a decade before, featuring micro-portions of food, artfully arranged on a plate. When their appetizers arrived, it was all they could do to keep from laughing. Francie's plate held one small ravioli dressed in a smidgen of cream sauce with one basil leaf for decoration, and Michael's salad consisted of two halves of a cherry tomato, each filled with four peas. "Why don't we go halvies?" Francie offered. "I'll take one of your tomato halves and two peas and you can have a quarter inch piece of my ravioli."

"They must be kidding," Michael said. "When we get back to the hotel, I'm going to shoot the concierge—and no jury would convict me—I have cause."

Their dinners were equally small—a tiny pomegranate-glazed quail with a scant tablespoon of wild rice on top, garnished with three asparagus tips, but the wine was abundant and appropriate to each course. For dessert, they each had an after-dinner cognac and a sliver of pear tart topped with a delicious ginger flavored whipped cream. When they left the restaurant, Michael said, "I can see why this craze didn't survive the eighties. Do you want to go out for a real dinner, or should we get a hot dog to tide us over to breakfast?"

"Neither—let's go back to our quiet, luxurious room."

They retired to their posh hotel for a very private night—just the two of them for the first time in months. Anticipation proved to be better than reality, because when the time was right for romance, Francie told Michael that she didn't feel well.

"Something didn't agree with me, or maybe the three glasses of wine and cognac were too much for me. Just give me a while to let it digest."

"I can wait," he said, "but barely."

The room was spinning when she ran for the bathroom, bent over the toilet, and lost her fancy meal from New York's latest "in" restaurant.

She got into bed and pulled the covers over her head. "Do you mind if we skip tonight?"

"The truth is, I feel nauseated, too, knowing you just flushed five hundred dollars' worth of food and drink down the toilet. But no worries." He kissed her forehead, "Good night, love, sleep well."

The next morning, Francie could barely manage toast and tea, but as auction time neared, she started to feel more normal, though a little weak. She silently swore never to have three glasses of wine and an after-dinner nightcap again. They taxied to Sotheby's and saw a line of limousines discharging passengers in front of the building.

"Do you think we fit in with this crowd?" Michael said.

"Sure, why wouldn't a poor girl from Ireland feel right at home with this bunch? And you—you're the only man here not in a custom-made suit."

"But some bidders here will be fighting over the paintings that I grew up with. Next month, when the furniture auction is scheduled, I expect it to be more unbelievable. The thought of elite people buying the bed I jumped on and sometimes wet; and the dining room table I spilled my milk on at least once a month never knowing it was special; and the sofa and chairs that my sweaty friends and I sat on when we hung out—it's remarkable. I feel smug just thinking that some hotshots want our threadbare Oriental rugs. They used to embarrass me in front of my friends."

They walked into a large auditorium furnished with comfortable armchairs and thick carpets. Every seat had a side table with bottled water, olives, chocolates, cheese and crackers. Bars were set up on both sides of the room, and those desiring soft or hard drinks simply had to ring a buzzer on their table. Michael buzzed for a waiter and ordered a glass of wine. "How about three for you, Francie?"

"Never again," she said, and ordered a Ginger Ale.

There was a balcony around the perimeter of the room with private booths for agents of telephone bidders.

Francie eyed the well-dressed "players."

"I've never been to a Broadway show, but this reality show has to top it," she said, enchanted with what she was witnessing.

The items were grouped in lots numbered in order of their presentations. The program showed that the Hanson lot was Number Five, the last one on the agenda. Lot One had about twenty items. The auctioneer presented each item individually, and the bidding proceeded speedily. The lot was gone in less than ten minutes. Most of the paintings and sculptures sold for between five thousand and twenty thousand dollars each.

Bidding on Lot Two lasted longer and was a little more exciting. The auctioneer controlled the bidding by starting with an opening amount of an ice-skating scene, *Figures on a Frozen River*, by Flemish painter Charles Leickert. Bidders raised a card to show that they were willing to bid that amount, and the auctioneer suggested a higher number. Those wishing to continue bidding raised their cards again. The auctioneer proceeded speedily, and bids mounted very quickly. Several agents on the balcony entered the bidding for their absentee clients. The skill of the auctioneer was remarkable. He seemed to wring out the highest amount possible until he said, "Going, going, gone," banged his gavel, and a thirty-five-thousand dollar painting changed hands in less than a minute. A breath later, the auctioneer proceeded to the next item. This lot was a bit larger than the first and the amounts bid were slightly higher.

Lot Three featuring mostly sea scenes, a popular subject, went quickly. The lots were listed in order of value, and the amounts were staggering.

Francie could feel her heart pounding when she heard the amounts bid. When Lot Four commenced, her head was spinning, and it went by with her hardly noticing the art except for the huge numbers it drew. She and Michael were dazed even before they had a clue of what was coming.

The Hanson Lot, Number Five, was next. A rumble went through the crowd. Michael and Francie watched wide-eyed when the bidding began. "Oh my God," Michael said, "We must have been rich all along, but no one ever told me. To think that I delivered newspapers from my bike when I was a kid to *learn the value of money!*"

The bidding was intense but polite, much higher than the appraisal value. Every piece of sculpture was sold, from delicate bisque porcelain Royal Copenhagen figurines to large clay and metal busts of the Swedish royal family. The climax was when the Hanson Collection of oil paintings was offered. The Statens Museum for Kunst, the National Gallery of Denmark, bought the entire eighteen-piece works of art for their permanent collection. The proceeds were well over ten million. The entire room applauded, and Michael, in his off-the-rack-suit, and Francie, in her Talbot's dress, stood up and bowed.

When it was over, Michael called his parents. "Did you know the value of your things?" he asked. His father said that he knew the art and antiques were valuable but the last appraisal for insurance value decades ago was conservative by today's standards.

He went on to explain, "The Hanson family was small, with only a few heirs—many of the generations had only one child—including my generation and my father's and grandfather's. As I was growing up, my parents were inheriting more and more art and antiques from old aunts and uncles and storing them in the attic. When they died, all their stuff came to Mother and me, and we just put most of it directly into the attic.

"We hardly ever looked at it until we decided to sell the house, and Francie called Sotheby's to come appraise it. We decided there was no point in keeping all of this under wraps—maybe someone else would want to buy some of it. We knew you didn't want it, so off it went."

Michael said, "I used to play up there with my friends. The stuff was so creepy, we pretended we were in a haunted house."

Michael told his parents about the excitement of the auction and the applause for the final total. "The art is going to be called *The Hanson Collection* in the Danish Museum of Art."

His father was pleased to hear that the art would be going to Denmark. "The core of the collection came from Scandinavia, mostly Sweden, when my fifth great grandfather emigrated. I guess the generations after him continued to add to the collection as the family prospered. Mother and I were overwhelmed with the amount of art that accumulated in the attic, so we never bought anything new for ourselves. Every once in a while, we rotated a painting or two from the attic to the living room. From the way you're talking, it must have brought in over a million dollars. Wait until I tell Mother—she'll be very excited."

"Dad, it brought in way more than that." When Michael told him the amount, his father was flabbergasted.

After a moment of silence, his response was, "We sure saved a lot on insurance!"

Chapter 27

After the excitement of the auction and the exhaustion from having been sick the night before, Francie was feeling lightheaded. They decided to go home that afternoon, one day earlier than planned. Back at the hotel, she lay down for a quick rest before they checked out to return to Philadelphia. Michael, on the other hand, was effervescent. "Let's live like millionaires and buy a summer home on the Irish coast," he told Francie. "I love Ireland and want to spend more time there. We could buy a place large enough to enjoy visits from your family and my parents. Wouldn't it be great?"

"Michael, don't let the money go to your head. We have a lot to think about before we even think of such a decision. Anyway, I am so tired I can't think of anything right now except getting home to Timmy and being back in my own bed."

"How about if I called the concierge to see if he can get us a driver to take us back home. Is that too much of an extravagance?"

"Sounds good to me. Just get me home."

They went straight to Michael's parents place to get the baby and to celebrate the good news about their bourgeoning bank account. Although they were only away for one night, Timmy looked to them like he had grown. "What's your secret?" she asked her mother-in-law. "Timmy looks like a giant!"

"It's no secret. We thought the same thing when Michael was a baby. We were always shocked to come home from a trip and see how big he really was. It seems that all parents picture their children to be smaller than they actually are when they don't see them for a few days."

"Mom, we saw him yesterday before we left. I doubt if that's enough time for us to forget what he looked like."

"Well then, Francie, I guess Dad and I will take credit. We gave him his Wheaties and he grew two inches overnight."

Michael's dad had bought a bottle of Dom Pérignon for the occasion, and his mother had taken out the Waterford crystal tulip glasses. They toasted and blessed their ancestors and thanked the twist of fate that made them multimillionaires. Francie added a note of solemnity when she made a toast of thanks to the life the United States had given her—her husband, her baby and her in-laws. "The money is grand, but it's icing on the cake, something unnecessary to decorate the wonderful life you had given me." She put her glass down after a sip or two, not wanting to push her luck after her sick feeling the night before. Then hugs and kisses goodbye and return to home.

Michael had an early class the next day, and Francie had a chance to sleep in. When she woke up with nausea again, she recognized the familiarity of the pattern. *Oh my God, is it possible?* She ran to the drug store and bought a pregnancy testing kit, and, sure enough, she tested positive. She called her doctor and made an appointment to see her that day—she wanted to be sure before she told Michael.

When her husband came home, she greeted him with a drink and a smile.

"What's this all about?"

"Congratulations," she said, "you're going to be a father!"

"I already am a father—oh, no! You don't mean....?"

"Yup, signed, the work is in progress, to be delivered in about five and a half months."

"Thanks for the drink, but I need a double."

"Should we call your parents?"

"Can you give me five minutes to get drunk first?"

She laughed and said, "Michael, the older you get the funnier you get."

She called his parents and told them the news. They hollered so loud, she was surprised that their neighbors didn't hear and call 9-1-1 thinking that they were under attack.

With a new addition coming, life started to get more complicated. Timmy would be a big brother by the time he was seventeen months. Someday he'd be explaining why he had two siblings, one twenty-four years older and another eighteen months younger.

Francie continued to work with her reduced schedule but prepared her staff and colleagues to be ready for her probable retirement. When she shared her news with her mothers' group, their reaction was laughter. "Didn't anyone ever tell you about birth control?"

"What's that? I'm an Irish Catholic. Do you have any idea what we think about those two words?"

Michael was nearing fifty-five and beginning to think about completely retiring from teaching. He had taught economics for almost thirty years and was ready for a change. For the past few years, a group in Washington had invited him to join their Think Tank, but he had always declined. Now he decided it might be just the thing. He would be required to spend two days every week in Washington, about a two hour train ride from Philadelphia. He thought it would be interesting to explore a new approach to economics rather than teaching, and he and Francie decided that it would be an exciting addition to his life. He notified the administration that this year would be his last, but he'd be glad to return now and then as a visiting professor if invited. The university president reluctantly accepted his resignation, saying that Michael had been one of the best-liked professors at the university, by both students and staff.

In May, at semester's end, the school gave him a retirement party, attended by a very pregnant Francie, a very squirmy Timmy, and Michael's proud parents, all of whom had attended Penn with the exception of Timmy—slated for the class of 2024. Department heads, faculty friends, important members in the world of economics, selected students and board members made tributes. Some were light and amusing, some were serious and complimentary, and some were as boring as canned potatoes. At the end of the evening, Michael was presented with a gift from the president of the board. "This is not the usual gift given to a retiring faculty member of Michael's standing, but Michael has shown remarkable skills in fields other than academics." He handed him a handsome rosewood box containing a sterling silver baby rattle for the baby yet to come, a sterling silver bowl and spoon for Timmy, and a first edition of *Charlie and the Chocolate Factory.*

The baby was due to arrive in about six weeks, and the house was ready for either boy or girl. Timmy's room was now the *big brother's* room, decorated in shades of blue with fire trucks and baseball pennants. The nursery was outfitted in neutral shades of yellow. This time they had most of the equipment in place—crib, quilt, baby blanket, onesies in unisex colors. The doctor told Francie that with her history of giving birth, anything could happen—long labor, short labor or normal labor. But this time they wanted to be sure the room was ready for the baby no matter what.

Francie and Michael had officially retired from their jobs in May, and now Francie had time to overhaul the garden before the baby arrived. She and her mother-in-law, with the help of a landscape designer, selected a mixture of annuals and perennials, as well as a variety of bushes and trees. The work had already begun, and they loved watching the progress. Timmy was part of the crew, and Michael's mother embroidered "Number One Helper" on the bib of a new pair of denim overalls to prove it. When the crew showed up, Tim was there with his overalls, bucket, rake and watering can to oversee the job. By the first day of summer, the flowers were blooming, and the bushes were growing. The landscaping made the house look like it should be in a magazine. Francie enjoyed it every day. As each plant blossomed or grew, she felt like a proud mother of each one.

The plan was in place for the baby's arrival at the end of June. After the experience they had with Timmy's birth, they were prepared for anything, but hoped they would have enough time to get Timmy to his to grandparent's place and to get themselves to the hospital.

This pregnancy had the perfect ending. On June 30, during an early, record-breaking heat spell that produced a failure of the entire southwest Pennsylvania's power grid, Francie had her first twinges of labor pains. Michael dropped off Timmy at his parents' place and drove Francie to Bryn Mawr Hospital with little time to spare. Six hours after Francie's first twinge, power was restored, and Audrey was born just as the delivery room lit up with a power surge. Michael swore that Audrey popped out glowing.

Three days later, Francie came home from the hospital and the fun began.

Chapter 28

Kate and Sean, now permanently living in Ireland, kept in close touch with Francie and cheered when they heard of Hanson baby number two—a girl! Kate couldn't travel to the U.S. right away for a post-baby visit, but she hoped she and Sean would get time away during the late fall. They had learned that working was not as easy as being students.

Their new life together as husband and wife—M.D. and PhD—had begun. He was appointed to the Royal College of Surgeons in Dublin as a pediatric surgeon, with surgical privileges at various hospitals in the city. Kate had turned down Cambridge's job offer and was hired as professor of economics at Trinity College, a much sought-after appointment. They settled into a small apartment in an area in Dublin popular with young couples. Sean's work was very demanding of his time—he made himself readily available to his young patients and their concerned families and was on call for emergencies. Kate designed her own curricula for the five classes she taught during the semester. She frequently consulted Michael by phone to ask his opinion and recommendations. She worked a pre-determined schedule at the college and spent a good deal of her week working at home so that she and Sean could see each other as much as possible. Their conversations at home were always interesting—he told her of the problems and successes of his work, and she told him about accommodating the peculiarities of some of her students.

Her lectures were popular, and she related very well to her students. She was quite exacting, presenting her material in a terse but pleasant way. She knew that theories and charts could be dull, and, with a nod to Michael's teaching methods, she managed to show her students that economics was exciting. Her goal was to make them see that in practice the global effect of the theories and practices of economics drove much of the politics of the world. She encouraged her students to meet her during her office hours, and often the time turned into gatherings of several committed students. At semester's end, there was a waiting list for her classes for the following semester.

They had a nice life in Ireland. They often spent their weekends with Sean's old friends and their favorite neighbors trying to get their bodies back into shape after spending the work week indoors in a stuffy classroom or a stressful operating room. Rain or shine, every Saturday they would plan a woods walk with friends, hiking for hours in the morning, stopping for a picnic or pub lunch, then walking into the late afternoon. At day's end they were physically tired and mentally invigorated, ready for a quick nap, romance and an evening at one of their favorite cafés with good friends.

Travel for the family between Europe and the U.S. became more difficult as the kids grew older; new babies were coming to the O'Conners in Ireland, and before long, another generation would emerge. Senior members were promoted in their careers and work schedules became more demanding.

Michael brought up his idea again to Francie about getting a place in Ireland. "The easiest way for your family and us to be together would be in Ireland. It would be great for our kids to get to know their only cousins. We could make it a summer destination every year. The kids could get to know everyone, and, for me, an only child, it would be great to experience life in a big family, especially your happy, welcoming one."

Francie was glad that Michael felt that way about her family and was gradually coming around to agree that it would be a unique way to use some of their money and to keep the family united. "Well, it's worth a trip to look around. Maybe my brothers and Kate could do some scouting for us and email pictures of their recommendations."

Francie put out the word to her brothers and to Kate and asked them their thoughts on Michael's idea. She and Michael had accumulated a large amount of savings from their earnings during their careers. Even before the family discovered the treasure trove in the attic, Michael and Francie were well-off financially. Michael's parents had created a trust fund for him when he was a baby and started one for Audrey, their new grandbaby, to match Timmy's. Francie's family didn't know the financial details of their sister and Michael's finances, but they knew they had a sizeable amount. She and Michael gave her brothers and Kate a price range they thought would be practical for the purchase of a very large house, or a smaller one with a guest cottage or two in the emerald green Irish countryside or in a tiny town near the sea. Michael hoped his Irish family would find a place by early autumn of the current year so they could purchase it in time for the following summer to celebrate Audrey's first birthday in Ireland.

Denis consulted a realty firm that specialized in that type of property and suggested that each brother investigate a different location and explore the environs of the area. Sean and Kate would join the hunt when their schedules permitted. They all were excited about the prospect of having a family compound established through the good graces of Michael and Francie. Who would have believed on that sad, sad day years before, when her parents banished her, that she would be able to provide a home away from home that would bring them all together?

Chapter 29

At age forty-six, Francie became a housewife. Although she had household help, her life became the raising of two kids seventeen months apart, planning breakfast, lunch and dinner with no end in sight, making playdates for Tim, and reading bedtime stories to both of them. She included her in-laws in much of her everyday life. They had been waiting fifty-five years to buy something pink for a grandchild, and now that they had one, they were addicted. They bought pink sweaters, pink pajamas, pink dresses, pink quilts, you name it, they bought it. Francie had to beg them to stop. Of course, Timmy continued to be an everyday part of their grandparents' lives. They stopped in for a short time each day, sometimes taking him to lunch or to a child's museum—always including Audrey in their visit by hugging her and having conversations in baby talk with her. Michael spent two or three days in Washington each week and enjoyed the stimulation of trading ideas with others in the economic and political Think Tank. When he was home, he was delighted to play the role of father, husband and son.

Meanwhile, Michael's plans to buy a retreat in Ireland were moving along. Property was very expensive in the Irish countryside, but Brian found a rambling house in Tipperary with a large amount of acreage, not too ridiculously expensive but almost at the top of Michael's budget. Denis found a mini-estate closer to the coast on several acres in Ballyshannon, Quin, in County Clare for a considerably lower price. A week later, all of them—Tommy and Margaret, Brian and Rosie, Denis, and Sean and Kate rented a van and drove to see both, about a two-hour drive from Dublin. They all thought the home in Tipperary was perfect—six bedrooms, four bathrooms and a three car garage with an apartment above. Though not near the sea, the grounds and views of the surrounding lush, green countryside were gorgeous. There was a small town a short bicycle ride away. They were elated. "Dibs on the apartment over the garage," Tommy said. Then they drove a little farther to the next property. This one was listed as a large country estate near the sea—seven bedrooms and four baths—in Ballyshannon, less than an hour's ride from Shannon Airport. It was hard to resist. The realtor told them it had just come up for sale and was *the find of the year.* The price was two-thirds of the cost of the home in Tipperary. The feel of the sea breeze made this one a shoo-in.

A few days later, in late November, Michael and Francie flew to Shannon to look at the properties. Their first stop was Tipperary to see the estate farther from the airport. They immediately fell in love with it. It had everything they wanted, but in fairness, they wanted to check out the other property in Ballyshannon. That night they stayed in the village in Tipperary so that they could get a feel of the area. Over dinner in their small hotel, they talked about the house. "Michael, it's so expensive. Can we afford it?"

"Think of it as an investment—not just in money, but in family. To me that is priceless. So, yes, we can afford it, but let's sleep on it and see how we feel tomorrow when we go to Ballyshannon."

The time of year to see this house couldn't have been better. The silver white birches lining the long, stone driveway were still afire with deep red autumn leaves. If this house were on a picture postcard, no one would believe it was real. When it came into view, Francie and Michael agreed that they never should have come there—now they were totally confused. They loved the house, the grounds, and the breathtaking water views from the cliffs. The price was lower, but they had already decided that they would not choose a house based on price alone.

That night Francie called Kate and asked her opinion. "I think they are both fantastic! However, if you're looking for a family retreat, I vote for Tipperary. That house had something that bespoke a home for all generations. Sean and I both felt the same. We thought that the other one was too close to Shannon Airport and that the surrounding area of Ballyshannon might become too commercial and lose its charm."

"Okay, love, we'll put one check mark in Column A. Now I'll call the boys."

In the end, it was unanimous—Tipperary it was. Michael called the agent the next day to put in the offering price the agent had suggested. It was accepted, and Michael had the funds transferred from his U.S. bank as a deposit on the agreed upon price. Everyone was happy. They filed the proper papers, arranged for the necessary inspections, and the house became theirs on a snowy day in December. The family who sold them the house was moving to Switzerland and offered to put them in touch with the caretaker, Jack, who had worked for them the past eighteen years and was familiar with everything in the house and on the property.

"Talk about the luck of the Irish," Francie said. This will make things so much easier for us."

In December, they flew back to Ireland for the settlement. The next day, when they met Jack, they hired him on the spot. They told him they would probably not be back until May or June, but since the sale of the house included all of the furniture, pots and pans, dishes, everything—including a garage full of first-rate tools and gardening implements, there was not much they needed, just two cribs for Tim and Audrey. He assured them not to worry—he would keep the house in good order until they returned.

Jack was so pleased that they had twins. "This house needs *babais* to bring it new life."

Francie said, "Not real twins, more like Irish twins, almost a year and a half apart. That should bring twice the fun."

"And won't my wife be happy to help when you need her," said Jack. "She's raised six of our own."

They planned to spend the whole summer at their new home in Ireland. Michael's parents would go with them to help get the children settled and to break in the new house. From there on, it would always be "open house" for everyone in the family.

Michael named the property *Tip Top*, and Jack had a sign made and posted it on the gate to the driveway. On the fourth of July, they held a combination celebration for the American holiday, Audrey's first birthday and a housewarming. Michael was eager for his parents to meet the Irish contingency of his family—and they came in droves—brothers, sisters-in-law, seven nieces and nephews, and Kate and Sean. Francie's oldest brother, Denis, now in his early 50s, came with his significant other—a surprise to everyone—named Liam, who turned out to be the life of the party.

Michael's parents stayed at *Tip Top* for a month, which they felt was long enough for them. "You know what they say about fish and house guests," his mother said. "We loved everything about being here. Francie, your family is a joy—and it was wonderful living here with our children and grandchildren, but now it's time for us to get back to friends of our own generation—at this age, you never know how much longer your friends will be alive."

Francie and Michael stayed until the days began to shorten, and on the first of October, they packed up and returned to their real home in Haverford. Their first year at *Tip Top* was over. They hoped it was to be the first for many generations to enjoy.

By November, Michael and Francie had converted the space above their garage in Haverford into a small apartment they would make available to foreign students at University of Pennsylvania. Francie thought if they could give even one student a home in his or her new country, they could help to alleviate the feeling of homelessness she had felt when she lived with her Aunt Agatha. In the years to follow, students of varied nationalities occupied that space. In return, some cared for the garden, helped paint the house, played with or tutored the children, played basketball with Francie during the week and with Michael and his friends on Sunday. They helped keep Francie and Michael in the loop of the thinking of young people.

Every student who lived there enhanced the lives of the Hanson family. They respected each other's privacy, but they often ate together, discussed various subjects from American TV shows to the strategies of applying their educations in various cultures.

Inspired by her discussions with their student guests, and after a few years of the family routine, Francie felt it was time to add something to her repertoire other than baby talk and pillow talk. She contacted Bryn Mawr College, just a few minutes by car from her home. She visited their philosophy department and spoke to Dr. Ellen Matthews about revisiting the subject of her original college major. Dr. Matthews studied Francie's credentials and said she was highly qualified to become a candidate for graduate school.

At her level, study was one-on-one with each professor, and she could arrange her course work and thesis with her advisor.

"When can I start?" she asked.

"We'll let you know when everything is in place, and after I appoint your advisor, you can consult with her to start whenever you both are ready. Given that you are raising two children, you will be happy to know that you can do seventy-five percent of the work at home, if desired. Of course, academic discussions with your professors are held on campus.

Francie walked out of there singing. She strolled around the campus with a light-hearted gait, explored the library, ran her hands over books in the stacks, and breathed in their aura. She felt at home again.

That night, she told Michael her plan, and he was happy that she felt able to juggle motherhood with student life. As for him, he had put his thirty-five years of campus life behind him and never looked back.

"Michael, just when I think it's impossible to love you more, I find new ways to love you. You make me a complete person—I can't imagine life without you."

A little later that evening, Francie and Michael were watching TV in the den after the children were asleep upstairs. Despite being middle-aged, they behaved like newlyweds when it came to lovemaking. Michael never needed much encouragement, and the remark Francie had made earlier egged him on to giving her that special look. She was struck with an emotion so powerful that it overtook her. *There is the man I adore who saved me from my grief and gave me a reason to love again.* She stood and walked to his chair, straddled him, burying her face between his neck and his shoulder. His response was to stand so she could wrap her legs around his waist. He kicked the door shut and they moved to the floor and slowly made love. He was careful to put the brunt of his weight on his hands and arms so he didn't hurt her. When they were finished, they lay panting side by side for a few moments until she rolled on top of him, kissing him inch by inch in a straight line from his lips down to where his body ended. He responded stronger than ever, finally drawing her up the length of his body to make love again.

When it was over, she cuddled against him until he blurted out, "Where did you learn that?"

"Professor, you know I read a lot of romance novels, and you know I'm an A student, so draw your own conclusions."

"Start practicing what it will take to earn an A-plus," was his response.

Chapter 30

Dear Reader,

You may be wondering what happened to Pat. I didn't forget him—I was just waiting for him to get out of his slump and begin his life anew. Read on….

After three years of feeling lost, Pat pulled himself together and started to live again. He had always been a highly respected barrister and now had become a judge. This position brought prestige, but more importantly for Pat, it involved a new set of challenges and surroundings different from the routine he had since he left Oxford.

He and Moira divorced, and she remarried. When she and Pat had first separated, she could not help feeling resentment for him, and her feelings eventually turned to bitterness. Now that she had a new life, she was more tolerant, and their relationship improved. The twins, Flip and Josh, suffered when their parents first separated, but now they seemed to fall into a rhythm that was healthy. The courts mandated their time with the boys, but since Moira and Pat wanted what was best for Josh and Flip, they had relaxed the mandate and tailored their visits to fit the occasion.

After Pat's appointment to the bench, he took the boys to the courthouse to show them his chambers. Once inside, he put on his black robe and white wig. The boys thought he looked *really cool* and took pictures of him with the instamatic cameras he had bought for them earlier that day.

He showed them the back passage to his courtroom and took them into the empty room. "Just before I walk in, the Clerk of the Court, says, 'All rise,' and everyone has to stand for the judge to enter. I open this door, go to my desk and pound my gavel to show that court is in session. Here's the high desk where I sit during the trial, and here is the gavel I use to quiet the courtroom, or when the trial is over."

Of course, they wanted to try the gavel, and they took turns saying, "Order in the court," and feeling very special.

Pat and the boys liked to spend time together, and, like so many divorced fathers, Pat always tried to find a fun experience. He took them to do the things he had enjoyed as a boy—the movies with popcorn, the circus with popcorn, the ice skating rink with popcorn, or the sporting goods stores (no popcorn, but usually a random purchase). He knew that in the not too distant future, they would rather be with their friends.

For the past few years, a popular social magazine listed Pat among the *Ten Most Desirable Bachelors* in London. He was still very handsome and vigorous, but the gleam in his eye had faded. He had dated a long list of women of all ages from middle twenties to middle forties. None of the more mature ones could compare to Francie, nor could any of the younger ones hold a candle to his daughter, Kate. He had had it with social life, but his friends were determined to keep him in the game. He didn't want to live the rest of his life alone, but he just couldn't get up the energy to keep looking for the right woman.

After a few months, the lassitude he experienced finally lifted, and he thought that he would like to do some traveling. The last vacation he had taken was more than ten years prior when he and Moira went to Spain.

He asked his friends for recommendations—and the consensus was Italy, definitely Italy—anywhere in Italy. He was not a fan of sightseeing, and what he really preferred would be an active trip, maybe hiking or biking from place to place, seeing outstanding history along the way. He researched a couple of tour agencies and found one that offered exactly what he wanted. The particular hiking trip he chose was fairly demanding and included seven days of trekking some of Abruzzo's highest mountains. The itinerary showed roughly four hours each morning of hiking mountain trails, usually on uphill climbs, followed by a two-hour break for a typical

Italian lunch and siesta. The afternoon activities varied every day, but most included a descent passing through villages and towns, each with its own personality and historic relics. Each day's trek ended in late afternoon at a villa or small hotel. Then a typical country Italian dinner—abundant fresh food and lots of vino. Most of the accommodations were a tad above rustic Italian with stone cottages, tile bathrooms, iron bed stands, and shuttered windows with million dollar views overlooking the countryside.

A van would transport their suitcases from inn to inn every day, so that after a day of hiking, their suitcases were waiting for them in their individual rooms. As rugged trips go, this one was very civilized but required all the participants to be in good physical shape.

The first day of the trip began at the Fiumicino Airport in Rome where their tour leader, Giulia (pronounced *Julia*), welcomed them all and introduced the group members to one another. There were a few attempts at conversation, but for the most part, everyone was happy to nap on the long drive to the medieval mountain village of Santo Stefano di Sessanio. The members of the group stayed in *albergo diffiso*—different cottage rooms scattered all over the village. There was no activity plan for that day until dinnertime, so they were free to explore the town, sleep off jet lag, or get to know each other. At seven that evening, they were to meet for cocktails and dinner at a small restaurant in the village.

Pat chose the nap option.

That evening, when they entered the restaurant, Giulia was seated at a small electric keyboard playing the popular tunes of Carole King. She was an accomplished pianist and singer, talents that came to her naturally from her musical parents. She played for her own pleasure and the pleasure of entertaining her guests.

Besides Pat and their guide, there were eight other people on the trip between the ages of late twenties to early fifties. The cast of characters included a married couple from the Netherlands (interesting, but talked too much); a married couple from the U.S. (very funny and willing to try anything); two female friends in their thirties from Wales (one divorced, one never married—both attractive and both looking for men); a Polish man in his forties traveling without his wife (quiet at first, but interesting once he warmed up); and a fifty-year-old single man from Canada (handsome, gay). The two married couples drifted to each other and the two single women and three single men grouped together. The middle-aged Polish man got the ball rolling by relaxing everyone with his observations of the Italians he had seen—men walking with hands folded behind their back talking with other men; women in black, walking and talking with other women in black; and young couples fondling each other's backsides. And then there was Pat, who spent most of the time looking at his watch and wondering why he was there.

Talk over dinner was tentative at first, but by dessert, the group became congenial. Pat forced himself to participate—the wine helped. However, early to bed was *de rigueur* so that they could be up and ready by seven thirty for breakfast and the start of the first walk—twelve miles up and down high hills and valleys.

Pat's room was pleasant, and he fell asleep to the sound of goats bleating in the distance.

The next morning, after a twenty-five-minute drive through a maze of narrow alleys, steps and tunnels, the troop began their hike from the village of Castel del Monte. From there, they set off for an easy two hour walk through grasslands and plains surrounded by some of the highest peaks of the Apennines. Around noon, Giulia led them down a narrow trail leading to a meadow where a picnic lunch awaited them. A long portable table, covered with a red and white checkered tablecloth had been set up by the tour company with a scrumptious meal—three kinds of sausage, a large smoked ham, olives, artichokes, sliced fennel, tomatoes, cucumbers, freshly baked rolls and ciabatta, local olive oil and five kinds of cheeses. Sliced melon, grapes, bottled water and the local wine, *Trebbiano d'Abruzzo*, were in abundance. The group had two hours to enjoy their repast and to rest, read, or enjoy the scenery.

Teddy took one look at the picnic table, and with his Polish accent, said, "When we get to the highest bluff, you can throw me off, because I've already been to heaven."

Eventually they arrived in Campo Imperatore and walked the final section in ninety minutes, circling back to Santo Stefano de Sessanio for one more night.

"This was our easiest day," Guilia told them. "We walked twelve miles. Tomorrow we walk about the same distance, but mostly uphill, to Sulmona. Dinner tonight will be a regional specialty of Abruzzo, *sagne e fagioli* (bean and noodle soup), and *Arrosticini*, (skewered lamb), with roasted potatoes and local vegetables. Dessert will be *pizzelle* served with cappuccino.

"Yum-yums" in various forms from all.

Olivia, one of the two single women with the group, said, "I hope I sleep better tonight. Those damn crying babies kept me up most of last night."

Guilia laughed. "In Italy, babies have no reason to cry. That crying noise was the sound of goats bleating on the surrounding farms."

The talk at dinner came much easier than the night before. The main topic was their occupations, and the group learned that Curt, the handsome gay man from Canada was a hedge fund manager. One of the girls, Vicky, was a computer programmer, and the other, Olivia, was a tile designer. They were neighbors in Cardiff, Wales.

Pat told them the story about the first time he ordered *Welsh rabbit*, and expected a cooked rabbit, not bread and melted cheese. Everyone laughed. Olivia said, "You're not the first one to make that mistake." The married couple from suburban New York—she a stay-at-home mom and he a partner in a New York law firm—were the fun couple. The other married couple owned a tulip distribution business in Amsterdam, specializing in purple tulips—they were the ones who talked too much. Teddy, the Polish man, was a teacher and soccer coach. That left Pat, the judge, and, Giulia, the group leader, who explained that before she led trips in Italy, she was a representative for Gucci designer sneakers. Everyone immediately looked under the table to see her shoes. "Danner Tramline boots—made in America," she said. "I save my Guccis for special occasions."

Most everyone went to sleep early, and Pat and Giulia were the last to leave. "Can I treat you to a glass of *Aurum*?" he asked.

"Sure, I'd love one. Let's take it outside where we can enjoy the cool air." They sipped slowly, the only way the super-sweet drink could be enjoyed. Without meaning to, they played the flirting game. The more he looked at her, the more attractive she was to him. Her tan skin brought out the whiteness of her teeth and her large, black eyes. She couldn't ignore his strikingly blue eyes, but his grin was one of the sexiest she had seen—a real accomplishment for a non-Italian.

"Would you tell me something about yourself so I can picture your real life? Or does everybody give you that line?" he asked.

"Some do, but to borrow a word from you Brits, most of them are *jerks.* Not you, though, I can tell by the expression in your eyes that you're not one of them. So, before I tell you about myself, how about telling me about the sadness in your eyes?"

"I hope you have plenty of time," he said, "because my story is quite long. We may actually finish our drinks before I'm done."

He told her the whole story, the one he had been carrying inside of him for almost thirty years. She was easy to talk to, and he spoke without hesitation about his recent divorce, his twin sons, the appearance of his older daughter after twenty-five years, and of Francie, his first love. Giulia took it all in.

When he was finished, she didn't speak for quite some time. She was deep in thought but finally sought out his eyes to look into. "I understand. I know what it's like to lose the love of your life. I could never talk about my past, but tonight, with you I think I can."

"I'm forty-three, and I live alone. No one has been able to fill the loneliness that descended on me twenty years ago when my husband died. I see others who have gone through similar experiences, but they all have made new lives for themselves. Somehow, I can't. Just when I think I have recovered, he comes back to my thoughts again.

"Gino and I fell in love when we were in college in Milano. Just like you and Francie, we met, and that was it—we knew right away that we would be together always. We spent our days and nights together, and when we graduated, we were married in Padua, my hometown. We settled in Verona, where Gino bought a travel business from someone who was moving out of the area. Together, we worked to expand by offering walking and biking trips in the area, similar to this one. We felt that there was a growing market for people who wanted active vacations. He ran the core business while I went out and scouted the area to design trips of varying lengths with quality places to stay along the way. I accumulated ten different trips, and everything was in place to introduce our idea to the public."

She paused, looked down at her hands and composed herself. "We went out to dinner to celebrate, then came home to cap off the night with lovemaking when I discovered a lump on his neck. The next day his doctor sent him to a specialist, and from that day, our life started to unravel. The doctor diagnosed a rare, fast-growing cancer. We went to Rome for more tests that led to immediate surgery. He died on the operating table. He was gone so fast I never had a chance to say goodbye. I called his family and could barely get the words out. I didn't know what to do or where to go. The hospital recommended a rooming house across the street from for me to spend the night. I barely dragged myself there. I was in a stupor all night."

Pat reached over, took the drink from her hand and put it on the table. Then he took both her hands in his and said," Please don't continue if this is too difficult for you," gently adding, "Your grief must be overwhelming."

"Actually, I'd like to continue so I can get it all out."

He nodded. "I'd be honored."

"The morning after Gino died, his father arrived, and we decided to fly Gino's body back to Milano for burial in a grave close to his grandparents' memorial. The entire week is a blur in my mind. I went back to my parents' home in Padua. They helped me survive the period when my thoughts and actions were paralyzed. I remained in a half alive state for three months. My music was a great help to me. I sat at the piano for hours. As I played, every detail I could remember of Gino's and my life together returned to me. Words and music flowed from me without any consciousness on my part, and finally I started to return to life somewhat cleansed and ready to live again.

"I moved back to our apartment in Verona. I followed Gino's and my plans to get the business going, although I scaled it back and eliminated the bicycle trips and developed the walking trips. It's now a successful business with a staff of sixteen guides leading trips all over northern and central Italy. We sell a variety of tours, and I have led all of them at least once. I'm constantly monitoring the accommodations and changing them if they don't meet our standards. One of the favorite things I do is interview new guides." Here she laughed. "They are almost all young, handsome or pretty, and enthusiastic—they keep me young. This is a happy business, dealing with people from all over the world on vacation and full of life. Some of our clients have returned three or four times. I consider many of them my good friends. Some even keep me posted about their important events, new babies, new marriages, new successes. They very seldom tell me the bad stuff, and that's fine with me."

She looked at Pat and he nodded, thinking to himself, *I know what you mean. I have walked around in that same daze, relying on my friends and family to keep me going.*

"Because the business is so successful, I am self-supporting. I love meeting new people, and I have an active social life, but at the end of the day, I am still lonely and only half alive. Tonight is the first time in years that I feel good about being able to end the day on a happy note."

Pat, touched by all she told just him, reached for her and they hugged as naturally as if they had known each other forever. They kissed, and both felt the magic.

"Let's think about this before it goes any further," Giulia said. "Sometimes when people are on vacation, everything looks better than it really is—like a shipboard romance. I don't think I could endure that."

They agreed not wanting to rush into anything but both feeling that something was happening to them. They went to their separate rooms with smiles in their hearts and the gleam back in Pat's eyes.

The next day was the third day of the trip. Pat and Giulia tried to look natural, but every now and then, they made eye contact that was decidedly intimate. The demands of the day's trip left no time for dallying. The walk was a long climb to a mountaintop castle, then a descent to a tiny town for a lunch. The chef welcomed them with his special ravioli made with fresh ricotta and fried sage, and, as always, more wine, this time a *Montepulciano*. The discussion over lunch was world politics, and by the second glass of wine, the whole group was ready to revolt against their country's leader.

The afternoon climb covered three miles skirting centuries-old ruins and a visiting the Oratorio of San Pellegrino to see thirteenth-century frescoes. At one point, he and Giulia walked side by side. The sun shone through the trees making a pattern of striped yellow sunbeams across both of them. In his heart, Pat knew that this was a message from Francie to tell him that Giulia was the one he had been waiting for. Then a van took them to the medieval town of Sulmona and their hotel, where they were to spend two nights.

During dinner, just about everyone took out their cameras and took pictures of the food and the company. One camera could have done the job, since they were all in the same place taking the same photos, but that would have been too easy. Later, the group broke off into small bunches and explored the village and environs to enjoy the *forte e gentile* (strong and gentle) feeling that the people and surroundings of Abruzzo are known for. Giulia signaled to Pat with a nod toward a *gelateria*, and the two of them set off in that direction. They bought small cones and sat at an outside table for two to enjoy their dessert. Giulia laughed from embarrassment when she realized that every lick of their ice cream was suggestive of something sexual and eventually, she had to turn her back to Pat so they could finish their cones in innocence. They took a short walk on a dark path in the woods. Pat couldn't stop looking at her—her expressions were delicious—the way her eyes flashed when she was excited, the way she pulled in her bottom lip when was concentrating, the way her face lit up when she was impressed. He told her that she fascinated him, and the melody in her voice when she spoke her Italian accented English was irresistible. He thought, *Everything she says sounds like a love song.*

She told him that he had the most appealing grin she had ever seen. She thought, *I know that grin—it's the smile of love.*

"That's it?" he said. "What about my blue eyes and my black curly hair? All you can say is I have a nice grin! What about my biceps?"

"Sorry, that's it," she said. "Black curly hair and big biceps are common in Italy, where men are men. And I've seen lots of gorgeous, blue eyes on Swedish men who are on my trips. But that grin—that's one of a kind."

So, he grinned, swung her around, kissed her and told her that if he was good enough for her, she was okay for him, too, even with her skinny legs.

She told him she needed another night before they got too close.

He said, "Just because I said you had skinny legs, you're going to punish me?"

"One more night, then maybe I'll reconsider," she replied. "And anyway, all Italian girls have skinny legs—in case you didn't know, it's very desirable."

The next day at breakfast, he made sure he grinned at her when he tapped his watch and said, "Twelve more hours!"

The day flew by. Everyone seemed to be energized, feeling their youth restored. The Italian adventure seemed to bring out the best. For their second night in Sulmona, the hotel owner's son lit a fire in the barbeque pit and served grilled trout caught that afternoon in a mountain stream. While the fish were grilling, waiters passed around bowls of *confetti*, the town's famous sugared almonds. After dinner Giulia gave Pat a wink and a nod to the door, prompting him to recommend the outstanding *gelateria* down the road to the others. While they all headed in that direction, Pat and Giulia sneaked into her room.

"Just to get in the mood, and since we're in the town where Ovid was born, I have a surprise in my secret bag." He took two items out of the bag—a loaf of bread and a bottle of wine and looked at her, saying, "a glass of wine, a loaf of bread, and thou…."

"That is so sweet," she said. "In fact, because it was so sweet, I will overlook the fact that Omar Khayyam, not Ovid, wrote those words. However, Ovid wrote *Ars Amatoria—The Art of Love*. What do you say about that?"

"Sounds good to me—that's even more my style!"

Their night together was a revelation to both of them. They didn't just have sex, they *made love* with a passion and depth that neither had had in years.

The next morning, Pat said "I never knew I could experience what I lost when Francie went away. Last night, I did."

And Giulia responded, tears streaming down her face. "I am the luckiest woman alive. This may sound crazy, because we hardly know each other, but I want to be with you always. The practical side of me says, *Wait!* It's too soon to feel that way, but I can't help feeling the way I do. I don't want to miss a minute."

"I feel the same way, but if I approach this with the maturity of a father of three, I say, "Let's at least wait a while to consider—I suggest three days is long enough, and if we still feel the same at the end of this trip, let's rush like hell!"

Chapter 31

Dear Reader,

I am not going to waste your time and mine by describing what happened between the time they "rushed like hell" and the time they were married, so suffice to say everything happened in superlatives: most romantic, most wonderful, happiest, funniest, etc. London became their home, and Giulia ran her business from there. She kept her small place in Verona to use whenever she needed an Italian "fix."

Back to the newlyweds later—now it's Francie's turn again. Read on....

When Francie began her advanced studies in philosophy, she reread the words of her former muse, Heraclitus, the Greek philosopher who espoused that the vicissitudes of the path of life are one and the same, that good or bad are built upon the other. At this point in her life, she considered his words to be ominous, an omen of bad things to come. She had been on an upward curve for decades—did this mean that she was due for a fall?

She concluded that the basis of life's philosophies should evolve not just on one premise, but many. Therefore, she began an in-depth study of Socrates, who believed that happiness was desirable and obtainable by those who had rational control over parts of their soul. At the time of Socrates, between three and four hundred years before Christ, the Greeks, like most ancients, had a pessimistic view of human existence. They felt that happiness came solely to those favored by the gods. To create one's own happiness was a punishable offense in Greece. But Socrates thought that happiness was part of the human condition, and that if one's soul was in harmony with truth, justice and goodness, one could obtain happiness.

Francie could relate very well to Socrates' observations, because she knew what it was to be in a situation that seemed hopeless. Her nature was to be happy, and she never gave up the idea that she could succeed in making her way if she continued to feed her soul with good thoughts and good values.

She enjoyed her studies, could not get enough of the teachings of the thinkers who freed the minds of the populace to think on their own. She had a way of gleaning the essence of her studies and the ability to write concise but inclusive theses. Her professors looked forward to their meetings with her as much as she liked meeting with them.

She was home much of the time—her studies came second to her children and husband—and her two growing youngsters continued to amaze her. Watching them was like unlocking the secrets of progress of the human condition. It fascinated her to see the first time they turned over, smiled, sat up, crawled, babbled, and then greatest miracle of all—speaking and understanding.

One day little Audrey came to Francie with a "boo-boo." It was a splinter that she must have picked up at the playground that morning. Francie kissed it and went for a needle to remove it. She was gentle with Audrey. She said, "This is what my Mum used to do when I had a splinter," and a feeling of homesickness swept over her.

Audrey asked, "Who is Mum?"

"She's my mother—I call her 'Mum.' She lives far away."

That was enough to satisfy Audrey, so Francie proceeded to try to remove the splinter. She lit a match and held the needle over it until it glowed red.

"Why did you do that?" Audrey wanted to know.

"The hot fire kills any germs that are on the needle so that I can use it on your finger."

"Did Mum teach you that?"

"Yes, she did, she was a very good teacher."

"Will I meet her some day?"

"Maybe, but let's get on with taking out the splinter."

Very gently, Francie rubbed the point of the needle around the splinter and worked it out through the place it had entered.

"There it is," she said. "Now that won't bother you anymore. Let's clean your finger with some soap and water and give you a Band-Aid."

"I'm glad that you don't live far away, Mommy," she said. "Then I'd be very sad."

"Don't worry, Aud, I'll always be here for you."

Audrey reached up and hugged her mother. It was all Francie could do to hold back her tears.

When he wasn't in Washington, Michael was home much of the day. At least twice a week, he took the children to the park or playground for an hour or two. He was usually the only father there and never took offense when someone said how wonderful it was that he spent so much time with his grandchildren. He didn't deceive himself—he was closing in on sixty—and he knew he looked it. He was still in excellent shape, so it was easy for him to keep after Tim and Audrey when they ran in opposite directions, from sandbox to swings.

Francie continued to see some of the other women from her mothers' group, who, like Francie, had growing families. As she became more and more Americanized, she enjoyed being silly with her friends. She laughed with them when they told stories of their days at summer camp, sneaking from their bunks at night to meet the boys. Some of them talked about summers in Atlantic City or Ocean City.

One hot summer morning they piled into two cars with all their kids and drove to Atlantic City. When the car crossed the causeway over the bay, Francie smelled the sea air, and she understood why they loved it. The kids played in the calm ocean while the mothers sunbathed on the famous soft white sand or swam in the surf, diving under the waves. The salty Atlantic Ocean exhilarated her. At lunchtime they surrounded a hot dog joint on the boardwalk, and her friends recommend that she get a doggie with the works. The combination of hot sun, salty air and a hot dog with the works made for the best hot dog she'd ever eaten. "I'll have another," she told the vendor, and she gobbled it down only stopping to say "Mmm." She remembered the delicious french fries sold on the boardwalk and sought out a stand to treat all of the others to some hot, crisp fries.

She told her friends what a nerd she had been in Ireland, spending her summers in libraries or studying, far from the lazy days on the beach that the girls had. "The Atlantic Ocean off Ireland is much colder than it is in New Jersey," she said. "Even ankle-deep, it's too cold to wade in for more than a minute. I can't believe that this is the same ocean. In New Jersey, the ocean feels like a warm bath."

Driving home with the group that day, she realized how much she enjoyed having girlfriends. They were fated to stay together until all their kids were grown. Francie and Sue became lifelong friends.

That night she couldn't wait to tell Michael about her day. She raved about it, as if she were the first one ever to discover the beach in Atlantic City. "Michael, the water is so warm and the salty makes you buoyant, even if you never could float before."

He indulged her, not telling her that almost everyone in Philly had been to the Jersey shore from the time they were kids, and to them it was old hat.

The next day when she awoke, she was red as a firetruck, making that trip to Atlantic City the first and last one of the summer.

PART V

Chapter 32

Just before she was forty-five, Francie started to feel that her youth was fading fast when an unforeseen turn of events presented itself. Her advisor at Bryn Mawr retired and was replaced by a youngish man. When she entered his office, her breath caught in her throat—he had the same boyish looks and black curly hair as Pat.

He smiled when he saw her and offered his hand. "I'm Kevin Patterson."

Reflexively, she offered him her hand and remained spellbound by his presence. He continued by asking her if he should call her Francie or Mrs. Hanson.

She found her voice and said with her usual smile, "Francie would be fine."

"Please call me Kevin," he said, returning the smile. "I have a feeling we won't have any problem relating. I just hope I'm up to the challenge of working with you after the raves I've heard from your former advisor."

The relating will be easy, she thought. *Controlling it will be the hard part!*

She looked at his degrees posted on the wall behind him. "Princeton, Harvard, Yale—your academic background is extraordinary, Dr. Patterson. I have no doubt that the challenge will be mine, not yours, but thank you anyway." She made a promise to herself not to be taken in by his compliment—and his looks.

"Kevin," he said to remind her. "Don't be shy."

He took a seat at his desk and beckoned her to sit opposite him. Then he went over his opinions about her work so far and assigned some new thoughts for her to ponder. He listed a few particular observations of three little-known German philosophers and asked her to come back in a week or so after she had a chance to digest their theories.

"The German philosophers are fairly new to me, and I haven't read anything by the three you suggest. I look forward to working on it." She felt a need to impress him and planned to be thorough with her report. *Oh, God, at this stage in my life, why am I trying to impress him?* She hadn't realized that she'd missed the company of a younger man.

When it was time for her to leave, they made eye contact and he told her he was looking forward to their next appointment. She held his gaze as long as she dared and replied that she was, too.

That night when she had trouble falling asleep, she knew she was hooked.

They had another meeting two weeks after the first, and the same magnetism was apparent. A week later, he proposed a lunch meeting at a small Italian restaurant in Bryn Mawr. Ignoring her good judgment, she accepted. She wasn't sure what she was hoping. For almost a month now, he was in her head most of the time. The day of their lunch date, she put on her sexiest lace underwear, sprayed her body with cologne and dressed in a light green (her color!) cashmere turtleneck sweater and a pair of well-fitting tan wool slacks. She added small gold and pearl earrings to brighten her face.

She knew exactly what she was doing.

He was seated at a small table in the back corner of the restaurant when she arrived. His choice of location did not escape her. Their conversation flowed easily, nothing deep, no secrets revealed. She told him that the cold, wet weather today reminded her of Ireland, that the one thing she missed the most was the vibrantly green grass of the Isle's spring and summer. The U.S. couldn't compete on that front, but for the most part, life in this country was superior in many ways—the choices, the opportunities, the influence of so many ethnicities on the culture.

He spoke of his grandparents' farm in Minnesota—helping with the harvesting of peas, corn and potatoes, swinging on a wooden plank from an oak tree, swimming in freezing lakes and sipping hot chocolate on cold nights. When they looked at each other, she feigned naivete, but hoped he would suggest something more than small talk, maybe a hint about going someplace more private. When he didn't, she felt disappointed, and more than a little relived.

She told him she enjoyed the lunch and the company, thanked him and rose to leave.

"It was my pleasure, Francie," he said. "Maybe we can do it again."

"Maybe," she said. "But next week, I'll see you in your office. Where it's all business."

She wanted him to know that she was in the game, but the next move was his. She grinned at him and made her way out, feeling his eyes on her.

That night she wrote in her journal, *Is it possible that I am the typical older woman trying to hold onto my youth? Or dreamy graduate student looking for a relationship with my advisor like the ones Michael told me about? Or am I the real thing? I hope I'm a special one to Kevin, but I have my doubts. Thank goodness he didn't let this become more than it should be—a flirt between two people who like each other.*

A few days later, her friends from the mothers' group met for dinner—girls' night out. They started with one bottle of wine and light conversation. When their dinner arrived, they ordered another bottle, and the conversation opened up. Francie asked them if they flirted with other men.

Amy said, "Of course I do. It's perfectly innocent. I have a 'work husband.' We flirt all the time. We both know it won't lead to anything, but it's fun and we look forward to seeing each other. Of course, our spouses don't know, so I'm holding you to utter secrecy."

Meg said, "I don't exactly have one, but I have one in mind, also just for fun."

Sue chimed in with, "I work in an all women physician's office, so, no, I don't have a work husband or a work wife, but I have all your husbands to flirt with. Why do you ask, Francie?"

"I have to tell somebody, or I'll burst, so here's another confidential confession," she said. "I've been flirting with my PhD advisor, and it's getting a little scary. I'd love it if you'd advise me to break it off, but you all offer nothing but encouragement."

"Even philosophers can't solve their own problems, Francie. Just keep it innocent," offered Amy.

All eyes turned to Lisa.

"Well, here goes," she said, and took a big gulp of wine. "You are all out in the world, and I chose to be a stay-at-home mom, so my choices are limited. I had no thoughts of looking for a thrill. So, dumb me got blindsided. I did a stupid thing—I had an affair with the carpenter who was redoing our basement. He was in my house every day for months, and we got into the routine of having coffee together, and from there, our relationship grew insane. There was something about his work shoes and the smell of his T-shirt that turned me on. I have no excuse except boredom, I guess—and the work shoes. Jeff came home early one day and found us, so that was the end of the carpenter. Jeff and I are still together, but our marriage is on the verge of collapse." She was sipping wine and crying. "Now you know why our basement is still only half done after all this time," she added with a sad laugh.

They offered their sympathies and sentiments to Lisa, then agreed all around with the adage, "If you play with fire, you may get burned," and ordered a third bottle of wine and ice cream with chocolate sauce.

That did it for Francie. She would find a way to get Kevin out of her head and her life. She had too much at stake to play games.

She was all business at their next student-adviser session, and she skipped the next one altogether. Kevin looked puzzled. But she detected a relief in him as well.

Chapter 33

When life interferes with living, one has to set priorities. Francie's thoughts were assailing her from multiple directions. She wanted to be a good wife, a good mother, a good daughter-in-law. She wanted to have a social life with her mothers' group and evenings with Michael and their friends. She wanted to connect with her biological father and her new family. She wanted to reconnect with her mother and Da. She wanted to see Kate and Sean. She wanted to be with her brothers and their families. She wanted to keep up with her studies at Bryn Mawr, and she wanted to continue to be on the board of Shea's Soup Company. She wanted to find the time to read a book for pleasure. Most of all, she wanted to alleviate the guilt she felt for flirting with Kevin.

That night at dinner, she broke down in tears and couldn't stop crying. She left the table, got into bed and pulled the covers over her head. When Timmy and Audrey saw their mother cry, they both started to cry. Michael didn't know what to do, so he called his mother.

When his parents arrived, Michael had calmed the children and was reading *The Cat in the Hat* to them. His parents took over the reading detail, and Michael went upstairs to see why Francie was so upset.

He lay down next to her and poked his head under the covers. "What's the matter, Francie? Does something hurt?"

"Yes, my brain hurts! Lately I don't know who I am. I need time to be myself again, whatever that is. I need to have a day, a week, a month with no obligations, no choices, no guilt. Is it wrong to want that?"

"Francie, darling, it's not wrong. I want what is best for you, and right now I think what's best for you is sleep—with no guilt. Whether you realized it or not, you've been on an emotional roller coaster for the past few weeks. Your brain is rebelling and needs a rest. We can talk in the morning, but just remember—there's nothing wrong that can't be fixed." He kissed her on her forehead, pulled the covers back over her head and tiptoed out.

The next morning, Francie felt much better, but she still wasn't her usual ebullient self. Little things annoyed her. Michael was going to Washington that day, and when he hugged her, she felt closed in, pushing him away after a few seconds. Everything seemed exaggerated—she knew something was wrong. After breakfast, she called her in-laws to thank them for helping last night when she was in a state of "who knows what."

Her mother-in-law asked if they could have lunch together that day. She said they needed a woman-to-woman talk.

They went to the Wayne Hotel, a quiet, suburban inn with a small dining room. After they ordered, she told her mother-in-law that she was worried about the way she felt. "Mother, could I be having a nervous breakdown?"

"Francie, I'll tell you what I think, but first let me ask you two key questions. One—have you been sleeping okay?"

"I used to, but actually no. For the past two weeks, I've been tossing and turning, visiting the bathroom two or three times each night, checking the thermostat to see if the heat's set up too high, and waking up exhausted."

"Question two—have you been perspiring?"

"Yes, it's been awful. Every once in a while, I have to go outside just to feel the cold air and get away from the heated house. At night, I kick off the covers because I'm too hot, then a few minutes later, I'm freezing."

"Francie, dear, what's wrong with you is natural. Every woman goes through it, some easily and some with difficulty. Francie, you're starting menopause—change of life."

"Oh my God! You mean I'm old enough for that? It never occurred to me."

"It's different for everyone, usually around fifty, though some start earlier. You were always ahead of everyone else your age, and you are in this too. I think you should make an appointment with your gynecologist to see what she has to say. You have more options than you think. I know, for me, I couldn't stand to be close to anyone—I felt claustrophobic. My doctor gave me hormones, and I felt better within a week. By the time a year was done, I was off the hormones and back to my old self, and without the bother of monthly periods."

"That's exactly the way I feel, like something has taken over my body," Francie said, unaware that she was fanning herself with her menu. She looked across the table and they both stated to laugh.

She followed her mother-in-law's advice and saw her gynecologist, who told her that at this time of life hormones are unsettled, and it's tempting to make an irrational decision. She said to Francie, "Some women actually fall into the trap of having an affair and often end up with a broken marriage when they need their husbands the most."

Francie felt a chill run through her body when she thought of her narrow escape. Her only consolation was learning that her feelings were normal; she could have kissed the doctor for telling her. Now she could put her guilt to rest and blame the whole flirty experience on menopause.

She called her mother-in-law to thank her for the advice.

"That's what mothers are for, Francie."

"I'm so glad I have you," Francie said earnestly.

"And I'm so glad I have you, too. Before you, I had no one to give advice to!"

The pills her doctor prescribed started to kick in after a week and life returned to normal. The episode made her realize that now was the time to think about changing some things. She had to prioritize her time. She decided not to pursue a PhD; she was perfectly satisfied with a master's, and she could earn that without the help of an advisor So, goodbye, Kevin.

Some of her friends played tennis regularly, and since she was finished having babies and had cut back on schoolwork, she decided to go back to her favorite pastime. Her friends' steady games had been going on for years, and they had always called her when they needed a sub. She enjoyed subbing, but she wanted to have a more regular schedule of games. Just as she did at Penn, she visited a neighborhood racquet club and asked about finding partners and opponents for singles and doubles. The pro pointed to a list of people needing partners and she signed up, listing her estimated ability. A day later, she started getting calls, and once the days and times were agreed upon, she was back in the game. She signed up to play twice a week. All the people she met were congenial, and just as she discovered on the courts of Penn, a social life evolved from the players, usually lunch with the girls. Her natural abilities and expertise returned quickly. She had forgotten how much fun it was.

Michael grew up playing on grass courts at an old established local club, the one his parents still belonged to, and he had been quite a good player at one time. The club was convenient to their home in Haverford, so the following summer, Michael and Francie became members. He hit with the pro a few times, and his skills quickly came back. He and Francie played a smooth game of mixed doubles and were much in demand. Michael hit a strong, deep ball, and Francie's specialty was hitting the shot at net to finish off the point for a winner.

Chapter 34

Even with taking time off to play tennis, Francie progressed quickly toward her master's. She would have her degree by spring, when her second year of study was finished. "I'll miss Bryn Mawr," she told Michael. "The campus is so small that everyone seems to know each other. My professors treat me as one of their peers. I guess my background measured up to their expectations. That and the fact that I'm older than some of them."

She would officially receive her master's at graduation in May. The ceremony and bestowal of her degree were just a formality. Nonetheless, Michael and his parents, as well as the two children, were on hand to celebrate. The kids surprised Francie by wearing miniature mortarboard caps that Michael's parents had made. When degrees in philosophy were handed out, all the professors in the department shook hands with the awardees. Francie and Kevin shook hands awkwardly, but when he leaned to her ear and whispered, "I'm engaged!" she smiled broadly, happy for him, happy for herself.

Now that she had more leisure, she felt it was time to start passing on the gifts she had been lucky enough to receive. She turned her attention to helping others in the way she knew best. The Hanson family had always been generous donors to the University of Pennsylvania, and Francie suggested to Michael that they establish "The Hanson Family Foundation" to provide assistance to foreign students. This project was a very personal one for Francie, as she knew firsthand how important a tuition free award was to a struggling foreigner. She would assume the position of running the foundation, hiring an assistant, reading the applicants' dossiers and serving on the selection committee.

Michael asked her if she was sure she wanted to add one more thing to her list of commitments. "Do you realize how much time it takes to run a foundation? And how much money?"

"Michael, we have so much more than we need. We and our children and grandchildren will always be taken care of. I think your parents would be honored to have a foundation in perpetuity named for them and their ancestors. I am more than willing to put the work into getting it going. Let's invite Mother and Dad over to the house for dinner, and we can discuss it together."

"Good deal," he said. "Be sure to make it early, you know they eat at four thirty."

She called them and arranged to pick them up the next day at three thirty, just before the children got home from pre-school, but early enough for some Grammy and Papa time before dinner.

The kids loved to play the card game, *War*, and their grandparents were always ready for a few rounds with them. Audrey and Timmy thought they were great players because they always won against Grammy and Papa. And Grammy always had a wrapped candy in her handbag for the winners.

After dinner, the children went upstairs to play until bedtime. It was time for adult talk without distractions from the little ones.

The senior Hansons listened to Francie's proposal, and without hesitation said they would be honored and delighted to take part in the foundation.

Her mother-in-law said, "Francie, if not for the funding you received as an undergraduate, we might not have had you as our daughter. I think Dad would agree that we'd love to pay back the school for giving us our happy family."

Within a week, Francie had laid the groundwork for starting a foundation. For years, she had used her marketing skills at Shea's, and now she applied them to a non-profit. She was in heaven.

During the coming year, many things changed in their lives. The health of Michael's parents had started to fail dramatically. They began to realize that age was taking its toll on them, and they thought it best to stop their summer travels to *Tip Top* and slow down. A year later, Michael's father quietly slipped away, succumbing to heart failure. After a lifetime of being together, Michael's mother joined her husband in death a few months later. Francie, Michael, and the children had been with them for a portion of every day through their failing health and passing. They were devastated. For Francie, Michael's parents had taken the place of the mother and father she lost when she was seventeen. She loved them unconditionally. For Michael, an only child, his parents had been his advisors, companions, sounding boards, and friends. They had seen him through his awful tragedy and helped make him the man he became. For the children, Papa and Grammy were their magical family who were always there to read to them, take them on outings, help them with their schoolwork, and love them. Papa died when Timmy was six. He put his favorite teddy bear—the one he used to sleep with when he was afraid of the dark—into the coffin to keep his grandfather company. A few months later when Grammy died, Audrey put her favorite book, *A Child's Garden of Verses*, into the coffin so that her grandmother could read to the children she met in heaven. Audrey was not yet five, but she had taught herself how to read before she was four. She read from the book almost every day. Her favorite poem was "The Swing," by Robert Louis Stevenson. Audrey told her mother that she imagined her Grammy in heaven, "'Up in the air…and looking down…on the garden green and the roof so brown,' just like the poem says."

Francie hugged her hard, in wonder at her little girl's sensitivity and maturity.

The day after his mother's funeral, Michael took Audrey to the book shop to buy her a new copy of *A Child's Garden of Verses*. Audrey kept it on her bookshelf for the rest of her life.

Chapter 35

With the loss of her in-laws, Francie became even more curious to find out what she could about her birth father, Robert Dugan. Her mother had told her he was a professor of history at Trinity College, so she Googled him. Wonder of wonders—and with a little help from technology—she came up with a retired professor of history named Robert Dugan who lived in Connecticut and had formerly taught at Trinity College and Yale University. The site described his credentials with dates of his achievements. She did a little math and determined that he was probably in his late seventies. Then she Googled Robert Dugan, Jr., the little boy whom her mother had taught to read, and found one who was in his fifties, a psychiatrist in Greenwich, Connecticut. The site showed his picture, and she definitely saw a resemblance to herself and to her daughter, Audrey. She showed Michael the picture and asked his opinion about phoning Robert, Jr.

Michael could not stop laughing! "Sure, why not? Maybe you'll find out that you have other half siblings, too."

"What do you mean?" she asked.

"Well, maybe the father—your father, got married again, in the U.S. and had more children—more half siblings for you."

"Well, you're right! Who knows? Maybe I'll find out that our next door neighbor is my sister!"

"I know this is not a laughing matter, Francie, so excuse me for laughing, but you have to agree, this is an absurd situation. If I were in the same situation, I'd be too curious not to call. I think it's remarkable that you waited all this time."

That was all she needed. She looked up the number of the office of

Robert, Jr. and put in a call. The secretary asked what the call was in reference to, and she replied it was personal and important. The operator said she would pass the message on to Dr. Dugan.

Hours went by, and Francie was sure she would get no response. She had already planned to call the next day when the phone rang. "This is Dr. Dugan. I understand you called about a personal matter."

Francie had given some thought about how she would begin the conversation, and she plunged in. "You probably never heard of me. My name is Francie Hanson, and the reason for this call concerns your father's history, not the subject he taught, but his personal history. But first, I'd like to ask you a question to be sure that I have the right person. When you were a young child, did you live in Dublin?"

"Yes, I did, but we left Dublin when I was eight years old."

Francie's chest tightened and she felt her heart start to quiver. "Do you remember a woman by the name of Eileen O'Conner who came to your house to tutor you in reading?"

"I haven't thought about her for years, but, yes, I have some fuzzy memories of a pretty lady who used to bring cookies to my house and help me with my reading. My mother had died and having a woman in our house was a great comfort to me. I don't remember her name, but I do remember her kindness, and that I was so sad when she stopped coming. Is this about her?"

"Very much so, but I'm warning you to be ready for some shocking news, both good and bad, involving both you and me. Is that okay with you?"

"I'll let you know after you tell me what it's about."

"Well, Robert—I hope it's okay for me to call you by your first name…."

"You can call me Rob—my father is called Robert."

"Rob it is, then. About a year ago, after a very long estrangement from my family in Ireland, my mother informed me that my father was not my real father. She went on to tell me about a sad, little boy without a mother, whom she tutored. His name was Robby." Francie heard his sharp intake of air on the line, realizing he suspected what she was about to tell him.

"Apparently my mother and your father developed a strong and serious affection for each other, which led to a love affair. When she realized that she was pregnant, she abruptly ended the affair without telling him the reason. My mother, being a God-fearing Catholic, was overcome with guilt. She stopped all contact with him, never telling him about her pregnancy. A short time later, your father and you moved away."

She paused a second and asked, "Are you still with me?"

Uh, yes," he said haltingly. "Please go on. Let me hear it all before I say something."

"Bottom line—I am the result of that pregnancy, which makes me your half sister. It took more than forty years and lots of extenuating circumstances for my mother to tell the truth about my biological father, and I am as surprised as you. I imagine your father would be, too, since he never heard from her again and had no idea that she was pregnant. Believe me when I say that my mother is an honorable woman, and so is your father. I have no reason to doubt what she told me is true. They were two people who fell in love and the result was tragic for both of them.

"Please think this over carefully. Rob. I would love to meet my biological father—our father—and you, but I positively do not want to create a problem for either of you, and I want to assure you that I have no ulterior motive. I would just like to meet my father and have a chance to talk to him. If you think he'd be upset, we don't have to tell him who I am."

"Francie, I'm shocked—I need some time to think. You're right about my father. He is and always was an honorable man, and I'm sure he'd want to know about you and your mother. I'd like to talk this over with my wife, then I'll get back to you. I think you and I have much to talk about. For now, I'll just tell you that Dad is close to eighty and in excellent health. I'll call you in a few days to take up where we left off."

Francie hung up and told Michael about her conversation. "I hope this is the last twig in the continuing growth of my family tree."

"With your family, don't be too sure, you crazy Irish woman," he said with a bear hug and his irresistible laugh. "Francie, you are the most amazing person to be able to come through all this without letting bitterness destroy you. Just when I think I love you as much as I can, I find something else to add to my list."

Chapter 36

Rob got back to Francie a few days later and invited her and her husband to come to Connecticut so they could meet. The next day, she and Michael set off to meet Rob Dugan at his home in New Haven. His wife opened the door, stared at Francie and smiled. "Your resemblance to Rob is remarkable. If there was ever be any doubt that you two are related, it's gone, now. I'm Theresa, please come in and meet the family. We're all in the backyard."

She was right. As soon as Francie looked at Rob, she felt she had known him all her life. Apparently, the feeling was mutual, as she could tell he immediately recognized her.

"Hi, Sis," he said. She recognized his smile—it was the same as hers. "Those are words I never thought I'd say. I've been an only child my whole life, and suddenly I have a sister and a brother-in-law, and we skipped right over the sibling rivalry."

She had to laugh. His sense of humor was even familiar. He took her arm. "Come meet our son—your nephew, David. He's a junior at Yale—third generation at the university."

"My pleasure to meet you," the handsome young David said, holding out his hand to Michael first, then to Francie. "My father told me you both are University of Pennsylvania alums. It's great to have an aunt and uncle from a rival Ivy League school. The Dugan family has been spending too much time in New Haven."

"Or maybe the Hanson family has been spending too much time in Philadelphia," Michael added.

Over wine and cheese, the long conversation began. The first thing Michael did was to warn them to take notes on their latest family member.

"There's more to this than meets the eye," he said. "This is just the beginning of a long list of names you're going to have to learn."

Rob said that his side was easy. "My father is an only child, my son is an only child, and I am, I mean *was*, an only child. Now that I have a half sister, I am only half of an only child, or whatever, so I'll begin—this shouldn't take more than a minute.

"Father is a quiet, sometimes lonely man. He's been on the faculty of Yale since we moved here from Ireland. He extended his original concentration of history to Political Geography, an area that focuses on how geography, topography and natural resources shape the politics of different countries. He's tops in his field. For two decades he was on the board of *National Geographic.* Now that he's about to hit eighty, he's fully retired. I'm lucky to have inherited a smidgeon of his intelligence, enough to get me through medical school without too many problems." He smiled at his new sister. "It appears that you inherited a good deal of it, too."

She grinned back and shrugged.

"I do remember more and more of your mother since you called. How kind she was to me when I was a lonely little boy. I never knew my mother—she died giving birth to me. Throughout my childhood, my father was so sad. The psychiatrist in me now knows he was suffering from clinical depression. We lived a quiet life in a house that felt empty. We had breakfast together with no conversation that I can remember, then he left for work, and I left for school, and we didn't see each other again until dinnertime. I played with the neighborhood kids after school, and their mothers kept an eye on me.

"When we lived in Ireland, Dad was professor of history at Trinity College with an impressive record in teaching, consulting and writing, but he had no idea how to handle a seven-year-old child with a reading problem. Anyway, my confidence started to fall. My father took a cursory look at my schoolwork and saw on my report card that I had poor grades in reading. He was baffled, and the school recommended a reading tutor. When your mother came along, she paid attention to me, tutored me, encouraged me to develop my natural abilities. It seemed that all I needed was some attention at home, and I got it from her. On the days she was there, my father seemed to come alive. I had never seen him happy before.

"My reading started to improve, and she and my father made me proud of myself. I started to fit in with other kids at school, and life at home became happy. Then, one day, with no explanation, he told me that Mrs. O'Conner wasn't going to come to the house anymore. I was devastated, and so was he, but I never knew why until you phoned last week."

"It was a nervy call to make," said Francie. "But I figured I had nothing to lose, and just look what I gained!" She spread her hands out to him and his family, smiling like a teenager.

Rob, holding tight to Theresa's hand, smiled back to Francie and Michael and in a husky voice said, "Finally, I have a family, and I couldn't be happier."

He paused for a sip of wine, cleared his throat and went on. "I'll bring you a little more up to date. We moved to New Haven to a house not far from here, where Dad still lives. As far as I know, his social life was absent except in academic and neighborhood situations. Looking back, I realize that he was twice burned and could not afford to strain his emotions for a third time.

"He retired from full-time classroom teaching when he was close to seventy, but he still maintains an office at Yale where he sees doctoral candidates. He and I have become closer in the past twenty-five years since Theresa and I married and David was born."

At this, David raised his arms and flexed his muscles, in the pose of a champ.

"Theresa loves to be with Dad, and they often spend afternoons together going to lectures, movies, or lunch at a neighborhood snack shop. He started to come out of his shell throughout David's childhood, and the two of them did special things together that Dad never had done with me—going to the zoo, and the circus; then later, when David was in upper school, they spent hours discussing history and politics. Now that David's a *Yalie*, my father has taught him to appreciate a good glass of wine before dinner, even though he knows he's aiding and abetting a minor below the legal drinking age."

"Have you told Robert about me?" Francie wanted to know.

"No, I haven't had the nerve. I don't even know how to approach it. But I see much of him in you, especially in the expression in your eyes."

He looked at his wife and back at Francie. "What would you think if I called him now and told him I wanted to stop over with some people I'd like him to meet? Then you could use your own judgment to decide what to tell him. Would that be too difficult for you?"

"Rob, after what I've been through, nothing is too difficult for me. I would love to meet him as soon as possible," Francie said, and proceeded to tell him everything that happened to her since she left home for University of Edinburg until now. "My adult daughter, Kate, is a professor of economics at Trinity College. Coincidence rears its head—it seems without knowing, she followed in the footsteps of her grandfather. My mother still lives in Dublin, and she and I haven't reconciled since I was sent away almost thirty years ago."

Theresa leaned over the coffee table and took Francie's hand. The two women looked at each other in what Francie considered sisterhood. It brought tears to her eyes, and she gripped the hand extended to her.

Michael excused himself for interrupting, and said, "This may seem daunting to you, but there are quite a few more twists and turns in the obstacle course of Francie's family. Don't worry if you get the relationships wrong. Francie and I have been married for twenty-five years, and I don't think I'm too shabby in the brains department, but there is no way I can keep score of Francie's family without a program."

"Rob," Francie said, smiling now, "don't think I'm crazy, but I have a strange question for you. Is your father a good dancer?"

"I can answer that one for you," said Theresa. "He's a terrible dancer, which I found out at our wedding when I lured my new father-in-law onto the dance floor. Why do you ask?"

"Finally, I have a legitimate excuse for my two left feet. I always wondered why everyone in my family were such great dancers, my mother included, and they all groaned when I approached the floor. Now I know I come by it naturally."

"For your information, Sis, I'm not such a hot dancer, either," Rob said, then he moved to the phone. "I'll just call to let him know we're coming so he doesn't think he's being invaded, then I'll grab a bottle of wine and we can get going."

"I'm coming, too," said David. "I wouldn't miss this for the world."

Chapter 37

Francie spotted Robert looking out the window when the group pulled into his driveway. He was obviously curious to see these people that Rob was bringing for him to meet.

Francie didn't think she'd be nervous, but when Robert opened the door, her heart skipped a beat or two. He was one of the handsomest, most distinguished-looking men she had ever seen. *Ma, you sure picked a handsome one*, she thought.

She searched his face to try to find a resemblance, and there, in his expression, she saw herself.

Introductions were made all around, the wine was uncorked, and the conversations began.

"Do I detect an Irish accent?" he asked Francie. She smiled and said she was about to ask him the same question.

"Yes, I was born in Dublin," she said, "but moved to the U.S. when I was seventeen. My Dubliner accent follows me wherever I go. They say you can leave Ireland, but Ireland never leaves you."

"My accent follows me, too," he said. "Just when I think I've lost it, someone tells me they love my Irish lilt. Rob came here young enough to lose it. He left it all behind."

Theresa told Robert that Francie and Michael were new acquaintances, and from there the conversation moved to all their occupations. The list of their academic achievements was impressive. David commented that there was probably over a million dollars of education in the room. The conversation shifted to their personal lives, and Francie told them about leaving Dublin for Philadelphia, her years at Penn, her marriage to Michael, their children and her career at Shea's Soup. "Maybe you've notice my picture at Shea's Soup and Sandwich spots.

"No way! I see that picture whenever I walk into the soup joint on Yale's Campus," David said. "That was you!?"

"Yup, that's was me in my twenties. I hope it doesn't spoil your appetite."

"Far from it," Robert said. "David and I go there often, and I always love to see that picture—it reminds me of a girl I knew when we lived in Ireland. You have a strong resemblance to her."

Rob and Francie looked at each other and both nodded that the time had come to tell the truth. Rob said, "Dad, Francie and I have something to tell you. I'll let her speak first."

"We're not sure that you want to hear this, so if it makes you uncomfortable, let me know and I'll stop," said Francie.

"Uh, oh, sounds ominous. Go on, please" he said.

"My mother is Eileen O'Conner," she said with gentleness in her voice. "Does that name sound familiar to you?"

"My God, Eileen O'Conner—your mother!" Immediately his eyes became moist. He swallowed hard and thought hard before saying, "I met her close to eight years after Rob's mother died, and I was still in mourning even after all that time. When she started to tutor Robby, she lit up our dreary house. She changed my life and brought me out of mourning, and I fell in love with her. She abruptly stopped coming to the house and refused to see me, and I never knew why. I just knew that to retain my sanity, I had to leave Ireland and the sad memories it held for me. I never forgot her—I still love the memory of our time together."

"Now comes the shocking part—so let me know if you're ready."

"I hope so," he said.

"Two years ago, my mother told me the story about her love affair with you. She discovered that she was pregnant, and she and Da knew that the baby could not have been his. They stayed together, and he forgave her. He loved her enough to raise the baby as his own.

"It took me quite a while to get up the courage to find you to tell you this story.

"Robert, I was that baby."

"Jesus God," he said, that makes me your father!"

Granddad, you rock, thought David.

Robert looked at her, tears now trickling down his face. He got out a large white handkerchief and blew his nose. "Give me a moment, Francie. Rob, a scotch would help, please."

He was silent for a few seconds, took a sip of scotch, and nodded. "No wonder. Now I understand, Francie, and I think she did the right thing to end our relationship. She owed it to her husband and family. But I want to thank you for being honest with me. I'm glad she told you her secret, and I'm glad you found me. I suspect she knows you well enough to have hoped you'd pursue it. I'm sorry it took so many years for us to meet. Let me say this loud and clear—I have a daughter! Could you come here and give me a hug?"

She was quick to oblige. "It's hard to believe, isn't it? Don't be surprised if it takes a while for it to sink in—I'm still working on it."

She sat back down. "But I have more to tell, of a serious note. Robert, the relationship I have with my mother is nonexistent and has been since I was seventeen. I once lived a roller-coaster life. I had a baby out of wedlock when I was seventeen. My mother banished me from our home and I was forced to give up my baby, Kate, a few minutes after she was born. I was sent away to live in America and didn't know anything about Kate for over twenty years. I was lonely and miserable. But everything changed when I married Michael. He is the finest man I have ever known. He has supported me and my crazy past in every way imaginable."

She held Michael's hand and went on.

"He has given me joy, security, children, parents who loved me as their own daughter, and laughter—especially laughter. We continue to have as much fun together as we did as newlyweds. No one could ask for more."

Michael was usually quite satisfied to let Francie converse for both of them. He loved watching her facial expressions and listening to the charming way she conveyed her opinions and emotions, but now he felt that the time was right to speak up. He looked at Robert and said, "Much about our backgrounds is similar, Robert. My first marriage, like yours, ended in tragedy, and years later, both you and I fell in love with women from the same family. My second chance at love continues to this day with Francie. I'm so sorry that your second chance was fated to fail."

Robert replied, "You are both so honest and so generous with your sympathy. I was not so lucky. Eileen and I both knew from the start that we had no chance to really be together, but we wanted to live in the present and not worry about the future. After we parted, I turned to my work to calm the loneliness I felt. I wish I had been a better father to Rob, but I honestly couldn't cope with my situation. Once he was grown and married, and especially when David, was born, I finally started to relate to him."

The father, son and grandson looked at each other and nodded, small smiles on their faces, all of which held such familiarity to Francie. Her Timmy had the same smile.

"I missed so much." Robert continued. "If only I could have put my sadness aside and focused on my son, but I was not man enough to do it."

"I turned out quite well considering you ignored me for years," Rob joked. "And actually, you were an excellent role model for me. I learned values, manners and not to allow regret to ruin my life as it did to yours."

His dad gave him a wry nod and then said to Francie, "I hope Rob agrees with me that we'd like you and your family to become a part of our lives. Being father to a new daughter at this late age makes my job easier—no late-night feedings, no school plays to endure, no dealing with a teenager—just enjoying the wonder of having another child. And I have a feeling that knowing you, Francie, will go far in making me forget any leftover regret still with me."

Rob smiled. "I always wanted a sister I could bug, and it's never too late to have one. Just remember, I was here first!"

David spoke up like a typical college student. "This story is like a soap opera with corny jokes, I think I'll have another beer."

"No more for me," said Michael "We have a long drive ahead and two little ones at home waiting, so I think we'd better call it a night. We all have so much to think about, and for a change, it's all good."

With hugs and handshakes all around, they were off.

In the car, the conversation about their new family didn't let up. To

Michael, every part of Francie's world was part of his. In their hearts, both of their families had merged into one and kept growing.

They were determined to keep up the budding relationship with Robert and his family.

"They were so nice, don't you think?" Francie asked Michael.

"My unemotional opinion is that Robert is a man whose life has passed him by. He could have had everything, but he never met the right woman to make him complete again. Today I couldn't help but think how lucky I am to have you, Francie. His story could have been mine. You turned everything bad in our lives into a stepping stone to something better. Where do you think you got that trait?"

"Luck? Timing? I don't know. Happiness has always been a magnet for me, drawing me back on course through sadness. My mother didn't have that compass and neither did Robert. But you did, Michael, and I think when we met, we helped each other create a new path to happiness."

She was quiet for a minute, and Michael let her be. Soon she started talking again. "I felt a definite tie to Robert, a familiarity from the start, as though our minds were in sync. I hope I can see him often, and I think I can learn more about myself from being with him.

"But now I have some deep thinking to do about my relationship with my mother. What would you say if I told you I'd like to re-establish it?"

"Francie, I support you no matter what you decide, you know that. I think your mother needs you—she cast you out of her life because of her weakness, or the domination of the Church. Or both. It took her so many unhappy years to realize how wrong she was. You have the power to help her. Don't let her suffer any longer. It isn't like you to be unforgiving. You can put it right."

Chapter 38

Dear Mum,

Here I am, hopefully back in your life after all these years. When I think of you, I picture our house in Dublin with you and the family, and I am transported back home.

When I left Ireland, I left behind my youth, my country, my home, my parents, my brothers, the boy I loved, and my baby. I exchanged all those things for misery and loneliness. As a child of seventeen, I had to make my own future in the home of an unloving, critical aunt who made me feel unwelcome from the day I arrived. I missed you every one of those days and years. How could I have done something so awful that my mother would throw me away?

It has taken me a long time to forgive you, but finally I realize that everyone needs a mother to love and I would like us to have our life as mother and daughter again. We have a lot to talk about and a lot of crying to do together.

I've said enough for now. Take some time to think this over and I'll wait to hear from you.

Love, Francie

She mailed the letter the next morning on the way to the park with Audrey. Michael was working from home, but when he heard them leave, he got up from his desk and went to the window. He watched Francie and Audrey practically skip down the street. Francie had a lightness to her step which made him feel a similar lightness of heart seeing his wife so happy. And he loved watching Audrey. What a joy to be the father of a daughter.

When they were out of sight, he went back to preparing a speech he was to give in Washington at the end of the week—still smiling, but relieved to have some quiet in the house.

Francie and her mother's group dedicated Mondays as mother and child day. Ordinarily the kids went to school or pre-school, but on Monday mornings, whoever was around got together at the park—with or without children—unless it was inclement. That day, Meg and Lisa were there with their kids, and the little ones all played together on the jungle gym and swings. The girls asked Francie about her weekend, and when she finished, they both said that her life was so full of drama, she should write a book.

"Not possible," said Francie. "It's an ongoing saga that would fill volumes. But the bottom line is that I'm here with you, living an ordinary life, raising kids, working down at Penn part-time, and cooking dinner, as if nothing else has ever happened in my life."

At lunchtime, they went their separate ways.

"Ready or not, we're home," she said through the closed door of Michael's office, then went to the kitchen to make a peanut butter and jelly sandwich for Audrey and tuna melts for Michael and herself. There was a chill in the air, so she heated up a family staple—Shea's tomato soup.

About ten minutes later, Michael came to the kitchen apologizing for taking so long. "I was on the phone," he said. "You got two calls. I'll tell you about them after Audrey goes to her room for quiet time."

"Sounds mysterious," she said. "But okay, if you say so…."

As soon as Audrey went upstairs, Francie listened to what Michael had to say.

"The first call was from Robert, your new father. He wanted to know if it would be okay for him to come to Philadelphia in a few weeks for a short visit to get to know us a little better and to get to meet the kids. He wanted to know if there was a hotel nearby where he could stay for a couple of days. He said that at his age, he didn't want to put things off too long. Meeting you ignited a spark in him that reminded him of his youth, and of your mother."

Francie immediately reacted. "If you agree, Michael, I would love him to come. How would you feel about him staying here, in the guest room?"

“If he’s comfortable staying here, it’s fine with me, if you’re sure you want him to see how you look in the morning.”

Ignoring his teasing, she asked, “What about the other call for me?”

“This one’s not so good, so brace yourself. Tommy called to say that your Da died in his sleep last night.”

Tears came immediately. She turned to Michael and hugged him, burying her face in his chest and sobbing.

When she finally stopped, she used the handkerchief Michael offered, cleared her throat and said, “He was a good father until the day he put me on a plane to America. His wife came first, no matter how irrational her decision was. I’ll try to remember the early days when we were a happy family, but it won’t be easy.”

She phoned Tommy in Ireland to offer her condolences and ask for details. He said that it was completely unexpected. Da had been in good health from what he knew. Though the relationship the brothers had with their parents had been distant for so many years, Tommy said, “We loved him, and we love Mum, Francie, but we just couldn’t abide them.

“Mum discussed it with us, and we decided to have a short wake at home, then a Mass at their church with burial at the church graveyard. They had very few friends, so we expect mostly neighbors and some cousins. The wake will continue through tomorrow. After the funeral, my Margaret and Brian’s Rosie will take care of the refreshments at home. The flowers we provide will say, *To our father, from all his children.*

“I think that will be very appropriate, and I thank you for taking care of it. Now I have some things to tell you that will probably shock you.”

“Nothing more about your life can shock me, Francie.”

“That’s what you think,” she said and continued with the latest chapter of her story. “When Michael and I were in England for Francie and Sean’s wedding, Mum called me at our hotel.” She went on to tell her brother all the details, including the part about learning that Robert Dugan is her biological father.

“Did I hear you right? Did you say that Da is not your real father?”

“Believe me, Tommy, when Mum told me, it was hard for me to believe, too. Straitlaced, God-fearing Ma had an adulteress affair, and I end up having a father I never knew! Until now."

"Here's the clincher. After two years of waiting to find my bio father, my curiosity got the best of me and I tracked down his son, Rob, my half brother. That led to a meeting in Connecticut with my father.

"They were lovely and welcoming. I am arranging to invite Robert here to spend time with Michael and me, and to meet his grandchildren. He's an old man, Tommy. He wants to get to know us while there's still time."

Tommy's voice turned sad. "Francie, does this mean that you and I are not true brother and sister? That you have a whole new family that doesn't include me?"

"Tommy, no, no, no. You will always be my number-one, and my real family will always be you and the boys and our parents in Ireland. In fact, when all this finally penetrated my head, I realized how much I wanted to be with our parents again.

"Before I knew that Da died, I did a lot of thinking and decided it was time to reconcile with them. This morning I mailed a letter to Mum, telling her I was ready to see her and Da and resume our relationship as parents and daughter. And now I get the news about Da. Really, Tommy, it seems the whirlwind is still spinning, and I am right back in it again."

"We're all in it, Francie. You're our baby sister, and you have that position for life, no matter who your real father is."

"Tommy, could you tell Brian and Denny what I told you? I don't think I can go through it again. And please tell them that they will always be my full brothers. Nothing could change that. Please don't say anything to Mum. If she hasn't told you about my real father, she probably has a reason. I'd like to tell her myself about meeting him, but, of course, I'll wait until Da has been properly respected."

Later that afternoon, Francie went to church and lit a candle for Da. As a tribute to him, the father she loved during her childhood, she returned every day for a week, and mourned a relationship that had never been restored.

She was surprised to find that the childhood sense of home she used to have in church was reawakening.

Chapter 39

Dear Reader,

You probably want to know what's been going on with Kate and Sean's married life in Ireland—and I do, too. The reality is that their lives are taking the normal course for newlyweds. He works at the hospital, she teaches at Trinity, they furnish their home with stuff from IKEA. Sean puts it together with many expletives beginning with the letter 'F.' Kate is his holder and cheerleader, telling him what a great job he's doing. In other words, right now their lives are mundane, so I'll get back to them when something interesting happens.

Instead, I'll go on to Pat. His life is much more interesting. Read on....

Pat and Giulia, Up a tree,
K-I-S-S-I-N-G.
First comes love,
Then comes marriage,
Then comes Giulia
With a baby carriage.

And so, it happened, a new Harrington appeared on the scene. Sophia, a surprise package, with Pat's curls, Giulia's black eyes, and her very own temperament—a mixture of the passion of Italy, the humor of Ireland and, so far, none of the sophistication of England. She was a dynamo.

Her parents delighted in her antics. By the time she was seven months old, she was speaking in short sentences. When she was a year old, she understood concepts. She asked her papà questions like, "Where do the colors go at night?" and "Why don't chickens drive cars?" Every day she did something outrageous. She shared her pacifier with the dog to make him happy. She threw her dolls out of the window to see if they could fly. She finger painted all the walls in her room.

Now that Pat and Giulia had a child, commuting between London and Verona became impractical, and once Pat got used to Italian ways, he found that life in Italy was much more fun than life in England. Just listening to the melodic Italian language made him happy. However, the many years of a successful legal practice and the honored accomplishment of becoming a judge made his decision to resign from the law a difficult one. The procedure of retiring from his position took almost a year. He knew that as an expat in Italy, the profession of law was out of the question for him. The quirks of the Italian system were virtually insurmountable. He had no regrets—it was time for him to move on and leave behind the status oriented society of London.

He joined Giulia in her travel business and instead of spending his days in the contentious legal system, full of crime, greed and injustice, he spent his time in a happy business, dealing with smiling people looking forward to and enjoying happy vacations. Working with Giulia was *molto gratificante*, and raising Sophia was a new treat every day. Life in Verona was nothing like life in London. Everything was intensified—the colors, the laughter, the pleasures of everyday life. He asked Giulia how she could have endured living in stuffy London when they were first married. How could she have given up Italy? Her answer was, "I did it for love, silly. And, long as we were together, I was home."

Pat's twin boys, Josh and Flip, now fourteen, came to Italy every chance they could get. They hiked and skied in the Dolomites and sailed and swam in Lake Garda. When they visited their dad, Giulia, and baby Sophia in Italy, they hated to leave. Their mother and Pat maintained a good relationship, but Moira discouraged too many visits to Italy for the boys. She wanted them to become proper Englishmen, to follow the traditions and lifestyle of their native country. Pat did nothing to try to change their future in the life they had been born to, but he did leave the door open to them to make Italy their second home.

Kate and Sean came for few short visits when they could get away for a long weekend. They, too, thought that life in Italy was like stepping back in time, off the treadmill of reality, but they knew that vacationing in a country was far different from living there. Kate hardly thought of Pat as her father, he was more like an older brother, an uncle maybe. She and Sean envied the ease that Pat and Giulia had with raising Sophia. She was such a happy, darling little girl.

"Do you think we could have one of those someday soon?" Kate asked Sean.

"Maybe next year," he said, "when we have a chance to catch our breath."

Chapter 40

Francie received a reply from the letter she had sent to her mother. It looked like tears had stained the paper, and through the runny ink, Francie read her mother's heartfelt apology and wishes for their reconciliation.

Life is so lonely now that Da is gone. I didn't realize how much he had done for me all these years, and how little I had done for him. I know now that I was not good enough for him. He deserved better. After what I did to you, I'm ashamed to say that I am turning to you for comfort. I'm not good enough for you, either, Francie, but I hope we have time to restore our relationship to what it should have been.

Would you feel awkward if I came to the U.S. to visit you and your family? Is there's a hotel close by where I could stay?

Love for now and always, Mum

Dear Mum, Francie wrote back, *we have plenty of room at our house, so let's plan to have your length of stay indefinite depending on how we both feel. Life has been fortunate for us, and we have no problems with money, so tell me when you would like to come, and I'll make the arrangements and pay for your ticket. We have so much to talk about, so please come soon, and we can start being mother and daughter again.*

As soon as her mother got the letter, she called Francie and said, "I'm ready this second, so please make the plans. We'll talk about who will pay for the ticket when I get there."

"Mum, after all these years of both of us waiting, I know for sure that the time is right. Your voice sounds happy and so young, like it did when I was a kid and we were all together. I'd love for you to feel that way again."

"I'll pray it will," said her mother.

Chapter 41

They were all there to greet her at Philadelphia Airport when she came through customs. Her mother hurried right to Francie, and they looked at each other, cried, hugged, looked again, cried again, and hugged again.

When they regained their senses, Francie introduced Michael and the children. "This is Grandma," she said to Timmy and Audrey.

Timmy offered his hand and said, "If you didn't know it, we had another grandmother who died, and now I'm glad you're alive so we can have you."

"And I'm glad I'm alive, too, so I can have you."

Audrey was a little shy, and whispered to her mother, "Am I supposed to curtsy?"

"If you want to, but a little hug would be okay, too."

Audrey thought a bit, then looked at her grandmother, curtsied first, and then hugged her.

"That's the best greeting I ever got from a little lady," she said.

"Do you mind if I call you 'Eileen'?" Michael said.

"Well, and wouldn't I be pleased, Michael?" she said with her Irish lilt.

"Grandma, you talk funny," said Timmy. "Could you teach me how?"

"Well, and wouldn't I love to do that?" she said with a wink.

They piled into the car and the talking never stopped until they reached Haverford.

"What a pretty city," Eileen said.

"Welcome to our home," Michael said, pulling into the drive.

"It's so grand, Michael." To Francie she said, awestruck, "I had no idea."

"Life has been good to me, Mum, like I said. Michael and I are lucky to have found each other and have been so happy here. Now let's go inside and I'll show you around. I know that the children want to show you their rooms."

"And wouldn't I be glad to see them," she said with a forced Irish vernacular, looking at the kids, "Who wants to go first?"

"I think Audrey should because I want to save mine for last," Timmy said.

"Is that okay with you, Audrey? Maybe you could show me your books."

"I have lots of books. Mommy says that I have my own library."

"Lead the way, then. Did you know that your mother had her own library, too, when she was a little girl?"

"I know, Grandma," said Timmy, "she's always telling us about it when we want to watch TV."

Eileen could barely believe how large the house was and how beautiful the furnishings. "Francie, this is like a palace," she said. "I've never seen draperies like yours except in a hotel."

Audrey took her grandmother's hand and led the way upstairs to her room. The first thing she showed her was her overflowing bookcase. "When I was little, my favorite book was *A Child's Garden of Verses*, but I gave it to Grammy to take to heaven so she could read it to the children there. Daddy bought me a new one and I still love it." She thought for a few seconds, twirling the hem of her sweater with her index finger. "But now my favorite is *Peter Rabbit.* It's about a rabbit named Peter who always gets into trouble. I can read it myself but when Mommy reads it to me, I like it more. She sort of acts it out. Could you read it to me tonight when I go to bed?"

"There's nothing I would like better, Audrey."

Timmy spoke up. "Come on, Grandma, let me show you my buildings."

Audrey said, "Don't mind Timmy, he's a boy and all boys like to build stuff."

"Audrey, are you sure you're just five? You sound very grown up, like your mother was when she was your age."

Timmy piped up with, "When I was little, I read books all the time, too, but now I'm into Lego and Lincoln Logs."

"I know about Lego," said Eileen. "But I don't think we have Lincoln Logs in Ireland. Can you show them to me?"

"Sure. Lego is harder because it's smaller, but Lincoln Logs are better because they look like real houses."

His room was filled with houses of all sizes that he had built. Eileen studied each one, oohing and aahing over their intricacies. "Did you know that your Uncle Denis is an architect? He designs houses. Maybe you take after him, because you design houses, too."

Francie had forgotten how much fun her mother could be, and how wonderful she was with children. Eileen was impressed with the children's abilities, although she thought that with the genes they inherited, she should not have been surprised. She and France talked about and mourned the loss of so many good years they could have had together, but they planned to make up for lost time as much as possible.

"Mum, not only did I miss having you, but I missed having Da. Why did he stop loving me? Did he ever really love me? I have so many wonderful memories of the two of us together. Once, he and I planted a garden, and when the first bean shoot came up, he woke me to come and see it. Then he made me oatmeal with honey for breakfast, just the two of us, and early in the morning when everyone was asleep, he read the funnies to me from the morning paper.

"I remember the day he took me to pick out Puffy from Mrs. Dougherty's litter of kittens. I promised I'd take good care of her, and Da taught me how to handle her with a gentleness I never knew he had."

She started to cry, surprising herself that her emotions had risen so quickly. "I cried for him when I heard he died, Mum. I'm so sorry that I didn't get to see him all those years. And now it's too late."

Her mother took a tissue from her pocket and wiped Francie's tears. "You're a good girl, Francie, and you always were. I knew it and Da knew it.

"He never stopped loving you. He resented me for becoming pregnant by another man, and he wanted to extend his resentment to you, but he couldn't. He loved you too much. After you were born, as soon as you looked at him and gurgled, he accepted you as his own. Our life went back to normal until you became pregnant. He felt it was his fault for not insisting that I warn you about the trouble that can happen when passion takes over reason—and for being too embarrassed to tell you himself like he had told the boys. From that day forward, he was never happy again, and neither was I. We missed you every day and didn't have enough courage to admit it. It was all my fault, Francie. I was too ashamed to tell you the facts of life, then too guilty to accept the blame of your pregnancy. I turned the blame on you."

And now Francie wiped her mother's tears.

After a few days, when her mother had adjusted to jet lag and was feeling full of vigor, Francie decided it was time to bring her real father into the new honesty between them.

She waited until the children were off to school and Michael was off to DC, and the house was quiet. "Mum," she said, "I have something important to tell you, but it may shock you, so do you think you want to hear it?"

"Francie, if it's sad, maybe I'd rather not know, but I think I can handle anything else."

"It's not sad, just, uh, shocking maybe? After you told me about my biological father, Robert Dugan, I spent two years mulling it over. Finally I gave in to my curiosity and tracked down his son, Robby."

"Francie, please bring me a drink before you continue—some whiskey would be fine. I'll just sit here and wait." She took out her handkerchief to wipe her brow, then nervously began clasping and unclasping her hands.

Francie came back with two drinks, one for herself. "I called Robby and told him the story you told me, that you were my mother and that his father was my father. He took it quite well, even thought I had to give him a couple of days to digest it."

"Is Robert alive? Oh, God, let him be alive," she said.

"Yes, he's alive and well, for an eighty-year-old. They live in the U.S., in Connecticut, a four hour drive from here. Michael and I drove there to meet them."

Eileen was in such deep thought that she was unaware of the tears streaming down her face. Francie handed her a Kleenex box and put her arms around her. "Mum, it seems that every time we talk, we need to be close to a box of tissues." They both laughed.

"We met Rob and his wife and son, and after a short time, we all felt like family. After a while, we all drove a few blocks to Robert's house.

"My first though when I met Robert was that he is so handsome—I can see why you fell for him!

"We didn't tell him who we were at first. We wanted to get to know each other a bit over a glass of wine. Eventually I told him about you and about the circumstances that led me there."

"Oh, my Robert, how did he take it? What did he say? He must have been shocked."

"I was very careful with his emotions. I told him very gently that I was his daughter. And, yes, he was shocked, of course. I could see the wheels spinning in his brain, then he nodded and said he understood that you did what you had to do. Just like that. He's quite the reserved fellow. But he put out his arms and told me he was so happy to meet me.

"Mum, he wants to come down to Philadelphia to meet our children, his half grandchildren, but I put him off until now. How would you feel about seeing him, or should I wait until you leave to have him come visit?"

"My heart is racing, Francie. I'm not young, and he's ten years older than I am. Do you think this is heart attack material for either of us?"

"Do you think it's worth it?

"For me, yes—for him, I wouldn't know, now, would I?"

"Think about it overnight, Mum. If you decide I should call him, I'll do it tomorrow."

The next morning, Eileen was in the kitchen when Francie came down.

"Francie, do you think it's too early to call him? I'd love to see him."

Francie phoned him at nine on the dot and invited him to come and stay with them for a few days if that suited him. She decided not to tell him anything about her mother. She wanted his trip to be relaxing—she knew he was not a man used to excitement. There was time to tell him after he arrived at the station.

"I can take the train from New Haven to Philadelphia and arrive in time for dinner tonight. Is that too soon?"

"Just let me know your schedule, and we'll be there to meet you at 30th Street Station."

"Deadly perfect," he said.

Chapter 42

The train pulled into the station that evening at six, and Michael was there to meet Francie's dad. Robert was in great humor, well rested from a two hour nap he had on the train.

Michael greeted him with a handshake. "Francie and the children are home making dinner," he told Robert.

They walked outside to the car, and before Michael turned the key, he said, "They want everything to be perfect. But first, I want to let you in on a little surprise that may come as a shock to you. Are you ready for another shock?"

"All I need for perfection is being with you and Francie and meeting my newly acquired grandchildren, and I welcome all surprises, as long as they're good ones. I just lived through the biggest one of my life, so I guess I'll live through another."

"Here is comes, point blank—Eileen is at the house. When you called, it was a pure coincidence, and she is dying to see you."

Robert started, grabbed the dash, looked over at Michael and said with a huge dawning smile on his patrician face, "And aren't I dying to see her, too!" in a pure Irish lilt.

Less than fifteen minutes after they left the train station, they exited the main highway and drove through the beautiful Main Line suburbs. "I've never been to Philadelphia. The Main Line area is gorgeous. Were you raised here?"

"Yes, I grew up in Haverford. When Francie and I were married, we bought a house close to my parents' house. Family means so much to Francie, and my parents became her parents, too." Robert turned to the window, silent.

"Almost two years ago, both of my parents died within a short time of one another," Michael went on. "But they lived long enough to see our kids, their only grandchildren except for Francie's daughter, Kate. They had sold their home and moved to a retirement apartment in the area. Francie and I still live in the same house we bought when we were first married. For over twenty years, we rattled around in it, hoping for children to fill the empty rooms, and it finally happened, in quick succession, I should add. So now, although I'm old enough to be my children's grandfather, I am happy to live in a noisy, sometimes messy home full of the sounds of children's laughter and never-ending questions."

Robert spoke up. "I missed all those happy years, and so did Robbie. Except for the short time that Eileen was in our lives, I didn't have the strength to pull myself out of my grief. Our home in Ireland, and the one in America were quiet places with very little laughter. The love was there, but without a woman, affection was missing for both of us."

Michael pulled into the driveway. Francie was waiting outside with the kids, who wore matching aprons monogrammed with *Kiss the Chef.*

"Timmy and Audrey, come meet your grandfather."

This time Audrey wanted to go first. She ran over to her grandfather, looked at her mother, and curtsied. Then she reached up for a hug. Robert was glad to oblige.

"That's the best hug I've ever had from a little girl. In fact, it's the only one."

Audrey reached up again and said, "Here's another!"

Timmy said, "Wow, I'm meeting a lot of new grandparents. My Grammy and Papa died, and another grandfather just died in Ireland. You look old, but I'm glad you're still alive because grandfathers are nice, and they like to explain how things work and they're never in a hurry."

Audrey said, "We have new grandmother, too—she's inside waiting to meet you."

Robert smiled and let them take his hands and lead him up the steps.

They came into the foyer and entered the living room. Eileen stood by the mantel, waiting. Robert looked straight at her for a full minute, drinking in the reality of her.

"Eileen," he said at last. "Is that you? How could you be so young?"

"Well, and sure it is me in the flesh, Robert," she said, almost shyly, like a girl.

He took both of her hands in his. "Let me look at you, Eileen. You are as beautiful as I remembered."

"And you are even more handsome than I remembered," she said.

They held onto one another's hands and continued to stare at each other with amazement and wonder.

"I never want to let you go," he said.

"Nor I, you...."

They hugged each other as naturally as if they'd been doing it all their lives. When they broke apart, Eileen said, "Oh, pardon us!" She was blushing. And Robert touched her cheek.

She recovered and to cover her embarrassment said, "Don't we have a wonderful family here? Our daughter, Francie and son-in-law, Michael, and their beautiful children?"

They still held hands as they beamed at the grands beaming up at them.

"I wish that Robby were here," Eileen said. "For years, I wondered how he was doing in school and if he was still so lonely. My heart went out to him." She turned to Robert and ran her palm along his cheek. "And to you."

"We have quite a bit to talk about, don't we Eileen?"

"I'm sure you do," said Francie. "Let's have our drinks and snacks, and sit for a while, just all get to know one another. Then dinner. When we're finished, the two of you can help put your grandchildren to bed. After that's done, there will be plenty of time to talk."

They munched on cheese and crackers, and sipped cocktails and wine. The kids had lemonade with a cherry floating on top.

Timothy snuggled up close to Robert, and Audrey climbed up onto her grandmother's lap. When dinner was ready, Audrey wanted to sit next to her new grandfather and Timmy wanted to sit next to his new grandmother.

Timmy announced that he and Audrey had made dessert. He ran into the kitchen and returned holding a tray of Tastykake chocolate cupcakes, a Philadelphia specialty, and a bowl of whipped cream.

"Magnificent," said Robert, "my favorite combination—chocolate and whipped cream."

The children were permitted to skip their baths that night. Eileen read to Audrey who fell right to sleep. Robert went to Timmy's room with him and inspected his Lego and Lincoln Log constructions. Robert could never pass up an opportunity to teach something, so when Timmy spun a wheel that was Part of his Lego construction, Robert gave him a short lesson on Isaac Newton's first law—the simplified version, "Once you give it a start, it keeps going for a long time."

Timmy took it all in. He was used to this kind of thing from his mom and dad.

When both children were asleep, Robert and Eileen tiptoed down the steps. Francie and Michael had finished in the kitchen and were sitting in the den. "You two can have the living room to yourselves. You have forty-eight years to catch up on. We'll see you in the morning." They got up, hugged both oldsters. "You can show Robert his room, Mum." She kissed her mother's forehead and Robert's cheek. "You two enjoy yourselves."

Michael hugged Eileen, shook Robert's hand and followed his wife upstairs.

Robert held her hand in his, just looking at her. "My, you are beautiful, Eileen."

She blushed but buzzed his cheek. She took his hand and kissed it, put it on her heart. "You were always in here, my love, but duty to my husband had to come first. I missed you terribly and never told Dan who Francie's father was. And he never asked. It took years for me to stop missing you. We stayed true to our wedding vows and raised a happy family until Francie shocked us with her teenage pregnancy. I was wrong to send her away. I was punishing her for my sin. It all came tumbling down around me, and the guilt returned. I ruined any happiness my husband, my children and I could ever have again." She wept against him.

He put his arm around her and held her close.

"I had no idea why you stopped seeing us. We both missed you so much. When I came home at night, I expected you. When I walked into the room where you tutored Robby, I thought you'd be there. I kept expecting you to call. Eventually I felt that the only way to get you out of my mind was to move away and start again. I found that a position at Yale was available, and I applied.

"My CV was reviewed by the search committee of the history department. After that, there were a number of calls and letters back and forth until I was on the short list. They suggested I come to New Haven so we could mutually evaluate one another. Robby came with me and waited in the front office during my interview. When it was over, they asked me to call Robby in so that they could meet.

"When they introduced themselves, Robby smiled, and said, 'Pleased to meet you.'"

Eileen smiled and squeezed his hand.

"When they extended their hands for handshaking, he looked them in the eye and returned a firm handshake." He patted her shoulder when he told her, "He remembered everything you taught him, Eileen. You taught him to smile and you taught him how to have confidence in himself, and I can't thank you enough for helping to create the man he is today, a successful psychiatrist and professor at Yale. Sure of himself, outgoing, content—nothing like the lonely little boy you knew."

Eileen interjected. "I worried about him after I left. I hoped he would remember all the things we talked about, especially how proud you and I were with his progress, not only in reading, but with gaining confidence. Apparently, it stuck, and he developed the social skills to handle himself with others and to enjoy life. Francie and Michael found him tremendously likeable in every way and are proud that they are part of the same family."

"Of course, it helped him to grow up here in the States. You know I got the job, and by the time the following semester began, I had bought a small house in Orange, Connecticut, where many faculty members lived. Robby had just turned eight and there were lots of kids for him to play with. The mothers were very nice—there was always a supply of cookies and other goodies for him to bring home."

He went on to tell her how he tried to find the right woman to marry, but after a few years, he gave up. His friends invited him to their homes for dinner—and often a single woman was there. He made small talk with them, but when the night was over, so were any thoughts of them.

"Eileen, I don't blame you for leaving me—your family came first. It was not until a few weeks ago when I met Francie that I knew the reason you left. For sure, you made the right choice, and I am grateful to your husband for raising Francie as his own."

"Robert, you have no idea how many candles I lit for you, Robbie and Francie throughout the years, all the time trying to keep my secret from God."

They squeezed each other's hands.

"I have had a very quiet life, but Robby has brought me much happiness. He has a wonderful wife, Theresa, and a son, David, who is, as he would say, a "cool" grandson. We live within a few miles of each other, far enough for us to have privacy and close enough to have frequent visits. I'm content with my little three-person family."

"You're in for it, then," she said with her beautiful smile.

"Eileen, could you tell me about Francie when she was a child?"

"Francie was always a wonder—smiley, happy and bright. She must have inherited her intelligence from you. My three boys are very bright, but nothing like Francie. She dazzled our family and her teachers with her abilities in the classroom and in athletics. She taught herself to read when she was three, breezed through every one of her classes, and she started at University of Edinburgh at age sixteen on a full scholarship. We were so proud of her—she was perfect in every way. I can't believe I sent my child away. I am so ashamed."

Eileen had to lean over and snatch a Kleenex from the box on the coffee table. She composed herself and reached for his hand again. "Francie told me that she brought you up to date with the story about her pregnancy and what came later, so I won't repeat it. I'll just add the part about me and how I destroyed our family's happiness.

"I was so selfish to put myself before my daughter. From the moment I discovered her pregnancy, all I could think of was my own sin—and there she was to remind me that the apple doesn't fall far from the tree.

So, I did the most terrible thing imaginable. Not only did I send her away, but I arranged for the Church to take her baby from her as soon as it was born, to be given away for adoption—yours and my grandchild. I told Francie she was no longer my daughter—our home was no longer hers. My husband arranged to send her to America to live with his older sister."

Although Robert held her, she could not look at him. She blew her nose. Determined to finish her story, she set her shoulders and continued.

"Robert, the story gets worse from here, so I'll try to cut it short.

"I alienated my sons because of my miserable behavior. I turned our house from a happy home to a place of grief. One by one, they moved out as soon as they could. I was a cold grandmother to their children, my very own grandchildren, and they never loved me—how could they?"

Robert started to say something, and she shushed him. "Let me get it all out, Robert.

"My husband Dan stood by me all those years. It takes two to make a happy home, and my misery made him as unhappy as I. Then, after twenty-five years of ruining everything around me because of my guilt, Dan and I heard that Francie was in England for her daughter's wedding. I finally came to my senses, put my pride aside and contacted her by phone begging her for forgiveness. I told her about you, her biological father. Her reaction was shock and confusion. She said she had made a life for herself in her new country without me. She had a wonderful husband and new family that Kate was now part of. She understood my guilt but told me that she still couldn't forgive me for 'throwing her away.'

"To this day, neither you nor I have ever met Kate, our granddaughter. We all have missed so much love."

She started crying again, taking the entire box of tissue, and continued.

Here, she broke down and sobbed. Robert just held her tight.

"Francie's husband's parents considered her their daughter and she loved them for it—called them Mother and Father. I wish I could have met them—I can see their goodness carried on in their son, Michael. A few years later," she went on shakily, "after her in-laws died, her curiosity about you got the best of her, and she was able to find you and Robby.

"Shortly after she wrote to tell me that she was ready to talk about getting together and invited me to come here. On the same day that she mailed that letter, my husband died in his sleep. It came suddenly, a shock. I cried for days thinking of what Dan's and my life could have been and how grateful I was to him. Then a week later, after the funeral rites were over, Francie's letter reached me, lifting my spirits and inviting me back into her life. I called her, and here I am!"

Robert took in what she had to say, offered his condolences for her husband's death and reached out his hand to hers. She took it to her lips and kissed it.

"Eileen, I'm so sorry for what I did to entice you into a love affair. Robby and I were so happy when you were in our house. In the short time you were there, you made it feel like a home. You were just what I needed to get me out of my eight years of solitude, living a bland life, moving between school and at home in a constant slump. Within the few months you were with us, you brought out the best in Robby and in me, too. How could I not fall in love with you? I was so taken that I never thought of the problems that loving each other would bring you."

"Robert, without our love, we wouldn't have Francie. And without Francie, you and I would never have found each other again. I never stopped loving Francie, the child of our love. My problem was that I loved her too much and expected too much of her. I lived my life through her, and then when she disappointed me, I abandoned her and ruined my family. Our home lost its laughter and became a place for our boys to flee from as soon as they could."

"It does no good to dwell on the bad things that happened in the past, Eileen. Let's hope we can make up for our mistakes. I made the mistake of taking you to my bed, and you made the mistake of making your family pay the price. But through it all, I still love you. Do you think we could possibly have a future together after all these years?"

"I came here at Francie's invitation, so that she and I could be reunited. My Dan had been gone for less than two weeks and I needed Francie more than ever. That was our original intent. I had no idea that she had made contact with you or that you and I could be together again. I love seeing you, but my first priority is to mourn my husband's death.

"We can certainly keep in touch, but I want to honor my Dan's death for a full year. He stood by me all these years. After that, maybe we could talk about a future together. I thank God for restoring my family to me. That I get you, too, is more than I deserve."

Now he took her hand and raised it to kiss her open palm. "I love you, Eileen, and I would wait forever for you to come back to me."

"Thank you, Dear, for understanding. We've waited this long—let's hope that time flies by for us.

They climbed the stairs to their separate bedrooms. That night they both went to sleep the happiest they had been in years. Maybe ever.

Chapter 43

The next morning, Robert said goodbyes to three generations—his grandchildren, his daughter and son-in-law, and his love, Eileen. He took the train back to Connecticut, a happy man with so much happiness ahead.

Francie could hardly wait to hear the details of what happened between her mother and Robert. She and Michael had heard only the outline at breakfast before Robert had to return to New Haven for an appointment. Michael was walking Robert to his cab when Francie closed the kitchen door to be alone with her mother.

"Mum, you got ten years younger overnight."

Eileen smiled, her wrinkles seeming to have disappeared. She told her daughter everything, including the hand kissing, the holding and hugging. And the agreement to wait a year before being together again.

"Francie, sharing this with you, my daughter, is the icing on the cake."

"Mum, I feel the same," Francie said, getting up from the table. "Now I have to get breakfast going for my hungry brood. Then I'll drive them to school—you can come if you want. After that we'll have a few hours to ourselves until we have to pick up Audrey after lunch, and then Timmy at three."

Timmy bounded down the steps, banging the rail along the way with the vigor of a typical boy, eager to see his new grandmother again. He was wearing his red Phillies shirt and jeans. Audrey followed daintily, dressed in the eclectic outfit of her choice, a checkered polo shirt, a flowered skirt, and striped leotards. Nothing matched, but she proudly twirled around for her grandma to admire. And she did, with a big smile.

After they dropped the kids at school, Francie's mother asked her if there was a church close-by. She was used to going to Mass every day and didn't want to miss two days in a row, especially now, while she was in mourning.

"Mum, I don't usually go to church, but when I heard that Da died, I went to a local church to say a prayer and light a candle for him. If you want to go to ten thirty Mass, I'd be happy to take you."

"Would you go inside with me, Francie?"

"No, Mum, not this time, I'll wait outside."

After Mass, Francie took her mother to a local Farmers' Market run by the Amish of Lancaster County. Eileen had never seen nor heard of the Amish, and found the sect quite interesting. The Amish women wore plain dresses, aprons and caps, and the men wore white shirts, black trousers and flat-topped, wide-rimmed black hats. The wares they sold were fresh baked breads and cakes, chickens, meats and cheese. Some booths had hand knitted goods or handmade wooden craft items. The aroma of freshly cooked food was too hard to resist, so Francie and Eileen sat at a lunch counter and ate sliced rotisserie turkey breast, roasted vegetables and a shared slice of fresh pear tart. On the way out, they breathed in the aroma of fresh donuts and couldn't resist. They each grabbed one and brought some home for later.

"How can we even think of eating dinner tonight after all of this food?" Eileen asked Francie.

"I think salad for us, take-out pizza for Michael and the kids, and everyone will be happy."

They enjoyed their day so much that having a serious talk seemed unnecessary. Being together felt so natural. They were mother and daughter again, a tie that proved to be stronger than all of those years they were apart.

After they picked up Audrey from school and put her in her room for quiet time, they sat down with a pot of tea for a quiet conversation.

"Being with you and your family is the most precious gift I've ever been given, Francie. I'm grateful for everything you've done for me, but I think I'd like to go home tomorrow. I still have things to do since Da's death, and I need a while in my own home to think about Robert."

"Whatever you want, Mum. I feel as if our visit couldn't have been better, so let's quit while we're ahead. It'll take time for all wounds to heal and old memories to fade, but now that I'm sure I have you in my life again, we can start rebuilding."

"God must have had a plan for us, Francie. Maybe he wanted to tell me that I had atoned for my sins and wanted me to move on."

PART VI

Chapter 44

Francie was approaching fifty and Michael was close to sixty. They had spent the past four summers in Ireland at *Tip Top*. It was an idyllic, relaxed vacation place, with family coming and going during the four months Francie, Michael and the children were in residence.

Kate and Sean had come every summer for a week, and last summer they came with their twin toddlers, Violet and Finn, and Kate's adoptive parents, Grace and James Mullins. This was the first visit for Grace and James, and now they could see why they raved about the place. Grace said, "It's like heaven on earth—tranquility juxtaposed with frenetic activity."

All the cousins got to know each other, and the older ones emailed throughout the year in anticipation of being together again in the summer. When the house overflowed with company, the kids pitched tents outside and camped in their sleeping bags. If Uncle Denis and Liam were there, they would build a fire pit and roast marshmallows and s'mores, an American treat that the European cousins loved.

Six months before Francie's fiftieth birthday, the day Michael and Francie arrived in Ireland, Michael surprised her with the tennis court he'd had built at *Tip Top* during the winter.

Francie was stunned. "Michael, you outdid yourself," she said, covering him with kisses. "Let's change the name of this place to *Tip, Tip Top*—it gets better every year." In bed that night, she showed him her gratitude in her favorite, very personal way.

"Want to play doubles?" he asked before they fell asleep.

They recruited Uncle Tommy as their private pro. He came every weekend, and Margaret and their four kids frequently stayed for a week or more. The tennis court was almost always in use, and the family coach was in great demand. With gentleness and strength, he drove them to play their best, no matter what their age. Francie loved watching—it took her right back to when her brothers taught her, giving her not an inch.

The younger kids never tired of playing hide-and-seek throughout the big house and all around the property, rain and shine. The older ones confided their secrets to each other, complained about their parents and ate nonstop.

Stormy days were filled with making soup, baking muffins, and playing cards and Scrabble with the whole family.

One sunny morning, Francie was in the kitchen spooning oatmeal into bowls for her family's breakfast, when she noticed lines of sunbeams coming through the shutters onto the table. For a split second, thoughts of Pat, and their everlasting bond leapt to her mind. She clearly pictured two teenage lovers in their hotel room in Scotland, striped by sunbeams, agreeing that they were forever united in the Universe.

Her family sat down to breakfast and her thoughts of Pat evaporated.

At that same moment, fifteen hundred miles away, Pat was outside on his pergola in Tuscany enjoying his usual breakfast—melon, ham a wedge of cheese and bread when he noticed lines of sunlight coming through the slats and falling onto the table. He had an instant memory of Francie and Scotland and thought, *I wonder if she still remembers our vow.* Giulia came outside with the coffee and his thought vanished in a flash.

In Dublin, Eileen continued to give thanks to God for returning her to her former happy self. Her sons and grandchildren relished the change in her and they became a family again. Adding to Eileen's happiness, Rob and his wife and son had visited her during the past spring when they were in Ireland. Although they were decades older, both could recognize the same smile and expression in their eyes from so many years ago. They hugged as if they were mother and son. "I never forgot you, Robby, and I hope that you remembered me."

"I had flashes of memories of a beautiful, kind woman who made me feel happy," he said. "That was you—and you still make me feel happy."

When Rob and his family returned to Connecticut, they were enthusiastic about encouraging their father to make plans for the future before he and Eileen got too old to enjoy it.

That first time Francie's mother came to Tip Top, Robert came with her. Francie and Robert developed a familial bond, often taking short strolls filled with details of the years they left behind. In late afternoon, Robert got into the habit of claiming a wicker chair by the tennis court to watch singles or doubles being played. On most days, Francie joined him, carrying a tray with tea and sliced cake. They talked about happy things—mostly about the return of love and the chance for a new life.

One night at dinner Robert and Eileen announced their plans to marry at Christmastime. Everybody, especially Audrey and Tim, made a big fuss. The adults discussed the logistics of getting together for the holiday wedding, which might be complicated, but they were sure they could handle it. Michael and Francie would have Jack open *Tip Top* for Christmas to welcome three generations of the Irish and American families.

But sadly, it was not to be. In late autumn, Robert suffered a stroke. Miraculously, he stayed alive until Eileen came to Connecticut to be with him at the hospital. Robert had lost the ability to talk, but when Eileen walked into his room, he was able to raise his hand to her and produce a weak smile. She sat next to his bed for hours, holding his hand, until he fell into a deep sleep and death took over. She was sad but also grateful. They had found each other and were able to share their love openly, with no shame. Few people experience the last phase of life to be the happiest, and they were two of the lucky ones, so deserving of it after their sad lives.

Francie had spent more than thirty years in Pennsylvania without any knowledge that she had a biological father and half brother, remarkably within a four-hour drive of each other. She was glad she had the chance to meet them, however short it was for her to get to know her father. They all liked each other from their first meeting. If only she had known him longer, she was sure that she would have found a great friend and confidant, one who might have advised her to accept the advances of her mother without delay. Rob, Theresa and David became part of their U.S. family, a treat for all four of the Hansons, especially around holiday time when they were together for feasts, gifts and stories. To Francie, the reality that she and her children had many of the same genetic traits as Robert and his family was incredible. She had grown up without giving any thought to her family's genetics, but once she met Robert, the effect of inherited genes became apparent to her. They celebrated their kinship, especially Rob, who had lived the life of an only child with no mother and no siblings. Now he had family. He and Michael often talked about their childhood wish to have siblings, and now the wish had come true for both of them via Francie.

Francie's Irish brothers were relieved their mother had finally shed her sour moods and feelings of guilt; they were able to reclaim her, the remembered mother of their childhood. When Robert died, they comforted their mother with loving words and understanding, and she was grateful for their support.

Timmy and Audrey were nine and ten when their interest and skills in tennis increased to the next level, and they signed up for neighborhood clinics on hard courts and lessons at their club's grass courts. By the time they were teenagers, they were playing for fun and competing on the club's team. The Hanson family of parents and children loved playing together, and they usually drew a crowd of spectators. They played the game as it should be played, with good sportsmanship, good competition, and lots of laughter.

Francie and Michael knew that within a few years, their kids, like typical teenagers, would be spending less and less time with them, so they added another activity to their family exploits. Every Sunday, they hiked or rode bikes through Valley Forge Park where there were miles of woods with marked trails, historic sights and bikeways along river and creek paths. They always stopped somewhere in the park for a picnic lunch, and each week, one of the four of them was responsible for choosing the menu and packing the backpacks.

At home, they had dinner together every night and discussed topics from politics to dress codes. Dinner talk was a free-for-all, and all subjects were welcome. Audrey suggested a few rounds of *Stinky-Pinky*, a word game that required making a two word rhyme from a definition. "In other words," Audrey said, "if I say, 'nighttime playground,' you answer, *dark park*." This game led to evening competitions and some very, very clever challenges. One night, Timmy said, "emotional menu," and twenty minutes later, Michael came up with "*mood food!*" Francie thought all week about hers—"pants divas." "Easy," said Tim, *"jeans queens."*

Without realizing it, these times together were forming the foundation of their adult values. While so many families around them struggled to find common ground, it was easy for the Hanson family—they enjoyed being together. And Francie, in particular, knew the joy of a happy, healthy family, and more importantly, the necessity of fostering it. She'd had it when young, and she was determined to maintain it through her children's teen years and on throughout their lives to make up for what she had missed.

Francie and Kate continued to speak by phone at least once each week, often by Skype where they could share experiences in action. Every day was a challenge for Kate and Sean during the first two years of raising twins. Being a pediatric surgeon, Sean knew more about caring for children than Kate, but she was a quick study, and before long, she was able to nurse both babies at once. When they started to eat solid foods, the twins' spirit of competition became apparent. Little Finn perfected his technique of grabbing Violet's food before she had a chance at it. Violet quickly learned to protect her food by biting Finn's arm. *You show him who's boss*, thought Kate.

Sean's family was local and visited regularly for typical cozy, uncomplicated family dinners. But because Kate was part of three families—her adoptive one, her biological one, and Sean's, there were frequent out-of-town visitors, mostly from Kate's brood of siblings, half siblings, uncles, cousins, and, of course, Francie and her gang from the U.S. The conglomeration of individual families, each with its own dramas and its own scripts, made for very interesting company.

In addition, Pat came to visit Kate, Sean and his twin grandchildren several times each year, sometimes bringing his own teenage twin boys from England and his toddler daughter, Sophia, from Italy.

Giulia, came less frequently, as the business took so much of her time. She was such fun to be with. Her warm, Italian attitude and happy laughter endeared her to them, and they wished they could see each other more often. Giulia, Francie and Kate were alike in that enviable trait—wherever they were, they lifted the mood of those around them.

Kate seldom initiated a discussed with her mother about Pat. She knew that her mother's marriage was very happy, and she didn't want to complicate things by bringing Pat into the picture. However, during her last visit to *Tip Top*, Francie asked Kate about Pat and his family. Kate told her mother about the back-and-forth visits between the European families.

"It's hard for me to believe, Mom, that Sophia, this beautiful, funny, Italian child, is my half sister. I think of her as my niece. Even though she is almost two years younger than my twins, they all get along like best friends. Of course, when our twins were born, and Sean was walking around like a testosterone king, Pat reminded us of his twin sons and jokingly claimed that our twins were due to his dominant genes. Sean chided Pat with, 'Dream on.'"

Francie laughed at this. "Sounds just like Pat," she said.

"Mom, I hope you'll have a chance to see Pat's three children someday—we're all connected, even though we're not all related."

"I hope so, too. Maybe I will someday." She paused, then asked, "How is Pat?"

"There's so much to tell. I'll start with the obvious—he is handsome as ever. If I am lucky enough to look like either of you when I am in my fifties, I can't miss."

Her mom blew her a kiss.

Kate continued, "After Pat and Moira divorced, he went through a period of profound sadness. It hurt me just to look at him. But when he met and married Giulia, his happy, secure personality returned.

"Like you and Michael, he and Giulia are truly in love, and, thanks to your advice, Sean and I are, too. Pat moved on to another phase of his life, to a new country and a new business. He became a partner in Giulia's tour company, and they have developed it into a highly successful business. Their clients love them and come back for more trips, or just to visit with them. Laughter fills their home and office, and now, with Sophia on the scene, Pat and Giulia have another reason for joy. Whenever we visit them, Sean and I leave there wanting to change places and leave our careers behind.

"The strange thing is that we feel the same with you and Michael. When our visits at *Tip Top* are over, we hate to leave. I can't help thinking that, if not for one not-so-small complication, the six of us could have been such good friends."

"Complicated stuff isn't it, honey?" answered Francie. "I sometimes wonder at it all. And soon after that, I'm always thankful that you found me."

"I love you, Mom."

"Back at you, daughter."

"Pat often tells me that I remind him of you. I keep him up-to-date on the fabulous *Tip Top* in Ireland and the fun we all have. Maybe through some turn of events, he and Giulia and Sophia will come, and the families will blend.

"Do you think that Pat and his family would ever be invited to *Tip Top*?"

Francie didn't want to give Kate any false hopes. "I don't see that happening soon, but who knows?"

Before the conversation ended, Francie told Kate how wonderful it made her feel when Kate called her, "Mom."

"I never thought that day would come, but it seemed to transition so naturally. I love it, Kate, and I love you, too."

Kate said, "I wasn't even aware I was calling you "Mom"—it's so natural for me—and I love you, too, whether you're Mom or Francie."

Chapter 45

Summers at *Tip Top* were like surreal interludes from Francie and Michael's real life in the U.S. Now that Tim and Audrey are in school all day, busy with classes and extra-curriculars, Francie spent two days a week at Penn keeping up with the Hanson Foundation. She found most of the foreign students she interviewed to be intelligent, inspired, and super achievers. She had to make difficult decisions concerning which students to accept. Their stories were heartrending, close to despair. During the first year, the Foundation accepted six students. Two received full tuition, room and board, and the other four received partial grants. All were offered jobs in the University system. Francie employed one female student in her office, bringing her staff to four.

The thrust of their jobs was to raise funds to grow the Foundation so that more scholarships and grants could be added. The endowment contributed by the Hanson family to establish the fund remained untouched except for additions. All of the bequests came from interest earned.

For two mornings twice a week, Francie was a volunteer teacher of an introductory philosophy course in the neighborhood public and private high schools. She still had one full day and two half days for her regular tennis games, her book club and an occasional lunch with one or more of the original mothers' group. She was good as a teacher—she loved her subject. and loved to demystify ancient philosophies. She presented the material in an interesting way, the way she had always seen it. She compared the great thinkers of Greece and Rome to the great thinkers of modern times. She brought the ancients alive by humanizing the way they questioned the logic of *their* times. She showed her students how from

400 BC onward, the greatest Athenian philosophers—Socrates, Plato and Aristotle—influenced Western thinking.

Once Francie humanized the trailblazing ancient philosophers in the minds of her students, most of them wanted to continue studying the classics in college. She was proud of the effect she had on young people by bringing her favorite subject into the realm of their understanding.

Michael continued to travel to Washington for meetings at the economic Think Tank. Francie could adjust her volunteer teaching schedule so that she, and sometimes the children, could join him in Washington for invitation only presentations at the Kennedy Center, and for other perks of Michael's position.

From his point of view, new formulas were emerging due to pressures from foreign economies, and some of the younger members thought that some of the old theories had outlived their relevance. Michael wondered if he were one of the old theorists who had outlived his relevance. Every so often he called Kate for a consultation. He respected her intellect and her viewpoint on up-to-the-minute theories. He looked forward to their conversations, and she welcomed his calls. They had an unusual affection for one another, not quite father-daughter, not just colleague to colleague or friend to friend. They were more like favorite uncle and favorite niece.

The next few years were fuzzy, a phenomenon from the point of view of Francie and Michael: the older one gets, the swifter time passes. In what seemed like only days, the kids went from asking for hot cocoa to asking for car keys, and the parents started to celebrate their ages in half decades rather than years. The kids were involved in extracurricular activities, and on some nights, they came home too late for dinner but in time for dessert. They would storm in the door with a quick, "S'up?" from Tim to his father and a big hug for his mother before he grabbed dessert and ran upstairs to his room. Audrey, cheeks red from cheerleading practice, would give her parents a big metallic smile, sporting braces on her uppers and lowers, run upstairs to change into jeans and a sweatshirt then come down for a bowl of cereal or poached eggs.

Timmy's development through his teenage years laid the foundation for the young man he would soon become. He had always been an excellent student and athlete. Now he achieved a trifecta and more—he was tall and handsome, too. The girls weren't shy. Thanks to Michael and Francie, he had his priorities straight. Athletics, particularly soccer and tennis, kept him busy after school and on weekends. He planned his time sensibly and devoted enough energy for studies, not only to allow him to excel, but to allow him to ponder what he learned. In this department, both Michael and Francie were to thank for encouraging dinnertime discussions and emphasizing the meaning of ideas behind the words he read. As he got older, he required his privacy and spent time in his room doing the things that all teenage boys do, mostly to the puzzlement of his parents.

"What does he do in there all the time?" Francie wanted to know.

Michaels advice was, "Leave him alone—try to remember your brothers at that age and trust that Tim is not planning to be a serial killer."

"Just promise me one thing, Michael—that you tell Tim all about preventing pregnancies and venereal disease."

"Don't worry, Francie, long ago and far away, I managed to be ahead of you on that. You worry about Aud, and I'll take care of Timmy."

Audrey was less than two years younger than her brother, and she was in her early teenage years, sneaking mascara to school, painting her toes turquoise, and doodling "I love so and so" in the margins of her notebooks. She, too, was super bright and cute, but still a work in progress. Francie had no worries about her, but then, Francie's mother had had no worries about her either, when she was a teenager. Francie made sure that Audrey clearly understood the facts of life, although Audrey was embarrassed that her mother was the one doing the telling. Her only response was, "I know, Mother, you don't have to tell me."

Unlike most families with teenagers, Francie and Michael and their kids continued to enjoy each other's company. Audrey liked Francie to go with her to shop for clothes, and they often made a day of it at the mall—shopping, eating, shopping, snacking and shopping. Those days were like running marathons and they usually came home exhausted.

So far, the kids had not asked about how Kate came to be their sister. They were still too wrapped-up in themselves to ponder that situation, so Michael and Francie left it alone for the time being. When the time came, which they knew it would, they would explain it truthfully, with no shame and no judging. Just, “It happened. End of story.”

Under Francie’s administration, The Hanson Family Foundation had awarded full scholarships to fifty deserving students so far, from twenty-seven different countries. Francie maintained a relationship with all of them, whether a yearly greeting or a continuing friendship. To Francie, each student felt like her own child and made her proud. Photographs of every graduate hung in a position of honor on her office wall.

Chapter 46

When the phone rang at eleven p.m., Francie knew that it portended bad news. Her brother, Denis was on the phone to tell her that their mother had fallen and broken her hip in several places. She would be undergoing surgery the next day to either stabilize her hip or replace it. "The surgeons will know more when the surgery begins, Francie. Right now, she's pretty well drugged because of the pain."

"Den, I'll be on the first plane out of here in the morning. I'll come straight to the hospital."

She told Michael that he didn't have to come; she could positively go by herself. Her family was there for her and she would stay at one of their homes. Michael could stay home with the kids without worrying about her navigating her way around Dublin.

The next day, with the five hour time difference, she arrived in Dublin in early evening. Tommy was at the airport.

"Tommy, I told Denis that I'd take a taxi to the hospital. You didn't have to come for me."

He hugged her, then said, "Francie, Mum's not doing too well. There was a lot of damage to the joint and she developed blood clots. If the doctors can keep them under control, everything should be okay, but we have to wait and see. She was in a lot of pain, and the medications controlling the pain seem to have affected her mind. She's hallucinating. But the doctors say that older people frequently hallucinate when on pain medication. It should go away when things stabilize, so don't be surprised if she seems to have lost her mind."

"Do you think she'll know me, Tommy?"

"We'll see. She comes in and out of the hallucinations, so she may know you when she sees you. Let's hope so. Sometimes she knows us."

They went right up to their mother's room. "Mum is asleep now," said Brian, then put his arms around Francie. "My little sister," he said, "you've had a long day. You must be exhausted."

"No more than you," Francie said. "Have you all been here all day?"

"Yes, but we've all been napping when Mum sleeps, so it's not too bad."

Francie said, "I'm so grateful to all of you—and to Margaret, Rosie, and Liam for your concern and support for Mum."

"Francie," said Tommy," we thought we lost our Mum to bitterness for so many years while you were away, but, thanks to you, she came back to us to be our good old Mum again. We're the ones who are grateful to you."

"It was a team effort, and Mum and I finally became a team instead of opponents, and you guys held everything together through all the years of grief."

About an hour later, their mother stirred. She looked up at the ceiling and said, "Robert, what are you doing up there with Dan? This is so silly—you and my husband don't even know each other." Then she looked around and saw all her children in the room with her. "Why are you all here? Did something happen?"

"Mum," said Francie, holding her mother's hand, "you're in the hospital. You had surgery on your hip. You fell and broke it, and the doctors fixed it."

"I did," she said matter of factly. "Just help me get up so we can leave now."

"Relax, Mum," said Brian. "You're here to recuperate, and we're all here to be with you until you feel better."

"Well, isn't that wonderful," she said. "But why am I in bed? I should be in the kitchen fixing something for you, taking care of you, my children. Did you see Da and Robert over there on the ceiling? They came to see me too."

The tiredness seemed to come in waves, and she said, "I think I'll just go to sleep now. I'm very tired," and closed her eyes a fell into immediate sleep.

Francie thanked Brian for telling her what to expect about Mum not having control of her mind. "Would you mind if I stayed here in the chair next to her for a while? You all can take a break—I'll be here holding her hand."

They agreed it was a good idea, and they left for the coffee shop downstairs for a dinner break.

Francie fell asleep in the chair holding her mother's hand. She didn't know how long she slept. The trembling of her mother's hand awakened her.

When she saw Francie, she smiled and spoke with clarity. "Francie, I am so sorry for the years we missed being together. I loved you every day while we were apart, but I was too scared and too selfish to back down. Banishing you from my life was the sacrifice I made for my sin. It was so weak of me, and so wrong."

"Mum, that's in the past. We're back together and what's important is the present." She took her mother's hand to her lips and kissed it.

"Francie, I can feel death coming. When I close my eyes, I hear God calling me, but I can't go until I make something right with Him. Will you do something for me to make it right? Will you take Communion once again—for me—so that I can rest in peace knowing that my daughter is in God's hands?"

With tears rolling down her cheeks, Francie told her mother that she always loved her, too, even throughout her abandonment. "I needed time to heal my pain after all of those years without you before I could take you back into my life. My happiness was never complete without you. These past few years have made my heart sing." She leaned over and kissed her mother's lips, and said," Mum. I will be happy to take Communion to honor your wish, and I pray that you rest in peace, knowing that your daughter loves you."

Her mother smiled again, squeezed Francie's hand and started to fade. Francie called for a priest.

The priest was administering last rites to their mother when the family returned. Francie explained. "Mum wanted to make things right with God. She feels she is close to death."

They nodded solemnly, and the three brothers and Francie hovered around the bed when their mother fleetingly opened her eyes and breathed her last breath, at peace. The doctor said that she had an embolism that reached the brain causing her to die suddenly, but with no pain. He was amazed that she felt it coming.

The next morning, Francie went to her former neighborhood church, the one her mother had continued to attend all these years, and made her confession. Three days later, her mother's funeral Mass was celebrated there, and Francie took Communion. When the priest offered the wafer, her mind was flooded with memories of making thousands of them in the kitchen of the Home for Unwed Mothers. She recognized the icon on the wafer as being the same one as theirs, and for a split second, she subconsciously evaluated the wafer for texture and taste. *Perfectly done.* She shook those thoughts from her head with a smile and returned to thoughts of her mother.

Michael and the children had flown over to Dublin for the funeral. The family and guests went back to Mum's home after the funeral for a light buffet supper. When the company left, the family quickly inventoried the house for anything they wanted to keep. The remainder was set aside for donation to *Enable Ireland* and other used furniture stores. Francie found some of her diaries and scrapbooks in the closet of her old room, and she packed them in boxes to take home, along with some of her mother's handkerchiefs and jewelry. All the cousins explored the basement. In one of the boxes, they found toys that had belonged to Francie and her brothers. Audrey came upstairs to show Francie a doll she'd found.

"You found Jeannie!" Francie said with delight, smoothing the doll's locks. "I had forgotten all about her. Mum must have saved her because she was my favorite doll. I took her everywhere I went until the day I started kindergarten. Sometimes my mother and Jeannie and I, would have a tea party when I came home from school, especially on cold, rainy days. I'm so glad you found her. She definitely belongs in the take-home pile."

Timmy and his cousins found all kinds of stuff, ranging from tools to fishing gear, old quilts to costumes, and holiday decorations to leather-covered book sets. They brought some of the treasures they discovered upstairs to take home with them.

Everyone stayed up late, the children playing together and the adults reminiscing about family times, summer ice cream cones, the spread of chicken pox to all the kids in one week, sports competitions, abandoned piano, flute, trumpet and drum lessons; but, most of all, what fun they all had together in the innocent days of their childhood. Michael listened with rapt attention, laughing at their stories when they did, but feeling more than a little envious of the experiences of a large family.

When Francie and Michael said goodbye, they all knew that a part of them was missing. The older generation was finished, and now their generation was elevated to the position of family elders.

Chapter 47

Timmy came home from school one day and announced that he had a girlfriend. He was sixteen and in love. What could be better?

"When can we meet her?" his parents wanted to know.

"It depends," he said. "If you promise not to give advice, criticize, embarrass me, or laugh—maybe soon."

"I promise," Francie said. "How about tomorrow?"

"Too soon."

"How about next week?" Michael said.

"I was thinking, how about in a month," said Timmy.

Michael and Francie looked at each other and said, okay, whatever he wanted.

"Tell us about her, Timmy. Where does she live? How old is she? What's special about her?"

"She lives about twenty minutes from here, in Radnor. Last year she sat next to me in English class. She's fifteen, and really smart, so she's in my grade. The best part about her is that she is so funny. She has a hilarious running dialogue with her version of what's going on in *Hamlet*, or *Catcher in the Rye*, or other stories we're reading. We had so much fun in class last year. The only thing dorky about her is that she plays field hockey, the most boring sport ever invented. She's in our Saturday tennis round robin at Merion and she hits an awesome ball."

Francie smiled blandly, watching carefully for her son's giveaways as far as how deep he'd fallen. *Did you kiss her yet?* she wanted to say.

"I'm warning you, Mom—don't come to Merion on Saturday to spy on us. I will not think it is at all funny. Anyway, I told you too much. Can I have the car now? I'll be back in time for dinner."

Audrey chimed in with a singsong, "I know where you're going, I know where you're going!" then moved on to kissing sounds," Smooch, smooch, smooch!"

Timmy ran out of the house, groaning.

Michael and Francie turned to Audrey, hoping she would be their informant, but all she said was, "I won't tell on my brother, so don't ask me."

A month later, Timmy came into the kitchen, banged the door shut, and said one word: "History!" And that was the end of his first romance.

In private, Francie and Michael gave loud sighs of relief.

"Postponed," Michael said.

"At least for the time being," Francie countered.

Chapter 48

While Timmy's hormones were raging, Pat's daughter, Sophia, six years his junior, was a little girl growing up in Verona, the home of Romeo and Juliet. She was a charmer, but at ten years old, still in the bud stage, not yet in bloom. She was very close with her parents and went with them whenever possible when they were scoping out possible destinations for their ever expanding travel business. Originally, the trips they offered were in north-central Italy—Lake Como, Milan, Turin, and the Piedmont area, but now their clients were asking for trips to Tuscany, so they started to map out the locales around Pisa, Florence, Siena and San Gimignano.

They loved the area and designed various trips featuring language, cooking, nature and art. They selected lovely small inns and villas to accommodate their guests. Some had their own olive groves and vineyards featuring the area appellation, mostly Chianti. The countryside was the pride of Italy, a symphony of rich colors and contrasting shadows, sunflower fields against tall Tuscan Cypress trees.

Before long, they had a waiting list for their Tuscany trips. The northern Italian trips maintained their high repute, but the Tuscan trips had become the most popular, and the favorites, too, of Pat and Giulia.

"How would you feel about leaving Verona and moving here?" Pat asked.

"I've been thinking the same thing for a while. Let's look around and see what would be best for Sophia. We probably have to be near Siena or Florence for the schools."

After months of looking, they bought a place in the country outside of Florence. The local school was fine for Sophia, and like most excellent students, she would go to boarding school when she was thirteen. One of the best of those was St. Stephen's in Rome, a ninety minute train ride from Florence, an easy commute for visits. Fortunately, Sophia was versatile and made friends easily. During the three years before boarding school, she was lucky to have excellent teachers who prepared her for the transition and the rigid entrance examinations at St. Stephen's. Pat, who was so well-educated during his youth, took it upon himself to give Sophia extra academic work at home, particularly in literature, history and political science. Giulia had graduated from the University of Padua, the second oldest university in Europe, and had always relied on her own intelligence to guide her through her studies. She was satisfied to let Sophia fine-tune her mind at her leisure, but she didn't mind Pat coaching her. That the two were such good friends had always been a positive in the family.

By the time she was ready for St. Stephen's, Sophia was a juicy adolescent, budding with the promise of future charms. Add to that her sharp mind and quick wit, qualities that seemed to run through all the family, including Pat's twin sons and daughter Kate. Pat took credit for being the source of the sense of humor, even though the three different mothers of his children happened to be hilarious—well, two anyway; Moira had her own style of wit, more sardonic. Sophia and Giulia simply ignored Pat when he boasted.

At least once each month, Pat went to England to see his sons, and to Ireland to visit Kate and Sean and their twins. They often spoke of *Tip Top*. Kate wished that Pat's boys could go there some day to meet her other side of her family—reminding them that she was not only Pat's daughter, but also the daughter of Francie.

With that in mind, though he knew a reunion might never happen, and as an extension of the Tuscan part of the business, Pat decided to add a wing to their existing home in Tuscany so they could have a large villa for clients, as well as a family retreat, similar to *Tip Top* in Ireland. The construction, allowing for the Italian red tape and the relaxed manner of the Italian workers, took a little over two years. The place was made of local tile, marble, with olivewood accents, and typical terra cotta tile roofs. The villa had six bedroom suites with shaded, private patios built around a pool, surrounded by olive groves, vineyards, native Cypresses. The views were classic Tuscany. There were two dining rooms, one indoor, and one al fresco, and a kitchen large enough to hold cooking classes.

Giulia chose the name *Casa di Tranquillità* for their new home and separate rental villa, and its name was well chosen—it personified the place. It was not unusual for clients to reserve the entire villa property for family and friends for a month or longer. Their location, about halfway between Florence and Siena, and not too far from the walled city of Lucca, was ideal. After spending hours exploring the area, their clients appreciated returning to the "House of Tranquility" at day's end.

Pat was a very robust sixty-five-year-old, still handsome, with the same boyish grin that had affected Francie O'Conner. Some of the color had faded from his blue eyes, and his curly hair was now a mixture of black and gray, but Giulia found him irresistible, and the feeling was mutual. She retained all the appeal to him that she had when he met her almost twenty years before. Even if Italy had not been the country of love and romance, theirs would have continued. Neither of them carried jealousies concerning the former loves they both had. They were secure with each other. Giulia loved Pat's children, Flip, Josh and Kate, as if they were her own, and his children loved her. Sophia was everyone's favorite little sister. To Italians, the mixture of parents might seem odd, but it worked for them. Even Moira had to laugh at the circumstances, but as long as her boys were happy, she was tickled by the family's make-up.

Just as it had for Francie and Michael, time raced by for Pat and Giulia. Suddenly they were ready to retire. For the past several years, the boys and Sophia had worked in the business and were ready to take over from their parents when the time was right. Flip ran the London office, Sophia ran the Italian office, and from his base in London, Josh took charge coordinating both offices and the marketing and advertising of all their destinations throughout Italy. Pat and Giulia stepped down, confident that the business was in good hands.

In the U.S., a similar reality was happening. With reluctance, Francie and Michael acknowledged that they were senior citizens. She was in her late sixties, with the energy of a girl, and Michael was in his late seventies, still funny, still brilliant, and still a little fresh. But no one escapes the downside of the golden years.

To add to the race with time, Kate was closing in on her fiftieth birthday, coming up in October.

Pat and Giulia were planning a family celebration at *Casa di Tranquillità* in honor of Kate's half century mark. They invited Francie, Michael and their children to their Tuscan complex.

Francie and Michael talked it over and decided that it was finally time for the family to become one, and this was the perfect occasion.

Chapter 49

Dear Reader,

Just to add a little clarity, I listed the ages of some of the players in the story. Maybe some of the outliers will meet and start their own romances. I haven't decided yet, but something may be brewing....

The natural twists and turns of life continued. The older generation had faded away and was replaced by the next. Francie was the matriarch of the O'Conner and Hanson families. There was a lull in new babies being born, and the younger generations of this complicated family were starting to find their own places in life. The one constant for Francie and Michael's family was *Tip Top*. It was the place all family could come to be together.

Kate and Sean were middle-aged. Their twins, Violet and Finn were in their twenties.

Tim and Audrey Hanson were in their twenties.

Pat's twin sons, Flip and Josh, were in their thirties.

And little Sophia was close to nineteen.

And, not to forget Robby Dugan's son, David, on the far side of fifty.

Chapter 50

When the Hanson family arrived at *Casa di Tranquillità* for Kate's fiftieth birthday celebration, the door was wide open, and talking and laughter were pouring out onto the lush Tuscan countryside.

Giulia came out to welcome them. Francie offered her hand in introduction, and Giulia pushed it aside to hug her. "*Ciao, cara,*" she said. "I have heard so many wonderful things about you." Then she hugged Michael, kissing him on both cheeks. "What beautiful children you have—Audrey and Tim, welcome to your Italian family." From that moment on, Francie and Michael felt they had known her forever.

"Come in and say hello to the entire family."

Kate was the first to get to them before the crowd surrounded them. Close on her heels were Sean, and twins Violet and Finn, who were happy to see their grandparents. Then came introductions to the ones they didn't know—Pat's sons, Josh, and Flip, and Josh's wife and kids. Flip had been married briefly, with no children, but was now divorced. Finally, they were introduced to Sophia, the child they felt they knew, since they had been hearing about her since she was born.

Little Sophia was now in full bloom. She resembled her father—his same black, curly hair and shocking blue eyes, but the face, form, and Italian passion came from Giulia. Sophia was a knockout. Francie's heart filled with happiness to see that Pat and Giulia's child was captivating and sparkling in every way.

After the introductions, Michael walked onto the loggia, and he and Pat were now deep in conversation, trying to keep a low profile until the greetings quieted down. Francie saw them together, and the first thing she thought was *there are the two men I have loved.* She crossed the room to say hello to Pat. There was no doubt that the love was still there between them, but that love was of the memory of two starry-eyed teenagers who no longer existed. Again, she confirmed that Michael was the right one for her, and always had been.

Giulia came over and sat with them, and Francie was glad to see the love and playful affection that Pat and she had for each other. Conversation among the four of them flowed as if they were family who'd seen each other the day before. Michael asked about the development of their travel business and raved about the elegant villa that was *Casa di Tranquillità.* Pat and Giulia told them that for years Kate described how beautiful *Tip Top* was and what fun they had every summer with the family. Michael said that their door would always be open to them, and Pat said that they would love to visit someday. Francie and Giulia agreed.

Conversation turned to all their children and grandchildren, whether shared or not. So much had happened during the past forty-some years, and they didn't want to miss any of the details.

Pat said both of his parents had died. His relationship with them had never been close after he left St Andrews, but he was glad that Moira had remained close to them. She had gone out of her way to make the boys available to them throughout their childhood, for which he was very grateful. His parents had never expressed a desire to meet Kate, and they seldom saw Sophia.

Francie brought Pat to the present day about her real father and the situation that she had learned about from her mother. Then they decided to end the discussion of the past and enjoy the here and now.

"I'd better get back to all of our guests," said Giulia, "especially Kate, the guest of honor, before her birthday is over!"

A sumptuous buffet had been set with the most succulent Italian specialties imaginable. Chianti and beer flowed, and *Limoncello* was on ice for after-dinner drinks. The dinner took more than two hours. Before dessert appeared, a small dance band arrived. Kate and Sean started off the dancing, joined by Pat and Giulia. Francie and Michael, whose dancing skills were nowhere near the others, joined in. Then they changed partners and Francie had the chance, finally, to explain to Pat why she lacked the dancing gene—because her real father was flat-footed on the dance floor.

"A likely excuse," he said, before changing partners again so he could dance with his daughter, Kate. The band played "Love Shack," and Pat and Kate danced like professionals. The rhythm was so compelling that everyone was on their feet dancing, switching partners and mixing the generations. The band played the song over and over, and it lasted over a half hour. No one wanted it to end—but the musicians were in a sweat and needed a break to cool off.

With so many attractive young people enjoying wine and champagne, it was natural for a liaison or two to be in the making.

Tim Hanson was now twenty-five, full of the virility of youth, with the long, lean body of his father and the Irish coloring of his mother. After his first romance at age sixteen ended, he had quite a few more. He came close to marrying his college sweetheart, but something was missing. He was looking for the perfection he saw in his parents' marriage. He and his sister, Audrey, had had very frank talks with their parents about life and love, and both parents beseeched them not to settle, even if everything else seemed right. "If the spark is not there, they're not the right one. Francie and Michael had found perfection twice—and told their children about it. "Wait," they said. "You will know it when you see it."

Tim took one look at Sophia and knew this was the one he had been waiting for. He saw her dancing with her brother, Josh, during the "Love Shack" dance-a-thon and had to get to her. When the band took its break, she walked outside to the patio to enjoy the cool, night air. He followed her and handed her a glass of champagne.

"I'm Tim," he said, "and somehow we're related, but I hope it's not biologically."

"I'm Sophia," she said, "and I'll toast to that." She raised her glass, and her eyes, *"Cin cin."*

He raised his glass to hers, "Cheers," he said.

And they were off and running.

Chapter 51

Dear Reader,

"Too predictable," you say? Maybe. But something else has been added to the brew. Lest we forget Audrey, looking adorable in her shoestring-strapped dress and spike heels. Read on….

Audrey was so busy watching her brother, Tim, make his move on Sophia, that she hadn't noticed she was being watched. Pat's son, Flip had his eye on her.

"What's a nice girl like you doing in a family like this?" he said.

"Sorry," she said, "That old line sounds like something my grandfather might have used on my grandmother."

He had the Harrington grin, and he couldn't keep it off his face when he heard her retort. "Before this conversation goes any further, is it possible that we're half brother and sister?" he asked.

"Just a minute, let me consult my genealogy chart. Are you an O'Conner, a Hanson or a Dugan?"

"No, I'm a Harrington, but Dugan is a new one to me. How did that one slip onto the chart?"

"My mother, who thought she was an O'Conner, is actually a Dugan—it's a long story, too confusing for words."

"Nothing is simple in this family, is it? So how is it that we've never met?"

"I know less than you do, and you're obviously much older than I am, so maybe if we go back to your beginning, we could deduce why we're here today."

"You're right, I am older than you, but I assure you I am not a dirty, old man. The numbers may say so, but in my head, I'm just a teenager."

"Point taken, but let's be honest, there are some years between us." Audrey said this in a blatantly flirty way—she couldn't help it, she found him so appealing.

"Do we agree that in this family age means nothing and anything is possible?" he answered, knowing a flirty look when he saw one.

Before she could answer, quiet was called for so that speeches could be made before the birthday cake was cut.

All of Kate's parents—Grace and James Mullins, Francie and Michael Hanson, and Giulia and Pat Harrington—were at the front of the room. To the multitude of immediate family, add Kate's brothers, Leo and Tommy Mullins; her half siblings Tim and Audrey Hanson; and her other half siblings Josh, Flip and Sophia who all joined the group at the front of the room. Pat welcomed everyone to Italy for the happy occasion of Kate's fiftieth birthday. Everyone raised their glasses to Kate, saying *Cheers, Salute, Slàinte, Hear, Hear, Good health*, and more.

Pat raised a glass to Grace and James Mullins, Kate's adoptive parents, saying, "To the wonderful parents who raised Kate to be the lovely woman she is today. Francie and I will be eternally grateful for the love and the family you gave her from the time she was an infant until now, and forever."

The Mullinses cried.

Next, he raised a glass to Francie and Michael, saying, "To Francie, who never stopped loving the child who was lost to her for twenty-five years, and to Michael, who never hesitated to welcome Kate as his own."

The Hansons cried.

Then he turned to Giulia, saying, "To you, my darling wife, for accepting Kate as your daughter."

Giulia had been crying throughout the entire toast. She just raised her glass and managed to croak out, "Salud."

Finally, to Sean, he said, "To you, Sean, in the role of husband, you deserve the Nobel Prize. You managed to fill the shoes of all of us to complete Kate by being her perfect husband. You are our son."

Sean cried.

"Kate is the only one related to all of us here in this room."

With that realization, everyone in the room looked around at the relatives they had in common with Kate. Some of the people exclaimed, realizing this for the first time.

"A few of you have not met before," Pat said, "but we all share something in common besides Kate—we are a family defined by love. So, here's to Kate, and to love, past, present and future."

A giant tiramisu was wheeled in and everyone shared in the birthday cake, birthday toasts, and then started dancing again. Now, two new couples appeared on the dance floor—Tim and Sophia danced with arms intertwined as if no one else was in the room. When the tempo picked up, Flip and Audrey hit the floor and before long a crowd surrounded them, watching them dance and clapping to the beat. Francie and Pat found each other's eyes and couldn't help laughing at the absurdity of the situation. Pat nodded to a side door to the patio, and Francie followed him outside. They walked down along a path to a quiet gazebo hidden in the woods. He reached for her hand, and they both felt the excitement of their youth. They recognized it for what it was—a look back into the past. "Oh, Pat, if only...." she said.

He nodded with agreement. "Maybe we wouldn't have lasted, so let's just be happy with what might have been and with what we have today." They embraced and he kissed her.

"Uh-oh, Pat, something is coming between us! Down, boy," she said laughing.

"Boys will be boys," he said with a shrug.

"I'll leave you alone to solve your problem like I had to do so many years ago at the Mullins' house. Good luck!"

That being said, she walked back inside to the party with a big smile on her face, a look of panic on his.

A year later, there was another wedding, this one at *Tip Top*. After a whirlwind period of dating and loving for both young couples, handsome

Timmy Hanson and vivacious Sophia Harrington's relationship fizzled out. But adorable, freckle-faced Audrey and blue-eyed Flip Harrington's romance grew into a deep, meaningful love.

After the wedding ceremony on the tented tennis court, the parents of the bride and groom saluted them with an international flair. A marching band appeared, complete with saxophones, trombones, tuba, drums, accordion, guitars, and mandolins and invited the entire group of guests to follow them with Audrey and Flip leading the way while they marched in a conga line around the property, down the road and back, playing lively Irish jigs and reels like "Ten Penny Bit," happy Italian songs starting with "Zooma Zooma," British Beatles classics like "All You Need Is Love," and American rock and roll, capping it all off with the jazzy, "When the Saints Go Marching In."

The marching set the tone for a wild Irish wedding with food, drink, toasts, talk and tears.

When the dancing began after dinner, the bride and groom, Audrey and Flip had the first dance. Then with tongue in cheek, Audrey called for their parents to join them. The dance floor became the common ground of past, former, and present liaisons. Francie started with Michael, Pat started with Giulia, Moira (remember her?—the mother of the groom!) started with her husband, George. They switched dance partners several times and came up with the funniest combinations. One by one, they started to giggle, until they all were bent over in hysterics watching the oddest couples—Moira and Michael, and Giulia and George. Pat and Francie were laughing too hard to even think of dancing.

Ironically, more than fifty years after Pat and Francie's romance, Audrey—instead of Francie—became a Harrington.

PART VII

Chapter 52

Michael was the first to die. His and Francie's life had become more sedentary and their trips to Ireland more infrequent. The ten year difference in age finally showed itself, and as Michael closed in on ninety, he started to fail physically and mentally. He died quietly a few months before his ninetieth birthday. Death came to him gently, just as it had for his parents. He had lived to see both of his children married. He managed to sing at Audrey's wedding and to dance with the bride, but at Timmy's wedding, he could only enjoy listening to the singing and watching the dancing from his wheelchair. Michael's life had been full, more than he ever expected. He had thoroughly enjoyed his role as the main supporting player in the cast of characters in Francie's life. His last words to her were, "You are the love of my life, and the only thing I regret about dying is leaving you."

The entire family was there for his funeral. Timmy eulogized him as a quiet, generous man, a humble genius with a brilliant sense of humor.

Although she knew it was coming, Francie felt a huge hole in her heart after Michael's death. She thought of him constantly in everything she did. She missed him from the minute she awoke, alone in their bed, until she kissed his pillow at night.

In her journal she wrote, *My life lost its compass. I feel like I am barely going through the motions of living. Without Michael, my life has little substance.*

After Michael's funeral, Kate and Sean, now in their early sixties, planned to spend a week or so with Francie, and maybe convince her to come with them to *Tip Top* for a while. Francie said she would consider it, maybe for the following summer. Sean had retired from his surgical practice, and he and Kate worked as consultants in their separate fields, pediatric medicine and economics. The twins were married and settled with their own families. Finn married an Irish girl, and they were making a life for themselves in Dublin, close to their parents and extended families. In accordance with Francie and Michael's wishes, upon their deaths, *Tip Top* would pass on to the care of Finn, their Irish grandson. The property was put into a trust so that all the generations could share in the pleasures of the Irish estate. To the delight of Francie and Michael, their granddaughter Violet, young Finn's twin, had attended University of Pennsylvania where she met and married her husband, Andrew. For the past twenty years, they lived in Princeton, about an hour's drive from Philadelphia. Francie and Michael had seen them often when they were undergraduates at Penn and continued to see them every few months when they moved to Princeton.

Violet had inherited the best qualities of her parents—Kate's infectious personality and Sean's fierce intelligence. Her grandparents' traits showed through with Pat's irresistible grin, and Francie's red hair and happy outlook on life. People liked her and she liked people. She related to all types and brought out the best in them. While at Penn, she majored in communications, a natural choice for her. Now that she was close to forty, she was a successful TV journalist and frequent talk show guest. Two of Andrew's and her children were away at college, and one was preparing for graduation from prep school.

She and Francie had grown extremely close. Hardly a week went by that grandmother and granddaughter didn't talk on the phone about all things, important or trivial—always punctuated with laughter. Violet planned to stay with her for a week after Michael's funeral, and since Kate and Sean were staying at the house, too, the funeral served as a mini reunion. The morning after the funeral, Violet approached Francie. "Nana, Mom and I love hearing the stories about your history. Your life is full of so many experiences, more than can be counted on both hands. Why don't you write a book?"

"Maybe I will someday, but first I have to see what comes next. It's too soon to think about it."

But she did start to think about it, and that night, after everyone was asleep, she went to the basement and dug through her storage unit to find the boxes of diaries, journals and letters she had collected since she was a teenager. During the past twenty years, she had written only sporadically in her current journal, but her personal thoughts and important milestones were all there in her stack of previous ones. At the bottom of the box of letters was the handkerchief she'd saved since her mother's death. She found the gold chain and heart that Pat had given her for her eighteenth birthday, and she rubbed her fingers over the heart and sobbed. She was alone, and she was overcome by the same feeling of homesickness and loneliness that she had felt as a banished seventeen-year-old. She cried into the handkerchief that still carried the familiar odor of her mother.

She came upstairs with the boxes and files, sat down at her desk and started writing. She would add the final chapter when the time came. She wrote every day for a year, reliving the life's experiences she thought she had forgotten. Somehow those memories came through her fingers during the act of writing. She wrote of her happy childhood, then her wonderful year with Pat. She wrote of the daffodils that he gave her and their trips through Scotland. She wrote of the day they were lost and freezing in the Scottish mountains, and their finding the cottage where the Thomsons and their three dogs welcomed them in from the cold.

So many memories....She wondered what happened to Rosemary, her roommate in the Home for Unwed Mothers, and hoped that she had found happiness. She often thought of Dean Ross, her second father for the years she was at University of Pennsylvania. She amazed herself when she thought of the success she had at Shea's Soup Company and at the family's unexpected windfall at Sotheby's. She thought of the loving feelings she had for Michael's parents who accepted her as their own daughter.

She thought of the canoe trip down the Brandywine with Michael, and all their Sunday travels and *afternoon delights* during their years without babies. She thought of the look on Michael's face when Timmy was born at home. She thought of how Michael was her hero, putting up with her uncertainties about Pat and having faith in their marriage. She thought of how she loved him and missed him.

Violet phoned her from work in the middle of the day, an unusual time for her to call. Francie was alarmed when she heard a catch in her granddaughter's voice. "Nana, I'm leaving work now and should be there within an hour. I have something important to tell you."

Francie was taken aback but knew the wisest thing to do was not to press Violet. She forced herself to wait with composure. "I'll be here, waiting," she said. *No questions*. Of course, she thought the worst—*something must have happened to one of the children*.

Violet arrived, eyes swollen from crying and began crying again when she hugged her grandmother.

They sat down on the couch, hand in hand, and Violet said, "My mother is in the hospital in Ireland."

Francie took a few seconds to digest what she heard. "Kate in the hospital? What happened?"

"There was a freak accident. No one knows how long Mom was missing until Dad came home to an empty house, with an empty garage, nothing unusual in itself—she must have driven to the woods to hike with the dog.

"By dinnertime, she still wasn't home. Dad made a few calls and then drove around the neighborhood looking for her car in different car parks at entrances to the woods. He spotted it, and started on the closest path, calling her name and the dog's name. After some time with no response, he sped home, called the Dublin police, grabbed a flashlight and went back to the woods, continuing to call out for her. By then, the police were there, helping in the search. They spread out, walking on different paths in different directions calling her name, and Rags' name.

Distraught, Francie interrupted, "Violet—just tell me if she's alive."

Violet, crying again, nodded. "Yes, she's alive."

"I think I need a scotch. I'll get you one, too."

They sipped their drinks and Violet continued. "It took an hour to find her. They heard Rags barking and followed the sound. Mom was on the ground unconscious, under a tree, the leash around her wrist, with a bloody head wound. They emergency crew took her to the hospital. She is in intensive care, still unconscious."

"I'm going, Violet. I know you are, too. Can we get on an evening plane?"

"I've already made reservations for you and Andrew. He's packing for me and we're meeting him at the airport. He has my passport. The plane leaves at seven tonight."

"Did anyone call Pat?"

"Finn called him right after he called me. Pat asked about you right away, and we told him that you'd know as soon as I got to your house. Pat should be on his way to Ireland by now."

Violet went with her to her bedroom to help with the packing. Francie was in her eighties, and though her mind was clear, in a circumstance such as this, anyone could lose track of their thoughts. Violet had just told Andrew what to pack for her, so it was easy for her to list the items her grandmother needed.

The first thing they did was to take turns washing their tear-stained faces, then they got to work. "Nana, I made a list of what you need to pack. I'll help choose. We can be out of here in an hour."

Violet was right. An hour later they were in the car, en route to the airport. Andrew was waiting when they arrived. They had less than an hour to spare before the plane started to board.

Andrew took charge at the airport, making sure the women were comfortable and helping to make the check-in procedure as smooth as possible. Francie thought what a fine man her granddaughter had married, very much like Michael. The plane departed on time at seven. All three of them were lost in their own thoughts. Francie remembered the first time, over sixty years ago, when she had flown in the opposite direction, her face turned to the window and crying almost the whole way from Dublin to Philadelphia, not knowing if her baby was alive. This evening she turned to the window to cry for the same reason—was Kate still alive? She slept for a while, awakening when dinner was served. She and Violet discussed sleeping accommodations once they got to Dublin, and Francie said she'd like to stay at the closest hotel or bed and breakfast. "You and your brother and family should stay at the house with your father without me to worry about."

Francie played with her food, eating a few bites, then fell into a fitful sleep.

They arrived in Dublin early in the morning in the pouring rain. As soon as they cleared customs, Violet called her brother. He was at the hospital with their father, the Mullins and Pat. He told her to hurry.

The taxi driver cut through the rain as fast as he could, and they arrived at the hospital forty-five minutes later. At that time of morning, the lobby was empty except for the eerie, lifeless feeling and stench of sickness and death.

Francie's knees went weak when she saw Kate surrounded on all sides by tubes, machines and tanks. Pat rushed to Francie to support her. She turned to him and buried her face in his shoulder. Violet kissed her father and brother briefly and went right to her mother, taking hold of her limp hand and speaking gently to her. "Mom, it's me, Violet, can you squeeze my hand or blink your eyes to let me know you hear me?" There was no response. Violet tried again to the same result. Sean put his arm around his daughter and said, "She's been like that since we found her in the woods. The doctors tell us to prepare to say goodbye." Violet turned to her father and her tears fell onto his chest. She had a fleeting thought about apologizing to him for getting his jacket wet. Finn joined them, crying as hard as his sister.

Francie and Pat moved to the Mullins and tried to comfort each other. All four of them were Kate's parents and all their hearts were breaking. Kate's brothers, Leo and Tommy were devastated. Francie couldn't stop squeezing Pat's hand, slowly getting her strength back. They went to Kate's bedside and talked to their daughter, trying to break through the coma. They took turns kissing her hand, both thinking that this miracle they made, the child of their young love, could not be leaving them. There was no response.

Not long after, Kate's breathing became shallow until it simply stopped. She was gone, gently, with no struggle. The nurse came in, checked her and told them, but they knew already, however hard it was for them to believe. When the nurse tenderly pulled back Kate's eyelid, they could see for sure that the light had gone out, and two by two, they left the room. Sean stayed.

They all knew what they had to do, so when Sean was ready, they went back to the house, a sad group of mourners missing the pivotal one in all their lives, their wife, mother, sister and daughter. They were still puzzled as to what had happened in the woods, but they agreed with one supposition—the dog had given chase to a squirrel or a fox, and before Kate could release the leash, she crashed headlong into a tree.

They sat at the house, transfixed by grief and disbelief. At the end of the day, Francie asked Pat if he would spend the night with her. She needed him, and he needed her. They said their goodnights and arranged to be back there by ten the next morning.

They went to the small hotel where he had stayed the night before. He showered while she changed into her nightgown and climbed into bed. When he came into the bedroom from his shower, she was fast asleep. He quietly put on a clean undershirt and boxer shorts, put out the lights and crept into bed, spooning her. They slept until the morning sunlight came through the curtains. They felt as one. As they lay in bed, he told her that his beloved Giulia had dementia and didn't recognize him anymore. He was mourning her as well as their daughter, just as Francie still mourned Michael.

Together they faced the loss of their daughter through the wake and the funeral, returning to the hotel at night.

When Violet and Andrew were ready to return to the U.S., Francie went with them. That morning in their room, she had said goodbye to Pat. A part of the life they shared was gone, but now they were together in grief.

For so many years when Francie needed comfort, she turned to her journal, and now when she felt the need more than ever, she wrote, *With every death, a part of me dies, and there is less and less of me. But I count my blessings and look to my children, my grandchildren and my great-grandchildren to love—and I thank God for my memories.*

She recorded the sudden death of Kate. The love she felt for the daughter she didn't know until her adulthood was unusual. She had never really mothered her, as she had mothered Timmy and Audrey, but she felt as close to her as if she were a younger sister. Her adoptive parents had raised Kate from infancy and, naturally, Kate considered them her real parents and loved them as such. Francie and Pat were grateful to them for encouraging them to share so many wonderful years with Kate.

She decided it was time to simplify her life, sell the house and start anew. The house sold quickly and the children helped her clear out the things she no longer wanted. She moved into Westfield and couldn't help but think how the years had raced by since she and Michael helped his parents with a similar move.

Francie insisted on taking the four-poster bed that she and Michael had slept in during their entire married life. She still changed his pillowcase every week. Each night when she went to bed, she ran her hand over his pillow and whispered goodnight.

Chapter 53

Francie continued to write her story in her journal when she felt the need. The next ten years were very difficult for her, as they are for most people who lose the ones they love. One by one, her brothers died, and with great sadness, she wrote, *Love and respect are strong emotions. They overpower the doubts I still have about my faith and compel me to go to Mass to light candles for those who have kept the faith. So many deaths, so many candles. I pray that my gesture hastens their arrival in heaven.*

She and Pat kept in touch through letters, emails and phone, but as the years sped by the time between conversations lengthened.

On her eighty-fifth birthday, she received a bouquet of daffodils from Pat, along with a note.

Dear Francie,

I forgive you for not remembering my birthday last year, but I'm still young enough to remember yours, even though I can't offer you a toast—my doctor has told me, "No more drinking." It interferes with my medication. But I think it's the other way around—the medicine interferes with my drinking.

My Giulia continues to decline. The ravages of dementia have taken away her sparkle and her ability to reason. Although she doesn't know who I am, I visit her almost every day, in a facility not far from here, and, sometimes she opens her eyes briefly and tells me I'm handsome, then says, "Do I know you?"

Sophia and her husband and children have redone the original wing of Casa di Tranquillità to accommodate her family and to give me my own private quarters. She and I have changed roles. Now she feels responsible for me—always telling me to watch my step or to hold onto the railing. When we go to a restaurant, she orders lunch for me as though I have forgotten how to read a menu. She greets me every morning, with a cheerful "Ciao," probably happy to see that I'm still alive. Thank goodness for daughters—no man should live without one. I seldom see Josh and his family, as airplane travel, even if just to London, has become such a hassle for them. My daughter-in-law, Elizabeth, is very attentive and fills me in on what's happening in rainy London while I'm here "living the life" in Tuscany. I'm glad that she and Moira were close. In fact, Lizzy was at her bedside when Moira died. Flip calls every week, too. I'm happy that he and Audrey have made their life in California. It's ironic that we have children living in three counties, but, since Kate died, none in Ireland. But even more ironic is that Moira was Audrey's mother-in-law.

I often think of the way our lives have played out, Francie, both of us loving our spouses and still loving each other. Isn't it incredible that your daughter is married to my son? When you look at Audrey and Flip, do you think of us? I do—and I hope they will be as happy as we might have been had we been able to remain together. Their children will have a lot of explaining to do.

Happy birthday, my first love. Enjoy the daffodils. And try to remember to send me a birthday wish on my day next year.

Love always, Pat

P.S. I wasn't going to admit it, but here goes anyway: I use a cane now. I guess I'm finally over the hill. Xxx

The next year, she remembered Pat's birthday but never had a chance to send him her wishes. He had died a few months before.

Chapter 54

Westfield had lovely walking trails through woods and fields. Although she was into her nineties, Francie continued to take daily walks. There were benches every so often, and she usually stopped once or twice to sit and observe the occupations of the birds, chipmunks, and squirrels that nature provided, and to restore her energy.

One day an elderly man approached her. "Do you mind if I share the bench with you?" he asked.

"Please, sit down and join me. I'm just watching the fascinating interplay between the little things that live in the world around us. The squirrels and the birds seem to be taking turns at the feeder." She held out her hand. "I'm Francie Hanson."

He introduced himself as Kenneth Samuels.

They talked a bit about what they liked or disliked about living in Westfield, and they agreed that they missed living in their own homes, but this was the next best thing. They could be independent but carefree.

"The sun feels wonderful, doesn't it?" asked Kenneth.

She smiled and said, "Feeling the warmth on my face and hands brings back so many memories to me. My husband and I used to take Sunday excursions and each one seemed to be on a sunny day. As I get older, I value the simple pleasures more and more—the warmth of the sun, the pleasure of a cup of tea and a cookie, even staying in bed for an extra hour in the morning."

He smiled in full agreement. "Aren't we lucky to be alive to appreciate what old age has to offer?"

When it was time for Francie to get on with her walk, she said goodbye to Kenneth, and both said that they hoped to see each other again.

Later that week, they met again on the path, and they were glad to see each other. They walked together for a while, with a minimum of talking in order to preserve their breath, and when they sat down, they found they had very much to talk about. After they went through the usual details about their families, they talked about their pasts. She told him that she had completed advanced studies in the classics and was a lapsed Catholic; he told her that he had been a professor of theology and an ordained rabbi, and he, too, had lapsed from his faith.

"I had too many doubts about religion and how it separated people. I chose to celebrate my ethnicity and to shrug off the constraints that lead to differences among good people. In my own way, I keep up with the holidays and continue to celebrate the traditions of my people."

Of course, this led to a discussion of philosophy, theology, faith, family and current beliefs. They agreed that these subjects could be discussed for years, and they didn't think they had enough time left to form any conclusions. However, they agreed that their thought-provoking, soul-searching revelations made for interesting discussion. They were both light-hearted and found their deep discussions uplifting. He asked her if she was familiar with the Philadelphia Ethical Society or the philosophy of Ethical Humanism.

"That's a new one on me," she said. "But I'd like to hear about it."

"It's a movement that focuses on a non-theist approach to honoring the worth and dignity of every human being, like the Golden Rule without the religious constraints. Of course, there's more to it than that, but I find the rationality and the simplicity of the message interesting."

"Let's put that on the top of our list for discussion the next time. It sounds like something I'd like to pursue."

The philosophy major in her surfaced and she pursued the subject by writing away for information about the movement. She and Ken had serious discussions about the problems of ethics in the world around them and the disparity of wealth and education between the haves and have-nots. They didn't reach any solutions, but their discussions put the issues into their thoughts adding substance to their life.

Francie and Kenneth's friendship evolved naturally. They enjoyed each other's company and looked forward to their visits. Serious discussions were just a small part of their relationship. Even though she was an old woman now, flirting still came naturally to her, and she flirted with him without trying. He courted her by sending her gifts delivered from a local chocolate shop, or gourmet cheese shop or flower shop. They changed their usual dinner arrangements so they could sit at the same table every night. He delighted in pulling out the chair for her, making sure she was seated comfortably, and handing her napkin to her.

Westfield offered activities after dinner, and they often went to chamber music concerts, movies, or lectures. Some nights they returned to her apartment, or his, for a short visit before turning in for the night. He started to call her *Dear*, and she smiled every time she heard the word. They shared stories of their past lives and past loves and spoke of their children and grandchildren. But most of their world revolved around the here and now. They welcomed visits from their families, but they were most content when everyone left and they were alone, but together. For their third anniversary of the day they met, he gave her a platinum and gold ring with bands intertwined in the form of a lovers' knot. She put it on her finger, just above the wedding band she hadn't taken off in over eighty years.

Francie wondered, *Is it possible that love can come to ninety-year-olds?* She and Kenneth found that it was, and it happened to them. Their love was different from those she had with Pat or Michael. It was one of affectionate gestures and quiet togetherness. Her admiration for him was boundless—he was a gentleman, a scholar, a companion and a wonderful listener. He loved to hear her stories and the lilt and laughter in her voice when she spoke. He was taken by her knowledge and brilliance, but mostly by her approach to life. She was happy—and she made him happy. How fortunate they were.

They were together every day for seven years, but Kenneth's age crept up on him faster than it did for her, and he slowly started to fade. Francie stayed by his side throughout. By the time he was bedridden, he had not had a woman in his bed for such a long time, and he asked her if she would lie beside him so he could have the comfort of feeling her next to him. She thought it was the most beautiful compliment anyone had ever given her.

She was next to him when he died. She kissed him and covered his face with her tears.

In her journal she wrote, *Kenneth was one of the greatest gifts that God ever gave me. Our souls related and he became a part of me. I didn't light a candle for him. I wanted to honor him and his heritage in his way. I asked the rabbi who ministers to some of the residents to teach me the traditional Hebrew prayer said by mourners. He taught me the Kaddish, a Hebrew prayer said all over the world to glorify God, give solace to the mourner and honor the dead.*

I looked at his picture on my bureau, and said the first verse:

Yitgadal v'yitkadash sh'mei raba
b'alma di v'ra chirutei,
v'yamlich malchutei,
b'chayeichon uv'yomeichon
uv'chayei d'chol beit Yisrael,
baagala uviz'man kariv,
v'im'ru. Amen.

Rest in peace, my darling.

Chapter 55

Her hundredth birthday approached, and for the year leading up to it, Francie wondered why her body continued to have the strength to live. Now her steady companion was her electric scooter that took her everywhere she went. She seldom left the campus, but she continued to scoot outdoors when the weather was fair. Her children came to see her when they could, but their own families took up most of their time. When Audrey and Flip came from California to visit, Francie imagined she was looking at a young version of Pat and herself. She delighted that their children's marriage was robust and happy, and she wished that Pat were alive to share her happiness for them. Timmy, tall and handsome like his father, came to visit Francie most Saturdays. Like Michael, he had met and married his sweetheart at Penn. They had four children, now grown with babies of their own.

Francie eldest granddaughter, Violet, Kate's daughter, was her most attentive visitor, and she and Francie grew even closer, like mother and daughter. Violet loved to listen to Francie's long history of experiences. Her grandmother always had another facet of her life to relate to Violet. She became Francie's transcriber, typing *Francie's Story* on the computer.

"Nana," Violet asked, "I've always wondered, how did the family make their money in the first place?"

"The Hansons were book publishers in Philadelphia for several generations. Then they sold the company to a New York publishing firm and continued to invest their money and live on the proceeds."

"Would it be foolhardy of me to take your manuscript to that firm in New York to see if they wanted to publish it?"

Francie laughed at that prospect, but said "Why not? Stranger things than that have happened in this family."

"Let's put our heads together then, and finish the story, Nana."

"We can save that for another day, dear. Now I need some quiet time alone to think. On your next visit we can take up where we left off?"

Francie closed her eyes and tried to imagine how her story would end. The feeling of homesickness came back to her, and the longing for home made her nostalgic. Where was her home? Her thoughts took her back to the Church, a place that had not been a regular part of her life since she left Ireland at age seventeen.

She asked the director of her retirement home to arrange for a pastoral visit from a Catholic priest to provide counsel for her.

Father Paul Welsh responded to the request and arranged to come on the following Sunday afternoon. He knew she was close to a hundred and expected to see a bent old woman in her bed. He was pleased to see an alert, well dressed, lady sitting in an easy chair with book in hand.

"Father Welsh, thank you for coming. I know I'm quite a bit older than you, but if you'd like to call me Francie, I'd prefer it. I think we have much to discuss."

"That will be fine, Francie, and if you'd feel more comfortable calling me "Father Paul," or even, "Paul," I'd be pleased."

She liked him immediately, and they fell into a discussion with ease.

"Father Paul, I'll begin by telling my reason for wanting to talk to a priest. It's pure and simple—I feel homesick and I don't know where to turn. That might sound ridiculous at my age, but let me tell you some of my background. I've had a wonderful life, but a feeling of emptiness entered my world when I was seventeen, and, after all of these years, it's returned."

She went on to tell him her whole story about mothers, fathers, babies, husbands, loves found, loves lost, struggles and riches, everything. Then, somewhere along the way, she lost the sense of home. She felt empty when she had to leave Ireland, her family, the boy she loved, and her baby. She turned her back on the Church when it turned its back on her, and she found a home in the U.S. with her husband and children. Eventually, she realized she felt the loss of a deeper sense of home, a fundamental sense of belonging. Occasionally she visited a Catholic church to honor a loved one or to give thanks, but those feelings of faith and belonging never returned. She lost her faith as a Catholic and replaced it with a trust in the philosophies she studied. The Golden Rule became her religion.

She watched Father Paul as she spoke, hoping she didn't sound too critical of the Church. "You might say that is wrong, Father Paul, but, for me, it seemed right.

"When my husband died, I gave my attention to my children and grandchildren, though I knew that something was lacking. Romantic love had faded from my life, and my thoughts turned inward. I often contemplate my life's experiences and their meaning.

"Without Michael, my house became a lonely place, no longer a home. I needed a new start, so I sold my house and moved here looking forward to the end of loneliness. Good fortune followed me, and I met a man, Kenneth Samuels, and fell in love again."

She stopped to think again, wondering if he would think love among ninety-year-olds was believable. She elaborated on the way love felt to her at this age.

"Our love was completely different. Our hearts sang in perfect harmony. We talked of life's experiences and theories about life's mission. Sometimes, we didn't talk at all, just spent times holding hands and reflecting. Our gentle love was a gift to be savored.

"When Kenneth died, a feeling of emptiness started to creep into my life again. Something was missing. I needed help to point me home. I wondered if I could find it by regaining my faith. So, I asked to see a priest to help me through this crisis. And here you are."

Father Paul had listened patiently. "Francie, I hope I'm up to the job," he said. "My first reaction is to say that if you return to the Church, you will find your home. The door is open to all believers. But I don't think it's that simple. Now that you've told me your story, I think that only you can honestly evaluate how you feel about the dictates of the Catholic church and your true feelings about God.

"I'm happy that you wanted to talk to a priest, and I am happy to give you my blessing. I hope that you have received some comfort and direction just by telling your story to me today, and I'd like you to keep thinking if the Church is the answer. May I come back next week so we can meet again?"

"I would love that, Father. I am so happy that we talked today. Even though I did most of the talking, your patience in allowing me to speak so freely helped me put my confusion into perspective. I have some serious thinking to do about my faith and the reason for my feeling of emptiness."

"Would you welcome my blessing?" asked Father Paul.

"Positively—I would never turn down a blessing!"

Chapter 56

She was glad to see Father Paul when he returned the following week. He told her that she had been on his mind, and he was eager to hear her feelings.

"I haven't reached a conclusion, Father Paul, but I am finding that the examination might be more revealing than the conclusion. I believe in God and don't feel the need for religion, but I miss the feeling of belonging that I had as a child when I went to church."

"Francie, let's start slowly. I understand the resentment you had when your mother forbid a marriage between you and a non-Catholic because of the rules she strictly followed. Her guilt misled her to believe that it was right to put the Church before the daughter who needed her.

"So, she sent you away, the daughter she loved, and banished you from the family—with no explanation except that you shamed them.

"The treatment you and the other pregnant girls received from the sisters at the Home was unconscionable. Experiences such as yours, and worse, remain a blight on the Church. I wish I could say something to make it better. All I can do is apologize for the Church that I love.

"The important thing is that deep in your heart a spark of the Church you felt was home remains. Is it strong enough to allow you to forget the resentment of the past and to return to the Church you left and to embrace it as home?"

Francie bowed her head and rubbed her forehead. "Father, my thoughts are so conflicted. What you say makes so much sense to me, but once I was forced to leave my home in Ireland, I relied on the teachings of many great philosophers to formulate my spiritual being.

"I need more time to contemplate the issues in my mind. May I call you again when I'm ready to continue?"

"Of course, Francie. Our conversations are a pleasure, and I will look forward to talking to you again, no matter what conclusion you reach."

He gave her God's blessing. This time she crossed herself.

Chapter 57

All of Francie's children, grandchildren and great-grandchildren—twenty-seven in all—came to celebrate her one-hundredth birthday at a party in the clubroom of Westfield. Add to that over twenty-five of her brothers' children and grandchildren from Ireland and England; four more from the children and grandchildren of her half brother, David, from the U.S.; and from Italy, the wonderful Sophia and her gang of kids and grandkids. Three of the many students who had lived in the apartment above the garage in Haverford came, as well as dozen beneficiaries of the Hanson Fund at University of Pennsylvania. The total was nearly a hundred relatives and friends from four countries who came to celebrate Francie's birthday. She received a beautiful card and a box of chocolates from Sue and Amy, old friends from her mothers' group. They had both moved to warmer climates and were now in retirement homes—Amy in Florida and Sue in Arizona. The three of them kept up with occasional phone calls and notes through the decades.

Some of the guests at the party were meeting for the first time. They marveled at the complications of the family relationships. They sang Irish songs, laughed about family secrets, lauded the guest of honor with toasts and tributes, and danced to the piano music played by Sophia who had inherited her mother's incredible talent. Francie enjoyed every minute of it.

The highlight of the day was a slide presentation that Violet had put together from the pictures of past and present that everyone sent. Francie watched much of her life's memories pass by her eyes, nurturing the most private ones in her thoughts. She saw herself at her first Communion with her brothers and young parents, and later, at the picture taken at her high school graduation. Her brothers' children had sent scores of pictures from that side of the family marking happy occasions. Francie's granddaughter, Violet, and her twin brother, Finn supplied pictures of their parents' wedding that showed a glowing Kate and Sean followed by more pictures from the years of children and grandchildren. Audrey and Timmy brought pictures of Michael, Grammy and Papa that they had gleaned from old scrapbooks found in the basement of the Haverford house. Sixty years of marriage had yielded scores of pictures. Sophia brought pictures of her parents, Giulia and Pat and an old picture of Pat from his high school graduation in a forgotten scrapbook that had passed on to him when his parents died. He looked exactly as he was when he and Francie met, over eighty years ago on the ferry from Dublin. Watching Pat on the screen took Francie's breath away. She could hear him saying, *Is this seat taken, Miss?*

The slides from Kate's fiftieth birthday at *Casa di Tranquillità* in Tuscany and the ones from Audrey and Flip's wedding at *Tip Top* in Ireland brought cheers from the crowd who remembered the outrageously good time they had on those occasions.

The final picture was of Kenneth, the love of Francie's golden years. Violet had obtained it from his family for this occasion.

When the slide show was complete, Francie made a short speech thanking her family for coming and for the wonderful slide show. "One hundred years of my life took less than twenty minutes on the screen. But to me, the days, months and years I lived seem to have gone by in a minute. My heart was broken by the loss of my loves, but my heart has healed with my memories intact. I have no tears for the time gone by—only smiles for the wonderful life and loves I had and those that are to come.

"Being old does not necessarily bring wisdom, but it does bring experience. So, my advice to you, based on my experience, is to cling to love, nurture it, make it grow and never forget the ones you love."

As the party drew to an end, Francie asked her children, Timmy and Audrey, her grandchildren, Violet and Finn, and Pat's daughter, Sophia to come back to her apartment for a few minutes.

Francie asked Violet to take out a box that was in her bottom drawer.

"I have something to give all of you from these items that I value the most.

"For Violet and Finn, the children of Kate, my first-born—Violet, here is a something I have kept hidden for most of my life, a gold heart and chain that your grandfather, Pat, gave me for my eighteenth birthday. I hope you wear it often and think of the young love Pat and I had that resulted in the birth of your mother. For you, Finn, I have something that I recently had shipped here from Scotland—a cashmere tartan scarf with the St Andrews University crest on it, along with an airline ticket to the town of Fife in Scotland, so you and your wife can walk the streets and trails that your grandfather and I walked while we were young lovers.

"To my Timmy, the miracle baby that we thought we'd never have, I give your father's class ring from University of Pennsylvania, and the first edition of Charlie and the Chocolate Factory that he received as a retirement gift from the University." Laughter followed that bequest, but Francie added, "Oh, yes, one more small thing—the Renoir painting of mother and child that was a gift to me from Grammy and Papa.

"For you, Audrey, my darling daughter, I have my diamond engagement ring and an emerald pin that belonged to Grammy Hanson. She waited seventy-five years for you, the first girl in the family. You made her the happiest grandmother in Haverford when you were born, and you continued to give her pleasure until she died."

She turned to Sophia, saying, "You are the only one here that is not related to me by blood, but I consider you a part of my family. Here is the engagement ring your father, Pat, gave me on the ferry when he asked me to marry him after our first year at college. In my head, I can still hear the applause of the people in the seats around us when I said '*Yes!*' It has a yellow diamond at its center, the color of daffodils like the ones he gave me on so many special occasions.

"Now I have something to tell you about the stack of books on the shelf behind me.

"When I started my first journal as a child in Ireland, I never imagined that I'd be alive one hundred years later to share my birthday with you, my beloved family. I have saved all my journals, and, with the exception of a few years, I still continue to add to my collection of thoughts and experiences. You are all part of my story. You have given my life joy and depth, and a story no one would believe could happen in one lifetime.

"Violet has been helping me put my journals into book form, and has promised, after my death, to have them published and distributed to all of the family. I hope you enjoy the story of a simple Irish girl whose life was determined by love."

She hugged each one, knowing she might never see all of them again.

Chapter 58

As the months passed, Francie grew progressively frail and spent more time asleep than awake. She had trouble getting her thoughts together, but Francie's story wasn't quite done, so she turned to someone who knew her best to finish it for her.

Dear Reader,

Francie came to me in a dream and asked me to finish her story. I told her that Violet was the likely one to write the ending, but she insisted that I was the one she knew from the start and she trusted me to write her final thoughts and words.

I hope I ended her story as she would have. So, here goes....

Francie could feel that her death was almost upon her and wanted to see Father Paul. He had last seen her just after her birthday, but a few months had passed since then, and he was saddened to see how she had fallen into decline.

"Father," she said barely over a whisper. "In my head, I believe in God but still have doubts about my religion. My heart tells me not to go to my final rest without saying my confession and receiving Communion. Could you do that for me?"

"I would be honored, Francie," he said. She bowed her head, and for the first time in his life, he cried while performing the rites. When he was finished, she told him that she had a request to ask of Violet and asked him to send her in to see her.

She labored to get the words out but gathered enough strength to tell her what she wanted. "There are four things I want to take with me when I die, Violet. The first is my mother's handkerchief. It's in my box of treasures. Please put it in my hand when I am in my coffin. The next two are the rings I wear now, my wedding ring from Michael and my lovers' knot from Kenneth. Please be sure they stay in place when the coffin is closed. The fourth is an envelope in the bottom of the box with the letter 'P' on it. Inside is a pressed daffodil from the first bouquet your grandfather gave me. Please put the envelope over my heart. I want them to be with me in my grave. All my other treasures are in my head and will stay with me through all eternity."

Violet kissed her grandmother, and Father Paul blessed her again. Then they quietly left the room.

Francie's last thoughts were of her loves—Pat, the boy she loved throughout her life with the intensity of a young girl; Michael—the husband she loved for his goodness, for rescuing her from a time of deep sadness, and for whom her love never stopped growing; and Kenneth—the man she loved for his intellect, his spirit, and his companionship—their essence and hearts came together in pure love. She missed them all and hoped she would see them after death.

The hint of a smile appeared on her face when she realized that her life had been like one of her favorite things—a romance novel, just waiting to be written.

And here it is.

About the Author

Sandy Ross Jacobs has been writing from the time she was a child in Philadelphia. Her travel articles, human interest stories and commentaries have been widely published in magazines, newspapers and literary journals. She has taught writing classes at Community College of Philadelphia and various educational centers in Pennsylvania and Florida. Many of her students have gone on to become successful writers in fields ranging from legal writing to fiction.

She and her husband live in Boca Grande, Florida.

This is the author's first novel. She wrote it in celebration of her 80th birthday.

Made in the USA
Monee, IL
12 May 2021

68444981R00204